THE GODDESS CALLS

THE CLAN'S CHOSEN BOOK ONE

LEXI MACQUEEN

1st Edition published in 2025 by Lexi MacQueen
www.leximacqueenauthor.com

Cover Design & Interior Formatting by Dream Echo Designs
Editing by Alexis Augustin

AUTHOR'S NOTE

To the people that craved to be something more, something unique and wonderous. This is for you, because how could magic not exist?

Or, if you just really want to know what it's like to get railed by a handsome man that shifts into a mythical creature, then this book is also for you.

TRIGGER WARNINGS

-Animal Cruelty resulting in death
-Biting (the sexy kind and the not so sexy kind)
-Blood
-Chasing (the sexy kind)
-Choking (sexual and not)
-Explicit language
-Explicit sex scenes
-Mental/Emotional abuse from a parent
-Oral sex during menstruation
-Rough consensual sex
-Roughish oral sex
-Semi-public sex
-Stalking (not the sexy kind)
-Threatening
-Violence

Are you still with me?
Good…Now, turn the page like the good little mate you are and read.

CHAPTER 1

KINLEY

"That's it, I'm fucking deleting all these damn dating apps."

I slam my phone down a little too aggressively, seeing that there is still no message notification from the guy I'm supposed to be meeting. He is twenty minutes late. He is the one that set this date up, and he's late; maybe he hadn't even planned on showing up. *Is it wrong to hope something terrible happened to him and that's why he isn't here? Geez Kinley, way to be a downer.* I really want to give him the benefit of the doubt, but the dates I've been on lately are turning me into a pessimist. All kinds of scenarios start swirling in my head. This isn't the first time I've been stood up, and it probably won't be the last. *What is wrong with men these days?*

I take a sip of my wine, hoping that maybe the crisp, bright flavors will dampen my anger. I rushed home from work to get ready for this, and I'm starving too! *Maybe I'm hangry. I really need to eat before I start snapping at people.* Even if he does end up showing, with the mood I'm in, I'm not going to be good company. It was a long day at work, and right now all I want to do is just go home. My stomach gurgles as the tempting scents of Thai dishes swirl around me. I'll order some food to go, and if I still don't hear from him I'll leave. My gaze wanders as I take in the eclectic decor; it's a weird blend of Thai culture mixed with mountain lodge chic, and for some strange reason, it works. It gives the place an endearing yet exotic vibe, but the spices that permeate the space are probably what really gets people in the door and keeps them here. I've ordered take-out from here before, but have never had a reason to sit down and eat. *At least he picked a place with good food.*

I wave the waitress down, and when she approaches she gives me a knowing look that I absolutely despise. I don't want her pity.

"What can I get for you?"

"Can you put in a to-go order for Chicken Pad Thai please?"

She looks me up and down after putting the order in on her tablet. "Girl, screw whoever stood you up. If you don't mind me saying, you're an absolute babe." She gives me another once over, taking in my knee length sapphire off the shoulder dress. I blush a little at her scrutiny. *Is she checking me out?* She leans in, before asking me quietly, "You're not gay by any chance?"

Well, that is not what I was expecting her to say. Too bad I'm not; she is pretty.

"Unfortunately, I'm very straight. Not that it does me any good when the guys I've been attracting are subpar at best. It's very flattering that you would ask though. I really like your tattoos by the way; they are so colorful."

I look at the beautiful swirling designs that run up her arms and on her chest. *I wish I was brave enough to get tattoos.*

Her warm smile lets me know I haven't bummed her out. "Thank you, hey let me go put your order in, I'll have them put a rush on it. Would you like another glass of wine? It will be on me."

"That is a tempting offer, but I need to drive home."

"I'll be right back."

She walks away, and I glance down at my phone one more time and see a message notification. *Ugh, finally! Maybe he had car problems. He'd really seemed like a nice guy.* I click the icon for the dating app and as I read the message my heart sinks, my stomach grows heavy, and then I get pissed.

> Brandon_06: Hey there, so I'm really sorry for wasting your time. You seem like a really great girl, but I'm just not into bigger girls. I thought I could get over that, but when I got to the restaurant I just couldn't bring myself to walk up to you. Hope you understand.

What the fuck! Had he shown up and then bailed when he saw me?

My eyes well up, and that makes me even angrier. A tear slips down my cheek, and I quickly wipe it away. I go to respond, to tell him how his pictures aren't fooling anyone about his premature balding. How he isn't even worth a pity blow job, but then I stop myself. This guy isn't worth the time; I can't let a stranger bring me down to that level. I'm not a mean person; I try really hard to avoid being that way. I have enough emotional trauma just from my mother. She gave me an up close and personal view of how not to treat people. *Thanks, Mom.* So, just because he's shallow doesn't mean I will be too. I'm so mad and hurt, but again he is practically a stranger. His opinion doesn't matter, but I do allow myself to be petty for a few minutes, just to get it out of my system.

Yes, I'm plus size, but my pictures on the app show my whole body. I'm not hiding anything. *I look good, damn it! Ugh, he's a stupid asshole. Probably has a small dick and is intimidated by my ass.*

I continue to berate shallow men in my head as I block him on my account, but then I decide to take it a step further and just delete the app. *I'm so done.*

I had enough put downs to last me an entire lifetime when I was younger, and I'm not going to allow it now that I'm an adult. I drain the rest of my wine and wait for the waitress to bring me my take out.

I can't change people's opinions on what they find attractive, but I can at least remove myself from the toxicity. I'm going to go home, cuddle my pets, and eat my food before I crawl into my comfy as hell bed. I'm perfectly fine without a man, even if I still want one.

With a full stomach and a heart that is heavier than I would like to admit, I crawl into my plush bedding. Sighing deeply as I inhale the comforting scents of mint and eucalyptus, letting the calming effects seep into me. I bury myself into the soft sheets until only my head is exposed. It has been an exhausting day, but I only have one more work day until I get a mini vacay with my bestie.

"I just need to get through tomorrow and then I can take a moment for myself."

The comforter indents as Indy jumps on my bed, his tiny paws sinking into me and making me wince as he purposely walks up the length of my body. *His feet are so pokey, even without his claws out.* It's too dark in my room to see him, but he soon bumps his head into my chest and I wrap my arms around his soft-furred body. I cuddle him close, and his purr rumbles to life.

"Next time I get the great idea to download a dating app can you just bite me, or scratch up something I enjoy? I don't think I'm cut out for that kind of dating anymore, Indy."

His soft meow is the only answer I get before he's kneading his front paws into me and his purring grows in volume. The vibrations soothe me until I'm lulled to sleep.

Dreams begin to stir in my mind. At first, it's just the usual nonsense. Until my dreams take on a more sinister theme, sounds and images that plague my very soul. I'm surrounded by darkness, so thick I feel its weight on my shoulders, pushing down, down, down while I fight to not crumple under it. The slap of my bare feet echoes loudly on the cold smooth floor. I have no idea where I'm going, but I am spurred on by an urgent need to keep moving forward. Something is waiting for me.

"Kinley! What do you think you're wearing?"

I hear my mother's loud angry voice, but I don't see her.

"Mom?" My voice wavers more than I'd like to admit as I turn in a circle, searching for her.

"Kinley, don't ignore me. You know no one is going to want you if you present yourself like that." The sneer in her voice instantly puts me on edge and I fight the urge to hunch my shoulders.

"Mom? I don't know what you are talking about."

An incessant buzzing fills my ears, but not loud enough to drown out my mother.

"I can't believe that after everything I've done for you this is how you treat me. Your appearance is a direct representation of me, Kinley. People will talk!"

My lungs labor to pull in the air that has suddenly gone thick and acrid. My heart pounds with the strain and my stomach roils. *I don't like this. I don't want to be here.*

"Mom, stop please."

"If only you looked more like me, then people would actually know that you are my daughter. People probably think I'm an awful mother when they see how overweight you are."

I shrink smaller and smaller. "Stop." I whisper as her voice continues to spew hate and ridicule. I still can't see her, but her words pierce my soul. My hands slap over my ears like that will be enough, but I know better; it never helped in the past. No matter how much I try to block the words from my mind, I can't shut her out. I'm not sure when her words become garbled, but suddenly all I hear is her screaming my name.

"Kinley! Kinley! Kinleeeeeyyyy!"

Over and over she yells my name, and soon the mental pain I feel turns to physical agony.

My mind can't make sense of what is happening. My vision becomes blurred, and soon my mother's cries are joined with others, including my own. I'm utterly blind to what is happening, but I can just make out the sounds of fighting amidst the cacophony of fear. It's too loud, and there is too much pain. *Goddess, the pain is overwhelming.*

"What is happening? Why does it hurt so much?" My words are so loud in my ears, even with the noises that surround me.

But then it all goes quiet.

I'm utterly alone. Flooded with pain.

It hurts to draw in breath. I'm rooted to this very spot, unable to escape, unable to make sense of what is happening. My breaths come out in gasps, echoing loudly in the silence.

I want to drop to my knees and curl in on myself. Make myself as small as possible, but I still can't move. I want to sob, cry out for help. But no words leave my lips.

Then I feel it. A shifting in the air. Goose bumps spread like a flash flood over my body. Something is coming.

Sinister energy fills the heavy air, and if I could vomit, I would.

Suddenly, unknown arms wrench me to the side and my back slams into a hard, immovable body. A moan of agony rips out of me from the force of my body colliding with the unknown person. I sense a dark figure looming behind me. Its hot, stale breath whispers in my ear. The voice, holding such cruelty, buries deep into my eardrums, freezing me in place when all I want to do is flee. A menacing growl reverberates down to my very core.

"You bleed so prettily, Chosen. I can feel the power in your blood. You will be mine once and for all."

I can't make my brain understand what it is talking about. *Blood? What blood?* Still not able to clear my vision, I reach down to where the pain is most intense. My hands meet a warm, sticky wetness. I tremble in disbelief; a keening sound breaches my lips as I realize it speaks the truth.

The being grabs my hand and brings it up by my head. I cry out in pain and revulsion as I feel it lick the blood from my fingers. It growls again in my ear.

"All this power...so delicious...You're mine Kinley."

Then everything goes dark.

I shoot upright in bed with a gasp, disoriented and drenched in a cold sweat. My eyes dart around the dark room until my gaze snags on the lit up screen balanced precariously on my side table. With a shaking hand I reach out to shut off the obnoxious ringtone.

"Ugh, why the fuck is my phone not on silent?"

It is so tempting to let it ring, but that dream had been too real, and no one ever calls me this early unless it is an emergency. I swipe quickly to accept without even glancing to see who it might be. I should have looked at the caller ID.

"Hello...?" I ask breathlessly.

An unknown male voice responds and my mood, already dark and troubled, gets even darker when I hear the overconfident words that ooze out of his mouth.

"Hey baby, what are you doing? I have been thinking about you like crazy. Have you missed me?"

I look at my phone screen, seeing it isn't anyone in my phone contacts; I have no clue who this imbecile is. My emotions are too high, and even if this is a mistake and he dialed the wrong number, I'm in no fucking mood to be having this conversation.

"Who the hell is this? And why are you calling me this early in the morning?! You know what, don't bother answering that." He stutters an attempt at a response before I'm smashing the End Call button.

Now I just need to remember how to block a number. Figuring that out, and safe from further unwanted booty calls, I think back to that disturbing dream. Hearing my mother's voice after all these years makes me shudder. Just that would have made that dream awful, but hearing that dark entity's voice, feeling him press against my body, having him make me bleed. I almost want to vomit, the smell of him, pine mixed with sulfur, combined with the iron tang of my blood makes me shudder in revulsion.

It's not new for me to have vivid dreams, they have become quite frequent the past few months. But it seems as though the dreams have gotten weirder lately, more real. There is an underlying sense of urgency that isn't usually present, and I definitely haven't dreamt about being stabbed before. I also haven't dreamt about my mother in a very long time. Last night's non-date must have triggered those happy memories.

"God that dream was so messed up."

Resigning myself to not understanding the hidden meanings in the twisted images that plague my dreams, I pull the covers back up and cuddle my comfort pillow. Glancing at the clock, I groan in despair. I only have thirty minutes left before I have to get up and get ready for work. I kick my legs in frustration.

"I'm never going to get back to sleep, damn it."

Dragging myself out of bed I groggily make my way to the kitchen, trying not to trip over my cat as he weaves his way through my legs.

"Indy, I swear to god, one of these days you're going to kill me." I curse; he just yowls at me which only makes me want to curse at him some more.

Finally making it into the kitchen without tripping to my death, I flip on the light and proceed to the coffee maker. *I'm going to need so much caffeine this morning.* I measure out the coffee beans into my coffee grinder and push down the button to pulverize them within an inch of their aromatic lives. Even half asleep and in a grumpy mood, I never miss any steps in making my morning coffee. Nothing could prevent me from making the perfect pot of the elixir of life.

My coffee machine is happily brewing my will to live when I begin hearing the tell tale stirrings of my dog on her bed in the other room.

"Beretta, are you getting up, love?"

I'm answered with the thumping of her tail hitting the nearby wall. I silently cringed at the force with which her poor tail is thumping into things. Finishing wiping off the countertop, I turn around just as Beretta, my very large and lovable Boxer mix, walks into the kitchen.

"Good morning Betta Boo, I hope you slept well…I did not."

Beretta just wags her tail and looks up at me expectantly.

"I guess since we are up early, we might as well go for a walk."

Beretta's ears perk at the word "walk," and she trots to the side door. I shake my head at her antics, laughing at her silly body wiggles of excitement.

"We gotta wait until after I put some clothes on and get some coffee, silly." Beretta cocks her head to the side and sees that I'm not going for her leash; she sighs and follows after Indy as he strolls by to go to the living room. A light grin spreads across my face, and I turn to pour myself a cup of freshly brewed coffee before Beretta decides to figure out how to walk herself.

After a brisk walk around the neighborhood, I leave a tired Beretta on her bed. She loves walks, and I was thankful she kept me motivated to exercise. I walk down the hallway into my bedroom, glancing longingly at my bed, before going into the bathroom to shower so I can get ready for work. As the water warms up, I give myself an assessing look in the mirror.

"It's gonna be a long day."

Having recently turned twenty-seven, I'm thankful to my youthful face for not showing the signs of sleep loss. My deep blue eyes show it, though; if anyone knew to look there, they would surely see my tiredness. I vaguely remember my grandmother telling me that the eyes were the windows into the soul, and mine were the clearest windows she had ever seen. My mother, on the other hand, had always scoffed that my eyes weren't the bright green that all Munro women had, but then again, my mother had always loved to criticize me.

Shaking myself out of that unhappy train of thought, I twist my long dark brown hair up into a bun, so I don't get it wet in the shower; I didn't have the time or desire to fully style it this morning. I always thought my eyes and hair were my best physical features. Men that didn't think I was too big typically thought my ass and boobs were my best features, which was ok if I was looking for a quick hook-up, but it was incredibly frustrating when what I really crave is a genuine connection.

I wouldn't consider myself conventionally beautiful, especially if one goes by today's beauty standards, but I know I'm beautiful. The older I get and the longer I stay away from my toxic hometown, the more I grow to appreciate my looks. I had embraced my fuller hourglass figure in college and began to appreciate my body more and more as the years went on. In fact, my goal for this year was to begin appreciating my body for what it was, even if at the moment I was only finding the flaws in my body and wishing I was thinner.

"Maybe if I was thinner, I wouldn't have so much trouble finding a good man…I'm so tired of all these losers."

Giving up on trying to stare myself thinner, I get into the shower and try with all my might to wash the negativity of the morning away so I can start my day with a fresher outlook.

9

CHAPTER 2

KINLEY

Before I leave for work I quickly pack a weekend bag, so all I will have to do after is drive home and pick Beretta up on my way out to Megan's lake house. It had been tempting to just take the day off, but being a teacher means I only have a handful of leave days during the school year, so I decided to tough it out and just go to work. It's going to be an easy day anyway, and it is Friday, thank goodness.

Walking out the door, I make sure to give Beretta and Indy an extra pet. They keep me sane, and I love them both.

"Be good you two. Beretta get lots of naps in today because we are headed to the lake after work."

As if she knows what I am talking about, Beretta's tail thumps against the wall in excitement. I usually bring Beretta with me when I go out of town. She is a large dog but is great in the car, and she makes me feel safe. She's an excellent guard dog. Plus, Beretta always loves going out to the lake. In fact, she is excited about any body of water larger than a puddle.

Indy is fine being left home. He has an automated feeder, and he loathes car rides. I had given up bringing him a long time ago.

The one time I left Beretta and Indy both home while I went out of town had been a disaster. I had gotten my neighbor, Mrs. Carden, to watch her and Indy. Somehow the poor woman got knocked over and almost broke her hip.

Needless to say, the woman wasn't willing to babysit the two monsters ever again. That woman still glares at me when she sees me checking my mail. It's so hard finding good neighbors. In fact, I never did figure out who the culprit was. I do know that Beretta and Indy are both capable of mischief, especially if they don't like someone.

Making sure I have everything, I throw my bag in the back of my car and begin my short commute to work. It only takes about twenty minutes to get there. I usually try to give myself a ten to fifteen minute buffer, just in case I run into a train or traffic. Because of everything that happened this morning, I'm leaving later than I want. Now I'm crossing my fingers that I don't get stopped and end up being late.

Singing along with the radio, I drive down the winding back roads. This is my favorite part of my day, when the fog is still in the air and everything is quiet. I love it even more when I can be curled up on a couch and enjoying it from inside.

I'm really hoping that today goes smoothly, and I'm really, really hoping that I can avoid my creepy coworker altogether. I love my job, but the last few months have been uncomfortable thanks to him. A shudder works up my spine just thinking about it. *Think happy thoughts Kinley.* Images of drinking an overly large glass of wine, or two, while enjoying the view of Lake Adger from Megan's back deck, are the only thing getting me through the next eight hours.

I met Megan in college. We had several classes with each other from the beginning but hadn't become good friends until our junior year. That year we had organic chemistry, and we trauma bonded while suffering through our professor's ruthless torture. We had barely passed; afterward we were inseparable until graduation.

She moved back home, and I moved to start my current teaching position. Even though we live a few hours away from each other, we

11

still keep our friendship strong; Megan is family. We're a part of each other's lives; we look out for each other no matter what. Lately, it's usually by phone, except for the random weekend when we can get free from life's commitments.

We just always seem to know what to say to calm down the other, which is exactly why I'm glad that we are getting together this weekend. I need some face to face time with my friend.

Pulling up to my parking spot, I sit for a moment. Mornings like this, when I'm feeling a little too raw, get me thinking about my life. Thinking about the things I'm thankful for and the things I want to work on. I have been pretty lucky the last eight years; even if I'm creeping up on thirty. My life could have been very different if I hadn't gone out of state for college, and if I hadn't met my best friend. I had even lucked out in finding my job, which allowed me to stay away from that depressing small town in Texas.

I had been seriously stressing about not receiving any potential job offers, and I was about to graduate with my undergraduate degrees in Biology and Education. I had every possible certification that I could get, but the jobs were slim pickings and the interviews even fewer. I had almost given up hope, but my prayers were answered mere weeks from when I would have been forced to move back home.

When I got the offer for a position to teach advanced science at a private school just an hour outside Knoxville, Tennessee, I didn't even hesitate, I accepted it immediately. The job had just been too good to pass up, and I hadn't even cared about not having a place to live. I accepted the job and moved to Tennessee without looking back. I would have loved to live closer to Megan, but that hadn't been in the cards. The money was too good to pass up, and it kept me far away from Texas. I had also been hoping I would have met "Mr. Right" by now, but my career was going great, and I couldn't complain too much about how my life was going. Things could be so much worse.

Sighing, I gather my things and start towards the side entrance of Mount Tyler Academy. It's going to be a good day. It has to be; it's Friday, and we have an extended weekend. I walk out of the parking lot, careful to avoid the oblivious teenage drivers, to the side door I always enter through, and I'm greeted by several of my students waiting outside by the door.

"Hey, Miss Munro."

"Good morning, guys."

A chorus of replies answer me as I walk through the door and make my way through the hallways to my classroom. Even with so much on my mind, I still have a job to do, and it is days like this that I'm really glad I love my job. Today's going to be an easy day for me though, not so easy for my students. It's test day, their first practical test of the semester actually. I'm confident in my students; I just hope they are confident in themselves—and actually studied the reviews I gave them.

By midday I'm starving and a little cranky from hearing my students moan about having to take a test four periods in a row. I'm always so hungry by this time every day no matter how many snacks I have on hand. I just finish cleaning up and pocket my phone when my doorway gets blocked. I groan internally as I see who is standing in my door. It's the math teacher, Mr. Allen Cracket, whom students liked to call Mr. Crack Head. To be completely honest, I can understand why they call him that. He's one of the most unfortunate men I have ever met. Allen is tall, lanky, and has dark greasy hair that he attempts to slick back but never seems to get it right. His nose is hooked and crooked like he broke it and never got it treated, and it's always red and runny. He constantly sniffles and blows his nose on his cloth handkerchief. Just thinking about how disgusting that must be by the end of the day makes me want to gag. His beady brown eyes always seem to stare at you from behind some of the most outdated glasses frames, and his wardrobe doesn't do him any favors. It's like he shopped in the clearance section of the local thrift store. If all of that wasn't bad enough he gives off serious stalker vibes, and I have watched enough serial killer specials to have at least some knowledge of it. And to my utter dismay, I happen to be his new fixation.

"Oh, hi Allen…did you need something?" I ask, plastering a fake as hell smile on my face. I secretly hope it isn't something I can't back out of, the man gives me the creeps.

"Well, actually, I was hoping you would give me the pleasure of accompanying me to dinner tonight."

Ugh, gag me. I have to try really hard not to laugh, and I school my face to not show the cringe that is threatening to break free.

"Um, Allen I'm actually leaving to go see my friend this weekend, so I can't."

"Well, I could come with you."

Red Flag Alert, Red Flag Alert! What the hell is this guy's major malfunction? My control slips from my face, letting my look of disbelief begin to show. But by the look on his face, I can tell he is being serious, and I have to think fast about how I'm going to get out of this without being a complete bitch.

"Allen, you're a nice guy, but I don't know you well enough to even consider bringing you with me to see my friend. I'm sorry, but no, you can't come with me."

"Kinley, how will we start dating if we don't spend time with each other outside of work?"

My mouth drops open at his audacity. I'm utterly speechless and so uncomfortable that I decide the best way to end his delusions is to lie.

"Allen, I'm already seeing someone, who I'm actually going to see this weekend, so I'm sorry, but we can't date. Now, if you will excuse me, I'm going to get some lunch."

I quickly shut my classroom door, holding my breath as I skirt around him. He always smells like moth balls and sweat. I walk away quickly before he can come up with some other bullshit about why he should come with me.

God, what a nut job! Why are these weirdos attracted to me?

I spot Cory and Trina as soon as I enter the cafeteria. Cory is the other science teacher at Mount Tyler Academy, and Trina is one of the English teachers. They are my work besties. I don't always see them during the school day, but I'm really happy that they happen to be getting lunch when I am. I wave to Cory and Trina and fall into line with them.

Perks of being a teacher: I can cut in line.

"Hey Kinley," greets Cory; Trina smiles and echoes him.

"Hey guys, I'm so glad I ran into you! You guys can hide me."

They give me a perplexed look and Cory asks why. As we work our way to the front of the line, I quietly explain my confrontation with Allen. Trina's wide eyes, arched brows, and gaping mouth would be comical in any other circumstance. At least seeing her reaction solidifies my weariness. I'm not overreacting.

"You have to be kidding. He is so weird, but I have never heard of him doing that to anyone. I wonder why he would do that."

Cory has a smirk on his face and says, "It's because you're such a babe, Kinley."

I glare at him.

"Ha, ha. If that was the case I would have a man by now, not creepers. And you better watch it or I'll sick him on you, Cory. Tell him you just love his crazy tie collection."

Cory looks alarmed. I'm pretty sure that Allen isn't into guys, but Cory doesn't know that. Trina laughs at us both before saying, "Don't worry Kinley; we will protect you."

We all make it up to the front of the line, pausing our conversation as we each grab food from the cafeteria workers. Being the best work besties, they decide to walk back with me to my room, serving as a buffer, just in case Allen makes another appearance. Luck is on my side—at least for now.

My luck continues through the rest of my day, thank goodness. I have a stack of tests that still need to be graded, but I'm thinking that those can wait until I get back from my mini vacation. I pack up all my things, shut down my computer, turn all the lights off, and lock the door. I breathe a sigh of relief that my weekend has now officially begun, and I'm damn well going to enjoy it.

I hurry my way out to my car, passing a few of my students that are still waiting to be picked up. They all wave and greet me. *I have some really awesome students.* Waving back, I tell them to have a good weekend and to make good choices. They are teenagers; there is always a chance for poor decision making over a long weekend. Their laughs at my response make me smile.

With a smile still on my face I get to my car, unlock it, and begin putting all the odds and ends that I tote along into the back seat. I really need to clean out my car. It's beginning to look like a hoarder lives back there. I make a mental note to clean it out when I get home so Beretta will have more room for the drive, but I'm distracted by the loud scuffing of feet behind me.

I turn, thinking it's probably a kid running to their car. Startled, I take a step back. Allen stands next to me, looking very determined to talk.

My mood immediately darkens. *Looks like my luck has run out.*

I was so close to getting out of here and not running into him. I mentally prepare myself for the insanity that I'm sure will come out of his mouth. I'm almost positive that he's going to say something awkward and ridiculous, and it will put me in a foul mood. I steel myself and ask, "Did you need something, Allen? I'm kind of in a hurry to get on the road."

"Yes, Kinley, I wanted to give you one more chance to change your mind about this weekend."

Fucking hell, I knew it. I didn't want to deal with him!

I roll my eyes, flabbergasted with his audacity.

"Allen, I don't have time to have this conversation, and I really don't know why you think that this is acceptable behavior."

I give myself a mental pat on the back for not using the variety of curse words that I really want to use. *Go me for being an adult!* I almost let a smirk slip through when his body stiffens and his beady eyes bulge behind his unfortunate glasses. He hadn't been expecting me to talk to him like that, but I honestly don't want to deal with him anymore.

"You didn't have to be so rude, Kinley. I come to you to ask you to go away with me, since I know we are meant to be together and all you do is turn me down. I think you should come and make it up to me."

I'm being punked, this can't be real. What the fuck is wrong with this dude?

"You have to be kidding; Allen I don't know where you got the idea that we are "meant to be together" but that is not going to happen. If I have done anything to make you think that, then I'm sorry, but this has to stop. We are co-workers and that is it. Now, I'm going because I have somewhere to be."

I turn away from him, hoping that will be the end of it, but just as I get to my driver's side door his hand snaps out and grabs my arm. I gasp and try to jerk my arm back, but he tightens his hold on me and pulls hard on my arm, causing me to stumble into him. My heart rate and breathing speed up as a spike of adrenaline courses through me. Being this close to him, I'm overwhelmed by his foul scent, sweaty moth balls mixed with something else that I can't place. I fight the urge to gag, that won't do me any good. *I have to get away from him.*

"What the hell do you think you are doing, Allen!"

There's no one else in the parking lot. No one else to see. No one to help me. My heaving breaths fill my ears, sweat glides down my back and beads on my brow. I'm all alone.

"Please don't leave, I just want to talk about this."

Letting the need to escape flood me, I rip my arm free from his grasp and leap away. I don't want to be anywhere in his vicinity. I find my voice as I attempt to reach behind me for my door handle.

"There is nothing to talk about, Allen, and don't you ever touch me again or not only will I be reporting you to HR, but I will also call the cops on your ass."

His hands raise in front of him as if in surrender, but something crosses quickly over his face that makes me even more uneasy.

"I'm sorry, Kinley; I didn't mean to make you mad." He wrings his hands before continuing. "You go and have a good weekend." An unnaturally high-pitched laugh comes out of his mouth and then he adds, "I'm actually going out of town as well, so I guess I will see you when you get back. Please don't be mad at me."

With that, he whips around and walks away, not even pausing to look back at me. I don't understand him at all, but I'm not going to stand there and think about that.

Wrenching the door open, I jump into my car and lock the doors. The urge to scream or cry is hard to resist, but the need to get out of here is stronger. My trembling hands make it difficult to get the car started, but I manage. *Thank god.* I have to take several deep breaths to calm myself down enough to even think about driving home. I do not need to get a ticket for reckless driving, that really would be the cherry on top of this shitty encounter. As soon as my tires hit the street, I breathe a little easier. *Fuck I need a drink! Megan better have more than one bottle of wine chilling.*

I'm so confused; nothing that I'm aware of has changed in the few years that we worked together. His behavior just doesn't make sense. Maybe Allen's going through something, but I still can't believe he grabbed me. My arm still stings where his hand had gripped so tightly. I will definitely have to speak with my principal when I make it back to work next week. For now, I'm going to put it aside and not dwell on thinking about him. I'm not going to let this incident ruin my weekend.

Driving home, I call Megan to let her know I'm going to be on my way as soon as I get Beretta. I just really need to hear her voice. Unfortunately, she doesn't answer, and I'm forced to leave her a message. *I'm a responsible adult, and I don't text and drive—at least not in a school zone.*

Pulling into my driveway, I check the mail—junk and bills as usual. When I push open the door, I dump the mail off on the side table as I walk inside and call for Beretta. Closing my eyes, I take in a deep calming breath. I let the familiar comforting scents of home envelope me. Citrus, vanilla, and a hint of cinnamon and sugar from the snickerdoodle cookies I made a few days before.

The clicking of nails on wood makes my eyes open as Beretta pops around the corner. She is her usual cheerful self, wagging her tail as she trots towards me. Licking my hand in greeting, I crouch down to hug her.

"Oh Betta Boo, I've had such a weird day."

She answers me with a big wet kiss up the side of my face.

"I wish you had been with me; then that dumb guy would have never touched me."

Straightening up, I walk over to the back door. I swear I hear her growl, but when I look down at her following me closely, she just wags her tail. Shrugging, I open the door and let Beretta out.

"Alright, go do your business; we have a ways to go in the car."

Nudging my hand with her nose, as if in agreement, she lumbers out the door.

Keeping myself occupied I make sure Indy has enough food and water. Then I look over the house one more time to make sure everything is in order. I hate coming home to a messy, cluttered house after being gone for an extended period of time.

Who wants to clean up when they have just gotten home from being out of town? Not this girl.

Satisfied with the cleanliness of my house, I race outside to clean out my car. Thankfully, there isn't as much to clean up as I had originally thought. Checking my phone I realize I need to get on the road quick. Back inside, I open the back door calling to Beretta. At the sound of my voice, her head perks up from what she is sniffing at, and she comes running. My stomach growls inconveniently. *Ugh, we need to get on the road, and I need to get gas somewhere along the way. Maybe I'll grab a coffee on the way out, too.*

Snatching Beretta's leash off the hook by the door and my bag, I'm finally ready to go. Flipping off the lights, I open the door. Beretta is already waiting for me, wiggling with excitement and a small smile spreads on my lips.

"Alright, baby girl, let's get on the road."

CHAPTER 3

KINLEY

The drive to Lake Adger is a pleasant one, especially once I get into the mountains. Beretta, of course, sleeps the whole way stretched across the back seat on the blanket I laid down for her. An audiobook keeps me company as I drive in the increasing darkness. I'm really looking forward to getting to Megan's. I am tired mentally and physically, and I just really need to sit back, relax with my best friend, and uncork a bottle of wine.

I only have about an hour left, but my gas tank is getting low, and I spy a gas station up ahead with decently priced gas. Pulling up to the first open pump, I roll down the back window before getting out of the car. You can never be too careful these days, and I know that if something shady goes down, Beretta will protect me in an instant.

Beretta lifts her head, notices that we aren't anywhere of interest, plops her head back down and goes right back to sleeping. She is definitely less scary when she is snoring.

Shivering slightly as the cool air brushes across my exposed skin, I skirt around to the other side of my car trying to avoid the questionable puddles. My nose wrinkles in disgust when I see the state of the pump handle. *Gross, good thing I have napkins in the car.* A large, rumbling truck pulls up at the pump next to mine, but that is all the attention I pay to it until I hear a whistle behind me a few minutes later.

Definitely not in the mood for that, I square my shoulders and choose to ignore whoever is attempting to get my attention, really hoping they will lose interest when I don't pay them any mind. Of course, it can never be that simple; the whistler just has to make himself known. I'm only halfway done pumping gas when he leans up against my car. These old gas stations always have the slowest pumps. If this had been a newer one, I would have been done already, and could have avoided what I'm sure is going to be an awkward encounter.

I wished for a man, and this is what I get; a booty call, a fucking creeper, and a whistler. Never again…maybe I should let a lesbian sway me to their side. I've heard the orgasms are better.

My skin prickles in awareness. *He's totally staring at me. So much for hoping he would go away.* Slowly, I turn towards him, looking him up and down.

It's a shame he is such an idiot—he is cute, just my luck.

"Is there a reason you're leaning against my car?" I give him a pointed look, raising my eyebrow.

"Oops, my bad, just wanted to come over and talk to your fine self."

Slurring his words slightly as he sways, he does manage to straighten enough so he isn't leaning on my car. My nose scrunches as his scent wafts towards me; he reeks of alcohol. That makes me a little wary, but he isn't being aggressive so I continue filling my tank.

"Do women really respond to that?" I huff.

"Ummmm, maybe?" He slurs.

Rolling my eyes, I give him my best disappointed teacher scowl. I don't have time to deal with a drunk guy, no matter how pretty he is.

I'm about to tell him off when Beretta makes her grand entrance. Lunging her head out the window, her bellowing bark echoes in the night air. The man startles hard and falls flat on his ass.

I snort as I reach over, cupping her squishy jowls as I coo at her,

"You're such a good girl, Beretta! Protecting mommy from unwanted attention!" I give her a kiss on her nose as her wagging tail begins beating against the seats. The pretty drunk man giggles, he straight up giggles, and then he hiccups. He struggles to get off the ground, but his level of intoxication causes that to be near impossible.

The commotion must have alerted his buddies to the fact that he slipped away, because the next moment I'm surrounded by three more men.

I'm in beef cake heaven; all three of the men that walk around the car are the epitome of the male species. They are all fucking hot, like pulled straight out of any woman's wet fantasy. I immediately stop smirking and concentrate on keeping my jaw clamped shut, since all it wants to do is drop in awe.

All three of them tower over me. They are all well over six feet, broad shouldered, and I see hints of dark ink on their skin. I would have loved nothing better than to jump any of them. But sadly, I'm not that type of girl. I might talk a big game in my head, but there's no way I will ever do anything that bold.

The tallest one looks from his friend on the ground, then to me and just shakes his head. Turning back to his friends, who are not holding back their laughter, he gestures for them to help pick up their buddy. I can tell right away that these three are not drunk like the wannabe Casanova. *Thank goodness.*

The tall one speaks up first, still eyeing me.

"I'm sorry about my friend ma'am; he isn't normally like this. To be honest he just had a difficult break up, and unfortunately he downed a bottle of Jack before we picked him up." His brow furrows with a hint of disappointment as he shifts his focus to his friend.

The drunken friend is now being carried off by the other two. A small smile crosses my lips at the spectacle.

"No harm done; I think my dog scared him more than he scared me."

That causes him to smile and I have to seriously resist the urge to clench my thighs together. *Kinley, get a grip, you just met this man... even if he is a heartthrob...and makes other things on my body throb. Jesus I need to get laid. Or maybe I need a better vibrator.*

Before that train of thought can continue and I make a fool of myself, Beretta comes to my rescue again. She lets out another loud, deep bark, baring her teeth at the man. That gleam in her eyes makes me realize that she is on the verge of jumping out the window. The man turns to look at Beretta as I move to open the car door to secure her leash before I let her hop out. I know she won't attack him, but I'm not going to take that chance of my dog getting hurt.

"Well, I'm going to let her out to stretch her legs."

That sounds lame, but I don't know what else to say. This man is making me dumb, and all the sensible words have left my brain. Beretta hops out of the car and sits down next to me, putting herself directly in between me and the man. There is a glint in his eyes, as if he approves of her standing guard.

"She is a beautiful dog...Dane mix?"

"Actually, she is a Boxer mix." Beretta looks up at me, as if she knows that we are talking about her.

"Not quite sure how she got so big though, or why she looks like a Dane, but I guess you never know with mixes."

She leans up against me, getting my attention. I move my hand so it rests on top of her head, rubbing her ear. The man's smile brightens.

"I can see the boxer...either way she is lovely."

"Thank you, I think so too." Her tongue lolls out of her mouth. "You hear that Beretta? He thinks you're beautiful."

That gets her tail wagging. *I really have the best dog in the world.*

"That's an unusual name for a dog," he says curiously.

Taking my gaze off of her, it lands back on him.

"Yeah, it's a long story, but it suits her."

As if Beretta is finished assessing the situation, she gets up, walks over, and sits right in front of him, looking up at him expectantly. He chuckles and crouches down in front of her. Which is exactly what she's waiting for. She licks his face from chin to forehead.

"Oh my god, Beretta! Get off of him." I gasp with embarrassment. I grab her leash, dragging her away from him. "I'm so sorry."

I glare down at her, but she is, of course, oblivious to my embarrassment. He's wiping his face with his hand and when I look

23

back up at him, he's chuckling.

"It's fine, no harm done. I'm Donovan by the way; I feel like we should be on a first name basis after that."

He holds out his hand while he says it, gazing at me with obvious interest. I automatically put my hand in his, and instantly feel a warm fuzzy feeling in my stomach as he wraps his hand around mine. I'm so engrossed in the feel of his hand engulfing mine that it takes me a few seconds to realize he's waiting for me to say my name. "Oh, my name is Kinley."

"Well Kinley, it was a pleasure to meet you, but I gotta get going if we want to reach Lake Adger before dark."

He gives my hand a gentle squeeze before letting it go and turns to walk away. This moment feels big, like a turning point. I'm not sure how, but I'm not going to waste it. I force myself to snap out of la la land and answer him before he gets too far away.

"It was really nice meeting you too. Hope your friend starts feeling better. Maybe I will see you around, since I'm headed that way myself."

The warm smile that spreads across his face stops my heart. He nods and proceeds back to his truck. Not wanting to seem too desperate, and hoping I have redeemed myself enough, I turn to walk towards the grass with Beretta trotting by my side. I might have also put a little extra swing in my step, making my hips sway in the hopes he was looking.

DONOVAN

I can't help myself.

I turn back and watch her walk away, my eyes tracking the movement of her hips, internally kicking myself for not getting her number.

But she's human.

Her intoxicating scent held no trace of my people, and I'm not in the habit of leading a woman on that I can't have. I shake my head, open the truck door, and get behind the wheel.

"So, you have a nice chat, Don?"

I glance over at Brent, and the big-ass grin on his face. "Yeah, Don, did you have a nice chat?" Aiden seconds.

"None of your damn business, so shut your mouths." I glare at them both and start the truck.

"Come on Don, we're just messing with you. Did you at least get her number? She had some rockin' curves. I would so tap that."

That makes me reach over and smack Brent across the back of his head hard. "Hey!" Brent rubs the pain away. "Damn, Don, that stings."

In the backseat, Aiden can't help it and starts laughing; he, unlike Brent, knows when to shut his mouth. I have always had a thing about not talking disrespectfully about women, and they know it. It probably has something to do with the women I grew up with, but Brent just never quite gets that.

"Maybe if you weren't such a slap dick, he wouldn't hit you," Aiden says when he stops laughing. Brent glares at him and grumbles under his breath, as Aiden just grins.

"I hope you guys took a piss, because I'm not stopping again until we get to the cabin," I tell them sternly.

I'm in a mood. My beast is stirring, putting me on edge.

"Yep, we did, that's how Cam got out. But if he hadn't you wouldn't have met that girl. So, maybe it was a good thing that he woke up from his drunken stupor and tried to hit on the closest female."

That makes me glance at Aiden in the rear view mirror; shaking my head I put the truck in drive and pull out of the gas station onto the highway. I can't help but look in my side mirror at the woman walking with her dog, and I silently hope I will run into her again, even if she is human.

KINLEY

I watch the big truck pull onto the highway and speed away as I'm walking back to my car with Beretta trotting along by my side. I really hope I haven't made a fool of myself and that luck will be on my side, and I will see him again.

I can't be that unlucky, right?

But then, I'm unlucky enough to have a coworker beginning to develop stalker-ish tendencies, so there's that. I can't help but think longingly about that tall, muscular, gorgeous man. His name's even sexy—Donovan. Just when I resolve myself to swear off men, a man like that slides into sight, and I can't help but pant. I catch myself sighing over the thought of him sliding over me—naked—and give myself a little shake.

Jesus Kinley, snap out of it, you only talked with him less than five minutes. A girl can dream though right?

I resign myself that he's probably a magical unicorn of a man, and I will never see him again; I smile down at Beretta.

"Ok baby girl, let's get on the road again. We are almost there, and then you can play with Travis, if he isn't in one of his grumpy moods."

I open up the back door, and Beretta jumps in. I quickly jump into the driver's seat and turn the car on. I'm so ready to be at Megan's lake house and crack open that bottle of wine that she promised is chilling and waiting for us to drink.

CHAPTER 4

KINLEY

Almost an hour later, I pull into the long drive that leads up to Megan's lake house. The house is all lit up with whimsical string lights and an eclectic mix of hanging lanterns. They give a welcoming glow to the white siding. My tires crunch on the gravel as I pull to a stop on the circular drive. The sun has long since set, and the clouds, that have been threatening to unleash, have gotten darker. Big drops of rain hit loudly on my windshield-a-tell-tale sign that, in moments, it will let loose. I quickly turn the car off and race to get the bags from the trunk. Beretta bolts from the car, beelining it to the porch. She doesn't even stop to take the stairs; she just leaps over them. I sling my bags over my shoulders as large drops of rain fall on my face. For a split second, I'm tempted to tip my head back and let it wash over me, but Beretta's loud bark gets me moving. Just as my feet hit the stained cedar planks of the wrap around porch, the sky opens up, and it starts to pour.

Well that was good timing.

I open the front door, setting my bags on the ground. *I will deal with them later.* "Honey! I'm home!"

Her laughter fills the air before she answers me. "I'm in the kitchen!"

Walking through the house, the tension in my body slowly recedes. I'm here with my friend, and all the bad stuff can be put on hold.

Upon entering the kitchen, I take in the sight of Megan opening a bottle of wine. Seeing that instantly brings a smile to my face. Megan is a tiny woman—about 5'2" unless it's a really humid day, and then her height increases an inch or two due to her curly black hair. She makes up for her height with her larger-than-life personality, and it takes a lot to get her down. I always tease her that she is the sun to my storm cloud; she makes my life brighter.

"I saw your headlights so I thought I would get the wine ready," Megan says as she pours me a glass.

"You're the best. I so need this, and possibly the rest of the bottle."

Megan gives me an assessing look. "Don't worry; I have two other bottles in the chiller just in case."

Hearing that makes me laugh. "I love how you are always prepared. Do you have snacks too? Cause I'm kinda starving. I haven't eaten anything since lunch."

"I did one even better. I ordered Italian; it should be here in a few minutes."

"Oh my god, you are amazing. Is it from that one restaurant by the pier?"

"Yep, I figured that you could use some good comfort food after listening to the messages you left me." A slight look of concern settles on her face.

"You have no idea. We have so much to talk about. I will grab the bottle if you grab the glasses, because your sofa is calling my name. I'm so exhausted, and I'm sure you are too."

We are on our way out of the kitchen when the doorbell rings.

"That would be the food. Let me go get that, and I will meet you in the living room."

Megan runs down the hall as I juggle the bottle and glasses, going straight to the living room.

28

I set everything down on the coffee table and stretch out on the sofa, groaning in relief at finally being done for the day. There's just something so relaxing about sitting in a room with floor to ceiling windows, big comfy furniture, a wood burning fireplace, and my best friend down the hall.

Megan's lake house was a labor of love. Everything she could do herself she did; for the rest she hired a local contractor. The end result is night and day compared to what it had been. Fixing up the lake house had gotten Megan hooked on renovating old properties, and she has been doing it ever since. It also gives her something to do that keeps her mind off of her marriage.

I'm so glad Megan decided to buy this property, even though it was such a dump at first. With a year of renovation, this property became one of the nicest places on the lake, and Megan is so proud of it. Though, there's a really big cabin across the lake that I drool over every time I see it, but it hasn't been for sale.

Megan had been married for four years, but it wasn't a good marriage by any means. They had known each other all of their lives and it had been a match her family had encouraged. I hated the bastard, but he made Megan happy, or at least at first. But for the past year and a half Megan had become nothing more than a nursemaid, rather than a wife. Not that she had much of a marriage before her husband found out he had a terminal illness.

Megan thought she had the perfect husband, until he started showing her his true nature. It started off with him putting his fists through walls and breaking furniture when he was angry. It eventually escalated, and he turned his anger towards Megan. Several times I had driven up to their house outside of Boston, fully prepared to commit murder. Megan had always convinced me not to, but I wasn't going to let my friend be beaten and abused.

Thankfully, it hadn't taken long for Megan to file for divorce and move out. She was almost free of him for good, too. Until one day, she got a call from his assistant that he had blacked out at work and was taken to the hospital. No one ever understood why she went to the hospital that day; I certainly don't, but Megan's never a person to leave someone by themselves in a time of need.

After seeing specialist after specialist, it was determined that there wasn't much hope for him. He had a brain tumor that was inoperable. A few days later Megan dropped the divorce proceedings and moved back in with him. It didn't matter who tried to convince her otherwise, Megan wasn't changing her mind. Her husband didn't have any living family or close friends, and she wasn't about to leave him to suffer by himself. She is entirely too good for him, but I can't fault her for being the better person. That is just who Megan is; it's why I love her.

I can see that taking care of her husband is taking a toll on Megan. Every time I've seen her over the last few months I get more concerned, but I know it will be coming to an end soon. Maybe with his death, Megan will finally be able to begin her own healing.

So I do what any good friend can; I stand by her and am there for her whenever I can be. Just like Megan had been for me all through college, when I had no one else.

The fire dances and crackles in the fireplace while I take a much needed sip of wine when Megan comes in carrying the food. She is followed by Travis, her short, squatty bulldog, and Beretta.

"Oh, that smells so good."

I reach for the food, but my leg gets jostled as Beretta plops her slobbery jowls onto my thigh. A pitiful whine is followed by more drool seeping into my pants, and I realize that I haven't fed her yet.

Better do that before she thinks she can partake in our food.

"I'm going to feed Beretta real quick. My poor baby, how could I forget? Does Travis need to eat too?"

"No, he ate an hour ago. Won't stop him from begging like a street urchin though."

I snort at her comment and, before my body decides that getting up isn't an option, I go make Beretta's food. As I mix up dinner for her, the loud ringtone of Megan's phone blares through the house and she quickly gets up to answer it. I can't make out what she is saying, but from the tone of her voice I can tell she isn't happy.

Setting Beretta's food dish down, I go back into the living room. The tantalizing scents of garlic, butter, and the variety of Italian spices fill the air and my mouth waters. I ponder if I should wait for Megan to get off the phone, but my stomach growls loudly and I know she would scold me for waiting anyway. I grab a take out container and don't waste any time digging in. I'm a few bites into my pasta dish, trying to hold back the moans as I fill my mouth when Megan's voice rises in anger.

"Why do I even pay you?! You know exactly where all the medications are. You better believe I will be talking to your superiors come Monday morning!"

Hearing that, I put down my fork and walk to where Megan is in the next room. She's sitting down with her head in her hands, and I kneel down in front of her.

"Megan, are you ok?"

I know she isn't, but when she looks up at me there aren't tears in her eyes, but a look of weariness.

"I knew this was going to be hard…but I don't know how much more of this I can take, and that makes me feel like such a bad person."

I wrap my arms around her and say the only thing I can. "Megan, I don't know of anyone else that would even consider what you are doing for Todd."

"I know, and I know it will be over soon, but they keep sending nurses that are so incompetent. This is the fourth one in three months."

"What happened to that one that you liked?"

"She is on maternity leave, but she will be back on Monday, thank God. I honestly didn't realize how much I counted on her 'til she wasn't around."

I stand and pull her up with me, steering her out the door.

"Come on, let's go eat before it gets cold—and if I remember correctly you said there were two more bottles of wine we needed to get through. We are falling behind."

Megan cracks a smile.

"You're right; don't want to let good wine go to waste."

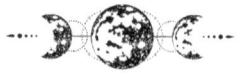

Two and a half bottles of wine later, Megan and I are sprawled out on the sofa and giggling uncontrollably.

"I cannot believe how bad your luck is with men," Megan says in between giggles.

"I know...you so don't need to remind me," I giggle. *I'm seriously buzzed.*

For no reason, Beretta gets up from where she's laying next to me on the sofa, jarring me with her sudden movement. My head swims slightly, but I'm able to focus when I notice her stalking towards the windows facing the woods. All the hair on her back has risen, and a deep growl fills the room. Hearing that makes us both sit up.

"Beretta, what's wrong, baby?"

Beretta, who usually never has to be called more than once, doesn't waiver from her spot by the window, and her growl becomes louder. My sense of alarm grows. I have never heard a growl like that come out of my docile, easygoing dog. Yes, she would bark and growl when she thought I needed protection, but she is straight up snarling, and that scares the shit out of me. I look at Megan who is equally alarmed.

"Does she ever growl like that?"

I shake my head, not taking my eyes off my dog as I ease up from the sofa and walk over towards her. I try to look out the window to see if I can find what she's so bent out of shape about. I'm almost to the window when Beretta moves in front of me in a protective stance, her growling turning into vicious barking right before she lunges at the window. I back away quickly, going to stand next to Megan, who's reaching for the phone, "Are you gonna call the cops? Cause I'm seriously freaking out. She has never done this."

As Megan starts dialing, Beretta suddenly stops. She gives one last bark and walks back over to us wagging her tail like nothing had happened. Megan and I look at each other, completely baffled.

"I have no idea what just happened," I tell Megan, before plopping back down on the sofa. "I'm too drunk for this," I mutter with a groan.

Megan sits down next to me.

"No shit, that scared the crap out of me…and I think my buzz has been officially ruined."

Beretta climbs back onto the sofa next to me. I drape my arm around her neck and hug her to me tightly.

"Beretta, you are going to give me gray hair."

As if to answer me, Beretta licks me on the cheek. Megan reaches out to scratch Beretta on the head.

"You're such a crazy girl, Beretta. I think I'm gonna be creeped out for the rest of the night now."

I sigh, "I'm pretty sure this is my week to be creeped out."

"Is that why I kept getting desperate sounding texts from you?"

"Yes! I have told you about the creepy math teacher right?"

She laughs and nods.

"Ok, so I have come to the conclusion that it was an incredibly bad idea to be nice to him."

Megan raises an eyebrow at me.

"No, I'm serious. Cause now he seems to think we are meant to be together, and he has gone full creeper mode on me."

"Creeper mode? Are you being overly dramatic?"

"No, I'm not being overly dramatic, Megan. He actually came up to me, asked me out, and when I told him I was going away for the weekend, he asked to come…and that isn't even the weirdest thing that's happened…it just keeps getting weirder and weirder."

Her mouth gapes in horror. "What? He seriously asked to come with you?"

"Yes! I can't make this shit up. And he wouldn't take no for an answer, so I had to lie and say I was seeing someone and that is who I was going away with. You know how much I hate lying; he drove me to do it."

Megan snorts. "I realized you had bad luck with men…but this is kinda ridiculous."

"Don't laugh! This is not funny because he didn't stop there. Megan, he fucking came out to my car when I was leaving today and tried to make a last ditch effort to change my mind about this weekend. Like I was being the unreasonable one! I finally had to get mean. I don't know what changed in the last few weeks. I've wracked my brain but literally can't think of anything. I'm taking crazy routes to my classroom just to avoid any contact with him, and that didn't even work. I've been hiding in Cory's room during my conference period so I'm not alone. And now that I'm saying this out loud I realize just how fucking crazy this situation is."

"Hmmmmm, I don't know. That is crazy, have you reported him at work?"

"No, I haven't...I should, shouldn't I?"

"Kinley, of course you should. That is harassment."

"I hate confrontation! Why can't I just go to work and have a satisfying day teaching teenagers that science can be cool...when all they really want to study is the opposite sex and how to get more followers on their social media?"

Megan puts her arm around me.

"I don't know lady...but seriously if he keeps doing that, you need to report him. But for now let's finish this bottle of wine and see if I have anything stronger in the kitchen, cause we need to get our buzz back on. Tomorrow we go on a man hunt, cause you, my dear, need a real man, and I'm going to help you find one. You will be my new project."

I sit up suddenly, remembering the four men that I ran into at the gas station.

"Oh my god! Megan, I almost forgot! I came in contact with the absolute man of my every sexual and romance infused fantasy!"

"Now this sounds promising, do tell me more."

I lean over and pour the rest of the wine into our glasses and hand Megan hers.

"Ok, so I stopped for gas, feeling a little down, when this drunk guy leans up against my car and starts hitting on me with cheesy pick up lines. I'm thinking my day has just gotten worse, when Beretta barks at him from the back seat of my car, startling him and making him fall on his ass."

"I hope this wasn't the man of your dreams..."

I wave my hands at her.

"No, let me finish! So I guess this guy had just gotten dumped by his girlfriend and got into the booze, or at least that was what the gorgeous man said. Megan, there wasn't one gorgeous man but four of them, including the drunk one. I was in heaven! So I didn't get the names of the other guys, but the really hot one's name is Donovan."

I sigh just thinking about the feelings that man stirred in me, making Megan crack up.

"Did you really just sigh? Good lord, girl, you need to get laid."

I smack her playfully. "Shut up, don't ruin my fantasy! Besides I'm not done with my story; so I was talking to him, trying not to drool— Don't roll your eyes at me, he was definitely drool worthy. Beretta butted in again, so I let her out and he thought she was beautiful, which she is." I leaned over to give Beretta a kiss on her head. "Beretta adored him. She must get her taste in men from me. Anyways, we had a nice little chat, and I found out that he and his friends are actually in this area for a guy trip. So if we are gonna hunt for a man for me…can we just go hunting for him? Because that man could make all my dreams come true. Well, for sure all my sexual ones."

Megan shakes her head at me in amused disbelief. "You're too funny. And I will try my best to deliver this Donovan man to you on a silver platter."

I can't help the giddy grin that spreads across my face as I drink the rest of my wine. We spend the rest of the night talking and drinking a stray bottle of wine that Megan happened to find in the pantry. When we run out of things to talk about, mostly due to the fact that our level of drunkenness supersedes our ability to form sentences, we drag ourselves off to bed.

Even with my level of intoxication, heavy images are still able to wrack my sleeping mind. The scenes that pass through my mind don't feel like made up dreams; they feel like memories. Memories I should not have forgotten.

"Come, my dear. Let's get you to the altar."

The crone gestures for me to lead the way, and as I move towards it, the crowd parts. The altar is breathtaking—filled with greenery, wild flowers, crystals, and candles. In awe, I can't help but want to weep and smile at the same time. I didn't want this, and I did not believe in it. Except at this moment, I can't help but feel that maybe I need to be here. Perhaps this was part of my pathway in life. I take my place in the center of a half circle of crystals, innately knowing where I need to be. The crone comes up right next to me.

"We all gather here today to welcome the Chosen; may her path be true and her heart be brave. May this be but the first step in her journey to restore The Maiden."

People are clapping and cheering. A sense of inadequacy washes over me. A beautiful elderly woman steps up to my side, gently patting my hand and clasping it with hers.

"Let us celebrate this new era for our clan. Let us cleanse our souls of negativity, and embrace the change."

The woman continues, never letting go of my hand. Her palm is so warm, and it grounds me like only a kind soul can do.

"We have been blessed with a Chosen. Only some of you know the true meaning of this. When the Goddess blessed us with a Maiden, Mother, and Crone, our Clan was strong, and the magic was balanced. Long have we waited for the fates to align. May the spirits follow the song of the Chosen into our souls and bring our Clan back to greatness. Come, let us embrace the touch of our Chosen, for only she may act as the conduit of our once great magic. Only she may instill the gift if you are found worthy."

I can barely breathe, for as the woman finishes her speech I feel the stirrings of something powerful deep within me. A power unlike anything I have ever experienced before bubbles up. A breeze gently brushes my cheek. An ache in my chest builds as if I long for something I have been waiting for. A whisper on that gentle breeze I'm not able to identify, but the feeling of longing intensifies as a single tear slides down my cheek.

The candles flicker, and the crystals glow faintly now that the magic is stirring. *But how? How is this all even happening? And why does it feel so right?* The elderly woman squeezes my hand, bringing my attention back to her, and her voice fills in my mind.

Don't be afraid. Let it happen. Your magic is ripening and will release as long as you don't fight your body. They will all come forward for the blessing touch. All you are expected to do is hold out your hand; be the conduit our people need. You were born for this; embrace your destiny.

She drops my hand and steps away from me, but surprisingly, I don't feel alone. I finally feel a sense of peace, a sense of belonging; maybe I can do this.

People quietly approach me, and as if my body has a mind of its own, my hand reaches out for them, and a song of power makes its way from deep within me. I'm not a musical person; I have never sang a day in my life, but this song that builds within me feels like the most natural thing in the world. It begins as a hum and gradually builds until it bursts from my mouth. I don't understand the words that come forth, but the power and joy weave into each note, and I know that the words are true. One by one, the people in my clan touch my hand reverently. Gone is the negativity from earlier; all of it is pushed away by the power building inside me, reaching out to each and every one of them as the song continues.

I don't see their faces as they brush their hands with mine; I only see the colors of their souls and how they grow brighter once they touch me. I don't understand this power, but I revel in it. They are all so beautiful as my song merges with them; it's all so beautiful.

Until it isn't.

My song halts abruptly as an excruciating pain erupts from my stomach.

"Mmmmmmmm, your pain is so delicious. I can't wait to soak up every last drop in person, my sweet Chosen," a voice so hauntingly malicious growls in my ear. My body begins to sink, but strong arms band around me. The male's voice holds so many dark promises that I don't want any part of. *I have to get away.*

"Noooo, please don't hurt me."

"Ah, your begging is almost as sweet. Beg me. Beg me to be merciful. Beg me, and I just might forgive all your past betrayals."

A sob chokes out of me. I don't know what he wants me to beg for. I haven't betrayed anyone. I can't think with all the pain that floods my system.

A feral snarl penetrates my mind—it feels near but at the same time so far away—a snarl that snares me and yanks me free from the brutal grasp of a male who demands far too much.

Another sob leaves me as my mind fights for consciousness, the snarl quieting as my eyes open. I blink rapidly, trying to clear the tears that cloud my vision in the dark bedroom. A warm, wet tongue swipes across my face, and I'm fully awake. A heavy, shuddering sigh leaves me as I wrap my arms around Beretta's neck.

She lays her big body down next to me; her head coming to rest on my chest. I probably squeeze her a little too tightly, but she doesn't protest. "Good girl, Beretta." I whisper into the darkness, my voice sounds so raw. *That was such a fucked up ending to a weirdly nice dream.*

I snuggle as close to Beretta as I physically can get and let her comforting warmth and soft snores lull me into a dreamless sleep.

CHAPTER 5

KINLEY

Bright and way too cheerful, sunlight streams in through the window the next morning, searing my eyes through my very thin lids. Blearily, I hiss in pain and attempt to roll out of bed as gracefully as one can with a hangover from hell. I make my way down the stairs, squinting my eyes to let in the least amount of light possible. Shuffling towards the kitchen, all I can think of is two things: coffee and aspirin. Megan must have been thinking the same thing since the coffee is already brewing and a large bottle of aspirin is out on the counter. She's leaning over the island with her face pressed against the granite top.

"I think I might be dying. Why did we drink that much?"

A groan leaves my body as I sit on one of the stools. "Megan, don't talk so loud; my head feels like it's gonna explode. But I think I might be in love with you for making coffee. Is it ready yet?"

I mirror Megan, resting my head on the countertop. "Oh, this makes my head feel better, so nice and cold."

Megan regains her will to move and stands up slowly. She grabs two coffee mugs, pouring coffee into both of them before returning to the island and sliding a cup towards me. I gingerly reach out to grab the cup in one hand and the bottle of aspirin in the other. I struggle for a moment trying to get the cap off the bottle.

"Damn these child-proof caps…They should make caps for when you have hangovers…They just magically disappear."

Megan snorts and then immediately groans. Holding her head, she mutters. "Kinley, don't make me laugh…it hurts."

I keep quietly cursing the bottle cap until I finally manage to get it off. "Ha, you stupid thing, I win."

Wincing at my loud words, I shake out several aspirin into the palm of my hand and pop them into my mouth, chase them down with coffee, and then slide the open bottle over to Megan. Megan proceeds to do the same and starts to shuffle into the living room. *Yeah, the living room is definitely a better idea, comfy couch.*

I follow close behind her, making sure not to spill my coffee as I slide off the barstool. We get situated on the sofa, and Megan squints out the window. "Thank God the clouds are starting to roll in."

"Yep, sunlight is no good for a hangover. I thought I was going to go blind when I woke up." I love cloudy days, and I am really hoping it will get cloudy enough to dampen the sunlight.

"Did you sleep ok? I thought I heard voices." Megan takes a sip of her coffee as she looks at me over the lip of her mug.

"Just a weird dream, Beretta woke me up before it got too crazy."

"I'm not surprised you're having weird dreams. Sounds like all the craziness is seeping into your subconscious."

"You're telling me, I've never had such vivid dreams before. I'm hoping the time away from home and the craziness will put a stop to them. It's starting to affect my sleep."

I see the concern written all over her face. "Do you want to talk about them?"

"No, the last thing I need is to take a deep dive into the hidden meanings of my dreams. I probably just need to lay off the super trigger-happy books for a little bit until things with work calm down."

Megan doesn't seem convinced. I know she loves all that stuff, but I really don't want to know why I'm dreaming about creepy bodiless voices and magical ceremonies.

"If you're sure. But if they get worse, you definitely should start writing them down. Might be a hidden message that you're missing."

I roll my eyes playfully at her; I know she is just worried about me.

"I'm sure the hidden message is to stop trying to date stupid men, and I already deleted all the dating apps on my phone, so I'm sure soon the dreams will stop."

"If you say so."

I don't bother responding, as I burrow into the comfy couch cushions. I don't want to think about my weird ass dreams. I'd much rather focus on wishing my hangover away.

We sit in silence, enjoying the sobering effects of our coffee, content to just be in each other's presence. Before long, Beretta and Travis scratch on the back door, signaling they want in.

"They are going to be so wet. Do you have any towels you don't mind getting muddy?" I ask as I slowly get up and walk over to the door.

"Yeah, let me go get them, and I will help you wipe the munchkins down." Getting up, she walks down the side hall to get to the linen closet. I go outside and wait with the dogs for Megan to join us. As I shut the door and turn to look at them, assessing the muddy mess that they have made of themselves, I notice that Beretta is carrying something in her mouth. Squatting down in front of her, I snap my fingers, and she immediately drops what she's carrying and sits down, her tail thumping against the deck. Reaching out, I pick up the object, grimacing at all the slobber.

"Whatcha got there, silly?"

I pick up what looks like a thick stick, but when I get a better look at it, I realize it's actually a bundle of jagged smoky crystals. I feel a vibration shoot through my hand, nausea roils through me, and I drop the bundle. Frowning down at it, I notice that the long, thin, smoky crystals are bound together by twine. I shudder with a chill of dread. *What the fuck is going on?*

Megan then walks outside with the towels in hand. She pauses when she notices me bent over. "What are you doing, Kinley?"

I straighten up and kick the bundle out into the yard. The feeling of dread instantly dampened.

"Oh, Beretta just brought up something weird and must have found it out in the yard. Have you had people over renting this place?"

"A few months ago, yeah. What was it?"

"I'm not sure, just a weird bundle of dark crystals. Beretta is always chewing on rocks, so that is probably why she had it in her mouth."

I swear I see Megan stiffen, but looking at her closer, I see no sign of recognition or distress.

"Weird. It's probably nothing."

I give her a sidelong look before answering her. "Yeah, you're probably right."

I shrug off the weird feeling and take one of the towels from Megan.

We thoroughly wipe the dogs down and trek back inside. Shortly after we are back in the living room, it begins raining, falling in a steady downpour.

"I love storms," I say quietly.

"Me too. I think they are so calming."

We both curl back up on the sofa, underneath warm, plush blankets, finishing our coffee. The dogs stretch out in front of the fireplace, enjoying the warmth on their bellies. All while the rain continues to fall.

Eventually, we shower and decide we are brave enough to think about eating. Having no desire to cook for ourselves, we climb into Megan's car and drive towards town.

The drive isn't a very long one. The roads are curvy and surrounded by lush vegetation on each side. Every now and then we get a glimpse of the lake through the trees. It ripples and rolls in response to the wind and the heavy rain drops hitting the surface. The chaos of it is beautiful, even if it reminds me of how fragile life can be. How each event, no matter how small, can stimulate a cascade of life-changing alterations.

In spite of that, the scenery still adds a soothing quality to the drive that helps my pounding head, even though the turns in the road don't help my stomach.

The tiny little lake town is welcoming, even on a dreary day like today. We spot a few vacant parking spaces and Megan maneuvers into the nearest one. Even though it's off season for this lake community, it's constantly bursting with life. Armed with sunglasses and umbrellas, we get out of the car in search of food, we tire pretty quickly and just go into the first place we come to. The cute little diner is a popular hangout for locals and tourists. As soon as we walk in we are greeted by the heavenly smells of diner food. My mouth waters instantly as the friendly, elderly hostess greets us.

"Just two today?" she asks.

"Yes, just two; could we possibly get a booth that isn't by a window?" Megan asks politely. The hostess looks us up and down and smiles knowingly. "Sure thing, dear. You girls just follow me."

We are quickly seated in a booth nowhere near a window. I wait a moment for the hostess to walk away before asking Megan. "Do we really look that hungover?"

"Do you really need to ask that question? First of all, we are wearing sunglasses when the sun isn't even out, we don't have makeup on, and if we took our sunglasses off our eyes would probably still be bloodshot. What do you think?"

"At least we showered off the booze smell," I say with a hint of a giggle.

Megan shakes her head and looks down at her menu. I follow suit, trying to decide what to eat. I'm debating the pancake breakfast versus the fried chicken Benedict when our waitress comes over.

"Hi ladies, what can I get you to drink? Maybe some coffee?"

I look up at her and ask, "Is it good coffee?"

"It's the best in town; we actually roast our own beans."

"I will have some, and could you bring lots of creamer too please?"

Megan also orders a cup, and the waitress leaves, weaving in between other tables to fetch our caffeinated goodness. When she comes back we order our food and practically dive into our coffees.

"Mmmmmm, she was right. This is really good coffee. I think I could live in this cup."

"Kinley, you are such a dork, but, you're right, the coffee is really good."

This place is filled with people of all sorts; it ranges from your average biker just passing through to your eclectic artist type who makes this area their permanent home. I love coming here even though I rarely make it into town. We usually stay at Megan's house and order in whenever we don't want to cook. If I didn't have a great job that I loved, this place would be enough of a temptation to make me want to never leave.

The food finally arrives, and we immediately dig in. Both of us are in such a hurry that we scauld ourselves. We fan our mouths and snort with laughter, trying not to choke on our food. That's not a deterrent though; the taste of the food is just too good. We just take extra care to blow on our food before shoving it in our mouths. We are just two girls enjoying our hangover brunch so much that we don't even notice the guy that stops beside our table until he clears his throat to get our attention. We look up mid bite. *No, it can't be.* I place my fork down, squinting up at him as I take in his familiar features. I internally gasp as I recognize him. *It is the drunk Casanova.*

If he is here, does that mean tall, dark, and handsome is too?

He waits until he has both of our attention before he asks, "Can I get you ladies a drink?"

I crack a grin and snort, Megan holds up both of our cups at the same time and says, "We already have drinks."

Undeterred by her response he continues, "Can I get you another?"

I can't help myself, I snort again and reply, "The refills are free. You don't remember me, do you?"

He gives me a perplexed look, studying my face for a moment and then shakes his head.

"We've met? Shit, we didn't sleep together did we?"

I scrunch my face in an amused grimace.

"Really? Do you make it a habit of sleeping with girls and not remembering?"

"Well, no…"

The look on his face is priceless. *Poor sweet fool*. I'm about to give him a break and explain, when the man of my dreams walks back into my life. The heavens open, tiny naked angels sing as I stare at the man I know would rock my world if he was so inclined. *Fuck me sideways and call me a good girl...Be cool Kinley. Don't fuck this up. This is our chance.* I get hot, bothered, and panicky just looking at him.

"Cam, what are you doing?" Donovan walks up behind Cam. Before he can answer I take a verbal leap of faith and answer for him.

"Oh, the usual, hitting on random women."

Donovan's focus hones in on me and instant recognition crosses his face, he cracks a smile, "Hey! This is a nice surprise."

"Wait, you know her, too?" Cam interrupts, he has a look of utter confusion on his face.

Donovan looks at him incredulously, "So do you, dumbass. You tried to hit on her last night when we stopped at a gas station, and you were shitfaced drunk."

While Donovan is explaining the situation to Cam, Megan whispers, "Is that the guy?"

I grin and nod; Megan fans herself with her hand and mouths, "Hot." She puts her hand down right as Donovan and Cam turn their attention back on us. Camden looks at me, "I'm really sorry, I feel like an ass now."

"Don't be sorry; I actually found it really amusing. You know, women like to be hit on, you just need to get better moves, and might want to stay sober while you're trying to do it."

He gives a sheepish shrug; the poor guy looks like a whipped puppy. "Is there anything I can do to make up for being a dumbass?"

"Well, it's always nice to get to know new people, but I think you can make it up to me by never using cheesy pick up lines on unsuspecting women ever again."

Cam grins and Donovan chuckles, "She let you off easy man."

I see that they are about to return to their table and desperately try to think of something to make them stay. Megan is one step ahead of me and takes over. "Would you guys like to join us for breakfast?"

A look of disappointment crosses Donovan's face.

"We actually just finished. I'm on my way to pay."

Megan, being the ultimate wing-woman responds. "Well, what are you guys doing tonight? We are going to throw some steaks on the grill; it won't be too hard to make a few extra…"

Both of their eyes brighten with interest. Cam looks at Donovan as if he is a child that really wants his parents to say yes. "Don't really have anything planned. I'm sure Brent and Aiden would be up for doing that too," Donovan answers.

Fuck yes! That's my girl! We smile up at them as Megan replies. "The more the merrier. You can bring the beer."

They both grin. "That sounds reasonable," Cam says.

"Oh, and Kinley is a great cook, hope you guys have a sweet tooth… since she will probably make something for dessert and stuff to go with the steaks," Megan throws in for good measure.

"Well, we are all suckers for good food. What time?" Donovan asks.

"How about seven?" I ask. I can't let Megan do all the work.

Donovan takes me in and nods. He moves closer to me as the conversation between him and Megan progresses. I catch a whiff of his cologne, hints of woodsy citrus filter into my nose. *Gosh, he even smells good, too!* His gaze is wholly focused on me, his eyes are such an interesting shade of blue, like the color was plucked straight from a crystalline lake.

"Seven sounds great. We will be sure to be there." His lips move but his answer doesn't register quick enough for me to answer. Yet again, Megan has my back.

"Great, ok, so you guys are going to need to know how to get to my place…which one of you is better at remembering directions?" Megan asks.

"That would be Donovan," Cam points out.

Megan describes to Donovan how to get to her place and even draws him a map on a napkin just in case he has any issues. She also puts my number down; when I spy that, Megan gives me a wink.

While Megan continues to give Donovan directions, he casually places his hand on the back of my booth and I'm hyper aware of how close his hand is to touching the nape of my neck. *This man has no right to be this distracting.* I need to focus on anything else before I make a dumb decision. Desperate to find something to steal my attention from the possibility of Donovan brushing his fingers on my neck, I shift my focus to Cam and talk to him, hoping that will do the trick.

"So, what have you guys been doing up here?"

"Oh, just doing some hiking and fishing. Donovan has a cabin that we stay in."

Interesting, I wonder which one.

"So you're just having a guy's weekend?"

He grins at me, a twinkle of mischief in his eyes. "Yes, ma'am."

"So, since you are bringing the beers, I'm going to give you a fair warning, you will be judged heavily on your beer selection. If it sucks, we might decide not to feed you."

"What do you take us for—redneck frat boys?"

That makes me laugh. "Hey, fair warning, so choose wisely."

Megan, having finished giving directions to Donovan, seconds me.

"Yes, please don't bring crappy beer, or I might accidentally burn your steak." She follows that up with a wink.

Donovan and Cam laugh and Donovan says, "Don't worry, we will bring you good beer. It's the least we can do since you are gonna feed us."

His grin melts my panties. *Good lord I feel like I'm in a cheesy rom com. Really, get your shit together Kinley.*

"Well ladies we will let you get back to your food. I'm sure Aiden and Brent are wondering what happened to us. We will see you tonight."

At that last part he looks directly at me and gives me a smoldering grin. I get instant warm and fuzzy feelings from that look; I feel like one of my giddy high school students. *Hold it together Kinley, do not go gaga like a teenager over their crush.* The guys turn and walk away, and all I can do is watch them. They round a corner and are out of sight when I turn to see Megan grinning like a Cheshire cat.

"You can thank me anytime for my quick thinking."

"Megan…I absolutely love you!"

"I know."

Megan and I finish our food and begin brainstorming what to make to go with the steaks tonight. We are going to need a lot of food; those guys look like they can eat.

Before heading back we stop at the local grocery store and get ingredients for the feast we are planning. What can I say, we like to plan parties, and we love to cook, especially for other people. As soon as we walk in, we divide and conquer. Megan heads off to go look at the butcher's case and I go straight to the produce section. We are women on a mission to capture men's hearts through their stomachs.

I decide not to go too fancy since I don't know what these men like or dislike when it comes to food. They look like they would all have a sweet tooth, giving me the great idea to make a berry cobbler for dessert. A pasta salad will go great with Megan's steaks, so I grab some veggies to go with it.

As I'm loading up my cart with ingredients, my skin pebbles as a chill runs up my spine. I straighten. Someone is watching me. My stomach clenches and I swallow the lump in my throat, dread blankets over me. I whip around, but there's only a woman and her two young children. No one is there. *Ugh, Kinley, get it together. You're just excited and still hungover, your mind is making shit up.* I shake it off and get back to shopping, but the unease still lingers.

Megan finds me in the baking section of the store. She's grinning from ear to ear as if she has accomplished something extraordinary.

"What are you grinning about?" I ask her.

"Oh, I just got eight huge, beautiful steaks from that stingy butcher for three bucks a pound!"

"How the hell did you manage that? Megan, did you show that man your tits?"

Megan gasps in outrage. "Fuck off, I would never!"

That makes me cackle. "Well, that price is a steal. You had to have offered him something."

"Kinley, you have no faith! I did nothing of the sort."

Megan scoffs at me primly. As if Megan knows I'm going to keep probing to figure out how she got such a good deal, she hurriedly changes the subject.

"So, what are all the fruits and veggies for?"

I arch my brow at her as if to say, "I'm not done with you yet," because I have been trying to figure out how to swindle that crazy old butcher into a deal ever since I started visiting Megan here. However, I go along with the change in subject because I'm anxious to get her opinion on the food choices.

"Ok so, the fruit is for a cobbler, and the veggies are for a pasta salad. Do you think those will be good?"

"Yum, cobbler and your pasta salad sound amazing. Just make sure you make enough so I can have left-overs, please. What else do you need to get?"

"Ummmm, I think I have everything for the cobbler except the ice cream, and I need to get the pasta and the ingredients for the dressing. And that should be it…oh, and we can't forget wine. Since we finished off your last bottles, I'm gonna need some while we cook."

Megan grins at me.

"Don't forget the guys are bringing beer, but I will go grab a few bottles for the rest of the weekend. You get what you need and we'll meet back at the front. Anything specific you want?"

"Oh yeah, um, get that really good Moscato that you got last time for funsies, please, and maybe a good red to go with the steaks."

"Ok, I will meet you at the front in a little bit." Megan walks off towards the wine, and I continue getting the rest of the ingredients.

We meet at the front of the store a little while later. Megan is loaded down with wine bottles and my cart is bursting with all the necessary ingredients for tonight's dinner. I also made sure to grab some extra stuff for breakfast. We hurry and pay for everything, get the cute bag boy to help load up the car, since it started to rain again, and we head back to Megan's.

CHAPTER 6

KINLEY

The house fills with the delicious aromas coming from the kitchen as we spend the rest of the afternoon talking and cooking—our two favorite things to do whenever we get together. By four o'clock I have finished the pasta salad and have it chilling in the fridge, Megan has the steaks marinating, and the cobbler is sitting on the counter waiting to be put into the oven a little later.

All in all, it turned out to be a successful day. We decide to enjoy the extra time we have by cuddling our dogs on the couch by the fire.

I nestle up to Beretta, and Megan is using Travis as a pillow. It has been a busy day, and thankfully my hangover has subsided. I sigh thinking about the guys coming over later.

"I'm so nervous. I don't think I have ever been this nervous about having a guy over."

"Girl, I wouldn't be nervous, didn't you see the way he was looking at you? He is so into you."

"You really think so? My perspective on men is so skewed; I don't even know what to think or how to act anymore."

"Don't worry about it; all you worry about is making sure that cobbler comes out of the oven fully cooked, and no one has any food allergies."

"Oh shit! I didn't even think to ask!" I burrow my face into Beretta's neck and curse some more.

Of course, Megan just laughs at me.

"Oh my god, calm down. I'm sure they don't have any allergies, people that do generally are forthcoming about that when someone is making them food. I was just messing with you."

I respond by throwing a pillow at her head, but it hits Travis instead. He wakes up with a snort and grumbles like a typical bulldog. A normal dog would have gotten up, but being his lazy self, he doesn't do more than raise his head and glare at us. Megan reaches back and gives him a scratch, and he settles back down, almost immediately snoring again.

"Megan…."

"Yes, Kinley, what now?"

"I didn't bring anything cute to wear."

"Girl, you crack me up. The man has already seen you bleary-eyed and hung-over; I don't think he will mind seeing you in jeans and a t-shirt. It's not like we are going to a club or a nice restaurant."

"Yeah, you're right. I'm being ridiculous."

"Just a little bit."

"I mean if my sunglasses and messy bun this morning didn't turn him off then very few things would."

"Exactly! It's the opposite of catfishing, you show him how little you care about your appearance and then reel him in by looking halfway decent."

I glare daggers at her as she laughs at me. "Fuck you very much."

We spend a little bit more time relaxing, and then at six, we decide that it's time to get dressed and be somewhat presentable. I can't catch myself a man of that caliber when I look like a bum. *Or can I? Megan is certainly under the impression that he is already hooked.*

I'm in the zone, putting on some makeup, fixing my hair, when I pause for a moment and just look at myself in the mirror. I want to look good but don't want to look like I'm trying too hard. I'm not a high maintenance kind of girl, and I don't want to come across that way. Just from our brief interactions, Donovan seems pretty laid back, which is perfect.

I just go with my normal makeup routine. Putting on a light touch of eye shadow, a thin line of eyeliner on the top and bottom lid, and to finish it off, I put on some falsies for good measure. I wear falsies everyday anyways, I'm not blessed in the lash department. I forgo foundation. I have a really good complexion, and I'm going for a somewhat natural look. Giving myself a final once-over, I'm pretty satisfied with the way my makeup turned out.

I have a brief silent debate with myself about whether to leave my hair down or put it up, but after really thinking about it I decide to put it up in a ponytail. The ultimate reason is because I'm going to be preparing food.

I give myself one last look in the mirror; I'm so nervous. This isn't the first date I have ever been on. At my age, I'm pretty used to it, but with Donovan it just feels really important. I have never felt this way about a guy I barely know, and it's making me so nervous. *It's weirding me out how much he's already affecting me, if I'm being honest.*

I'm as ready as I'm going to get, so I turn the light off in the bathroom and go downstairs to see what I can do before the guys get here.

Megan has already beaten me into the kitchen, but it looks like she doesn't need any help. I'm still feeling a little anxious and need something to do with my hands, so I decide to make cheddar biscuits. I have about thirty minutes till the guys arrive, and one can never go wrong with cheddar biscuits.

Megan is busy taking the steaks out of the marinade and letting them sit out so they can get to room temperature before she puts them on the grill. Not wanting to distract her, I walk past her and get out mixing bowls and the ingredients I'm going to need. When in doubt, bake something.

"Kinley, what are you making now? The guys will be here soon."

"I decided I wanted to make cheddar biscuits."

"Bringing out the big guns, aren't ya? If that man doesn't fall in love with you because of those biscuits, then there is something wrong with his head."

"Thanks, Lady."

Her reassurance calms my nerves a little, and a smile spreads across my face as I get to work mixing the batter.

Travis's obnoxious barks and the scrambling of his nails digging into the hardwood alerts us to the presence of someone at the door.

"You keep working, I'll go get it." Megan says as she wipes her hands off and walks to the front door.

The deep timber of male voices filter down the hallway amid Travis's continued raucous. I take a moment to breathe deep and still the giddy butterflies that are circling my middle. *Chill out Kinley, tonight is going to be great.*

Aiden is the first to come into view, followed by Cam and Brent. My hungry gaze locks onto Donovan the minute he appears, talking with Megan. Her voice is cheerful but there is a slight crease in her brow. Did something happen?

"Donovan, I will take the beer and put it in the fridge to chill. If you guys want to make yourselves at home, feel free. The bathroom is down the left hall and the first door on the right. I'm going to go get the steaks. Oh, and Kinley is in the kitchen."

They let her pass and she smiles over her shoulder as she walks by. She's almost to the kitchen when she pauses and turns back around.

"Don't mind the bulldog; he just naturally doesn't like anyone."

Hearing their conversation while I was cleaning up, set the butterflies in my stomach in a whirlwind. Megan walks into the kitchen, puts the beer in the fridge and then leans up against it.

"Is everything ok? You looked confused?" I ask.

Absent-mindedly she answers, "Hmm? Oh, no, everything is fine, I was just reminded of something that I can't quite place." *Weird.* Turning to face me she adds. "I don't know how I'm going to make it through the whole night. Those men are beautiful."

That makes me snort. "I thought you said you were done with men and were permanently closed for business?"

She snatches a towel off the countertop and swats at me. "Wipe that look off your face, I'm still married."

"In name only, so don't start with me, Megan. You're allowed to have a little fun, so just chill out, and enjoy the beautiful men that are lounging in your living room."

She rolls her eyes and is about to say more when the guys walk into the kitchen. If I didn't already have eyes for Donovan it would have been hard to choose between all of them. Even just in jeans and polos, they have cleaned up really nice. Donovan is the first to speak.

"Anything we can do to help?"

"Well, you guys can grab a drink out of the fridge. Really the only thing that has to be done is grill the steaks," I tell him.

Aiden then speaks up, "I grill a mean steak if you need any help."

Megan picks up her beer, hands him the tray of steaks and as she walks past him she says playfully, "Sure, follow me."

Aiden takes it in stride and follows her dutifully out the back door onto the deck, but before he shuts the door he calls out, "Cam, grab me a beer."

Camden hops off the barstool he was perched on and walks over to the fridge, browsing the selection of beers that are already available.

"You ladies sure do have a nice selection of beer in here."

"Megan loves her beer, and when she finds something she likes, she tends to keep it in stock."

That must peak their interest because Donovan and Brent walk over to the refrigerator to have a look for themselves. Brent reaches over Camden and pulls out a beer, analyzing the label.

"Where did she get this one? I have never heard of it."

Peering around his shoulder I recognize it instantly. "Oh, that one.

That is from her family's brewery; it's very good."

Camden turns away from the beers and says, "Wait, her family owns a brewery?"

"Yep, just outside of Boston. It's a microbrewery, so you're not going to be able to find it this far south, but her brother ships her some every few weeks."

The guys look intrigued and grab a few of Megan's beers out of the refrigerator for each of them. They pop the tops using the built-in bottle opener on the island. Camden takes his and one for Aiden and goes outside, too, while Brent and Donovan take a seat on the island stools. *Aaaaand now all of their attention is directly on me. Shit, be cool Kinley.*

"So, did you guys find the place ok?" I'm kind of at a loss as to what I should talk to them about. It's pretty intimidating, being stared at by two large, absolutely gorgeous men.

Gosh they are huge. Goodness, Brent has his hands tattooed...I wonder what else is tattooed.

Hearing the rumble of Donovan's voice as he answers me snaps my focus back to them and not my wayward thoughts.

"Yeah, we didn't have too much of a problem finding it; we almost missed the driveway though."

"Don, don't lie, you totally missed the driveway, and then we spent the next mile and a half looking for a place big enough to turn his truck around," Brent grins at me as Donovan scowls.

I can't help but laugh.

"Yeah, the driveway is really easy to miss."

I give Donovan a sympathetic look. "I keep telling Megan she needs to clear out some of the brush that is blocking the driveway from view of the road. I still sometimes miss it, especially when it's dark out and I've been here many times."

At that, Donovan gives me an appreciative smile. *If he keeps smiling at me like that I'm going to do something stupid. I just know it.*

"So, what smells so good?" Brent asks. *Oh, that one is trouble for sure. He looks like pure sex. I bet he gets any girl he wants.*

"That would be the biscuits." I check the clock on the oven. "Which probably need to come out now."

I turn away from them, getting a small reprieve from their assessing gazes, and grab the oven mitts off the counter and turn toward the oven to see if they are done.

While I'm focused on that, I'm completely unaware of what is going on behind me. But Megan sees everything from out on the back deck. Thankfully, out of the corner of my eye I see her waving at me through the glass door. As soon as she sees my eyes on her she subtly gestures behind me and wiggles her eyebrows as a wicked smirk plasters across her face.

As I bend over to look in the oven I see in the reflection of the glass what's going on. Brent is leaned over getting a good look at my ass, his hands clenching like he wants nothing more than to fill his hands with me. I'm shocked and outrageously flustered. I don't think I've ever had a man look at me like that. Then I notice Donovan, who is also looking on in admiration. I see the exact moment he notices where Brent's eyes are, because he elbows him in the side and lets out a quiet growl. Having the breath knocked out of him, all he can do is look at Donovan with feigned innocence. Donovan gives him a dirty look, shaking his head no, which Brent returns with a very devilish grin. Just as Donovan is about to smack Brent, I open the oven and take out the tray, breaking my view of the two men. I'm flushed and a little frazzled, so I'm careful to turn around slowly while the tray of biscuits is in my hands. I can't stay bent over like that forever, and I can't make them aware that I saw everything. So I put on my best haughty expression and ask sternly.

"What are you guys doing?"

"Nothing," they both say at the same time. Guilty expressions dance across both of their faces.

"Doesn't look like nothing to me. Why do you both look guilty?" I ask as my eyebrow rises and I give them one of my best teacher looks. Donovan and Brent both look at each other and then back at me.

"How do you know we look guilty?" Brent asks suspiciously.

"Because I have seen that look on too many teenage boys not to know what a guilty face looks like."

Donovan tries to pull off his best innocent look and replies. "I don't know what you're talking about."

56

That makes me shake my head. I grab a spatula, letting them think I have given up, when I know exactly what they have been up to. Smiling to myself, I take the biscuits off the cooking sheet, placing them onto a plate to cool. Brent, the sly devil, reaches out as if to snatch one off the plate, but I quickly tap his hand with the spatula, making him draw it back quickly.

"They are hot, and you can wait," I scold him.

Donovan smirks at Brent as if to say, "She told you."

"What kind of biscuits are those?" Donovan asks charmingly.

"They are cheddar biscuits."

"They smell really good, Kinley. Did you make them from scratch?"

"Yep." I grin proudly at Donovan.

Brent keeps eyeing the biscuits like he's just waiting for me to turn away so he can snatch one. I eye him and sigh, lifting the plate to him.

"Fine, you can have one, but if you burn your mouth it's your own fault."

That makes him grin wide and he quickly takes one off the plate before I can change my mind; I then move the plate close to Donovan.

"You can have one, too."

"Why, thank you."

I smile shyly, picking up my beer and taking a sip to give myself something to do other than panting at this man and begging him to take me. I also have to admit that Brent is just as easy on the eyes, he's rocking that bad boy biker aesthetic with his shoulder-length wavy brown hair and almost all visible skin covered in ink. Goodness gracious, if they both keep looking at me that way I won't be held responsible for what I do. *What in the world are these men doing to me? I never act like this.*

The guys both take a bite of the biscuits and moan in appreciation. *Holy shit, that is sexy. Fuck, I need to do something productive before I crawl onto their laps.*

I turn away to let them enjoy their biscuits and go to the refrigerator to get the pasta salad out.

"Kinley, did you say you're a teacher?" Donovan asks in between bites of biscuit.

Did I say that?

57

With the pasta salad in hand, I turn around and answer him. "Yes, I am. I teach advanced sciences at a private high school."

"Wow, I wasn't expecting that."

"Did you think I taught elementary or something like that?" I ask with a smirk.

"Well, actually yes."

I narrow my eyes at him slightly, set the pasta salad on the countertop and take another sip of my beer before saying, "I won't hold it against you. At least not for long."

"That's very generous of you," he replies with a grin.

He takes a long drink from his beer and gives me a look that makes my stomach flutter and my thighs clench in anticipation; I really hope that I don't screw this one up. This man does things to me with just a look that no man has ever been able to accomplish going all the way. I will be damned if I let him get away without at least satisfying some of the curiosity that is brewing.

Brent clears his throat, breaking the moment. Snapping out of it, I blurt out, "So, what do you guys do for a living?"

They blink at me for a moment before Donovan answers.

"Well, I'm a police officer in a city just outside of Knoxville. Aiden is actually my partner," Donovan admits.

This just keeps getting better and better. My inner girl practically squeals with excitement. I found him incredibly sexy before that admission, but now that I know he wears a uniform, perfect. Trying to contain myself, I turn my attention to Brent, waiting for him to answer. Before he can utter a word, Camden opens the back door followed by Megan, both are laughing. "What's so funny, Cam?" Brent asks.

"Oh, Aiden tripped and accidentally poured beer on the grill, and nearly burned his eyebrows off."

That gets a chuckle out of Donovan and Brent.

"Are the steaks almost done, Megan?"

I move to stand next to her while she washes the platter the raw steaks were on.

"Yeah, he is just waiting for me to bring this back."

"Oh, good, I'm starving. I will get the table set real quick."

I open the cabinets with the dishes and eye which dish set I want to use. Megan walks back outside with Camden and Brent following close behind. As I'm counting to make sure I have the right number of plates, a warm, comforting heat brushes up against me. I still as Donovan asks if I need help. An unknown feeling shudders through me at his close proximity. *What is this man doing to me?*

"Um, sure. If you could just take these and put them on the table, then I can get the silverware."

I turn, looking up at him as I hand over the stack of dishes. Our hands brush, and I barely stop the gasp leaving my lips. I drop my gaze, unsure what to do about all the feelings rushing through my body. I thank him and move to get the silverware. *I'm in so much trouble. Be cool Kinley, be fucking cool!*

We get the table finished just as everyone comes in from outside with the steaks. Megan grabs the pasta salad, I grab the biscuits, and we all sit down to eat. All throughout dinner, I can't help thinking that this feels so right.

We eat so much that the guys end up sprawled out in the living room, groaning in their fullness. Before Megan and I join them, we load up the dishwasher, since the guys helped clear the table and put the leftovers away.

"Go sit down, Megan. I will be there in a minute, I just need to put the cobbler in the oven and set the timer."

"Kinley, you're going to make me fat with all this food!" She replies with a snort.

"Hey, someone's gotta make sure you're eating, and since I don't see you nearly enough, I have to make up for it when I do," I murmur with a wicked grin. "Besides, you didn't eat nearly as much as those guys. I'm really glad I decided to make everything in triple batches. I didn't know guys could eat that much."

"Kinley, not one in the bunch is under six feet, I'm surprised they didn't eat even more than they did."

"Yeah, true, at least they appreciate our cooking."

"That's an understatement; I swear the sounds they were making were on the verge of being obscene." Megan covers her mouth to keep from laughing.

"Go back in there before they start wondering what we are doing," I swat at her with a towel to get her moving.

Megan scampers out of the kitchen towards the living room, leaving me to quickly put the cobbler in the oven and set the timer. But as I stand there, I decide to make coffee; coffee and cobbler is a perfect ending for this night. I set it to brew and go out to the living room. I pause, assessing the best place to sit; there are only a few choices. I can either sit next to Donovan or Aiden. Megan took the only single chair and the glint in her eyes tells me she did it on purpose. Donovan spies me looking as well and pats the seat next to him. *Well, that's settled.*

While the cobbler bakes, we all just relax, keeping nice and warm with the coffee and the fire Camden and Brent started. Even without the fire, I would be warm. The occasional brush of Donovan's hand on mine and the pressing of his thigh against my leg is enough to give me a heat stroke. His fingers tangle with mine and I spy a hint of a smirk as he answers some question Megan asks. *He is such a tease!*

The conversation throughout the night is comfortable, like we have known each other for years. The guys are very laid back and open about themselves. They had all grown up together and saw each other often at community functions, and then, when they graduated from high school, they all decided to go into the army together. If they didn't all look different, you would have thought they were brothers. And in a sense, they are.

Brent looks gruff and is covered in tattoos, but he is actually the jokester in the group and has one for almost everything. He has us all laughing more than once, sometimes to the point that there are tears running down our faces. I do get the impression that even though he is quick to joke, he can be incredibly serious when it's needed. He gives off predator that likes to play with his food vibes at times, which both intrigues and unnerves me. He never specifically says what he does for a living, but he does say it keeps him busy traveling, and when he isn't traveling, he lives in a very secluded cabin, about an hour away from Don. When they aren't coming out to Donovan's lake house, they usually meet up at Brent's.

Camden is the quieter one, unless of course he has some alcohol in his system. But he gives off silly boy next door vibes, probably because of his sandy blonde hair. He works as a computer specialist for the F.B.I. in Knoxville, but he is thinking of getting on with Brent doing whatever he does. There are moments that he gets a pained look on his face, and then he snaps out of it and joins in on the conversation. Later, when he goes out of the room to get coffee, they tell Megan and me that his girlfriend of two years left him a few weeks ago, which is the reason for the guys' weekend. They wanted to get him out of his funk and spend some time away from his apartment and work.

Aiden and Donovan are very similar; they are partners in the police department in Knoxville, both tall with dark hair, they even live a few blocks away from each other. Donovan is more of the leader of the group, but Aiden is a close second. Aiden and Donovan are actually cousins, which explains a lot.

Whenever the four of them need some time with nature and to get away from work they come to Donovan's cabin, which just happens to be across the lake from Megan's. Donovan's grandparents used to own the cabin on Lake Adger, but, unfortunately, it had been sold. Donovan, having had such fond memories of the place, bought the cabin back as soon as he could afford it, and the four of them have been staying there every time they can get away.

At about midnight, after the cobbler is devoured and they can peel themselves off the couch, the guys decide that it is time to go. They give each of us hugs goodbye, nearly lifting us off the ground. *Gosh, they are all strong, and smell so good.*

"Tonight was really fun; I'm glad you guys could come over," Megan tells them.

"It was Camden's night to cook, and he can't make food worth a damn unless it's in a microwave. So thank you for saving us from him," Brent tells us with a grin.

Camden goes to smack him, but Brent dodges and runs down the hallway towards the front door with Camden close behind. Megan looks at Aiden and Donovan, an eyebrow raised.

"Do you ever feel like the parents with those two?"

They both smirk and say simultaneously, "All the time."

I walk Aiden and Donovan to the door while Megan lets the dogs out. As we walk out onto the porch, Camden has Brent in a choke hold. The sight makes me pause and wonder why it's so hot. Their muscles strain as Camden fights to subdue Brent, and Brent tries to break his hold. My head cocks to the side as I continue to stare. I've never seen anything like this in person. Aiden sighs, heading down the stairs to break them up, leaving Donovan and I on the porch together.

"What are you thinking about that has that look on your face?" He whispers in my ear, causing me to jerk my attention back to the large man next to me.

"Um, I've just never seen anyone fight like that in person. How do they even move like that?"

Donovan chuckles, his body still so close to me and his mouth just a breath away from my ear.

"They are just playing. If they were fighting for real it would be a lot more intense, and probably bloody."

That mental image makes me shiver, or maybe it's from Donovan being so close. He gently turns me to face him and I get lost in his deep blue eyes.

"I'm glad we ran into each other again," he says quietly.

"I am, too," I smile shyly.

"How long will you be staying with Megan?"

"I'm leaving Monday since it's only a three day weekend for me."

He studies me, as if he's trying to solve a puzzle, but the heat in his eyes makes me want to know what he's thinking.

"Well, if you two get bored, you can always come over and we can feed you. And I would like to see you again."

He has a hopeful look on his face, and I just know that if we had been alone, he just might have kissed me. It becomes incredibly hard for me to think of anything else but wanting him to lean down and put his lips on mine. I need to see him again; I need to see where this could go. The feelings swirling around inside me can't be ignored.

"I will talk to Megan, but I'm sure she will be up for that."

Someone in the truck honks the horn, jerking us out of the moment. Donovan shoots them a dirty look over his shoulder before bending down and wrapping me in a warm embrace. My arms automatically come up to encircle his waist. He's so tall and his body is so firm. I keep my hands still, fighting the desire to let them roam across his muscled back. His scent fills my lungs, and it both calms and arouses me. A small sigh leaves my lips as I hold onto this man I barely know, but can't help but be drawn to. A deep rumble stirs from his chest, the vibration light on my cheek. Another loud honk from the truck breaks us apart, but not before he slips something into my hand. I stare at him, at a loss for words as he walks down the steps. At the bottom, he turns, looking at me from over his shoulder.

"I will be seeing you, Kinley."

He jogs the rest of the way to the truck, his long legs eating up the distance, and jumps into the driver's seat. The engine roars to life, and still I stand there as the truck drives down the driveway and out of sight. I can't explain exactly what makes me stare into the darkness. *Am I hoping I will see the truck come back?* I'm not sure, but an emptiness burns in my stomach that I don't like. My hands clench, the crinkle of paper drawing my mind back to what Donovan slipped into it. I look down; on the folded piece of paper is his number and a note underneath saying "I hope to hear from you soon." Butterflies swarm in my stomach and I can't help the grin that spreads across my face. He will be hearing from me, that is for damn sure.

I run into the house to show Megan, not even caring that I'm acting like one of my high school students who finally got their crush's number.

CHAPTER 7

KINLEY

Sunday morning dawns to a clear sky and a brisk fall breeze. It's a perfect morning to sit out on the back porch drinking our morning coffee while we watch the dogs romp around on the grass.

"If I could stay here forever, I would," I break the silence with my pondering.

"I think that once Todd passes, I'm going to move down here permanently," Megan says absently.

That makes me turn to her with concern. "I thought you were going to move closer to your brother?"

Megan shakes her head.

"No, I need to have some space. I love my brother, but I can't handle him being so negative about the whole situation, and don't even get me started on the rest of my family."

"You really think it's getting close to that time?"

She sighs heavily. "The nurses are thinking so, and he is barely conscious anymore. I'm hoping that he will just slip away in his sleep."

I take her hand, squeezing it gently. In this instance, the best thing I can do is to just let her know that I'm here for her. We don't talk after that. For a while, we just sit in the silence of the morning, drinking our coffee, but I never let go of her hand.

I'm not sure how much time has passed, but both of our cups are empty. The dogs have both gotten a chance to lie in the sun as it rises just above the trees. It's beginning to warm up, and as if our minds are linked, we both get up and make our way back inside, calling for the dogs to follow.

I take both of our mugs, having snatched Megan's out of her hand, to the kitchen sink to be rinsed. Megan looks on as she perches herself on the countertop, before breaking her silence.

"Kinley, let's do something fun today. Why don't you call that hunk of yours and have him round up his boys to meet us down on the lake. I feel the need to lie in the sun and look at sexy men in their swim trunks."

A smile creeps up my face, thinking that's a great idea.

"That's the spirit; I will call him right now and see what they are up to."

"Did you bring a sexy bathing suit? You need to make that man drool and pant at the sight of you."

I take a moment to think about what I packed, and then remember that I do actually have a sexy bathing suit.

"I do! I wasn't really expecting to use it, not knowing if we were gonna go on the lake. I'm so glad I had the foresight to pack it."

I run upstairs to grab my phone and the piece of paper with Donovan's number. The butterflies slowly creep back in as I plop on the bed. I feel like a teenager calling a boy for the first time.

Goodness, why am I so nervous? He told me to call him, he gave me his freaking number. Get it together, Kinley, and call him.

I take a deep breath and dial his number. It rings a few times and then he answers, "Hello…"

At the sound of his deep voice, I panic for a brief moment before I find the words.

"Hi, Donovan? This is Kinley." *Ugh, so lame.*

"Hey, I was hoping I would hear from you."

Just hearing the happiness in his voice calms me down and a silly smile spreads across my face.

"So...the reason I'm calling is because Megan suggested going on the lake and having some fun. She has a boat down at the dock and she was wondering, if you guys weren't busy, if you would like to join us?"

Hearing him chuckle does things to me that I don't really want to admit to myself yet.

"So, only Megan wants to see us today?"

"Oh no, I want to see you, too," I hastily blurt out. I can feel my face flame with a tinge of embarrassment. *Smooth Kinley, really fucking smooth.* My embarrassment subsides a little when I hear the grin in his voice.

"Good, what time should we meet you two at the dock?"

"You're coming?"

Tension that I don't realize is there fades from my body.

"Of course we are. We were planning on going to the lake today anyway, but two pretty girls is an even better reason to go."

Fuck yes!

"Great! How about in an hour?"

"Sounds like a plan; see you in a few."

We hang up the phone at the same time, my heart pounding with excitement. I can't help but wiggle with the giddiness that courses through my body. I'm so glad I packed a sexy bathing suit now. Needing to tell Megan that we only have an hour to get ready and be at the boat, I race down the stairs to tell her the good news.

Forty minutes later we are dressed and have a cooler packed with drinks and snacks. The dogs are loaded in the car, Beretta with her water toy held firmly in her mouth and Travis with his life jacket on. I have just heaved the cooler into the back when I notice Megan looking me up and down.

"Well you are definitely going to test his control today."

"What do you mean?"

"That man is going to take one look at you and get all hot and bothered. Whether or not he throws you over his shoulder and carts you off to have his way with you is going to let you know how in control he is."

That makes me grin.

"That is one of the nicest compliments you have ever given me, Megan. I have a cover up so I won't completely blow his mind though."

Taking in my bathing suit, I guess I don't look bad. "In all seriousness, you think this looks alright? Not too bulgy?"

"Kinley, I ought to smack you. Of course you look alright; you look amazing. You're a man's wet dream, all flat and curvy in all the right places. I would kill to have your ass and your boobs."

That makes me reach over and scoop Megan into a hug.

"Thank you for that. I'm trying really hard not to get swept up by this guy…but I can't help wanting to look good for him, too."

"That's smart. I know it's been a while since your last relationship and you're right to want to hold back and not get carried away, but just don't keep too much of yourself closed off. Let him see the real you."

God she's going to make me cry if she keeps going. With one more squeeze I let her go. "You're the best friend I could ever ask for."

I grab my cover up off the back seat and slip it on.

"Ok let's get this show on the road and go meet those men."

"That's the Kinley I know and love."

We get everything unloaded from the car and are working on stowing all of our gear and coolers on the boat as the guys walk down the dock towards us. They are a sight. It's really a wonder that we have never run into them before; they definitely don't blend into a crowd. All four men are dressed in board shorts and cotton t-shirts. Brent and Camden are carrying coolers. Aiden is carrying a kneeboard. And Donovan, goodness, carrying a bag with what looks like towels, makes me want to drool.

It has to be illegal for a man to look that good.

Brent is the first to jump aboard the boat, his movements way more graceful than any large man should be.

"Hello ladies, you two are sure looking good today."

He has a roguish grin on his face as he gives us both a once over.

"Oh hush," Megan tells him as she blushes brightly, which makes me smile. Megan deserves to be appreciated.

The rest of the guys get settled on the boat, stowing their gear and getting comfortable. Megan is bantering back and forth with Aiden, Brent, and Camden, but Donovan is eyeing me hungrily. He sits right next to me, his body heat radiating into my hip and arm.

I look up at him as he leans down close. Quietly so no one else can hear, he whispers in my ear. "That cover up is just see through enough to be a tease. Maybe you should show a little mercy and take it off."

His boldness causes my cheeks to heat, but I can't help letting a little playfulness shine through.

"I don't know if it would be merciful," I reply cheekily.

He growls in my ear. Goosebumps spread over my skin, and before I lose all my good sense and straddle his lap in front of our friends, I give his thigh a pat and get up to help Megan get the dogs settled. *Be smart, Kinley. Don't let his sexy talk and rippling muscles addle your brain!*

It doesn't take long for us to get the boat out on the lake. The sun is out, not a cloud in the sky; the water is calm and there is hardly anyone else here, we are in our own little world.

Megan is about to sit down to get the boat started, but Brent is practically bouncing up and down, begging Megan to let him drive.

"Megan, you have to let me drive this baby. Please, please, please."

"Sheesh, how old are you? You can drive, but if you crash my boat, I will inflict extreme bodily harm on you."

"Baby, that sounds like foreplay to me."

She punches him in the arm. "If you're gonna drive, do it before I take the keys back."

Brent slides into the seat behind the wheel and starts the boat up, steering it out into the lake. Content that Brent knows what he's doing, Megan sits down next to me.

Quietly she asks, "So what did Donovan say in your ear earlier?"

"Well, it was along the lines of the cover up being a tease."

"Seriously? Oh man, this is going to be fun to watch. So…you want to go sunbathe?"

"Megan, you have a truly devious mind. But I think we should wait until we figure out what the guys are wanting to do."

"I already know what Donovan wants to do, but not on my boat."

I shush her to keep her quiet. She's about to say more but can't because Aiden, Donovan, and Camden sit down next to us.

"So, have either of you been on a kneeboard?" Aiden asks.

"I have, but not in a few years," Megan admits.

"What about you, Kinley?" Aiden asks.

"Nope, never have. I'm not sure I want to either; it kind of terrifies me."

"It's not hard, so if you decide you want to, then just let us know alright?" Aiden stands up and looks at Megan.

"Come on, Megan, I have a running bet with Brent that a girl is going to show Camden up at kneeboarding. It looks like you're that girl."

Camden objects loudly. "Hey, that's not cool."

That has the others laughing. Megan stands up, taking her cover off, and grabs a life vest out of a storage bench. I remain seated, watching with amusement as Aiden watches Megan with a very appreciative look. *Hmmmmm, that would be an interesting pairing. Maybe we were both meant to meet these guys.* Camden and Aiden help her get on the board and put it in the water, and I become very aware of Donovan taking the empty seat next to me.

Turning to look at him as he holds out an already opened beer, I take it and thank him before taking a swig of it, trying to gain some liquid courage.

"So, what is your schedule at work like?" I ask, hoping to keep the conversation on neutral grounds. Work seems like a safe topic.

"Well, I work evenings Monday through Thursday, and I have Friday through Sunday off."

"That sounds nice, only having to work four days a week."

"Yeah, it is. It allows for time to recover from work."

"I can't complain about my schedule. I get awesome vacation time. Though, there has been talk about modifying our schedule to a four day school week to be more similar to a college setting."

"Really? I probably would have gotten better grades in school if I had to be there less. I was never one that liked to sit still. I guess you could say I'm a man of action." There is a glint in his eye that makes me wonder what kind of actions he would excel at, but then he continues,

"So, Kinley, what do you do when you're not working?"

I think for a moment. I'm kind of a boring person. I'm about to answer, but Aiden's excited cheering turns our attention to Megan, who's kneeboarding like a pro.

Keeping my beer in hand, I stand up and start cheering her on. Donovan is right there next to me, shouting encouragement.

"Camden, you're so going to get whooped by a girl!"

Megan does it for a little longer and then lets go of the rope. Brent quickly slows the boat down and loops back around to pick her up. As the boat pulls up beside her, Aiden reaches down and pulls her in. She's grinning from ear to ear.

"I didn't think I was able to do that anymore."

"That was amazing!" Aiden exclaims, before turning to face Brent. "You totally owe me a hundred bucks."

The guys continue to give each other a hard time, and Donovan decides to go next on the kneeboard, since Camden knows he's beat. I almost choke on my mouthful of beer as I watch in awe as Donovan takes off his shirt. He has a six pack for days and is built like a dream. Holy shit, the tattoos that cover that man! They are a beautiful mix of blacks, grays, and vibrant colors. His upper torso and back are covered in intricate designs, and I'm mesmerized. I have to school my face so it doesn't show my disappointment when he puts the life vest on. Megan hands me a napkin. I look down at it and then look at her confused.

"What is this for?"

Megan smirks at me. "It's to wipe the drool off your face."

I shove her playfully and hand the napkin back. Brent, having seen me push Megan, walks over and puts his arms around us. *Hmmmm, he smells really good.*

"Don't fight ladies…there is plenty of me to go around." That gets us both laughing at him. We scoot out from under his arms and walk over to the bench seats to watch Donovan on the kneeboard.

DONOVAN

After a few hours we get tired of the kneeboard, and Brent puts the anchor down so everyone can go swimming. It's early fall so the water is a little chilly, but with the sun shining bright, it is a nice reprieve from the heat. *Not that cold temperatures bother me anyways.* I'm itching to get in, my swim the other day was nowhere near long enough to sate my need. It's been harder lately not being near a body of water that is large and secluded enough for me to fully embrace all parts of me. I've been so unsettled, like I'm unconsciously searching for a missing piece, but I can't for the life of me figure out what that could be. Maybe it's time to take a trip home.

The loud bark of Kinley's dog, Beretta, takes me away from my thoughts, I grin widely at how eager she is to finally get in. She launches herself overboard after Camden throws her toy. Megan's bump on a log, Travis, is quite content to continue lying in the sun on the deck. *His doggie life vest is hilarious.*

Brent chases Megan around the boat, and when he finally catches her he throws her overboard. She is screaming obscenities at him until she hits the surface. Brent jumps in after her and swims circles around her, laughing as she cusses at him. Megan calls out to Kinley to come help her get the "asshole". I'm grinning so widely that my cheeks are starting to ache. These girls are something else.

Aiden and I are lounging in the seats drinking beer, when I choke and almost spit beer all over the boat. Kinley has just taken that tease of a cover up off to jump in; she's absolutely stunning. Her body is full figured and curved to perfection. She looks all soft and plush. The black and teal backless one piece hugs her curved body just right. She takes my breath away—literally. Her full, bubbly ass is barely covered, and I'm desperate to sink my teeth into it. I'm taken aback at how strongly I'm reacting at just the sight of her. I could blame it on the long dry spell, but I don't think my reaction to Kinley has anything to do with that. I haven't needed that kind of connection in a long time, but the need to just be in her presence floors me.

When she turns, I'm stunned at just how far the front of her suit plunges between the valley of her large breasts. There's just a hint of her belly button; I want to run my tongue up the middle of her body until I get to her lips.

Aiden pounds me on the back to get me breathing again. Coughing, I still can't take my eyes off of her. Right before she jumps in, she glances back at me, and with a naughty smirk, she gives her hips a little wiggle. *Goddess, the way her ass jiggled. What I wouldn't give to take a bite.*

"Holy shit man, I'm a goner," I mutter quietly to Aiden.

"I know what you mean, man. Megan is a little firecracker, and she is way off limits.

I give him a sly look, "Megan, eh?"

"Yeah, I know. There is just something about her."

"So, what are you going to do about it?"

"Absolutely nothing, Don; she is married." I can see the resignation written all over his face, but I know there is nothing I can do for him, he's too honorable to even think about crossing that line.

We finish our beers and jump in the water to help the girls dunk Brent and Camden. The six of us swim and horse around for the rest of the afternoon, only stopping to drink beer and eat some of the food we brought. I absolutely love being in the water, it calms my very soul.

When it starts to get dark and the others are all chilled from swimming in the rapidly cooling water, we all get back into the boat and get ready to go back to the dock. Megan and Kinley are curled up on the bench seats, both wrapped in towels. Camden is sitting across from them, and Brent is sprawled out on the floor right next to Beretta and Travis. I take the wheel and drive the boat back. Aiden stays close to me, helping to spot anything that might obstruct our path. With practiced ease, I pull the boat up to the dock and coordinate with Camden and Brent to get the ropes and tie the boat down. When the boat is secured, I go over to the girls; they look like they are asleep. I don't want our time together to end just yet, so I do what any self respecting male would do. I ask them to dinner.

"How about we take you ladies out for dinner at the diner in town?"

KINLEY

Opening my eyes, I peer up at Donovan. His warm smile is so infectious.

"That sounds great. Can you please carry me, I don't think I can move now."

I lift up my arms and give him a pitiful look. He threw me around while we were swimming several times, so I'm almost positive he can carry me off this boat. I'm too tired to move. He chuckles and calls to Aiden, who comes over. "What's up, Don?"

"It seems like these ladies are all worn out and need to be carried. I will take Kinley, and you get Megan."

Donovan scoops me up, and I can't help but snuggle into his sun-warmed skin. Aiden picks up Megan. She starts to protest but then decides not to when she realizes how warm and strong Aiden is as well. *That's my girl!* I grin up at Donovan as he walks up the dock with me in his arms. I'm having a pure girly moment, basking in his strength, not quite believing that I'm in fact being carried. When you are a bigger girl, it's a rarity to find a man that can pick you up, let alone carry you a distance. For that alone I'm going to do whatever it takes to keep him. *I wonder if he could throw me around during sex? Pin me up against a wall and fuck me? Ooooooo shower sex! Fuck! Now I'm horny, god damnit Kinley! Calm your tits!*

Donovan yells at Brent and Camden to grab the dogs and the coolers, and I smirk at their faint grumbles about the short end of the stick.

"Thanks for carrying me," I say quietly to Donovan.

"Kinley, any way I can get my hands on you. I'm happy to do it."

That admission causes me to blush, and my stomach dips at Donovan's grin. When we get to Megan's car, Donovan sets me down gently, allowing me to open the doors so Camden and Brent can set the stuff right into the car.

"Did you girls want to change first? Or are you ok going to dinner the way you are?"

"Well, we need to take the dogs back, so we might as well change. Give us thirty minutes."

Once everything is loaded into the cars, we drive back to Megan's house formulating a game plan to get the dogs fed and us cleaned up in a timely manner.

"Megan, I've never been this interested in a man before. It's weird right? Is he perfect or am I just jaded by subpar men?"

I look over at Megan who is nodding in agreement.

"I wouldn't say that it's weird, just not the norm. He is really great, Kinley. Hell, they all are. I can't believe how much fun I had. Today was perfect, and now four gorgeous men are buying us dinner." Megan smiles widely.

It is so good to see her smile, her cheeks will probably be sore tomorrow from how much she smiled today. It has been too long since she had this much fun.

Soon we are pulling up to the house and we quickly get to work taking the coolers out and setting them in the kitchen to be dealt with later. The dogs rush into the house only to sprawl out on the living room floor. Neither of them move a muscle while we race around the house, trying to get ready.

There isn't time to shower, so we both just dry off, put our hair up into messy buns, and throw clothes on. Messy buns are adorable.

I'm upstairs trying to quickly decide what to wear when I hear Megan call out for me. All she does is call my name, but from the sound of her voice I know immediately that something is wrong.

Just in a bra and panties I race downstairs, leaping down the last two and running into Megan's bedroom.

I find her sitting on the bed holding her phone as I skid into the room. She looks up at me with tears swimming in her eyes, and my stomach sinks. "What's wrong?"

"It's Todd. They don't think he is going to make it much longer. I have to go back tonight." Her lip quivers slightly before she takes a deep breath. Then right before my eyes, I see her putting her mental armor back on piece by piece, until she composes herself. "I have to go. Are you going to be alright up here by yourself?"

"Oh, honey, I'm so sorry. Don't worry about anything here. I will lock up the house and take care of everything. You go, and be safe driving, alright. Do you need help packing?"

"No, I will just change and load Travis in the car. Tell the guys I'm sorry."

"Don't worry about them; they will completely understand. Do you need me to go with you? I can take some time off work."

"No, you enjoy the rest of your weekend. I will call you when I get back, ok?"

I help Megan get Travis and her bag in the car and watch her drive out of the driveway. My heart breaks for her. Brushing a tear from my cheek, I turn to go back into the house and call Donovan.

CHAPTER 8

KINLEY

"Kinley, are you going to be ok?" Donovan asks, the concern in his voice evident.

"Yes, I will be ok. I'm just worried about Megan."

"Do you still want to come out for dinner? I can come pick you up if you would like."

"That would be nice. I'm ready to go now if you are ready."

"Ok, I will be there before you know it."

The phone call ends and I pace around the house for a few minutes while I wait for Donovan. Beretta is watching my movements, and if I didn't know any better I would say she looks at me with concern. I absentmindedly pat her head, rubbing her ear for good measure.

I see headlights flash across the front windows. *That must be Donovan.* I grab my purse from the kitchen island on my way out, making sure to put my phone in it. I don't want to forget it in case Megan calls me.

I'm going to worry about her until I know she gets home safely, and even then I will still worry about her. It just doesn't sit right with me that she's determined to see this through to the end by herself, not wanting to burden me or her brother—as if she could ever be a burden. Megan once told me that she didn't think she would be strong enough to do what needed to be done if she leaned too heavily on anyone else. I absolutely don't agree with her, but my feelings don't matter. I have to let her do what she needs to do.

With a deep breath to help clear my head, I pop out the front door, making sure to lock up the house. Lock secured, I turn around in time to see Donovan opening his truck door. He hops out and walks up the stairs to me, eating up the distance in a matter of seconds with his long legs. Not even pausing to say hello, he wraps his arms around me and holds me close. I sink into him, letting his warmth and comfort envelope me.

Why does it feel so good to be in his arms?

Donovan peers down at me with warmth and a hint of concern in his eyes.

"Hi there."

Seeing his smile gives me warm fuzzies. If I wasn't hungry and trying to be good, I would pull him inside and lock the door. This is a man that can definitely make me forget my worries. He brushes a lock of hair off my forehead, the gentle caress sends tiny shivers through me.

"Are you sure you're ok? If you're not up for going out, you absolutely don't have to."

His genuine concern is unexpected, but I guess I shouldn't be surprised, nothing about him is expected. The way I'm drawn to him is something I never thought was possible.

"I'm ok. I promise. Getting out will help keep me from fixating on what I can't do for her. Thank you for coming to get me."

"No problem at all." His eyes drop to my lips, they are filled with wanton desire, and I bite my bottom lip in response. *Oh my god, is he going to kiss me? Please let him kiss me.*

His hand cups my cheek and his thumb slides across my lips. "Mmm so soft, I need to taste these perfect lips."

He leans down, but it doesn't register in my head until his lips meet mine. God, his lips are the kind you can sink into. They draw me in, making me want more. He takes my breath away. When he gently nips my bottom lip, I gasp, and my mouth opens just enough for him to take the opportunity to deepen it further. His tongue dives into my mouth, caressing my tongue. *I need this man, and I need him to kiss me like this often.*

His arms draw me in closer. I cling to him, wrapping my arms around his neck. He is so tall that I have to stand on my toes to get closer, when what I really want to do is hop up and wrap my legs around him. I sigh into him, knowing that if he wasn't holding onto me, I would melt into the floor.

We come up for air, and I get lost in his eyes. They are breathtaking, deep blues with hints of green. He places one more soft kiss on my lips before he straightens up, unlinking my hands from around his neck. He looks down at me intently—so many emotions swirl in the depths of his eyes.

"We better get to the diner before the guys start eating the table from hunger."

All I can do is nod in agreement; he kissed me speechless. He takes my hand, his large fingers engulfing mine fully; he has such large hands. He leads me down to the truck, opening up the passenger door and helping me up into the seat. *Such a gentleman.*

Sitting in Donovan's truck, I can't help the small smile that stays on my lips, which are still tingling from that amazing kiss. As Donovan gets into the driver's seat, we just look at each other. His answering grin helps wash away some of the anxiety from the last thirty minutes. I relax back into the seat as Donovan starts the truck and heads down towards town.

The diner is busy, but as soon as we walk in the other guys zero in on us. We might as well have a big flashing neon sign saying "just kissed." Just that one look at the two of us gets Brent grinning from ear to ear. We barely sit when he asks Donovan, "So, Don, does she taste as good as she looks?"

My mouth drops. Donovan moves to hit him, but Aiden beats him to it. Donovan gives my thigh a light squeeze under the table when he sees my cheeks stained pink. My blush deepens further as his touch sends tingles all throughout my body.

The guys settle down enough so that the waitress can take our drink order. As we all concentrate on looking over the menu, Aiden breaks the silence. "Kinley, is Megan alright?"

I put my menu down, instantly noticing the genuine concern in his face.

"Honestly, I'm not sure. She doesn't want to talk about it much. She knows how sick he is and that he isn't going to be around much longer. She has been taking care of him so long that I don't think it dawned on her that it was going to end."

"Tell her that I send my condolences."

"I will; I'm sure she will be glad to hear that."

"Yeah, tell her she is in our thoughts," Camden adds.

"Thanks guys, it means a lot."

Donovan gives my thigh another comforting squeeze, his thumb brushing my skin briefly before releasing me. I have to hold back a shudder; his touch just feels too good.

The rest of the evening is a welcome distraction. The guys are just great to be around, but I can't help but wonder about Megan. I try to stay in the moment, periodically glancing at my phone to make sure I don't have any messages, but my phone notifications remain zero.

It doesn't go unnoticed, every time I look up from my phone one of them gives me a kind smile. I'm thankful to have met them, especially Donovan. They make me feel like I belong in their group. I so rarely get that feeling from others. I just really want to keep all of them; they feel like they are meant to be in my life.

"So most of you live around Knoxville, right?"

They all nod, giving me their full attention.

"Maybe if you are in my neck of the woods, you could all stop by for dinner. If we plan it with enough notice it would be a good excuse to drag Megan out of her hobbit hole, too."

"Kinley, to sample more of your cooking, I will go anywhere," Brent replies playfully.

Camden and Aiden second that, but Donovan leans close to me before responding, "Well, I plan on seeing you sooner than that."

A blush pinks my cheeks, and the guys laugh. It's getting a little embarrassing how much these guys are capable of making my face heat up.

It gets late, and the diner is emptying when we all make the decision to call it a night. Donovan drops the guys off first.

Thankfully his cabin is close, because I practically have to sit in Camden's lap. These guys are all well over six feet, not a one of them is skinny, and there is only so much room in Donovan's truck. We barely pull into the drive when the guys start piling out. I can barely make out the cabin in the dark, but it looks like it is two stories.

"Don't you guys turn outdoor lights on when you leave?"

Brent snorts at my question. "Why waste the energy when the cameras are all infrared and have night vision?"

I have no response to that, but I guess it makes sense that Donovan would have an intense security system with his profession. On my way around to the front seat I get pulled into hugs from each of them; they all give good hugs. Brent, the last one, lifts me off my feet and murmurs in my ear. "You make sense, Kinley; be good to my boy."

As he places me gently back on the ground, I look up at him, and even though it's dark, I can see he is being genuine.

"You don't need to worry about me, Brent. I don't play games."

That seems to satisfy him because he waves at Donovan and heads towards the cabin with the others.

The drive back to Megan's is entirely too short, but before Donovan leaves, he walks me back up to the house. As soon as we climb up the porch steps he gives me another heated good night kiss. His lips are warm and soft against mine.

The only thing keeping me standing is the sturdy door behind me. The grin on his face tells me he knows exactly how much he affects me. I can't help but think how easy it would be to just ask him in, but I also don't want to run the risk of running him off by coming off as desperate. I'm going to see him again. With as much chemistry as we have I just know it. I have time to wait. Besides I can't let myself get too caught up, I just met this man. Even if he is stirring strong feelings, I can't let that cloud all my senses. *Why is dating so difficult?*

Brushing a stray hair off my face that has fallen out of my messy bun, probably from his hand holding the back of my head as he kissed me, he tells me sincerely, "If you need anything, Kinley, don't hesitate to call me. If I don't answer right away just text me and I'll respond as soon as I can. Alright?"

"I will, Donovan. Be careful going home."

He pulls me away from the door and gathers me up in his arms for one more kiss. A kiss that is entirely too short and leaves me wanting so much more. He makes sure I'm steady on my feet, chuckling softly when I wobble a little. He waits for me to go inside, turn the lights on, and lock the door before he leaves. He's definitely one of the good ones.

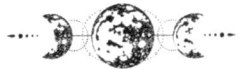

It's late, but I'm way too wired and amped up to go to sleep, so I change and decide to relax in the living room. I call Megan before it gets too late, and I talk to her briefly. She's a few hours away from home and is planning on driving until she can't.

I make her promise to call or text me when she stops to confirm she is safe for the night. The only comfort I get from talking to Megan is that she sounds better. Her voice is stronger, and it has lost the tremor that worried me so much when she initially left.

I make a mental note to check how many days off I have left. I'm going to need to make plans to go up to her house soon. Maybe if I have enough, I can go earlier, or stay longer and be with her.

I'm not sure how long I lay on the couch cuddled up close to Beretta, but it's long enough that I'm just starting to doze off. Megan has the best taste in furniture, and I freaking love this couch. It's so comfy.

My eyes are closed and vague images filter through my mind, when I'm startled awake by Beretta springing off the couch and launching herself at the windows facing the back yard. She doesn't even give a warning growl, she just goes into a full on rage of barking and snarling. I gasp in alarm, trying desperately to scramble off the couch.

Grabbing up my phone, I go to flip on the outside light switch, almost terrified to see what is out there. I can't see anything or anyone even with the lights on, but Beretta won't stop. She pushes me away from the glass doors, putting herself in between me and whatever is outside. I know that there are bears in the area, but they have lumbered up onto the porch before, and Beretta never acted like this. *This just isn't making any sense. What the hell could be out there?*

I grab her by the collar and give her the command to stop, but Beretta remains on alert even after her barking ceases. I stroke her head, and say as calmly as I can, "Betta, my good girl, it's probably just a wild animal."

She lets out another growl.

"Shhhhh baby."

Her keen eyes never leave the darkness.

I keep looking out the windows, scanning the surrounding woods to determine what could have set her off, but I still can't see anything. I'm about to turn the lights off, convinced that whatever startled Beretta has moved on, but out of the corner of my eye, I see movement.

My stomach drops, and before my brain can really process what I'm seeing, Beretta is snarling and lunging at the glass door again. A figure all in black walks out of the shadows onto the deck. An involuntary scream leaves me as the figure stalks up to the glass door. They are covered head to toe and I can only make out their eyes. The figure's eyes burn with hate and something more sinister that I won't let my brain decipher.

Unconcerned with the big dog snarling at them with only a thin window pane separating them, they reach out and stroke the glass, their fingers squeaking as they drag them down, as if they will reach through and caress my face. I'm momentarily frozen; I can't believe what I'm seeing. *Who is this person? Why are they here?*

Question after question slams through my mind in a matter of seconds. It's all I can do to force myself to snap out of the terrified trance I'm in. I lunge for Beretta's collar, commanding her to come, as I run out of the living room. I barricade myself and Beretta into an interior bathroom, praying the glass doors are strong enough as loud booms echo through the house as the person bangs on the door trying to get in. I fumble to unlock my phone, thanking God that I managed to keep a hold of it.

Without even thinking, I press the button to call Donovan.

The phone rings a few times, and with each ring my panic grows, when I finally get a sleepy answer. I barely hear his gruff, sleepy "Hello" before I blurt out in a panic, "Donovan! There is someone outside trying to get into the house!"

It takes every ounce of strength to not let out the sobs that are threatening to burst from me. I don't think I have ever been this scared before. I can't let this person hurt me or my dog. I need help. I need Donovan.

"Whoa, Kinley, say that again…what's going on? I'm getting dressed right now, ok? Take a deep breath and tell me what happened again."

"Someone is trying to break in! I don't know how long the doors will hold up!"

"Ok, listen to me carefully. Get into a bedroom or bathroom without windows…and don't come out until I call you. Can you do that for me?"

"I already am."

A small sob escapes my mouth, before I clamp down my quivering lips. I will not fall apart now.

"Good girl, just stay there no matter what. Can you still hear them?"

"No, it just went quiet."

I try desperately to calm my breathing. It won't do me any good to go into a panic attack.

"Kinley, I'm coming right now. Ok? No matter what, you stay in that room and don't come out until I tell you otherwise. Kinley, talk to me…"

"Don, I'm really scared."

He keeps me on the phone as he wakes up the guys and they race to the truck. I hear the engine roar to life and tires squeal, but still Donovan remains on the phone with me, doing his best to keep me calm.

"Kinley, I'm coming as fast as I can. Ok, hon? I even have the guys with me…can you hear anything?"

"No, and I don't know if that is a good thing or bad."

I clutch the phone in one hand and Beretta with the other. I can't stop shaking. Beretta's growls have stopped, but her entire body is tense, the hairs along her back raised. She is intently listening for the intruder as she keeps her body in between mine and the door.

The time seems to stretch endlessly, and I can't help pleading with him to hurry. A feeling of pure evil and darkness washes over me, threatening to steal all of the air from my lungs. Beretta's deep snarls start up again and grow in volume. I just know that if they don't get here soon, something terrible is going to happen to me.

CHAPTER 9

DONOVAN

Rage burns through my body, my beast rearing up inside of me at the thought of Kinley being in danger. If I find anyone out there I'm going to make them pay for scaring her. I hear every panicked breath over the phone, every tiny sob that escapes her. I have an uncontrollable urge to lay the corpse of her tormentor at her feet. This woman who has captivated both me and my beast will fear no one if I have anything to do with it.

My body vibrates with the need to change, but I hold it together so I can bring her comfort.

"Ok, Kinley, I'm going to hang up the phone. We are just about to pull up in the driveway. Remember, don't come out until I call you."

I quickly hang up the phone, leaping from the still moving truck. Brent curses me for not waiting for him to put the truck in park. I bark orders, and the four of us spread out and scan the area surrounding the house. We are going on a hunt.

I'm not sure what is going on, but something is setting off all of my senses, and looking over at the others I can tell they are feeling something similar. A sense of wrongness permeates the area. Negativity and desperation vibrate in the air, and as I draw in deep breaths I scent hints of sulfur. I take in another deep inhale and motion for the guys to fan out. If anyone is still here, we will find the fucker and make them regret scaring my girl.

Everything in me wants to rush into the house and get to Kinley, but the stronger urge is to eliminate the threat to make sure whoever has been trying to get in isn't still lurking around. I can't explain why I feel so strongly towards her this quickly; it's enough to almost distract me entirely. But not even my driving need to protect her is enough to dampen my heightened senses or my years of training as I sweep the area, making my way to the back of the cabin.

I don't find any evidence that the perp is still around, but I definitely find proof that someone has trekked all around the house looking for an easy way to get in. My lip curls in a snarl as I note the footprints at every window and exterior door. I'm careful not to step in any of them, but the more I find, the angrier I get.

Several times I have to pause and take deep calming breaths because I know that if my beast gets loose, I will surely trample all of the evidence and break down doors to get to Kinley. *Goddess, that will definitely get her running if she sees me like that.*

I catch a glimpse of Brent and Camden as I get to the backyard by the deck, a second later, Aiden shows up.

"Did you guys find anything?" Aiden inquires.

When they all nod yes, my stomach drops and I can't contain the low furious growl. Brent shines his flashlight on the ground, right on a pair of fresh footprints.

"I don't know what you guys found, but these are all over the place out here and I followed them around most of the house."

My eyebrows furrow, and a frown tugs at the corners of my lips at the grim looks on our faces.

"If I find that creepy mother fucker, they are going to regret it," Brent growls.

We all grunt in agreement. I want to let loose and rage. The urge to storm inside, pick her up in my arms, and take her back to my house is monumental. I want to stake my claim on her so no man dares to try to take her from me. Somewhere within the short time I have known her, I have begun to think of Kinley as mine. Even though she's human, I have an innate need to protect her. I'm beyond fighting it, and I don't think any of my Clan brothers would object.

Out of the corner of my eye, I notice Aiden's body twitch, his nostrils flaring as he takes in a deep breath. I turn to him fully.

"What is it, Aiden?"

His eyes narrow as he inhales deeply again.

"I think there is a ward around the house."

"What kind of ward?" I ask warily.

"I'm not sure. It's not any magic I'm familiar with and it definitely wasn't present when we were here before."

"Could it be in response to a potential intruder?" Camden asks.

"That is possible, but isn't this Megan's house?" Aiden ponders.

"It is," I reply slowly, thinking of what that means. Does that mean Kinley isn't actually human, or does that just apply to Megan?

"We don't really interact with other magical communities, and not all magical beings give off strong enough scents to detect them. It's not like we all go advertising that we are Clan. Maybe Megan and Kinley aren't human after all," Brent offers.

"If Kinley had any magical gifts, I don't think she would have called, nor would she have been as scared as she was," I add.

They all nod, milling over the possibilities.

"Well, none of that matters. Someone tried to break into the house, and it doesn't really matter who is magical because I'm pretty sure that ward is the only thing that prevented the intruder from gaining entry into the house. The three of you collect some evidence; there are footprints at every window and door along the side of the house. Cam, you might be a little rusty working a scene, so if you need help call out to Brent or Aiden. We have enough connections between all of us that we can run the evidence and see if we can get some answers. I'm going to call Kinley to get her to let me in. I'm going to see how she is before I decide if I will be coming with you all or not."

"We will call you if we find anything else," Aiden tells me. "Hey Don, we could all stay. That is, if Kinley is ok with that."

I pause as I think for a minute. "I'll ask Kinley if she is ok with that, but the cabin has some of our work equipment there, and it would be easier to process everything we can get from the evidence."

Brent nods in agreement, "You're right, my computer and everything is in the cabin. I doubt anyone is going to come back tonight, especially after us all trudging around out here. We will see if we can collect anything and then head back. You know, you could just get her to come back to our place."

He pauses, thinking about something and then continues.

"Oh, hey, ask Kinley if there is any type of surveillance equipment on the property. I might be able to tap into it and see if I can get any evidence of the perp being on the property."

I nod, and start dialing Kinley's number as I walk back up towards the house. She answers on the first ring, her voice still trembling. "Don, did you find them?"

"We found some footprints; the guys are going to see where they lead. I wanted to make sure you were ok. Could you let me in?"

"I will be right there."

Kinley hangs up the phone, and I watch from the back porch, seeing her open a door on the first floor and rush over to unlock the deadbolt. I have to reach down to catch Beretta from going out the door. I definitely don't need her trekking through the mud and potentially contaminating evidence. Pushing a bristling Beretta back in before I can walk through, I notice the smudge marks from someone banging on the glass. *Thank the Goddess they didn't break in.*

I have barely stepped into the room when Kinley launches herself into my arms, causing me to almost lose my balance. I adjust quickly, holding her soft body close to mine. I can feel her body trembling, and instead of putting her down, I swing her legs up and carry her to the couch. Her whole body sinks into me, and she clutches my shirt tightly, her pretty blue eyes are swimming with unshed tears. Seeing the panic and fear still etched on her face, I silently vow to myself and my beast that we will do everything in our power to prevent her from feeling this way again.

I cup her cheek, brushing my thumb lightly against her soft skin as she quietly asks, "So, you only found footprints?"

"Unfortunately, yes. There were a lot of them, but as far as I saw that was all that was left behind. The guys are still looking though, so they might find something else."

"Should I call the cops?"

I'm honestly surprised that she didn't call the police instead of me. Maybe she's having the same reaction as I'm having for her.

"I think we've got it handled. I'm glad you called me, though. Here, let me make you a drink to relax you. That sound ok?"

The last thing we need is human cops involved. We learned a long time ago that when it comes to matters of the slightly magical, human cops just muddy the water. Even if Kinley is human herself, the fact that she's connected to me would be enough to impair their senses.

I usually use that to my advantage when I'm at work. I'm damn good at my job and have the records to prove it. Aiden and I have an innate sense for the subtle links in a case. Maybe it's a hidden gift of ours, maybe it's just a part of our Clan nature; we never questioned it. I'm not even really sure that what happened tonight is supernatural, but there's something off—especially now that we know about the ward. I'm not going to take the risk and lose any potential lead because a human police officer got involved. We have learned to work around it when we are at work, but I'm not willing to do that when Kinley could suffer the consequences. She's too important.

Kinley nods, and my heart softens for her even more with the level of trust she's giving me. My lips brush her forehead, my beast finally beginning to calm as her body loses some of the tension and fear.

"Will you be ok while I go make you a drink?"

"Yeah, I'll be ok." Her voice is still quiet and there is an edge of nervousness, but I take her at her word. Standing up with her still in my arms, I savor her nearness for a moment more before setting her back down on the couch, handing her a blanket to cover up with. I'm almost to the kitchen when I see her motion for Beretta to get on the couch. She hops up and curls up right next to Kinley, resting her head in Kinley's lap. She strokes Beretta's head. That is a good dog; there's a bravery that most animals don't have when faced with danger. I know that she would protect Kinley with her very life if need be, and for that I'm incredibly thankful.

It doesn't take me long to find what I need to make a drink for Kinley. She doesn't seem like the fussy cocktail type, so I go with something simple. Eyeing the very expensive single malt whiskey, I add a few ice cubes and pour a few fingers worth.

I eye my surroundings, noting the lack of security. Maybe I should ask Kinley if she will be ok coming back to my cabin tonight. We won't be alone, but she will definitely be safer there than here. Goddess knows I want to be alone with her, but her safety's worth the sacrifice.

Kinley is exactly where I left her when I walk back in, and I can't help but think how lovely she is. Even with the stress of tonight, there's a glow about her that draws me in.

I reach over the couch to hand Kinley the glass when the guys knock on the back door. Kinley startles hard at the noise, almost spilling her drink. Beretta raises her head and growls, the deep timber of it makes, even, me pause. It makes me wonder what sort of person would have the balls to persist after hearing that. She doesn't growl for long, and they both calm seeing that it isn't strangers.

I motion for Kinley to stay where she is as I let the guys in. I don't want Kinley to get up; she needs to relax. The guys come in, being careful not to track dirt into the house.

Kinley takes a sip of her drink. Tasting how strong it is, she shudders, and I can't help but chuckle.

"Sorry, hun, I figured you could use something strong."

A small shy smile graces her lips in answer.

"Did you find anything else?" I ask, turning my attention to the guys as I sit down next to Kinley. Draping my arm over her shoulder I pull her into me, hoping some of my warmth and strength can ease her fears further.

"We followed the tracks down to the road, but we didn't see any cars or people. I don't know what to do. Whoever was out there is long gone now." Camden and Aiden nod in agreement with Brent.

"Kinley, would you be ok coming back to my place tonight? I don't really trust the security here. I know it's a big ask, and we are still getting to know each other, but I don't think it is safe for you here. If that doesn't work for you, then would it be ok if I stayed here with you? Just in case anything else happens."

I watch her as she mulls it over. Her face is so expressive and I wish I could hear the thoughts that are running through her mind.

Did I overstep by asking her to come back to the cabin? I know human women don't think the same way Clan women do. Will she think I'm asking for too much even suggesting I stay here? But she did call me tonight when she could have called the police. She at least trusted me enough to do that.

There is no way in hell I'm leaving her alone tonight. If she isn't ok with either option I will shift and watch from the trees.

"Would it be weird if I stayed at your place? We just met, and I don't want you to feel obligated to watch out for me. The fact you came out tonight is enough."

The guys chuckle as I shake my head.

"No, it wouldn't be weird, Kinley. There is plenty of room at my place. In the end, it is ultimately your choice, but I won't feel good leaving you alone tonight."

The other's nod in agreement, and Aiden seconds my statement.

"None of us are going to be ok with leaving you by yourself tonight. Your safety is our number one priority right now. I promise that it won't be weird for any of us if you come over."

I see her resolve to remain distant disappear with Aiden's words.

"I can't leave Beretta."

"We can always use an extra set of eyes. Especially since she has proven what an excellent guard dog she is."

Beretta's ears prick up and her head tilts as she studies me with an almost too perceptive gaze. *Was that a hint of a nod or am I seeing things?*

"Oh thank you, Don. I would feel so much better having her with me." Her bright smile brings my entire focus back on her.

If she keeps smiling at me like that, it's going to be incredibly difficult for me to keep my hands off her.

It doesn't take very long for us to pack Kinley up and get her and Beretta in my truck. It's a tight fit, especially now that Beretta is in the back seat with Aiden and Camden. I make Brent drive back, and persuade Kinley that, since it is such a short drive, it will be ok if she sits in my lap. A part of me feels like I'm taking advantage of her vulnerability, but my beast and I are very much in agreement that we crave her closeness.

The cabin is still dark when we pull up. We left in a hurry to get to Kinley and didn't even bother turning on any lights as we rushed to dress and get to the truck. We all have decent night vision.

Holding Kinley's hand, I lead her up the porch steps and into my cabin. I guess you can't really count it as a cabin—it's more like a lodge due to its size. With five bedrooms and over three-thousand square feet, it's a decent-sized lake house.

I flip on a light switch, letting warm light fill the space. The guys and Beretta trail in behind us as Kinley takes in the massive living and kitchen area. By her look of awe, I can tell she loves it just as much as I do, but I also see how tired she is.

"Come on, I'll show you where you can sleep tonight. I'll give you a tour in the morning."

KINLEY

Don leads me down a long hallway, the walls are lined with lightly stained reclaimed wood and black and white photos of nature scenes are hung periodically. One striking image of a large cascading waterfall catches my eye, and I pause.

"I'll have to take you there someday. It's even more beautiful in person." Donovan's voice whispers against my neck as he takes in the photo with me. I shiver, and with a slight turn of my head, my lips brush his beard-covered jaw. He's so much closer than I thought. "Did you take these?"

His lip quirks up and his eyes twinkle, but he's still gazing at the photograph. "Yeah, most of the photos here I've taken over the years. It's one of my few hobbies, kept me out of trouble when I was deployed."

My hand cups his face, tilting him towards me. Everytime I learn something new about him I have this urge to connect on an even deeper level, like I won't be satisfied until I've discovered all of him. I press my lips to his. It's just a brief kiss, but I just had to. His smile is bright and there is a tenderness in his eyes that makes my heart beat just a little faster.

His fingers twine with mine and he pulls me down the rest of the hall and up a black metal staircase. This mix of wood and metal makes his house feel edgy, but it still has a warmth that is welcoming. I think I love it even more than Megan's. Don opens up a set of large wooden double doors, the only ones on this floor, and gestures for me to enter after he flips on the lights. As soon as I walk in I know this is his room, his masculine scent fills the space. The ceiling is vaulted making the room feel even larger. The wood paneling behind the massive bed is painted a dark charcoal grey and there is a large stone fireplace on the adjacent wall bracketed by floor to ceiling windows. I bet the view in the morning is amazing. I turn to look at him questioningly.

"Is this your room?"

"Yes, I figured you can sleep in here so you won't have to wait for me to make up a bed."

"Um, and where are you sleeping?"

Donovan didn't seem like the type of guy to pull the one bed card, and I don't even really know if I would protest too much. I want to be close to him, but it's too soon, right?

He chuckles, his eyes glittering with humor.

"I'm going to be downstairs, the first door on the left."

How is it possible that I could be both relieved and disappointed with that answer? Because I am, and it confuses the hell out of me. Tonight has been a roller coaster, that's for damn sure, so I guess I should be grateful that he isn't the type of guy to take advantage of my weakened emotional state. But I really freaking want to cuddle and not be alone. I guess I will have to settle for being surrounded by the pillows and sheets that smell like him.

If he notices my inner turmoil he chooses not to comment on it. He stays close to the doorway. *Is he holding himself back, too?*

"There is a bathroom through that door," he gestures to a slightly ajar door to my left, "Feel free to snoop, and try to get some rest. I know it's been a stressful night, but I promise you'll feel a little better after some sleep. If you need anything, holler; one of us will come running. You're safe here, Kinley."

Before I can think about it and lose my nerve, I step close to him and wrap my arms tightly around his middle.

"Thank you for everything tonight."

He wraps his arms around me, squeezing slightly.

"Thank you for trusting me enough to call me. I know we just met, but I will do anything to keep you safe."

He is so warm and his words are so sweet that a tear almost spills from my eye. I'm still scared, but being here in his arms and his house makes the fear ebb to a manageable level. He gently releases me and gives me a nudge towards the bed.

"Go climb in and try and get some rest. I'll be close by if you need anything."

Sleep is short-lived. Even surrounded by the comforting scent of Donovan in his enormous bed, the nightmarish images can't be held at bay.

Hooded figures dressed all in black stalk me through the house. There are so many of them, around every corner, and no matter how fast I run, I can't escape them.

Scents of sulfur and ash choke my lungs. Hands reach for me with dagger-like black claws glinting with menace. Milky white eyes glow in the darkness. Sobbing, I desperately try to fight them off. I'm not strong enough. I'm not fast enough. Claws dig and rip at my clothes and skin. Screams rip out of my throat. I don't want to die—this isn't how it ends.

"Help! Please!"

My screams are so loud they echo in my ears, and the clawed hands continue their brutal savagery on my delicate skin. I just know I'm dying; the pain is too much to bear. I'm reaching my mind and body's limit—and then everything suddenly stops.

My agonized screams no longer shred my throat. The clawed figures no longer tear at my body. The darkness no longer surrounds me. Everything is bright, and I'm all alone. I turn, taking in my surroundings, but there's nothing except for a large mirror. I feel compelled to walk towards it, my figure growing within it as I draw near.

I take in my image. I'm dressed in my normal sleep clothes. Both my skin and clothing are unblemished, even though it felt like the claws were shredding me alive just moments ago. I'm completely untouched, and utterly alone.

I stare endlessly, unable to look away. Something is coming. I can feel it. The first thing to change is my eyes; they began to glow from within. My familiar blue eyes take on more and more tones of violet until they shine like a neon light. My mouth gapes open at the change, and that's when I notice my teeth have elongated and sharpened too. The only thing I can compare them to are teeth similar to a wolf.

What is happening?

Something stirs within me, trying to break free. A burning sensation begins in my stomach and continues until it becomes an all out pain. A red stain seeps through my shirt as I helplessly stare into the mirror.

My hand creeps to my middle, trembling as my fingers touch wetness. I'm terrified, but I have to know what is happening. I raise the fabric inch by inch. A wound is slowly exposed. Blood streams down my stomach, soaking the band on my shorts.

It's so red. I never noticed how it could be such a vibrant shade of red.

I pull my shirt all the way up until the bottom of my breasts show, and that is when I truly become terrified. Carved in jagged gruesome letters is the word "MINE". I scream and scream. I scream at the pain. I scream in horror.

Phantom hands grab me from behind, and they are covered in bright red blood.

A strong grip holds me steady as I thrash awake. I need to get away from that mirror, from the pain, from whatever keeps finding me in my dreams. I fight, desperate to break free. Sobbing in deep gasping breaths, I struggle to get away, but they hold me tight.

My ears register the gentle murmuring of soothing words meant to calm me, meant to guide me back to safety. A lamp has been switched on, casting the room in warm gentle light. *I'm not in that room, there is no mirror, no cruel blood-covered hands.*

Blinking the nightmare away, I take in my surroundings. They are all here. Camden and Aiden stand next to the bed, grave concern etched on both of their faces as they look down at me. Gentle, soothing strokes bring my eyes to the two men that are on the bed with me and my ever present guardian, Beretta. Brent holds my wrist, his thumb gently stroking my skin. My eyes meet his, seeing nothing but understanding. Beretta is draped over my thighs, as if she had been attempting to stop my apparent thrashing. Her small quiet whine makes me want to reach out to her, but my body won't obey me.

"Kinley, baby, you're safe... You're safe."

Hearing Don's gentle voice speak those words brings my attention finally to him. His body is so close to mine, his hands holding me, anchoring me to the present. Seeing my eyes connect with his makes him relax his hold on me. His hand comes up to brush away the tears I know are still glistening on my cheeks.

"There you are. Take some deep breaths for me, ok?"

I attempt to take a deep breath, but all that happens is a shuddering gasp. I'm hyperventilating.

"Try again, baby. Follow me."

He takes one of my hands out of Brent's grasp, placing it on his bare chest as he takes a long, slow, deep breath. My lungs strain to follow suit.

"There you go, just like that. Now, go again."

With my hand on his chest, guiding me, my breathing evens out and slows. My head clears as the panic fades away with each breath.

"That's my girl. I'm not going to let anything hurt you, Kinley. I promise."

His protective words and calmness soothe me further. Wiping my tear streaked face, he speaks to the guys. "I got it from here, guys. Go get some rest."

They shuffle out of the room. Brent gives my hand a squeeze before he also takes his leave. My mind finally registers their various states of undress. Even through the fog of my nightmare, I can appreciate how ripped they all are. Their backs all look like they have been carved from the finest marble, their skin various shades of tan. I don't realize I'm staring until Don takes my chin and turns my face back to him.

"Do you want to talk about it?"

I shake my head. How do I explain anything about that strange dream when I don't even understand it myself? He doesn't push, and I'm grateful for him. He slides down into the bed alongside me, tucking me in close to his body until my head is resting on his chest and my arm is draped across his stomach. Beretta graciously makes room for him, but doesn't leave the bed. She just moves to my other side, her back resting against mine. I reach back and run my hand up and down her side to not only ground myself in reality but also for comfort. No matter how much safety I feel from Don being here with me, he'll never replace Beretta's soothing presence.

"I'm not going to leave you alone tonight. I absolutely do not expect anything from you. I'm just going to hold you so you can get some sleep."

I nod, my face brushing against his warm chest, grateful that he didn't make me ask him to stay.

CHAPTER 10

KINLEY

I'm slow to wake. The sun is just peeking into the room, and I sleepily wonder why my pillow is moving. Gradually opening my eyes, the previous night's events come back, flooding my mind, and I shudder at the memories.

Last night really sucked, but in all the chaos, a bright calming light helped me out of that darkness. My eyes soften on the still sleeping face of Don. Somehow, in the night, I ended up completely on top of him, legs straddling one of his, and as I attempt to shift my weight, I become very aware of his hard length pressed against my thigh. *Oh my god, he is huge!*

I'm silently trying to figure out how to get off of him without waking him when I'm startled by him saying, "Has anyone ever told you how cute you look when you blush?"

Hearing his voice causes my body to jerk, which then almost causes my knee to connect with his balls if he hadn't grabbed ahold of my thigh just in time. I shyly look up at him, his playful smirk letting me know he isn't mad at my accidental attempt at unmanning him.

"Careful, your thigh is in a sensitive area."

I swear I think his eyes flash, but it happens so quickly I dismiss it instantly.

"I'm sorry, I must be heavy. I'm not sure how I got on top of you."

His chest rumbles beneath me, his hands flexing on my thigh and back.

"You're not heavy, Kinley." His fingers trail up my thigh, stopping just shy of the curve of my ass, I almost push back into his touch. "Besides," he growls, "I think it's pretty obvious I like you just where you are."

His hands knead my body gently, his hips rolling as if to emphasize his point. My whole body heats with desire, my breath coming out in small gasps. Don eyes me intently, breathing deeply as if inhaling something sweet.

"Kinley, I won't do anything you're not ready for, but I'm going to be honest with you. If you don't tell me you don't want this, I'm going to strip you out of these tiny shorts that have been driving me fucking crazy and feast on you."

My mouth gapes open. He just grins at me.

Shit, Beretta! I whip my head to the side where I know she should be, but the bed is empty. I crane my neck around Don's big body to search the room but notice that she is nowhere in sight. *Hmmm, one of the guys must have come and gotten her.* When my eyes land back on Don, he is patiently waiting, but his eyes are blazing with desire.

"What's it gonna be, baby? You gonna let me devour this?" His hand cups between my legs and my eyes widen. "Or am I gonna get up and make us breakfast?"

"The first one," I stammer out.

He flips me underneath him before I can even blink, grabs the sides of my shorts and rips them off. I let out a small yelp, and he just chuckles as he spreads my thighs wide, stopping to admire me with hungry eyes.

"Goddess, you have a pretty pussy."

I don't think any man has ever uttered those words to me, but I don't doubt the sincerity of them. Nudging my thighs even wider, he lays down right in between my legs, and I hear him growl before he says, "Your scent is fucking amazing."

He spreads my lips apart and swipes his tongue up my center. I whimper, my back arching slightly, and grab the hand that is on my thigh.

"Fucking hell, baby, you taste fucking delicious, too."

It has been a very long time since I had a man anywhere near me naked, and I have never had a man eat my pussy like it is his favorite pastime. He feasts on me like he is a man starved. I can't contain the loud moans that he wrenches from me.

"Such a good girl, let me hear how much you like my tongue."

His words ramp up my desire, and all I can do is hold on for dear life as he sucks on my clit and thrusts a finger inside me. My fingers weave through his short cropped hair. My hips grind against his face as I desperately try to get as close as possible. He continues to work his finger in and out, keeping up a rhythm with his tongue. My thighs shake as my body nears orgasm.

"That's it, come on my tongue like a good girl." Don growls and adds a second finger, crooking it up towards that bundle of nerves inside me. I scream out his name as my orgasm races through me, but he keeps pumping his fingers into me, pushing my orgasm higher and higher. Wringing my body of every last bit of pleasure, before I go limp.

He continues to stroke me lazily with his tongue, causing me to shudder. Looking up at me, he grins, keeping eye contact as he sucks his fingers clean and groans.

Holy shit, that is hot.

I'm a panting mess and if I could, I probably would have orgasmed again just from that sight.

God this man is filthy, and I fucking love it.

Don sits up, his cock straining against his boxer briefs. I move to pull him out but he stills my hands.

"Baby, I would like nothing more than to get inside of you, but I don't have any protection on me."

I groan and flop back onto the bed.

"Can I at least help you out? Relieve some tension?"

That makes him chuckle.

"I like to think of myself as a strong man, but if you get your hands on me I'm not going to want to stop until your pussy is wrapped around my cock."

I swear under my breath. This man is speaking straight to my pussy. I have to clench my thighs just to try and relieve the ache. I really, really want him inside me, but responsible sex is important—I guess. Feeling sassy, I let a little bit of my inner brat out.

"Fine…but it was going to be my mouth, not my hands."

Donovan lunges for me, and I leap off the bed, but not before he swats my ass. Just out of reach, I grin at him before sticking my tongue out. His eyes light up, and a predatory grin spreads across his face.

"Kinley, you run from me, and I'm going to chase you."

I shiver, hearing him growl those words at me. *So fucking hot!* My inner self is squealing in delight. So, feeling extra brave and sexy, I whip my shirt off, throw it at his face and take off running. I don't even know where the fuck I'm going, nor do I think of who might also be in the house with us—I just fucking run.

My blood is pumping; my pussy is drenched. *Who fucking knew I had a chasing kink, but I do, big time.* I'm not paying attention, just running, so of course I don't hear him come up behind me. I'm taken by complete surprise when his arms come around me and pin me up against a wall. The breath is knocked out of me and he grinds his hard cock against my ass. I don't know if I should giggle or whimper, I'm so fucking turned on.

His hands grip my sides and squeeze as he leans down to growl in my ear. "I warned you."

I'm breathless from running and excitement, and I must have been delirious because I can't help the words that leave my mouth.

"What are you going to do about it?"

He smacks my ass harder than before.

"Kinley, do you want me to fuck you bare? Because if you keep running from me and running that mouth, that's exactly what you're gonna get."

I have no idea what comes over me. Never in my life have I allowed a guy to even think about going without a condom. And now here I am, pressed up against the wall naked and panting after this gorgeous man, praying he will fuck me.

It's like something deep inside me has woken up and wants nothing more than to have this man inside me. A raw primal need rises up, so I say the only thing I can.

"Better catch me then."

Taking him by surprise, I push back with all my strength, managing to shove him off and make a break for it. This time I do giggle as I run away.

I don't run for long, because I'm not even remotely trying to get away. Thank goodness he catches me when he does, because I make it down a hallway and I'm almost positive I hear male voices coming from the room ahead. That would have been really embarrassing. Donovan grabs me, swinging me up over his shoulder and squeezes my bare ass, making me squeal.

I catch a glimpse of movement, and peaking up through my hair, I try to see what it could have been, but the hallway is empty.

It doesn't take long for Donovan to push through the bedroom door, tossing me on the bed. I bounce and try to roll off the bed, attempting one last escape, but he comes down on top of me, putting a stop to that. I gaze up at him. His eyes are bright and full of lust, and I can't help the grin that spreads across my face. I'm so incredibly aroused. I feel like I will combust if he doesn't get inside me. This is so much fun.

He must not care too much for my humor because he rocks his hips against mine, shoving his hard boxer brief clad length against my naked pussy. I gasp, my hips arching up against his. I grip both sides of the elastic band, desperately trying to shove them down.

"Please," I whine in a breathy moan.

His desperation matches mine. He instantly lifts off me and shucks his boxer briefs off in one smooth move. Finally just as naked as I am, I take in his impressive physique. His body is amazing, and holy shit, his cock is huge.

He quickly pulls me to him. Lining up with my entrance, his eyes meet mine as he thrusts into me. My back arches, my eyes roll back, and I scream as I feel his first thrust into my body. I pant as my body works to adjust to his very large invasion. It has been so long since I had any man inside me, and none of my vibrators come close to his length or girth. My legs tremble in his hands. He pauses, breathing heavily, waiting while my body relaxes enough around him so he can move.

"Goddess, you feel so fucking good. Are you ok?"

I nod. "Yes, please don't stop."

"Baby, there is no way in hell I'm stopping now."

He slowly rolls his hips, causing my eyes to close and an obscenely throaty moan to leave my mouth. I hold onto the sheets and him as Donovan slowly pulls out of me until just the tip rests in my channel. His eyes are now zeroed in on where our bodies are joined, his tongue swiping his lower lip as he thrusts back into me hard.

He is so deep, but I need more. I need him to own my body, I need to be able to feel him even when we are finished.

"Harder," I beg.

He adjusts his hold on my legs, pulling me with him as he positions us so I'm hanging off the side of the bed with him standing between my legs. And then he proceeds to fuck me hard and fast, picking up a deliciously punishing rhythm. Wrapping my legs around his waist, I hold onto him as one of the best orgasms I have ever experienced punches through me.

"So fucking tight. Give me one more, baby."

He groans in my ear before he kisses and sucks his way down my neck until he gets to my breast. God, my body is so sensitive. When he sucks my nipple into his mouth, I detonate again. He roars his release, thrusting deep and hard inside me, his cum filling me in hot spurts.

Holy shit, that was the best sex of my life, and Jesus, he came inside of me. And yet I'm not freaking out. Do I suddenly have a breeding kink? You can't develop a kink after one time, can you?

We are both breathing heavily, my hands idly stroking up and down his arms, zoning out in my post-orgasm bliss.

"Kinley, baby, look at me."

My eyes trail up his body until they meet his, and I stare into his beautiful blue eyes, sleepily smiling at him.

"There you are, you had me worried for a second."

I giggle.

"Still alive."

Chuckling, he gets up off me and gently pulls me to my feet, ignoring my protests. I just want to curl up on the bed with him and bask in post sex cuddles.

"Come on, smart ass. Let's go get in the shower."

Somehow we manage to get all cleaned up and dressed, much to my disappointment. If we had been in this house alone, I would suggest we just stay naked. Though he does give me another orgasm in the shower while he washes me. He insists we both need breakfast, so here I am, awkwardly hanging out in the kitchen with Don and his friends.

We were not quiet during any part of what we did earlier, and they are not shy about letting us know they could hear everything. At least now I know I can't die from embarrassment because if I could, I certainly would be dead.

"Well, good morning," Aiden drawls, a wicked grin plastered on his face. Three pairs of eyes zero in on us, and I can't decide if I want to strut around because I literally got the best orgasms of my life or hide behind Don. I choose a combination of both. I stand at his side and meet their amused and heated gazes.

"So, Cam and I have a bet, and we need your help settling it, Kinley." Brent's eyes hold so much wicked amusement that I dread what he is going to ask.

"Ok?"

"Two or three?"

My eyes narrow at him. "Two or three what?"

He chuckles. "How many times did our dear Don get you off this fine morning?"

Don growls, but I reach out a hand to him before he can tell them off. This is a test, and I will be damned if I'm going to fail, no matter how embarrassed I am.

"Who bet what?"

"I think it was three, but Brent thinks it was only two." Cam informs me, his eyes twinkling with playfulness.

I hold both of their gazes. "You're both wrong—it was four."

They all stare at me for a moment before they all burst out laughing. Glancing up at Don, his eyes shine with approval.

Don takes their teasing in stride, and thankfully most of their teasing is now pointed at him. I do have to hold in a laugh a few times, especially when Brent tells him that he must not have been doing enough cardio if I had been able to run as far as I did. *Fuck, I knew I had seen something after Don had thrown me over his shoulder. Now I'm all embarrassed again.*

I think he can sense that I'm starting to get a little too uncomfortable, so he clears them out so we can eat our breakfast, just the two of us. It isn't that I don't like his friends; they are just kind of a lot. Especially before I have even finished my first cup of coffee. I can't blame them for their teasing—we had been very out in the open about our fucking, and after this cup of coffee, I'm going to face any further teasing head on.

We eat in comfortable silence. With Don, it isn't awkward. I also don't really know what to say; I have no idea what has come over me. I have never been this forward about sex. I don't regret it, but I'm definitely going to have to get a Plan B on the way home, because I have to be somewhat responsible.

I finish my breakfast and get up to rinse my plate in the sink while Don finishes his own. I still cannot get over how amazing the sex was with this gorgeous man. *Maybe I should buy a lottery ticket. I'm never this lucky.*

I pause with my hands under the faucet, there is so much I should say, so much I should ask. We barely know each other and have taken giant leaps since the beginning. I should be freaking out, but I'm not. My brow furrows slightly. *Maybe that should be the real worry.* I'm so wrapped up in my head, I absolutely don't notice Don coming up behind me. He gently grabs my hips and turns me around, steering me away from the sink so he can lift me up onto the island countertop.

"You're thinking too hard. You doing ok? Not having regrets?"

He is so thoughtful, and I can't help but smile at him. Placing my damp hands on his shoulders, I lean in and kiss him.

"No, definitely no regrets, just trying to figure out what came over me."

"Well, it wasn't me. I came *in* you."

I snort and he grins at me, but then he clears his throat and gazes at me with sincerity.

"But seriously, I don't want you worrying. I'm completely clean... but there is the matter of possible pregnancy. I don't make a habit of leaving a deposit."

"Honestly, I wasn't worried about you not being clean, but I'll stop at a pharmacy on the way back, so no worries. I don't take birth control, because I don't have sex often enough to warrant the side effects of it."

"Ok good, I wasn't worried about you being clean, either. I just really didn't want to accidentally get you pregnant without us actually going on a proper date first."

I roll my eyes at his cheeky grin.

"Oh, so getting me pregnant after our first date is fair game?"

His eyes get a hungry gleam, like he would be one-hundred percent on board with that, and my crazy ass doesn't even feel alarmed by that. There has to be something wrong with me.

Together, we finish cleaning the kitchen. After we finish, I let him know I need to get back over to Megan's to clean up there, because I have to get on the road in a few hours. Like a gentleman, he takes me back. The guys wave goodbye from where they are crashed out on the living room couch. Which is also where I find Beretta, lounging in between Aiden and Camden. *She is such a little hussy for belly rubs.*

When he pulls up in front of Megan's lake house, he makes sure to open my door, not letting me out until he has kissed me senseless. Against my lips he murmurs, "I'll be seeing you soon, baby."

Still tasting him on my lips, I quickly put the house back in order. I remind myself to make sure to call Megan on my way home and check up on her, too.

With the house cleaned up and nothing out of place, I lock up, load my car, and get on the road. This has definitely been a weekend to remember.

CHAPTER 11

KINLEY

Pulling into the garage, I sigh in relief at being home.

Beretta snorts awake when she feels the car shift into park. She lets out a big yawn and sits up, stretching her neck and plopping her big head on my shoulder. I absentmindedly reach up and stroke the side of her face.

"Betta, this was a weird weekend."

She gives my cheek a little lick, as if to let me know she is in agreement.

Finally mustering the energy to get out of the car, I get to work unloading everything. There's no way I'm going to be able to sleep tonight if I don't unpack everything. I lug in my bag, and everything else that I brought. While I mutter to myself about why the hell I had packed so much, Beretta goes straight to find Indy, who is probably sleeping somewhere. For being a cat and dog, they are really cute together.

My first destination is the kitchen to put all the food and drinks away before they go bad. I can't stand being wasteful. Getting everything sorted into its correct spot, I'm about to walk out of the kitchen when Indy brushes up against my leg. The touch startles me so much I let out a squeal. I'm not proud of it, but after the weekend I've had, I'm allowed to be jumpy.

"Oh, Jesus, Indy you scared the crap out of me."

He just looks up at me like I'm insane, and honestly I probably am going a little crazy. The highs and lows within the last three days were really astonishing and I'm struggling a little to work my way through it.

I'm ecstatic that fate led me to meet Don, and holy hell that man can fuck like a God. Just thinking about all the ways he made me cum, makes me shiver. I'm still sore in the most pleasant of ways. I can't even really remember the last time I had sex. *Has it really been more than a year?*

God-like sex aside, potentially dealing with a stalker wigged me out to no end. *But that really isn't likely. Right?*

I'm sure it's just some dumb ass local that gets his rocks off scaring people. I do appreciate the attention to detail the guys had shown when searching the area around the house, and their insistence that I didn't stay at the house alone. Especially after the nightmare I had.

God, they are really getting weirder and weirder lately. Maybe I should see someone about that. Do they even have people to see for weird, traumatizing dreams?

That thought has my mother's voice creeping into my mind. Her sickly sweet voice always put me on edge, especially when she was criticizing me. "We don't show people our weaknesses Kinley; that's just not what we do. You suck up your issues and get over them."

I have to be losing it to have her hateful, toxic words slithering into my mind. I need to unwind before I spiral into a dark place.

Ugh, and I'm also worried about Megan. Todd hasn't passed yet. It seemed imminent when I talked to Megan earlier. His physician stated it would most likely happen in the next few days.

Normally, I would tell Megan everything, but I don't want to burden her further. So, I absolutely don't tell her about the incident Sunday night with the unknown stranger trying to get into the house. Nor do I mention waking up with Don, or the mind blowing sex that followed.

I know she will give me hell about that later, but it definitely isn't the time to parade around how many orgasms I received. Not after she had to leave.

I will tell her later, when the time is right. I take a deep breath to calm and center myself. *Look at me being all zen and shit.*

I'm going to run myself a bath with a big scoop of epsom salt for my very sore bits. Then, I will either read a book off of my very long TBR list, or catch up on a Netflix show.

And not to forget the unprotected sex, I need to take that pill I picked up on the way home. There is no use dwelling on things I can't control. I learned the hard way a long time ago that I couldn't. I need to give myself a little mental reset before work tomorrow.

I even have some new bath bombs I've been meaning to use, and now feels like the perfect time.

The steam from the bathtub is pleasantly fragranced from the bath bomb, and I'm submerged as far as I can get into the hot water. That is one thing that sold me on this house, the tub. I have a new monster romance loaded on my Kindle app, and am just about ready to start reading when my phone pings with a text notification.

A giddy grin spreads across my face.

Don: Hey…you make it home ok?

Me: Yes I did

Don: Would it be weird if I said I miss you already?

Oh my god…this man is perfect.

Me: It might be…guess we are weird together…

Don: You missing me too, baby?

Me: Well you did kind of play into my damsel in distress fantasy this weekend, so I can't help it, and you left a lasting impression on me this morning.

Don: I'm here to serve… , how are you feeling otherwise?

Me: You served me well, lol…I'm good, just relaxing and trying to get in the right headspace for work tomorrow.

Don: lol I would like to "serve" you again…is it too soon to ask when I can see you again?

God damn, I am going to orgasm again just thinking about all the ways he serviced me.

Me: No…I've been wondering the same thing. What is your work schedule like?

Don: Well, I don't have any big cases right now, so I'm usually off Friday thru Sunday. Want to get together this weekend?

I am such a sucker for a man that takes initiative…

Me: Not to sound too eager, but yes, I would really like that. Did you make it back ok?

Don: Yeah I got the guys dropped off and made it home in pretty good time, just relaxing now. What are you up to?

Oh man, should I tell him I'm taking a bath…yep gonna do it…he made me all hot and bothered this weekend…it's only fair to return the favor…

With a naughty smirk I text back.

> Me: Oh just relaxing in the bathtub. Was about to start a book I've been looking forward to.

My grin spreads further as the call screen pops up. I guess he's still a little on edge, too. I quickly accept the call and shiver as I hear his gravelly voice over the line.

"Are you sore, baby?"

Oh fucking hell, I'm a goner.

Trying desperately to play it cool. "Well, a lot happened this weekend, ya know with going out on the lake, a potential stalker trying to break in…"

"And…"

"And it could also be from your huge cock."

A surprised bark of laughter answers me.

"Woman, you're going to get me all riled up if you keep talking like that."

I can't help but snort. "Like you weren't already."

"You're right, I have been since I left you this morning. So when can I see you?"

"Friday?"

"You got it. I can pick you up, if that works for you."

"Yeah, that works."

"Perfect, we will iron out the details during the week. Oh, that reminds me, I wanted to give you an update on what they guys got around the house last night."

"Did they find anything?"

"Not exactly, but they found some clues that they are still trying to iron out. Aiden and Cam wanted me to ask you if you or Megan had any previous run-ins with any of the locals? They didn't find a vehicle, so we all were under the impression that they would have had to walk in."

"Not that I can think of. Whenever Megan and I are up there we usually keep to ourselves. Do you think it might be someone I know?"

"It is highly possible, but right now we are just being overly cautious. Kinley, I don't want you to worry; we are just covering all avenues."

"Ok, I appreciate all the work that you are all doing. It's like I was meant to run into you guys this weekend."

"You have no idea how thankful I am of that as well. I'll let you get back to soaking."

I can hear the grin on his face. "Don't wear out your hand, big guy."

"You're a sassy little thing. Goodnight, baby. I'll talk to you tomorrow. I have a few things I need to get done tonight."

"Goodnight, Don."

The call disconnects, and I start thinking that it is going to be a long week.

DONOVAN

I end the call with Kinley, rubbing my chest to soothe the ache that just won't seem to go away since I met her. A rumble deep within me lets me know that my beast is just as enamored with her as I am. This has never happened before, not even my exes instilled this much need. I'm very much at a loss for what to do. I need to talk with the guys; there has to be something deeper going on.

Sitting down at my desk, I pull up the video chat app and call the other three. Aiden is the first to sign on and Brent and Cam shortly follow. It helps that we frequently video chat, conferencing with each other whenever we have cases or Clan matters that need each other's expertise, so they are quick to respond when they get the app notification.

"Hey, big man, you miss us already?" Brent grins, and I flip him off.

"This is serious. I can't get the idea out of my mind that the situation with Kinley isn't the ordinary type of issue."

They all visibly straighten.

Aiden is the first to respond. "What do you mean, Don?"

"You met her. She's calling a little too strongly to my inner self for me to think she is just another human woman."

"Now that I really think about it, I definitely got some vibes from Megan, but I didn't feel anything from Kinley. Especially with that ward, I think Megan is more likely the one to have put it up," Cam chimes in.

"Could the whole intruder situation be linked to Megan instead? I mean, it is her cabin. Maybe it was a coincidence, and Kinley just happened to be there and they took notice," Brent ponders.

"That could be, but I don't think Kinley is human. You guys didn't see how much she drew my beast right to the edge..."

Brent chuckles, "Goddess, I fucking wish I had, especially since you walked out smelling so fucking sweet. And the noises."

He groans and my beast rumbles.

"What I wouldn't have given to have gotten a close up of that."

A growl slips out, my canines lengthening. I'm helpless to my beast's reaction as I bare my teeth at him through the screen. Brent, the fucker, just grins as he leans back in his chair linking his hands behind his head and purposefully flexes his muscles. I know he's provoking me on purpose, but I can't help but rise to the challenge.

"Goddess, you have it fucking bad, man." His eyes shine with mirth, and all I want to do is reach through the screen and smack the shit out of him.

"That's what I'm trying to fucking say. A normal human shouldn't be able to affect me this much."

Aiden taps his chin in thought. "I don't know, Don. She is too old to not be putting off more magic if she was Clan. Maybe she's a half breed, or some distant relative of hers was. It happens sometimes when we go outside the clan."

"What's her last name? I could dig a little and see if anything pops up of interest," Cam adds as he reaches over to switch on an additional monitor.

I sigh, frustrated with all the uncertainty. "Munro, but I don't know of any Clans with that last name."

"You never know, but if she's somehow linked, I will probably find it. You know she could also be a fledgling witch, or any other type of magical creature." Cam is already typing away on his keyboard.

"So, Don...when are you seeing sweet Kinley again?" Brent asks, not bothering to diminish his shit eating grin. I almost don't want to tell him.

"Friday."

Aiden grins, "You fuckers owe me $100!"

Brent and Cam protest.

"Did you shits seriously bet on me going out with her again?"

"Of course we did. Just so you know, I was the only one who had faith in you," Aiden states proudly like I should be thanking him for believing in me.

"You are all fucked up for that."

Brent gets a mischievous glint in his eye.

"So, Don, if she is Clan, can I get in on that action too?"

A growl rumbles through my chest and bubbles out of my mouth. My muscles tense as I hold back my beast.

"Come on, all the times we shared before it was fucking epic, and you're the only one out of these fuckers that can keep up with my moves."

"Shut the hell up, Brent. Your limp dick could never," Cam mutters while he busily types in whatever program he's in. Brent scoffs in outrage and Aiden and I laugh.

"Well, that's my cue to go. If any of you find anything of interest, let me know. Aiden, I'll see you tomorrow. Brent, are you going on any jobs soon?"

He unlinks his hands and leans closer to the screen. "Ummm, I might have one or two potentials. Do you need me to hang out? I can always pass them over to someone else."

"If you could. I just have this gut feeling something is up that might need all of us."

"Yeah man, sure, you know I got your back."

"Thanks, I'm gonna hit the rack."

We all sign off, but I sit for a minute while my computer powers down. They all might think it's Megan, but there are just as many clues pointing away from that idea. One thing I can wholeheartedly agree on is this is not a non-magical problem.

CHAPTER 12

KINLEY

The week flies by, and thankfully, nothing too eventful happens. There are no more creepy run-ins with Allen. I think me threatening to talk to HR got it through his head that I'm serious about not wanting any of his advances. I should probably still report him, but I'm in too good a mood. Everything just goes smoothly and I'm grateful for it.

Cory and Trina both notice my good mood. Cory teases me during lunch Tuesday.

"Kinley, did you get some dick this weekend? You sure look like you had something good happen. Something relaxing maybe?"

I'm not one to kiss and tell. There is only one person that I ever spill all the dirty details to, and that is Megan. While I do want to talk about Don, it's still too new, so I just end up laughing him off.

"I just had a great weekend, some much needed girl time on the lake."

I talk to Don every day. The more we talk, the more my attraction for him grows.

There are no new changes with Todd, so Megan is doing ok. And it's finally Friday; in a few hours I will be out with Don. The butterflies in my stomach are a riot, and I'm a giddy, anxious mess.

I feel a little crazy, because I've never reacted to a man this strongly before. I don't have a ton of dating experience, but I also am not a young, naive little girl. There is just this unexplainable feeling that meeting Don is going to have a profound effect on my life. I just pray it's a good one.

The school day is finally over, and I quickly pack up, trying not to run out the door. There is more than one instance in which I'm tempted to shove some slow moving kids out of the way so I can get to my car faster. When I finally make it, I give myself a mental pat on the back for not succumbing to the urge of shoving or yelling at teenagers to get here.

I quickly throw my bags in the back seat and am about to climb in, when I feel a heavy feeling in my chest, and the hair on the back of my neck rises. I clasp my chest, as my heart pounds erratically. *What is going on?*

I look around, but there are so many people in the parking lot, no one stands out. And just as quickly as it came, the feeling goes away, my heart rate decreases. *Well, that is fucking weird.*

I shake off the feeling and get into my car, and I don't waste any more time getting out of there. I have just enough time to get home, feed Beretta and Indy, and get myself cleaned up.

Don won't tell me exactly what we are doing tonight, but he did say to dress casually. Now I just have to figure out if I'm going to wear jeans or a dress. *Would it be too slutty to go without panties?* It is a little embarrassing how much time I pondered that question.

An hour and a half later, I'm dressed, the pets have been fed, and I'm pacing a circuit around my living room while I wait for Don to pull up to my house. I've rearranged the pillows on my couch twice and refolded my throw blankets at least that many times. I'm a mess, and with the way Indy is glaring at me, I think he is going to take a swipe at me if I don't stop my fussing.

I know he is on his way, because he texted me earlier saying he was. I have no reason to be this anxious, but I can't help it. This man is amazing, and not one red flag has popped up, which is extremely surprising.

Was that a red flag? No! Don't overthink it…

I reach for a pillow that still doesn't look properly fluffed but I jerk my hand back when Indy hisses at me. I huff at him, but I still need something to do, so I go and check myself one more time in the mirror. It's going to be a little chilly tonight, so I decided on some black leggings and an off-the-shoulder cream sweater that just barely covers my butt. I don't work out a ton, but I have a killer ass, so I might as well highlight it. Maybe I should add Pilates to my weekly routine? I have a feeling I'm going to need the added flexibility.

I let my hair down, putting in some loose beach waves, and I kept the makeup I already have on. I have been blessed with really great skin, and I'm thankful I have never needed a full coverage makeup routine.

I know I look good, but there is always a nagging voice in the back of my mind that makes me doubt it. I have worked really hard to overcome that inner voice over the last eight years.

Ugh, I have to stop doubting myself…Don is amazing…I am a fucking catch…I just needed to find a man…and he is a man…shit, did I put deodorant on…

My phone ping interrupts my anxious thoughts and I run over to grab it. Don is here. A smile I can't even begin to stifle spreads across my face. Taking a deep breath to steady my nerves, I walk out of my bedroom and towards the front door. I notice then that Indy and Beretta are both sitting on the couch, watching me. My white harlequin tuxedo cat and my large black dog make quite the picture standing guard in my living room. They look like they are going to lecture me on my curfew.

"Do I look ok guys?"

They blink at me, and I giggle a little, because it is silly to think they would answer me.

"Be good you two; don't wait up!"

I walk out the front door, and there he is, leaning up against his truck. He is so handsome, it takes everything in me not to sigh and bat my eyelashes at him. He pushes off his truck as soon as he sees me, prowling up to me. Without even a pause to greet me, he sweeps me into his arms and kisses me.

I don't even need to think; my body instantly responds to him. My arms come up around his shoulders, anchoring me to him.

Too soon, he gently breaks the kiss, his deep sigh bringing even more warmth to my belly.

"How do you always smell so good?" He breathes in my scent deeply. "If I didn't have plans I was looking forward to taking you to, I'd be very tempted to persuade you to let me into your house right now."

I know if he insisted, I would let him, too. I'm utterly infatuated.

Still trying to catch my breath after that kiss, all I can seem to do is blink at him.

Touching his forehead to mine he murmurs. "I missed you this week."

I melt a little, he is so sweet.

"I really missed you, too. So, where are you taking me tonight—or is it still a mystery?"

I need to steer the conversation to something that isn't going to make me burst into flames of lust. His sweetness, paired with the sultry look he is giving me, isn't helping my resolve. So, dinner seems like the safest option.

"Well, I guess I could give you a hint. There is food there."

My eyes roll. "I would hope so, I'm starting to get hungry."

"Come on, let's get going, before I get distracted again by how good you look and smell."

There I go blushing again. It is getting a little ridiculous how much he makes me blush. Is this normal?

"Hey, don't forget to lock your door."

He smirks at me as he turns back towards his truck. I frown at his back, because if he hadn't reminded me, I would have completely forgotten.

Door officially locked, I quickly follow after him. I wasn't lying when I said I was getting hungry.

I catch up to him, his hand reaching out to take mine as he then leads me over to the passenger door and opens it for me. *I guess chivalry isn't dead.* I hop up into the truck, and I might have wiggled my butt a little in his face. His deep groan as he shuts the door makes me smile mischievously, and I watch him try to adjust himself slyly as he walks around to the driver's door.

We drove for about thirty minutes, talking about our day. It feels nice and normal. I loved messaging and talking on the phone with him throughout the week, but physically being in his presence is one hundred times better. Don holds my hand, brushing my knuckles with his thumb as he drives, and even though it's wreaking havoc on my hormones, I never want him to stop.

"I hope you're ok with drinking tonight." His deep voice pulls me from my thoughts. The restaurant we pull up to is actually a brewery.

"I thought you said there was going to be food," I look over at him with a raised eyebrow.

"It has a kitchen. They actually serve food that compliments what beers they have on tap."

"Oh, that sounds interesting."

"Plus, they have a really great patio out back."

He turns the truck off and climbs out. Following suit, I circle to the front of the truck. He reaches for my hand as I draw near, tucking me in close as we make our way inside.

The back patio has a rather romantic view of a river with a small waterfall. The hostess directs us to a table with bench seats. I go to sit across from him, but before I can, Don pulls me in close.

"Sit next to me. It's a little chilly out, I don't want you to get cold."

He slides onto the bench and pats the section right next to him, causing fluttery wings to stir in my stomach. *He's so perfect; please let this be real.*

"It's so pretty out here. If the food and beer are as good as the scenery, I can't wait."

"The company is definitely top notch," he says quietly as he pulls me in close to his side.

"I'm really glad we were able to get together so soon. I know it's probably going to sound silly, but I really like spending time with you."

"It's not silly at all, Kinley. I feel the same way; we have a really great connection."

I smile up at him. It's nerve-wracking, confessing things to someone I still don't entirely know. I really want him to know that it doesn't feel like a casual thing for me.

"I'm really glad we met Don. I don't think I have ever felt comfortable with someone the way I feel with you."

I can tell he is going to say something in return, but the waitress arrives. Don, being more familiar with the brewery, orders the flight based on what I tell him I like in beers. The waitress is also exceptional, and gives us many good options for food that will complement the flight. We end up ordering a little bit of everything and share.

Throughout the entire dinner, he is touching me in some way. Some touches are subtle, some more lingering, like his hand resting on my legging clad thigh. One time in particular, he strokes his hand up and down my thigh. With each upward pass his hand gets closer and closer to the apex of my thighs, until he stops. He's nearly there, if he moved just an inch higher his hand would be right where I need him to be. I shiver at the thought of him cupping me, pressing his warm palm right against my mound.

"Are you cold?" He asks, his lips close enough to my ear that I can practically feel them brush against my skin.

"No, you feel really nice. Uh, I mean it feels really nice—nice out—out here on the patio."

His deep chuckle is answer enough. He knows exactly what he is doing. He is winding me up on purpose. I scrunch my nose at him.

"Just so you know, I find it incredibly cute when you get flustered."

My eyes roll as I attempt to get back to my food. His hand stops my head's progress as he gently takes my chin and tilts my face back up to his. His eyes blaze with desire, and I swallow hard.

"I also find it incredibly arousing when you get sassy."

"I'll keep that in mind, Don."

We grin at each other, and I giggle as all the giddy feelings swirl inside me.

We continue eating, and I probably drink a little too much, but it doesn't matter because I know I'm safe with him. I'm all tingly, and I don't think it's just from the beer. Our conversation flows effortlessly and more than once I almost choke on my food from him making me laugh. When he starts asking deeper questions that is when my eating pauses entirely.

"Kinley, where did you grow up? Your slight accent tells me you didn't grow up in this area."

"Yeah, I didn't. I moved here for my job. I grew up in Texas until I went to college and then moved out here."

"A Texas girl? You're pretty far from home."

I laugh, but it comes out strained. "Yeah, I don't consider it my home. I haven't for a long time."

His eyes assess me, his face showing concern.

"So no family that are worth visiting?"

I shake my head. "No, I'm an only child, and I have no family to speak of. I was happy to leave when I went to college."

"I'm sorry to hear that. Is that why you are so close to Megan?"

"Yes, Megan is my family." I smile as I say those words.

"I have a much younger brother, so it felt like I was an only child for a while, but I grew up with so many cousins and close friends that it was always crowded." His chuckle is warm and affectionate. I can tell he really loves his family, immediate and extended.

"Aiden and I drove our parents nuts, especially when we were teenagers. I think they all sighed in relief when we all decided to enlist together."

"It sounds like you are close to your family."

"We are. We all go back frequently, for holidays and family gatherings."

"I honestly wouldn't know what to do with a large family. The thought is kind of terrifying," I laugh lightly.

"You did good around the guys. If you can survive them, then the rest of my family would be a piece of cake."

"Are you inviting me to meet your family, Don?" I ask playfully.

Leaning in close so his eyes are level to mine, he says with pure sincerity. "Kinley, with as much as I think about you, I think it's inevitable that you will meet my family."

Holy shit, maybe he did feel as strongly as I was feeling towards him.

He kisses me softly, his lips are so warm. That warmth spreads quickly from our mouths through to the rest of my body. I pull away reluctantly, because I'm two seconds away from climbing in his lap. His eyes sparkle with amusement and desire.

"We should probably finish our food before we get in trouble for PDA."

"PDA isn't an arrestable offense. We would just get a stern talking to."

"Ok, Mr. Police Officer, I still don't want to get in trouble."

We finish our food and drinks pretty quickly after that. Not only is the food and beer great, but being out with Don feels like a puzzle piece locking into place. I feel like I can share anything with him, and he won't judge me. I don't like speaking about my past and my family, but I feel like I can with him. *Is this how people normally feel when meeting someone that they have a true connection with? Or do we have something really special?*

Once the check is paid, Don leads me out of the restaurant, his hand resting gently on my lower back. I just love how much he touches me, as if he too can't bear to not be close to me. The night has gotten chillier and even with his comforting warmth, I'm ready to get out of the cold. When we reach the passenger door, instead of opening it, he leans me up against the passenger side. Looking at him questioningly, I wait for him to speak.

"This might be a little presumptuous of me, but would you like to come back to my house tonight?"

He must see my brief hesitation, so he quickly continues.

"I only ask, because my house is only about fifteen minutes away, but I'm more than happy to take you home if that's what you want."

"Oh, yes I do…want to go to your place, I mean. Sorry, I was just trying to think if I left enough water for my pets."

I look down where my hands are fiddling with the hem of my sweater. His body bracketed around me, blocking out some of the chill of the night air.

"Why do you seem nervous all of a sudden?"

His quiet question makes me look up, his eyes twinkling in the light of the overhead lights. Before I can answer, he continues.

"I know we've been intimate already, and teasing the hell out of each other all week, but if you're not ready to go further tonight, I'm really ok with taking you home. I'm a big boy. I can handle it."

"What? No, that's not it at all! I guess I just didn't want to seem too over eager." My hands trail up and down his sides. His body tightens like the string on a bow, waiting to be released. "I want you."

Donovan sighs in relief, his hand coming up to thread in the hair at the back of my head. His lips brush over mine teasingly. "Kinley, the only thing holding me back from getting back inside you is these tight as hell leggings." He slips his other hand down to my ass for emphasis. "And the fact that we are in a well-lit parking lot."

He crowds in even closer and rolls his hips against me. Nipping my lower lip, sucking on it gently, he draws out a whimper from me. My breath shudders out of me. My hips roll against his. A tortured groan leaves his lips as his head drops to my shoulder. His hands grasp my sides to stop my rocking. With what seems like a lot of effort, he pulls his body away from mine.

Growling into my neck, he says, "I'm gonna need a sec, then we can leave."

I can't help my amusement, and a giggle slips out of my mouth. Groaning, Don moves further away from me, guiding me to the side so he can open my door for me. He gives me a playful swat to the butt as I climb in. I haven't even gotten my seat belt secured before he makes his way around to get behind the wheel. *Someone is eager, but hell, so am I.*

Feeling mischievous, I decide to see how far I can push him. So, as he is pulling out of the parking lot, I quietly ask him. "Would now be a good time to tell you I'm not wearing any panties?"

Donovan's head jerks towards me as he swears. His nostrils flare and his jaw clenches as I smile at him sweetly. There is a glint in his eye that reminds me of a predator eyeing its prey. Shivers of anticipation roll through me as he proceeds to peel out of the parking lot, gunning his truck's engine.

It takes a little less than seven minutes to get to Don's house. I can't help but laugh the entire way. As soon as the truck is parked and the engine is turned off, we both hop out. I get caught up admiring the dark grey siding and rustic farmhouse touches, so much so that I don't even notice when he quickly comes up behind me and flips me onto his shoulder. I gasp and flail a little; being carried is still so foreign to me. So, in a little bit of a panic I grab onto anything I can get my hands on, which happens to be the upper part of his ass. He grunts and swats my ass, making me squeal.

I honest to god just squealed...What is wrong with me...Jesus, he's strong...and God, he has a firm ass.

He jostles me slightly, opening up the front door, and it shakes me from my inner monologue. I get brief glimpses of a nice rustic looking living area before he takes the stairs up to the second floor two at a time.

"Jesus, Don, how strong are you?"

He chuckles. "Strong enough, baby girl."

My core instantly goes molten at that term of endearment. I hear him growl, and I'm plopped onto a very large bed.

"Did you like me calling you that?"

The tone of his voice causes me to gulp and I quickly nod my head.

"I can tell."

My forehead furrows slightly. *How would he know that? Ugh, don't overthink shit, stay in the moment.*

Donovan wastes no time in removing my leggings and getting up close and personal with my newly waxed pussy. And if I wasn't wet already, I would have been just from his look alone.

"Fuuuckkk," he growls out. "When did you do this?"

He doesn't even look up at me, just stares, entranced and licking his lips.

"Yesterday," I gasp, right as he puts his mouth on me.

My legs get hooked over his shoulders, his fingers join his mouth, and he wrings the orgasm that has been slowly building since dinner right out of me. I'm completely taken by surprise yet again, by how easily this man gets me to climax. I try desperately to catch my breath as he pushes off of me, his lower face glistening with my release.

Why is that so fucking sexy?

125

I track his movements as he reaches back to pull his shirt over his head. My brain is barely functioning, so of course, I can't stop the snort that leaves my mouth. I get stuck thinking that I've never seen any man but a stripper take their shirt off like that. Quirking up a brow, he gives me a questioning look, and I quickly wave him off.

"Don't mind me, just really enjoying the show."

I continue to eye him hungrily, as he tosses his shirt onto a chair. I get an uninterrupted view of all the beautiful artwork on his body. I really want to trace those tattoos with my tongue.

There is a twinkle in his eyes as he chuckles and shakes his head at me. I prop myself up while he continues getting undressed, removing his pants and boxer briefs. I have every intention of undressing myself, but understandably get very distracted when his cock springs out of the top of his boxer briefs. My mouth waters at the sight, and I know I will never be able to live with myself if I don't get a taste.

Quietly slipping off the bed, I rip off my sweater and bra, haphazardly dropping them to the floor. Stepping close to him, I don't even hesitate as I reach out and firmly grasp his cock. He sucks in a breath, making a satisfied smile creep across my lips, and it grows wider as he groans in response to me stroking his hard length.

I marvel at how big he is; my fingers barely meet. Feeling his eyes on me, I tilt mine up. I'm completely taken aback; he looks at me like there is nothing more important in the world. Not wanting to break eye contact, I kneel, watching him as I lick up the length of his hard cock.

A groan of pleasure leaves his lips, his eyes closing for the briefest of moments. He cups my cheek, his thumb stroking my face, as I lean forward, sucking the head of his thick cock into my mouth. I know I'll never get him all the way in my mouth, but I'm sure as hell going to try.

Fingers gently weave into the hair at the nape of my neck, and a slight squeeze gives me all the encouragement I need to continue. I won't call myself a pro by any means, but something about the way he looks down at me with that hungry gleam in his eyes makes me want to devour him and give him as much pleasure as he's given me.

My mouth moves down as far as I can, until he reaches the back of my throat. Making sure to breathe through my nose, I relax as much as I can to try and take him deeper. His hips give a slight flex and he manages to push in a little farther before my gag reflex kicks in. He pulls out immediately, apologizing sheepishly.

"Sorry, your mouth just feels so good."

I stroke his length from base to tip a few times before saying, "Did you want me to stop?"

"No, I don't, but I'm not going to last too much longer if you have your mouth on me."

I playfully give his tip a flick with my tongue, and he growls softly.

"Well, tell me when you've had enough."

Not waiting for him to answer, I bring him back into my mouth, running my tongue along the underside as I bob my head.

"Goddess, you're taking my cock so well…such a good girl."

Holy shit, hearing those words leave his mouth makes me moan around his cock.

"Baby, can I fuck your mouth?"

That makes me pause for the briefest of moments, and I look back up at him.

"If I get too rough, just tap my thigh and I'll stop, but I really want to fuck your pretty mouth."

A moan quietly escapes my throat, and I nod around his cock before I pull off to catch my breath a little. I'm so turned on, I'm panting. He rubs a thumb across my puffy bottom lip. "You ready?"

"Yes." I gasp out as I open wide for him.

His hands bury into my hair as he guides me back onto his cock. His thrusts are shallow at first, allowing me time to adjust.

"Don't forget to tap," he reminds me before his hips pick up a more forceful rhythm. All I can do is hold onto his thighs, my nails digging in slightly as his hands and hips work my mouth over his cock.

"Such a good fucking girl," he growls through his clenched teeth.

His thrusts get rougher, and I have to work hard to breathe through my nose. He is just so big, and my throat can only take so much before I choke. My eyes water as he gets farther and farther down my throat. His growls of pleasure make me want to keep going, but I have to tap his thighs when I reach my limit. He immediately slows and pulls out of my mouth, I cling to him as I gasp for air. He has other ideas though. His hands leave my hair and he grabs me up by the waist, bringing me off the floor.

His lips crush against mine in a desperate kiss. He thrusts his tongue into my mouth, mimicking what his cock had just been doing. I cling to him as he grabs the back of my thighs, pulling me closer to him.

Not one to let my legs dangle, I wrap my legs around his waist. Moaning into his mouth, I can't help myself as I grind my weeping pussy against his stomach. I'm so consumed with our kiss I don't even notice as he turns and guides us both onto the bed. As I register the coolness of his comforter, he breaks the kiss, and I'm helpless to stop the whine that leaves my lips. It gets louder as he moves away from me.

"I have to get a condom, baby."

At least one of us is thinking somewhat clearly, because I certainly would have just impaled myself on him if the decision had been left to my sex-addled brain.

He quickly grabs a condom out of his side table and efficiently sheathes his length. He prowls up my body, settling himself between my legs. I'm absolutely vibrating with anticipation as he positions himself right at my entrance.

"Baby, you're soaked."

"Please, Don, I need you."

Needing no further prompting, he pushes his cock into me in one powerful thrust. I cry out as my body desperately tries to adjust to the sudden intrusion. Even as wet as I am, it's still an uncomfortable stretch having him inside of me. I hold onto him as he sets a furious pace, letting me know without words that he is just as desperate for me as I am for him.

We chase our orgasms, reveling in each other's sweat-slicked bodies. Everything just feels so good. I unconsciously claw at his back as I get closer and closer to that gloriously brutal peak. I would normally have been embarrassed about moaning so loudly if I wasn't already out of my mind with pleasure.

"Come for me, baby," Don growls in my ear.

His teeth graze my shoulder as he reaches down between us, circling my clit and pushing me over the edge. My body seizes, my inner muscles clenching down on him, triggering his own orgasm.

I'm not even sure how long we lie there, breathing heavily, clinging to one another. Don kissing along my neck and collar bone slowly brings me out of my languid stupor. Supporting his weight on his elbows, he pushes up so he can peer down at me.

"Goddess, you're beautiful." He speaks in hushed awe, a grin spreading across his face as a blush spreads across mine.

"Why do you say that?"

"Say what? That you're beautiful?"

"No, Goddess. It's just unusual."

"It's just a thing my people say. It's a part of our culture."

"Your people? Like your family?"

"Yeah, our Clan's religion has a goddess for a deity. It can get a little confusing, but we aren't Christian. Is that a problem?"

"No, not at all. I'm not religious. I never have been, for as long as I can remember. What do you mean, though, when you say your Clan? Is your family Scottish?"

He chuckles. "Something like that, my family history is actually pretty complicated, but we do have origins in Scotland and the term Clan just stuck."

"That's interesting. I think I have family from Scotland, too."

"Really?"

"Yeah, but my family history is kind of fuzzy. My parents didn't have any living relatives so there isn't really any way for me to know for sure."

He nods in understanding, but it almost looks like he has a hopeful look on his face. Gently, he strokes some stray hair off my cheek, leaning down further until his lips are hovering over mine.

"Stay the night. I haven't gotten nearly enough of you after waiting a week," he whispers into my lips as he kisses me tenderly.

A shy blush creeps up my face. "It's only been four days."

"Close enough. I can't seem to get enough of you."

He grins at me as he gets up and moves to what I could only assume is the bathroom.

CHAPTER 13

KINLEY

Needless to say, we don't get much sleep. I wake up clinging to a pillow that smells like Don, and I hum in appreciation at being surrounded by his scent. Not feeling him behind me, I crack my eyes open and peer up from the bed. I wonder where he went, but I'm too comfortable to have any desire to get up and hunt for him. Pressing my head back down, I do what anyone else would do and push my face further into the pillow, inhaling the woodsy citrus notes. A deep chuckle interrupts me. Too tired to be ashamed, I don't even bother picking my head up as I mumble in the pillow.

"Don't judge me; you have the best cologne."

I feel the bed dip as he plops down next to me, his arms winding around me as he pulls me flush against him.

"Baby, I don't wear cologne. That's just all me."

"Of course you don't."

The noise that leaves me is a pitiful groan as he starts kissing down my neck, slowly making his way to my breasts. There isn't one part of my body that doesn't feel sore.

"Don, I'm so sore. How can you still want more?"

"Because I just can't seem to get enough of you."

He buries his head between my breasts, nibbling at me playfully.

"You're going to suffocate if you don't quit."

"Best way to die in my opinion," he mumbles, his short beard tickling my skin as he presses up against me. His hips rock against mine suggestively, but that pressure just makes my bladder protest.

I pat his shoulder. "I'm going to pee myself if you don't get off me."

Thankfully, that gets him moving quickly. "Yes, ma'am."

No longer caged in by him, I scramble off the bed as quickly as my very sore body will let me. I barely make it into the bathroom. I sigh heavily at the flashbacks of all the positions Don put my body in during the night. *No wonder I'm so sore.* A rush of heat sweeps through me, and I silently scold my pussy.

Down, girl. You can't possibly take any more of that monster cock. Ugh, would it be weird if I asked him for an ice pack? I'm one-hundred percent going to have to start adding pilates or something into my workout routine. That, or we were going to need to start stretching before we fuck.

After thwarting several more seduction attempts from Don, I finally persuade him that feeding me and taking me home is the smarter option. He plies me with delicious kolaches and coffee to make up for nearly breaking my vagina with his battering ram of a cock. He snorts coffee out of his nose when I say as much. I do feel a little bad for that, since he has to pull over so he doesn't crash his truck. He then proceeds to tell me he is going to paddle my ass if I do that again.

But is that really much of a deterrent? Nope, it sure isn't.

Donovan pulls up to my house without further incidents.

I can be good when I want to be.

Plus my nether regions are sore as hell, and I don't want to test if he would, in fact, spank me.

Like the gentleman he is, he walks me up to my door, his hand gently settling onto my lower back. We are almost to the porch steps when I feel his hand tense and he pauses, glancing around. "What's wrong?"

"I'm not sure; let's get you inside."

With my keys already in hand, I make quick work of getting the door open, getting a strange vibe as we step inside. Goosebumps spread across my skin as I glance around, but I don't see anything. I'm instantly distracted by what is waiting on the other side of the door. Sitting like sentinels ready for battle are Beretta and Indy, both looking frazzled and pissy.

"What's wrong, guys?" Not that they answer me.

Indy prowls right up to me, grumbling in irritation. Brushing up against my leg, he looks up at me pointedly, as if I'm responsible for whatever is going on. I raise my eyebrow at his antics, but he doesn't stick around. He pads off through the living room and back towards the kitchen. My eyes go to Beretta next, but she just huffs at me and follows Indy.

"I'm not sure what that was about, but I feel like I'm in trouble."

Don wraps his arms around me, nudging me inside.

"You better go make it right, baby; I've heard cats can hold a mean grudge." That makes me snort, and I give him an incredulous look over my shoulder. He just smirks down at me.

"I was going to invite myself in, but it seems like you'll have your hands full with those two."

He nuzzles my neck, his beard grazing my skin and making me shiver. He drops a quick kiss to my shoulder, before straightening back up. I turn around in his arms, snuggling into his warm chest. I feel so safe with him.

"Want to make the most of the weekend and come out with me and the guys tomorrow? I doubt they would mind, and I really want to see you again before work takes up our time."

"Yes, as long as the guys are ok with it."

"I'll ask them today, but I don't see it being an issue."

"Ok, text me the details, and I'll meet you tomorrow."

Don leans down again to brush his lips against mine.

"I'll see you tomorrow then."

I walk him out, getting that weird vibe again as I cross the threshold of my front door. Shaking off the feeling, I pull him down for one more kiss before he leaves.

"Drive safe," I whisper against his lips.

DONOVAN

Kinley goes back inside, so she doesn't notice me taking in the front of her house, analyzing it for anything amiss. I inhale deeply. There is something off, and I can't place it, but I also can't continue loitering outside of her house. A few minutes pass, and I'm still no closer to figuring out what is triggering my senses, so I climb in my truck and give Aiden a call. He answers just as I pull out of Kinley's driveway.

"I didn't figure I would hear from you at all today. Did the date with Kinley not go well?"

"No, it went great actually. But speaking of Kinley, I just dropped her off. There is a very distinct scent that wasn't there last night. I can't place it, but you and Brent are the ones with the best noses. Do you think one of you could do a drive by?"

His playful tone changes when he answers. "I can't, but I'll call Brent. Can you describe the scent? I'll relay it to him so he can be aware of what he's sniffing around for."

"Yeah, I kept getting hints of sulfur, pine, and something else that I couldn't figure out. Tell Brent to be low-key when he gets to her house. Her dog and cat are a little too observant."

"Will do. You notice anything else?"

"No, I didn't want to alarm her by asking to search around, but I didn't see anything out of the ordinary out front."

"Ok, I'll get Brent on it. You still on for tomorrow?"

"Yeah, about that, I kind of asked Kinley to come. You think Brent and Cam will mind?"

"Geeze, Don, you got it bad, huh?"

"You have no fucking idea. My beast is absolutely obsessed with her. I'm barely keeping him in check, but it's worse being away from her."

"Really? Shit, Don, you might need to call my Mom or Grandma about this."

"Shit, you might be right. I have no clue what's going on, but all I do know is that I need to be around her."

"Man, I don't envy you, but Kinley is great. Bring her along tomorrow. I'll give Brent a call now, and I'll tell him to call you after he's done."

"Thanks, man. Oh, and I got a little more information on her last night. She is from Texas, but she said she doesn't have any living family. That wouldn't make sense if she was Clan."

"Hmmm, yeah. I highly doubt that, too. Well, let Cam know that information. Maybe it can help him figure out if she is potentially any other type of magical species."

"Maybe, I just have this feeling she's not human. It just doesn't make sense to have this strong of a reaction otherwise."

"We will figure it out, Don."

I end the call, and as I drive home, I contemplate if I should call home. My Aunt and Grandmother are the heads of our Clan, but I don't want to call them prematurely and get them all in my business. They are meddlesome on a good day; if they get wind that I'm contemplating a mate, they will go feral. Better to leave that for another day, because I also need to figure out what is going on with Kinley, and why strange things keep happening.

KINLEY

I spend the rest of my Saturday relaxing and baking. When I get the text from Don saying that it is officially ok to come tomorrow, I feel it's only right to come bearing gifts. And what little I know about these guys, is they sure do love food. So I will ply them with sweets for allowing me to intrude on guy time. Just as I'm pulling my double chocolate brownies from the oven, my phone rings. Cursing silently, I quickly put the brownies on the hot plate and answer without looking.

"Hello."

When no one answers right away, I glance down at the screen to make sure I actually answered it. Frowning, because the call has been accepted but it's an unknown number, I answer again.

"Hello, is anyone there?"

But no voice answers me. *Is that breathing?*

Still not getting a response, I hang up. Stupid spam calls. Setting my phone on the island, so it's out of the way, I turn back to my baking, almost missing Indy sniffing at my phone and hissing.

"What has gotten into you today? First the cold shoulder and now you hate technology. What's your deal?"

With a flick of his tail, he jumps off the counter. I shake my head in exasperation as I turn back to check on the brownies, but I swear I hear a faint voice say "Danger." Goosebumps spread across my body as I whip back around, but all I see is Indy staring at me. Nothing else is amiss, and even though I'm thoroughly creeped out, I shake the feeling off as best I can.

"Geeze, Kinley, you need a nap or some coffee. You're losing it."

Eyeing my brownies, I focus back on my baking and decide that brownies alone might not be enough. So, I get out the ingredients to make peanut butter cookies. An hour later, I pack up my offerings and pour myself a glass of wine, because if I have coffee now, I will be up all night. After not getting much sleep the night before, I definitely need sleep so I don't look like a swamp monster tomorrow. Dark eye circles are not a good look when you are trying to keep a gorgeous man interested. Hot Mess Kinley is not to be brought out until he is properly snared. I snort to myself. Honestly, I think Don will like me no matter what I look like. He is such a good man.

Wine in hand, I decide that the best way to end my evening is to snuggle up on the couch and binge a few shows on Netflix before bed.

THE GUARDIANS

Deep into the night, as our mistress sleeps peacefully in bed, we keep watch. Foul, tainted energy kept us both on alert these last two days. Our magic is strong and unwavering. We chose our mistress, and no one will take her from us. Nothing will breach this home.

Their attempt had been laughable, but we are both still on edge. We both knew that one day, powerful beings would come skulking about, trying to obtain her, for we know how special she is.

It had been against my better judgement to begin unraveling the geas put upon her, but my companion had provided a good argument, even though I was loath to tell her so. The geas had been strong but hastily done, and it didn't take us long to begin unraveling those threads that held my mistress in the dark depths of her mind.

I growl at the thought of whoever had done this to her, but thankfully for my mistress, I'm more powerful than some old magic wielder. The magical community these days left much to be desired, but even our vast power could still not fully wipe the geas' effects immediately. It will have to fade slowly so as to not harm our mistress. My powers snake out, feeling the thread's strength ebbing.

"It won't be too much longer now."

My companion nods in agreement. "Probably why that male was sniffing about."

I scoff. "At least he has potential. Much better than some of those detestable humans she has brought home."

"Do you think the foul one will return?"

"If they know what is good for them, they won't."

As the night wanes and fades into dawn, we stand vigil, because we will do whatever is necessary to protect her.

Whatever is necessary.

CHAPTER 14

DONOVAN

As I get ready the next morning, I mull over the conversations I had last night with Aiden and Brent. Brent came over and Aiden connected over the phone. Brent scoped out Kinley's house, cataloging all the scents using his beast's incredible sense of smell. Not even he could place the smell, but he did mention there were similarities to some of the scents he picked up the night Kinley had the intruder at the lake house. Much to my frustration, we hadn't been able to come to any conclusions.

What we did realize was that something much bigger was going on with her. They both kept bringing up my need to be around her and how that was potentially linked. I'm still not sure, but I'm convinced that meeting her can no longer be considered a coincidence. It feels like a brush of fate, as my Grandmother would call it, and I'm not going to ignore it.

The guys busted my balls about it, but I'm looking forward to seeing her again today. I miss her in my bed, in my arms, the uncontrollable sounds she makes when I'm inside her.

My beast rears his head up and snorts in agreement at that thought. I'm really going to have to figure out how to reveal him to her. I know it's only a matter of time before he breaks free. It's a battle of wills with myself and the creature I share a soul with whenever Kinley is around.

But how can I bring her into my world without utterly terrifying her?

I tug at my hair in frustration. It's much too soon to be thinking about this. I dread calling my Aunt, but if these urges keep up, I'm going to need help.

Swiping a hand over my face, I sit down in my sitting room, looking out into my wooded back yard. It's still early, and dew coats the grass and the trees making everything shimmer. I sip my coffee, savoring the taste. It's going to start getting cold soon. With the cold, comes ice.

I'm going to have to take some more trips up to the lake house before the freeze sets in. It's the only place close by that I can safely fully enjoy myself. I sigh, thinking how much time that will take away from seeing Kinley if I don't let her in on my big secret first. This is going to get complicated.

KINLEY

I check my GPS again, squinting through my windshield. *Where the hell am I going?*

I swear I'm in the middle of nowhere, and I'm really praying my signal holds strong. I'm seriously contemplating calling Don, and begging for him to come find me. I even double-checked with him before I left to make sure I had the correct address. But I'm straight up in the woods, on a tiny ass dirt road.

At this point, I don't even care if I do sound like a damsel in distress. I hate being lost. I pick up my phone and begin to slow my car, when I see a break in the trees up a little ways. Even if it isn't a house, maybe I will have enough space to turn around.

Luck is on my side, though. As I pull through the longest driveway in history, I see a massive modern style cabin and several cars parked out front. Seeing Don's truck, I sigh in relief and pull up to the nearest space. Thank god I found it, because now that the anxiety is wearing off, I really need to pee.

Hopping out of the car, I move around to grab the treats I baked the night before. Hearing a leaf crunch behind me makes me whirl around, fully prepared to sacrifice the treats by throwing them at whatever is coming up behind me.

But it's just Brent, sporting a very devilish smirk.

"Jesus, Brent, you almost made me chuck brownies at you!"

Or piss myself—thank god for Kegels.

His forest-green eyes light up as he zeroes in on the sweets I have in my arms.

"You baked?"

I nod.

"Damn, Don has all the luck."

A blush spreads across my face at the compliment, and at the look of hunger that flashes across his face. I pray that look is purely for the baked goods, because I don't want to dive into that train of thought. I'm relieved when Don walks down the front stairs, his long stride quickly eating up the distance between us. Even though it has been less than twenty-four hours since I last saw him, my heart pounds in my chest.

A somewhat predatory grin spreads across his face as he gets closer to me. Smoothly taking the containers out of my hands and passing them off to Brent, he then pins me up against my SUV and kisses me senseless.

I barely register the bark of laughter from Brent before I respond in kind. My hands grab onto Don's shoulders to keep myself from melting into a puddle, my lips desperate for his. His large hands find their way down to my ass and lift me up. I gasp, giving him the perfect opportunity to thrust his tongue into my mouth. We cling to each other, our bodies burning for one another, completely tuning out our surroundings. Nothing matters more in that moment than being in his arms, his mouth on mine, and his body pressed between my legs.

A deep voice calls out, maybe Aiden's.

"If you start getting each other naked, I'm totally watching."

Laughter follows, quickly dousing the flames of our lust. I disentangle myself from Don, hiding my head in his chest, embarrassed that I let myself get so swept up in the moment.

Jesus, Kinley, you're out in the open, and you were practically dry humping this man.

Donovan breathes in deeply for a moment, as if he too is composing himself.

He tilts my head up gently with a finger under my chin. "Hey, don't be embarrassed. It's fine. They are just giving me a hard time. It's all good."

I can tell my face is still flushed, so I nod up at him, still not able to find my voice. Leaning down, he places a gentle but swift kiss on my lips before pulling me into his side and guiding me up to the house.

"Are you hungry? We've got food on the grill out back. Aiden is the grill master; according to him, anything can be grilled with enough effort."

I giggle at that. "Yes, I am actually starving. I thought I might have to eat what I brought because I was getting worried that I was lost."

"Baby, you should have called me. I would have made sure you weren't lost."

"I was actually about to when I saw the trees open up."

"Good girl."

My mouth drops slightly. *My goodness, this man gets me all riled up.* Shaking myself out of my lust brain, I follow his lead up the stairs. As soon as we enter the door, I'm greeted with the sight of Camden perched on the arm of a very rugged leather couch. His gray eyes twinkle with mischief as we walk inside. I can sense Donovan about to scold him and put him in check but, feeling a little sassy, I beat him to it.

"I will take back all of my brownies and cookies if you say what I think you're going to say, and no one will get any of them."

I hear panicked shouts just before Brent and Aiden bolt around the corner, of what I assume leads into the kitchen, both with a brownie in hand. They give Camden death glares and he mimes zipping his lips.

Not willing to let a little embarrassing situation get the best of me, I dive into helping with food, or at least I try to. The majority is already done, and the guys seem to have everything under control, so I ask where the plates and silverware are.

Brent, who is close by, helps me get the plates down—short girl problems—and shows me where the silverware is. With my arms full of dinnerware, I follow Aiden outside to set the table on the deck.

The view from the deck is beautiful. Large deciduous trees line the whole property. The leaves of the trees are just starting to get hints of red, orange, and yellow. It's so peaceful out here. I take a deep breath and just breathe in the nature that surrounds me. The closing of the grill lid jars me out of my slight trance, and I get back to setting the table.

The food the guys make is delicious—stuffed burgers with all the toppings, grilled corn, and an antipasto salad. With as much food as they pile onto my plate, I'm not going to need to eat dinner later, let alone be able to walk out of here. We eat, drink beers, and the guys tell hilarious stories about each other. They have graciously allowed me into their world, and I really don't want to leave.

Camden holds out the bowl of pasta. "You want more, Kinley?"

I lean back in my chair and groan. "I literally can't eat another bite, so full."

Donovan leans over, kissing my forehead. "Let me get your plate."

"I can get it."

"Nope, I got this."

"Yeah, Kinley, you hang out. We have a system down for clean up. It won't take long," Aiden tells me as he grabs a few plates and heads in.

Brent and Camden follow, laden with trays and bowls, leaving me on my own. Well, if that's what they want, who am I to get in their way?

Groaning, I stand up, stretching like that will suddenly relieve me of that too-full feeling. Walking over to the railing, I admire the scenery. It's so beautiful here, so peaceful. I close my eyes, feeling the cool breeze brush against my face. A whisper of fabric is all the warning I get as strong arms wrap around me. I automatically know it is Donovan. His tantalizing scent wraps around me just like his arms do.

"You're so beautiful," he murmurs as he leans down and nuzzles my neck, placing a kiss there.

I never realized how much of an erogenous zone my neck was until Don.

"How are you doing? I know the guys can be a lot."

"I'm having a great time, Don; they are great guys. I like that you have such a close relationship with all of them."

He nuzzles my neck with affection.

"Good, I'm glad you are having a good time. Kinley, I want to keep seeing you. Exclusively. Would that be ok with you?"

I turn around in his arms, gazing up into his deep blue eyes.

"I would like that so much. Can I tell you something? It might be too much because we haven't known each other for long, but I need you to know how I'm feeling."

"Of course, you can tell me anything."

I take a deep breath, keeping my eyes trained on his to see any potential change in emotion. I'm nervous to say this to him, but something pushes me to tell him.

"I've never felt the way I do for you with anyone else in my entire life. I can't explain it; it doesn't make any sense. But I...I need...ugh, this is sounding crazy."

He smiles softly. "It's not crazy, Kinley. Remember when I was talking about how my people believe in a Goddess?"

I nod my head.

"In my culture, we believe that when we meet the one that is meant to complete our soul, we form an immediate connection with them. An emotional and physical connection. We don't question it; it is Goddess-blessed, this connection. Do you understand what I'm saying?"

143

"Are you saying that what I'm feeling is because we were meant to find each other? That our souls are connected?"

"In a way, yes. Kinley, I haven't been able to stop thinking about you since we first met at that gas station. You're in my every waking thought. I need to be near you."

Oh god, he does feel the same way.

"So you don't think I'm crazy for feeling this strongly so soon?"

He chuckles and shakes his head. "If you're crazy, then we are crazy together. I don't think there is anyone more perfect than you, Kinley. I truly think we were meant to meet and be together."

"I'm not good with emotions. I'm not good at expressing my feelings. With you I want to, but it's hard for me to believe that it's real. Megan is the only person I have let in, and it scares me that I want to do that with you."

"I understand; I know this is a lot. We just met, and it probably didn't help that we were intimate, but Goddess, help me, I wouldn't change a damn thing. No matter how much I want to push and go the speed of light with you, I can be patient, Kinley. If you ever feel overwhelmed, or if I'm pushing you too fast, just tell me, ok?"

I smile up at him shyly. He is such a good man. More than what I think I deserve, but in my heart, I know that he is the one I have been waiting for, the one I need in my life. Standing on my tiptoes, I reach up and place my lips gently on Don's. His arms come around me, cradling me to him as he deepens our kiss ever so slightly. A throat clearing behind us pops our little intimate bubble.

"We leave you two alone for even a minute and you're already all over her, Don," Camden jokes from behind us. This time the interruption only makes me grin before I push away from the railing, purposefully brushing my body up against Don. Hearing him growl only makes me grin further, and I side-step out of his hold. I'm feeling really good about everything.

"So, what do you guys usually do when a woman isn't crashing your guy time?"

"We sacrifice ripe young Maidens under the Moon," a gruff voice whispers behind me.

I faintly hear Donovan reprimand Brent before my mind goes black and I'm transported to somewhere else.

CHAPTER 15

KINLEY

Flames from large candles surround me; crystals of various shapes and sizes glow between lush greenery with flowers woven in, and voices sing an ancient powerful hymn. Power pulses through me—strength, vitality, and passion fill my soul. It all bursts from my mouth, in the most beautiful sound I have ever heard. The beauty of it makes me want to weep. This is my purpose, this is my calling. I have been chosen for this.

That song unlocks something inside me, and I need more. I crave it.

Just as suddenly, the joy is ripped from me, and all I feel is pain and despair. I cry out in anguish.

No, this isn't how it is supposed to be!

People are screaming, and cruel laughter fills my head. My chest and head pound with fear and anger.

Snarls rise up from deep within me. *How dare they desecrate this beauty!*

I want to do something, anything, to make the pain and cruelty stop.

I have to save them. I don't even know who they are; I just know they need me.

A male is calling my name, pleading for me to come back.

Come back to him? Can I even do that? Yes, I need to go to him. That feels right, he feels right. He feels like home.

Where is this male?

The sound of his voice is faint, and I can't find him. There is so much agony it's making it difficult for me to find my way to him.

"Help me," I hear myself plead.

The male voice gets louder, more urgent. "Kinley!"

Is that my name?

"Baby, snap out of it!"

That voice is so familiar. He is safe. He will protect me. He will help me save them.

"Please, help me." My voice trembles with shock.

"Kinley, come back. You're safe. You're with me."

My body is beyond my control, shaking with the fear and the emotions of all those people.

"I can't… I can't… I can't."

"Kinley, you can. Come back to me. Now!"

A snarl of dominance fills my ears, pushing me over into the present. I gasp, my eyes finally seeing what is actually in front of me.

I stare into the bright glowing eyes of Don.

"Breathe, baby, you need to breathe."

My breath is heaving out of my chest. *Am I having a panic attack? Why does this keep happening when I'm with him?*

"Watch me, babe. Breathe with me."

His stern command helps me focus on him, slowly matching his deep breaths in and long exhales out.

"Good girl, keep breathing, just like that."

My muscles slowly relax as my breathing finally gets under control. As I finally become more self aware, I also realize that four very alarmed men are staring at me.

Their eyes are all so bright. *Why are their eyes so bright? Are they glowing?*

147

"Kinley," Donovan says sharply. "You're zoning out again, baby." He strokes my hair, pushing stray strands away from my face. "Has this ever happened before?"

"No, what happened, Don?" I croak out. My throat is raw; it feels like I have been sick, or screaming. I bring my hand up to rub my face, and am horrified at what I see. Blood is dripping off my fingers.

I cry out. *Was the blood and pain all real?*

I frantically look down, searching for where the blood came from. Then I see Don's arms, covered in deep scratches.

A broken sob leaves me. "Oh my god, Don, did I do this?"

"Baby, don't worry about that. I'm fine, I'll heal. I'm way more concerned with what just happened to you."

Aiden crouches down next to us, crowding in on my other side.

"Don, we should get her into the house. Get you two cleaned up, and then we will figure out what happened."

Don doesn't hesitate; he just scoops me up into his arms, cradling me close to his chest. Cam quickly opens the door for us.

"Don, use the master bath; there's more room in there," Brent calls out.

Aiden leads the way through the house into a huge bathroom with dark slate tile and a massive glassed-in steam shower with several shower heads. If I had the mental capacity to be in awe, I'm sure that is what I would be in. But I'm just so numb.

In a slightly hysterical whisper, I can't help but ask. "What does Brent do again?"

Brent doesn't even hesitate to answer me as he strolls in; he just leans in close to whisper while I'm still in Donovan's arms. "Princess, if I told you, I'd have to keep you for myself and never let you leave."

I give him a startled look, and he winks at me. Donovan gives him an almost feral glare. Utterly confused about how to feel, I glance around and notice all of the guys staring at me intently, as if my head is about to spin around.

Why are they looking at me like that? What the fuck happened outside?

"Guys, I'm going to start freaking out. Why are you all staring at me like that?"

148

Donovan gently sits me on the cold black granite countertop, looking directly into my eyes. "Kinley, I'm going to be honest with you, but I don't think you're going to like my answers."

"Don, you're scaring me. What happened?"

Aiden quickly steps around Don and nudges him out of the way.

"Don, you're not helping. Go clean up your arms, I'll get her cleaned up."

A deep rumble leaves Don, his shoulders tense and his fists clench as he takes one menacing step toward Aiden.

How is he making that sound?

But Aiden doesn't budge. "Don, I know, but one thing at a time."

Camden gets in on the action, giving Donovan some sterile gauze pads and saline solution and moves him over to the next sink. All I can seem to do is stare, at a complete loss for words. Aiden must sense my turmoil ramping up because he quickly moves in front of me.

"Hey, Kinley, deep breaths for me, ok? You're ok, nothing bad is going to happen. You've got the four of us now and we won't let anything get to you, ok?"

I nod my head, trying to make sense of what I'm feeling, but I still have no clue what is going on. Aiden just takes control, gently cleaning the blood from my hands. His touch centers me, helping me stay in the moment.

"How did I hurt Don?"

I look up into Aiden's eyes, pleading with him to answer me.

"Whatever you were experiencing stimulated your claws to come out."

I gasp. *What the hell was he talking about?*

"What? I don't have claws!"

"Oh, you do, but it's ok; we are used to claws." He smiles slyly.

My head shakes frantically. "No, I don't. What the hell are you talking about? People don't have claws."

I look around at the others, all with sympathetic, understanding looks on their faces.

They all believe what Aiden just said. They aren't this cruel, are they? Oh my god, did they drug me? Is this what this is? Am I coming down from a bad trip?

But that doesn't ring true, as soon as I think it, my mind automatically dismisses it. *But the claw thing has to be false, right?*

My eyes land back on Don. He doesn't answer my questioning stare. He just nods.

I feel myself spiral, but Aiden quickly brings my attention back. "Kinley, turn and look in the mirror. You're not human."

A pit forms in my stomach. *What does he mean I'm not human?* Unable to stop myself, I slowly turn my head and look over my shoulder. This time a sob does break free.

"My eyes. What is wrong with my eyes?"

The blue of my irises has completely disappeared. What stares back at me are the most intense electric violet I have ever seen, and they're glowing brightly. My stomach roils. I'm going to be sick; I just know it. Saliva pools in my mouth, and I can't help the small gag that sneaks free.

"Shit, Kinley, are you going to be sick?"

Brent doesn't even wait for me to answer. He just swoops in, and deposits me in front of the toilet, tucked away in its own private alcove. I heave, but my stomach doesn't yield the food I ate earlier. Thank god for small mercies. A gentle hand brushes soothing circles on my back as I work to get my stomach under control. I don't want to humiliate myself further and vomit.

"It's ok, princess, we've got you."

Realizing the soothing hand belongs to Brent stirs something in me, but my brain shoves it aside just trying to keep my shit together.

"Here, Brent, see if this cool cloth helps. Put it on the back of her neck."

Brent does what Aiden tells him to, and the coolness helps calm my nerves and stomach further.

"You think you're done? Don is getting antsy."

I hear the humor in Brent's voice, and a part of me wants to smile, but I'm so freaked out, all I can do is take a deep breath and nod. Brent shuffles me over to a teak bench in the middle of the room and gently guides me down.

Not able to resist being away from me any longer, Donovan pushes Brent out of the way and cups my face gently in his hands.

"Baby, it's going to be ok. There is nothing wrong with you. You're so fucking perfect. I can't believe how lucky I am to have found you. I'm not sure how you went this long without knowing what you are, but it's ok. We can help you with that."

"What do you think I am, Don?"

"You're Clan, baby. You're like us. I don't know how this is possible, but I'm so fucking thankful."

No matter how sweet he is being, his words make no fucking sense. I push him away, attempting to stand. Hands reach out as my legs wobble, but I steady myself before anyone can help me. I take several steps back. I don't want to be in a vulnerable position. They are all too close, staring at me, assessing my every move. I need space. I need room to breathe. It's making me feel like a caged beast.

"I don't know what any of this means, Don! None of what you are saying makes sense. This isn't some fantasy novel. People don't fucking grow claws and change their eyes! I must be having a fucking mental breakdown."

Not wanting to stand in front of the guys and break down fully, I go to leave, but Brent is blocking the doorway.

"Move, Brent."

"Kinley, I can't do that right now. You're freaking out, and if we let you go, you could get yourself or someone else hurt."

"Kinley, look at me, baby," Don pleads quietly. "I know this sounds fucking crazy. I know you're scared, but we can explain and help you."

I can't help it; the quiet pleading in his voice makes me turn around, but I know fury and pain are etched all over my face. When I'm this upset there is no hiding what I'm feeling, so I don't even try to spare him from seeing it.

"Don, none of this makes sense. I don't understand what is going on, and I'm so confused. I told you how hard it is for me to share my feelings and trust people. I want to believe you because you said you felt the same way and that felt so real. But if all of this is true, my whole life has been a lie. How am I supposed to trust anything...anyone?"

My voice has a broken edge, and the dam holding my tears back threatens to break. I know that once that happens, talking will no longer be an option, so I hold onto what's left of my sanity. I'm not a pretty crier; I sob and hyperventilate to the point no words can escape me. And now is definitely not the time for that.

Don takes a deep breath as if steeling himself against the pain he sees within me. "Baby, no, you can. What I said earlier was completely true. You are a part of me, and now I know why. We really were meant to find each other. I know we just met, but you know you can still trust me. You can feel I'm not lying to you. I don't know what happened to you, but I really need you to believe that we are here to help you. We can show you, ok? Can you just give me a little more time?"

His words are so sincere that I find myself wavering. I desperately want to put my faith in him, because he is right. I can sense that he's telling me the truth, that I really can trust him, but my mind is refusing to fully give into that idea. I have never felt this strongly for anyone in my entire life, and no matter how crazy it sounds I just can't walk away. There is also a part of me that just really needs to know what is happening. Squaring my shoulders, I meet his eyes and give a small nod. The tension leaves his face, and for some reason that makes me calm further.

Don clears his throat. "We're gonna need to go outside for this I think. Brent, lead us out."

Outside in the backyard they all stand around me, but, thankfully, I don't feel overwhelmed—yet. Don steps closer to me, not touching, but close enough that I can feel the warmth of his body.

"Deep breaths, ok?"

Still not trusting my voice, I nod again. He then turns to Aiden.

"Can you shift? You're probably going to be the one to scare her the least."

Aiden rolls his eyes and takes a few steps away from us, quickly removing his clothes. I begin to protest. *Why is he taking his clothes off?* But before I can make a sound, or even begin to process what Don had actually said, I feel it. A hum of energy fills the air around us, a soothing vibration, and Aiden transforms into the largest and most beautiful wolf

152

I have ever seen.

He is massive; he towers over me. His proud wolven head lifts, assessing me with his piercing gaze, and his tall erect ears perk forward listening intently. He is beautiful, and I want to weave my fingers into his coat. It looks so soft, and it's the darkest and richest brown. His coat actually matches his hair color when he is a man. That is such a strange thing to say, when he is a man. *Is he still? Is he aware of who we are when he's in this form? Can he communicate like this?*

I'm too stunned to speak, but as I stare into Aiden's eyes, something stirs deep inside myself. An energy builds, and it causes the others to look at me like they can feel it too, but it disappears as if it isn't ready to be felt. My brows crease at the loss, trying to pull it back, but instead what I find is Aiden's voice in my mind, clear as day.

See? It is possible for you to have claws.

I startle a little, and finally find some words to speak out loud. I turn my eyes to Donovan."So, you're saying I'm like him?"

My lack of hysterics must have eased the guys further; I can feel them all relaxing, still on alert, but the tension is fading. I'm not even sure why I'm not freaking out. Have I reached my limit? Or am I not reacting because a part of me recognizes what they have been saying and what I'm seeing is the truth?

"Similar, yes. Until you actually turn, we have no idea what your beast actually is, but we all felt her. Just now, and when you were in that trance earlier."

"You should have turned at a much younger age. You should never have been kept in the dark. It's incredibly dangerous for you and for our people to have one of us not know what they are," Brent states quietly, almost as if he is being careful not to spook me.

Don and Camden nod in agreement and a gentle huff from Aiden lets me know he also agrees. Don tentatively reaches for my hand, and his hesitancy clenches my heart. I don't want to hurt him, and it feels wrong to see him question if I will allow his touch.

"Let's go back inside and we can talk some more. We promise to answer any of your questions to the best of our ability, and if we don't know the answers, I know people who do."

153

"Ok." I take his hand, his fingers gently weaving through mine. That touch gives me confidence to ask what I have been silently wondering since I saw Aiden change.

"Wait, what do you turn into, Don? Do you all change into wolves?"

"Baby, I don't want to scare you. You've been through so much in less than an hour."

That makes me frown, and I attempt to take my hand out of his, but he doesn't loosen his hold.

"You said you would be honest with me." I feel my teeth bare at him and see in the reflection of his dark blue eyes that mine are still violet, glowing even brighter than they were earlier.

He swipes his other hand over his face, still refusing to let mine go. He looks at Brent and Aiden.

"If he goes after her you're gonna have to block me. Cam, you get her out of here if I do."

That makes me go still.

"Why would you come after me?"

Camden moves first, stepping closer to me. Don gives my hand a squeeze before he stalks away from me. I can see his back muscles ripple under his tight cotton shirt.

"Because he wants you; his beast sees you as his. And right now, your emotions are all over the place, and he's barely keeping himself in check."

Energy builds and flows around Don, his eyes stare into mine and glow a haunting shade of blue. He quickly removes his clothes. His voice deepens to a harsh growl.

"Don't run."

And then he changes into a monstrous horse, at least 18 hands high at his shoulder and built like the largest of draft breeds. There is just so much of him, I don't even know where to look first. His eyes, the same deep blue with flecks of dark green, contrast sharply with the rest of his face. His coat is as dark as a night with no moon. his mane, full of wild waves, drapes along his massively muscled neck. A large Roman nose ends in flared nostrils. But his mouth is all wrong, lips pulled back much further than a normal horse, as if his jaw would open and swallow prey, not grass. Razor sharp canines protrude past his lower and upper jaws. *God, what kind of mythical creature is he?*

He paws the ground with his massive four toed hoof, which is more claw-like, as if preparing himself to charge. He snorts and paces, his eyes never leaving me. And as if in answer, what had shied away inside me earlier perks up again. A desperate whine escapes my mouth, and my body bows. Whatever is inside me desperately tries to break free at the sight of him. Not to run from him but to him.

His head rears up as he hears my whine of pain, of longing. My hand involuntarily reaches out to him.

Mate, my mate…

I hear chants in my head, over and over. As if he can hear it too, his control snaps, and he charges toward me, his hooves thundering over the soft grass. He is coming for me.

Cam breaks my eye contact, scooping me up as if to run, but my body has a mind of its own, and I struggle against him, desperately trying to get to Donovan.

"Cam, let her go. She's going to hurt herself trying to get to him. He's in control, I can feel it." Brent shouts and Cam immediately puts me down, backing away quickly as I lunge forward.

We reach each other at the same moment. Don bows his mighty head down towards me. My arms attempt to circle his neck, but don't come close to reaching. I surely would dangle off the ground if he decided to lift his head higher. He towers over me, but he cradles me close to his body, nudging me closer with his chin resting along my back. Deep chuffs leave his mouth as if trying to soothe me, sensing the turmoil that rages within me.

I've got you, baby. I've got you.

His deep voice whispers in my mind. It's like a warm, comforting blanket. I don't understand anything that has happened, and I can't explain why I feel this overwhelming need to be with him. I just know, and as I press my body against his, a small door inside my soul quietly unlocks and releases a little bit of myself that has been hidden away. A small, quiet song spills out of me. I didn't know I could sing, let alone know the words, but I know the feelings it provokes. The words of this song are about coming home.

Don's body shudders against me, muscles rippling. Astonishment and wonder trickle through that link in my head and know it's from him. As my song builds, songs of beasts join me. A stallion's trumpet, a roar, a loud screech of a bird of prey, and a howl all join in. All the while, Don's beast stands here with me, soaking in the haunting melody, bracing me against his chest with his large head. The song slowly fades, leaving a feeling of hope and of loss. As the final note stills on my tongue, my world goes dark, and I collapse at Don's feet.

CHAPTER 16

KINLEY

Sunlight peeking in from a nearby window shines brightly on my face, drawing me out of a deep sleep. Cool, silken sheets are draped over my body, and I revel in the softness against my skin. My stirring body brushes up against a large warm one. Strong arms tighten against me with my movements, as if anchoring me to them so I don't drift away.

My eyes crack open, and I'm met with an unfamiliar room. Alarmed, I turn over quickly to see who is in bed with me. Don's ocean blue eyes stare back at me, and my sudden anxiety eases.

"Hey, you're ok. We stayed over at Brent's," He tells me, like he already knows what I'm going to ask. He draws me back down into his arms, but I startle up again, trying to leap out of the bed.

"Fuck, work!"

"Woah, hold on, baby. We took care of that, we called in for you."

My brow furrows in confusion.

"What? How would you know how to do that? I don't have any sub plans, oh my god. I'm so fucked."

"Baby, calm down. Look at me, please."

My lips tremble slightly, and I desperately try to hold it together as best I can. I just manage it before I chance a look into his eyes. He is sitting up in bed now, and distractingly naked. I can't help it as my eyes travel down his perfect, rugged body. He doesn't let me stare long, though, before he brings my chin up.

"I called your principal. I told him you were very ill, in another city, and would be stuck there until you were better enough to travel. He said he would talk to your department chair and get something set up while you're gone. It's all taken care of. I had no way of knowing how long you would be out, and I knew you would be upset about work. I figured you could use some time to process what happened yesterday."

My mouth gapes open a little at how thoughtful he was about getting my work figured out.

"Now come and lay back down. I need to hold you a little bit longer. You scared the shit out of me and the guys last night."

I can't argue with that, so I snuggle back down and use my finger to trace along the lines of his chest tattoo.

"Don?"

"Hmmm?"

"Did you really turn into a black horse last night?"

I'm secretly hoping it was all a fever dream.

He sighs and pulls me in tighter, my face smooshing a little into his hard pec.

"Well, I'm not actually a horse. I actually shift into a Kelpie."

I snort at the ridiculousness of that statement.

"Really? You're gonna talk semantics with me now?"

"Yes... completely different species."

I groan, thumping my head lightly against his very hard chest, which flexes under my forehead as he chuckles.

"And Aiden really turned into a wolf?"

"Yes."

"God, none of this makes any sense. How is this possible?"

Before he can respond, the door clicks open, I yelp and burrow into

Don. With his back to the door, I'm completely covered from view, but I still hide.

"Did someone say my name?"

Aiden strolls in, plopping down on the bed behind Don. Don rolls over giving him a reproachful look, but by Don rolling over, I lose part of my body shield. I scramble to grab as much of the covers as possible and pull them up under my chin. I don't care how comfortable they were with nudity; I'm not. Cam peeks in shortly after.

"Oh, hey, are we having a meeting?"

Aiden grins at Cam and nods, and before Don can tell him no, Cam yells down the hall for Brent.

I'm completely mortified, silently wishing that I could turn myself invisible and run far, far away. *Wait, are invisibility powers a thing, too? I'm going to have to ask about that.*

Don looks back at me, taking in my beet red cheeks. The ass just grins at me.

I whisper-yell, "What the fuck, Don?"

Yet again, I get no answers because Brent struts his way into the room, taking in the scene before him.

"Come on, guys; you are stressing her out." Don tries to reason with them, but it lacks conviction.

The other three just exchange looks and grin at each other. Suddenly, as if they choreographed it, Camden and Brent take a running leap, tackling Don and Aiden onto the bed. With roars of laughter, they jostle and wrestle around. My precarious hold on the sheets fails and my tits and ass are now on full display.

Seeing more than one hungry gaze, I shriek. I've had enough. Abandoning Don, the covers, and the bed, I make a break for it to the en-suite bathroom and slam the door shut.

Bracing my back against it, Don yelling at the others comes through clearly from the other side, "Gods damn it, you fucking idiots, this is not the time for your fucking childish tactics."

Thuds are next to filter in, like fists hitting flesh. My best bet is to just hang out here for a few, collect myself, and maybe find some food when I'm brave enough to go back out there. My stomach gurgles in hunger.

Checking that the door is actually locked, I straighten and walk over to the vanity, groaning as I look at myself in the mirror. Honestly, I'm pretty sure I've looked worse. I guess that's a plus. My hair is definitely a mess and needs a good brushing.

Surprisingly, I still look like me. My outward appearance doesn't betray what I went through last night.

I wonder how long I actually slept. At least my eyes aren't fucking purple anymore. *What is going on with me?*

Steeling myself and taking several deep breaths, I decide to work my way through the shit show that is currently rocking my life. Pulling from my years of experience with compartmentalizing, I unbox everything one at a time.

Alright, Kinley, do we get the fuck out of here and ghost the shit out of him? Or do we take a shower, put our big girl panties on and figure out why we are a shit magnet all of a sudden?

"Holy shit! They turn into animals," I whisper to myself, trying to keep quiet, and then my mind goes to some of Don's more interesting attributes.

Don turned into a Kelpie horse thing... oh my god, is that why his dick is so big... what the fuck, Kinley... way to stay focused.

"Ughhhh, fuck my life! Shower it is. I can't walk away from all of this. I can't walk away from him." I rub my face, trying to ease some of the tension at my temples. This is all so much to deal with, but I can't deny what I'm feeling for Don.

Guess my compartmentalization skills are rusty.

With my mediocre mental pep talk complete, I turn to the shower and pray that I'm doing the right thing.

The shower restores a little bit of my confidence, and when I can't justify staying under the warm water jets any longer, I get out and brace myself for what I'm going to find beyond that door.

I wrap myself in a very fluffy towel that shockingly wraps completely around me. If I remember, I'm definitely asking Brent where he gets his towels.

Steeling myself, I unlock the door and find Don sitting on the bed, waiting for me. He must have also showered while he waited, since his

160

hair is wet and he also put pants on, but his upper body is still bare. All his muscles and ink are on display and so very distracting.

"Come here, baby."

He holds his arm out for me, beckoning me to come closer. I don't hesitate. I walk right up to him and rest my head on his shoulder as he wraps his large arms around me, cocooning me in his warmth and surprising safety, even after everything that happened last night.

"I got you some clothes. They'll be baggy, but you'll be cozy."

He stands up, tilting my chin up so he can softly kiss me on the lips.

"I'll let you get dressed. We are just finishing up making breakfast. Come out when you're ready."

He closes the door gently and leaves me in silence.

It doesn't take me long to get dressed, and a few minutes later I'm making my way out to find the guys. It doesn't take me long, I just follow the noise and the delicious smells.

Pausing in the doorway to the kitchen, I watch everyone work together to put out the food. Aiden spots me first and comes up to me, putting an arm around my shoulders and giving me a little squeeze.

"You doing ok? I know we are a lot, and what we sprung on you last night is probably messing with your head."

"I'm coping, for now, but I have so many questions."

"Good. We will help as much as we can. You can count on all of us, not just Don. You are Clan, and we protect our own."

I still don't really know what that means, being "Clan," but I feel his sincerity. He gives me a reassuring smile before leading me into the kitchen. Camden spots us then, scooping me up in a big hug, causing me to squeak. *I have been making the most undignified noises lately.*

"Umm, Cam, why are you cuddling me?"

I hear a quiet, trilling sound. *Was that coming from him?* I search for Don. I don't really need him to rescue me, but it's still a lot at once. Before he can intervene, Brent snatches me from Camden. He gently sets me on my feet.

"Don't mind him, he's just a little touch-deprived since his break up."

"Why are you all being so affectionate all of a sudden?"

Brent is the one to answer, "It's a Clan thing, and with as much power as you were throwing out last night—Well, it's been a really long time since we have all been around such a powerful female, so we are kind of soaking it up still."

"We don't get home very often, and females are kind of like power supplies. We get a recharge when we are around them. The more powerful the female, the bigger the recharge," Aiden adds.

"Ok, firstly, we need to talk about this whole Clan thing, because you all say it like it means something to me, when it doesn't. And um, secondly, this isn't gonna turn into a reverse-harem type of thing, right? Because you guys are great, but..."

I drop off, getting embarrassed when every single one of them gives me heated looks.

Don growls and quickly tells me, in a very deep grumbly voice, "Fuck no, you're mine. They can get their own."

Brent, still next to me, brushes up against me as if he can't help himself.

"You ever get tired of him, we will be happy to fill in."

"Jesus, Brent the only reason you're not bleeding right now is because I know it will upset Kinley. So, knock it off. We are so off-topic. Kinley needs to eat, and we need to figure out why she can project power but not shift. Also, she has questions that deserve answers."

That seems to get the guys focused back on the problem at hand. We all manage to get through breakfast without any further incidents or come ons. I still can't believe how different the guys are acting now that they have determined I'm one of them. They were friendly before, but now they are downright caring, like I'm now an integral part of their group. It's so weird, but also kind of nice. I'm fully accepting that something is off with me, but I'm not convinced that I can actually change into anything. Though, that would be pretty cool, I guess.

I try my best to explain what I saw and felt when I apparently went into that trance last night. None of them really know what to make of it. I do find out that during the trance thingy, I had been projecting so much power that it almost caused them all to shift.

"Only powerful females have that capability, Kinley. Which is why we are so stunned that you don't shift. It looked like you were about to

162

when you clawed up Don," Camden states.

"We are pretty high up in the hierarchy of our clan, but we aren't privy to enough to know what is going on with you. But if anyone would know, it would be our clan council, and maybe then we would be able to shed some light on your circumstances," Don says comfortingly, while stroking his thumb over my knuckles. He hasn't left my side during the entire conversation.

"I don't feel all that different, though. I grew up in a normal home, not in a clan."

"It's ok, baby. We will figure it out."

"Ok, so can you explain to me what you all are now? We keep dancing around it and I still have no idea what a Clan is. How does that lead to you having powers that turn you into creatures? Do you have any other powers lurking around that I should be aware of?"

They chuckle good naturedly at my list of questions. Don looks to Aiden, like he is asking him to explain.

"Ok, I'm going to give you the cliff notes version of Clan history. It is long and complicated, but I'll try to give you enough information that we can answer your questions as best we can."

I nod my head, thankful to maybe get some answers.

He continues, "Ok, so in a Clan, you have a council, and that council is led by three women: The Maiden, the Mother, and the Crone. These three women link us to our power source, which is basically nature, and supposedly to our Goddess. They keep the logistics hush-hush, because they don't want other magical beings trying to hijack our power supply."

Holy shit, this is a lot.

"Centuries ago, the Clans, before we officially were the Clans, had connections to Druids. Druids also have connections to nature, but they worship the Horned God. The Horned God is the counterpart to our Goddess. If the legends are true, the Horned God is very much the trickster and craves imbalance. The Druids were a Patriarchal society, and the males craved the power that the Goddess had bestowed on their females. Males were overpowering females, taking what didn't belong to them. I'm sure you can imagine what atrocities they were willing to do all in the name of their God?"

I nod, trying not to think of all the horrific things people did for the sake of their religion. Hell, what people still do, for the sake of their religion. I shudder at the thought.

"But how did you all get here? How were the Clans established?"

"How my Mom tells it is that the Goddess came to the females and showed them a way out. In the dead of the night, the Goddess gave them the powers to shift into birds. Any female that was willing to brave the journey left. They fled to a new world, carrying their young with them. Even some of the males, who were disgusted by the Horned God's wishes, fled with them."

"I always loved that part of the story," Camden interjects.

They all give him knowing looks that I don't understand, but I'm too focused on the story to ask.

"The Goddess guided her children to a land where they could live in harmony with nature, and so the Clans were born. She then taught them that in order to channel her powers, they would need the three strongest. Three is a sacred number for us for that reason, and that is how the Maiden, the Mother, and the Crone came to be."

"Are you born with your powers?" I ask. Pictures of baby animals romping around is alarming, but also freaking adorable. Don's voice draws me away from an extra adorable image of a foal romping around with his Kelpie's coloring.

"No, baby, we aren't. When we turn thirteen, we get to participate in the yearly ritual. The Maiden's song opens our soul up, so that our beast can link with us. Our shifting isn't instantaneous. It takes us a year, sometimes two, to have a stable bond with our beast. Once that happens, we start learning how to shift."

"Is that why I can't shift? I've never participated in any ritual."

"I don't think that is what is going on, Kinley. You have a beast. We can all feel her," Cam answers. I frown at that, but he continues.

"I've been trying to research your past. Before we knew you had Clan connections we were trying to determine why Don was so drawn to you, and also why there were magical signatures at Megan's lake house that night."

"Wait, you researched me? Why didn't you tell me? And what do you mean magical signatures at Megan's?" My eyes narrow at all of them.

"Baby, we thought you were human. We can't go telling humans about magic unless it absolutely can't be helped, and we still don't have any answers," Don says gently.

"Oh."

"Anyways, there is no Clan anywhere close to where you grew up. In fact, there is no Clan in Texas at all, which is weird. I'm completely stumped, and I don't have the clearance to go through Clan documents for that information. Eventually, we will need to consult our council to help us, but we won't do that until you are ready."

A frown mars my face. I should be able to remember if I had been a part of a magical community. Right?

"If it's any consolation, we also don't know how you've passed for a human this long. It should be impossible, yet here you are," Brent adds.

"Lucky me, I'm a magical being with no known backstory or access to my magic."

Brent chuckles. "It could be a lot worse. You could have had that episode last night around humans, and be locked up, most likely."

"Jesus, Brent, thanks for that image," I grumble sarcastically.

"You're welcome, Princess." His devilish smirk irritates the crap out of me.

I rub my forehead, feeling the beginnings of a headache. This is entirely too much information to process, but I'm the one that wanted to know. And then a thought occurs to me. My dreams.

"Um, so I'm sure you are aware that I have pretty vivid dreams. I don't really talk about them because they are pretty graphic and honestly never made sense. They are just something that I deal with." My eyes meet all of theirs and each one of them nods in encouragement, wanting me to continue. Don siddles closer, pulling me into his body, giving me strength to continue.

"I honestly thought they stemmed from unresolved childhood trauma. My parents, before they died, weren't people who should have had a kid." I can sense the air shift, their concern growing, but now isn't the time to unpack that.

"Recently, actually just before I met all of you, my dreams changed."I blow out a shaky breath thinking about those awful images.

"How have they changed, baby?"

I meet his eyes and resolve myself to divulge what has been consuming my sleeping mind. "There is always this dark figure. I never see his face." My brow scrunches as I remember his painful touch. "He calls me his Chosen, he hurts me…everytime. Claims that I'm his over and over. No matter how much I try, I can never escape him." Deep rumbling growls fill the room as they listen and I stop.

"Keep going, baby."

"He's not the only thing I dream of. There has been a woman too, she leads me to an altar. I'm always so stunned at how beautiful it is. I never know why I'm there but she guides me into a ritual. There are so many people there, I feel like I should know them, but I don't. I sing to them." I glance up from my hands that I have been clenching in my lap. They all have guarded expressions and my lips tilt in a slight frown. *Why are they looking at me like that?*

Aiden sits forward, his eyes boring into mine. "What do they call you in these dreams, Kinley?"

Don tenses next to me, as if he too is waiting on bated breath for me to answer. Hell, they all are. I don't even need to ask what he means because I already know. My gaze doesn't leave his as I say the words I worry will have repercussions that I'm not ready for. "The Maiden."

Aiden has his phone in his hand as soon as those words leave my lips.

"Who are you calling?" my voice wavers with uncertainty.

"My mom." He holds the phone up to his ear, his other hand tapping on his thigh as he waits for the call to be answered.

"Why her?" Don's hand eases up and down my arm, making me realize just how stiff I've become. Aiden doesn't answer me, though, and I don't have the patience. "Why her, Aiden?" there is a sharpness to my tone that I normally would hold back.

"It's ok, baby. Let him see if she answers."

I can't sit still, so I scoot out from under Don's arm and pace as the phone seems to ring for ages. It rings and rings and I know it's only been mere seconds but I'm so agitated I want to pick something up and throw it.

166

The silence is broken by a cheerful woman's voice. "Hi! This is Willow. I'm on a retreat right now and am unavailable until the 20th. Please leave a message and as soon as I'm back I'll contact you right away."

I glare at Aiden and say, "Tell me why you called your mom."

He rubs his brow, "Because if your dreams aren't just dreams but memories then this goes way beyond our knowledge. My mom is The Mother of our Clan. Our Clans are all interconnected. If something went wrong and a Maiden was missing she would know."

"They might not be memories, though." Even I don't believe the words I just uttered and neither do they.

Don's comforting hand massages the back of my neck. I lean into his touch, desperately needing something to keep me anchored in the present.

"Look, we can try to contact Ashira later since Willow isn't available. There isn't anything that can't wait until tomorrow, though." Brent's words are a soothing balm to my agitation, but now I need to know who Ashira is.

"Who is Ashira?"

Don's deep voice rumbles soothingly into my back as he answers, "Ashira is our Clan's Crone and is also Aiden's and my grandmother. Brent is right, we can wait until tomorrow to call her and see what she knows."

Maybe I shouldn't have said anything about my dreams, but it's too late to take it back. I'm also not sure how I feel about Don and Aiden being so closely related to their Clan's governing figures. Does this change things if I really am supposed to be a Maiden?

There is so much I still don't know, and it makes my head hurt just thinking about it. I need to make a list of all the questions so I don't forget. I sigh heavily. I really need a time out from all of this. "Is there anything else I need to know? Or are we done for now?" I sound so tired and a little lost even to my own ears.

"I think that is about it for now. If you think of any more questions, just let us know, and we will try to answer them. I'll let you know if we learn anything as well," Aiden says gently.

"Baby, why don't you go lay down? This was a lot of information, and after yesterday, you could use some rest and time to process."

"But I really need to get home and check on Beretta and Indy."

"No, you don't. Cam and I can do that while we are out. You should take it easy," Brent says smoothly.

It takes very little convincing from Don before he's leading me back to the room we slept in last night. Once he tucks me into bed, I give up. The bed is so comfy and I am really tired.

"I'm going to just be down the hall. I need to make a few calls for work."

"Can you come lay down with me after? I don't really want to be alone right now."

Don's gaze warms and then softens. Brushing my cheek with his fingertips, he leans down and kisses me sweetly. "I won't be long; I promise."

I pull the covers up higher and try my best to close my eyes, pushing away the stress and uncertainty that is threatening to take over. I have overcome so many things in my life already, so I can do this, too. I will put my trust in Don and hope that everything will be ok.

CHAPTER 17

KINLEY

I must have dozed off, because when I do wake it's dark out, and I'm starving. Don isn't in bed with me, but I can tell he must have laid down with me at some point, because the bed is indented on the other side. I waste no time getting up, taking care of my needs in the bathroom, and then go find the guys and some food.

I spot Camden in the kitchen, but no one else.

"Hey, pretty girl. Everyone else is outside on the deck. You want me to make you a plate?"

"Actually, I'm starving, so yes, please. Oh hey, did you and Brent find my house ok?"

"Yeah no worries, we got the pets set up with their auto feeders, they had plenty of water, and the dog door is all good to go. Oh, we also got your mail while we were at it, and your bag of clothes is in the closet of the room you are staying in."

"Thank you, Cam. It's a big relief that you guys did that for me."

"It was no problem. We might joke around a lot, but we take care of our own. And you're important to Don, so you're important to us."

Getting a little choked up, all I can do is nod. He finishes making me a plate and we both go outside. I sat down in the open seat next to Don. As soon as I'm seated, he pulls my chair closer to his before leaning over to kiss me.

"You feeling any better?"

"The nap definitely helped."

He nods in understanding, and gives my thigh a little squeeze of reassurance.

"I'm really proud of you for how well you're taking everything."

Cam nods in agreement as he sets my plate down in front of me and we all dig in. The guys dominate the conversation while we eat, with talk about work and other random things. Every now and then I'll speak up but for the most part I just listen, and I can't help but be thankful for a small sense of normalcy. We are just a group of people enjoying a meal and conversation together.

Realizing my glass is empty, I go inside to refill my water and put my dirty dish away. While I'm rinsing off the plate, I notice my mail stacked on the counter. Drying my hands, I flip through the stack making sure there's nothing important that needs to be taken care of, like a bill. A few pieces of junk mail, some really early black Friday sales ads, and a white envelope with my name on it.

Hmmm, I wonder what neighbor put that in.

I open it, not thinking much of it, and gasp immediately dropping the contents on the floor. Pictures with a note scatter everywhere. I'm helpless to look away as I stare in horror. There is picture after picture of me and Don during our date, and after when we were at his house.

Why the fuck is all of this happening to me?

The back door opens, Don and Brent walk in, but they stop short, immediately going on alert when they see me. I must look a mess, eyes brimming with tears and pure panic etched on my face. They both rush to me.

"Baby, what happened?"

All I can bring myself to do is point to the pictures scattered on the floor.

170

"What the fuck."

Don crouches to pick them up, but Brent stops him before he touches anything.

"Don, don't touch anything without gloves. Kinley, was this in the mail we brought from your house?"

I numbly nod again as I watch Don race out of the room to get gloves. Brent gently takes me by the shoulders, lifting me onto a bar stool. Blocking my view of the pictures.

"Just sit here. Ok? We will pick it up. It's going to be ok."

Hearing Brent say that, triggers a breaking dam inside of me and a sob breaks free. I've finally reached my limit, and there is no stopping the torrent of tears.

"Shit, Kinley."

My body falls forward and I end up leaning into his chest as I sob.

"It's—not—ok—nothing is—ok," I manage to get out between sobs. Brent gently wraps an arm around me, holding me to him.

Cam and Aiden must hear the commotion, because they walk in with alarmed looks on their faces when they see me sobbing into Brent's chest.

"Brent, what the hell happened?" Aiden asks.

"Just go help Don find the gloves in my office. Cam, go get my kit out of my SUV."

They rush to do what he asks without further questions.

"Kinley, I need to ask you some questions, and I need you to calm down so you can think clearly. I know a lot has happened the last few days, but we are going to help you."

It takes me a few moments to get myself under control. But it still takes a few more deep breaths before I can even begin to think somewhat clearly.

"Ok. I'm ok." My breath shudders out, and I sniffle.

"You're not ok, and that's completely fine."

Don, Cam, and Aiden all come back into the kitchen at that moment. Seeing me calmer, Aiden nudges Don over to me.

"Take care of her. We know how to do this."

That makes me balk.

"Don, the pictures!"

"It's ok, baby; I'll get them. Just stay right there with Brent."

I watch Don anxiously as he begins to collect pictures through my bloodshot eyes. There are multiple pictures of Don and I naked. Pretty sure there was also one where his cock was shoved down my throat, and I have no desire for anyone else to see that. It's a violation. That thought makes tears swim in my eyes again, but Brent brings my focus back to him.

"Hey, why don't we go sit in the living room where it's more comfortable. Would that be ok?"

I instantly recognize the placating tone—a tone I have used many times on students in high stress situations. I slightly resent it, but understand why he's doing it. I take my gaze away from Don and Aiden collecting the contents of that envelope and nod. Gently, he ushers me into the living room, getting me settled onto the couch and drapes a throw blanket over me.

He sits on the sturdy wood coffee table in front of me, taking one of my hands to comfort me.

"Ok, I'm just going to ask a few questions so we have a baseline of information. There is a good possibility that this is linked to the incident at the lake house, but before that, has anything out of the ordinary happened that could be linked?"

I shake my head.

"No, nothing like this has ever happened before. I've lived in the area for four years, and nothing has ever happened that would cause me to question if someone was watching me."

My voice rises slightly with an edge of hysteria. Brent strokes my hand and comforting rumbles make their way to my ears. I can feel the tension coming from the kitchen, rolling in waves in response to my stress.

"It's ok, Kinley; you are safe here. Ok, I'm going to need to ask some personal questions. Is there anyone you've dated recently or met up with that has gotten aggressive or possessive of you since you lived here?"

"I don't date much, I'm so busy with work. Don is a fluke; it's been over three months since I've been on an actual date, and that was a one and done. He was so boring, I didn't see him again."

"Would it be possible to get me a list of the guys you had contact with?"

He pauses at the incredulous look I give him.

"I swear this is just to rule out any potential threats to you. Don isn't a jealous guy."

"I can try."

"Alright, what about work? Any disgruntled parents or coworkers?"

With just the mention of work, I think of Allen and how strange he has been acting lately. Could it really be him, though? Brent sees the change on my face.

"Who at work, Kinley?"

"I don't think he could be it; it couldn't be."

"Kinley, tell me who and why you are thinking about him as a potential suspect."

"It's another teacher." I look up at him and he nods for me to continue.

"Allen Cracket. I think he's been at the school for two years. He's been acting weird starting around the end of last school year. It's kind of escalated recently, but I figured he was just weird. He got aggressive when I turned him down before I went up to the lake last weekend."

Brent's eyes narrow, "How did he get aggressive, Kinley?"

"He grabbed my arm pretty hard when I told him no. But he backed down immediately when I told him to. He hasn't spoken to me since."

"I'm going to need all the information you have on him. Did you report him at work?"

I shake my head in shame. I know I should have, and I'm very much regretting not doing so now.

Brent gives my hand another squeeze. "Hey, none of this is your fault. He fucked up when he thought he could come after you. We will take care of this."

My breath shudders in and out. I desperately want to fall apart, but I hate feeling out of control.

I notice Brent look behind me, and he nods. I turn around just in time to see Aiden walk out and go down a hallway, but then my eyes meet Don's. I search his face, looking for signs of anger or disappointment.

To my relief, I see none, but something on my face causes him to come around the couch. He sits next to me, pulling me onto his lap. Wrapping his big arms around me, he pulls me in close, resting his head atop mine as he deeply inhales my scent.

I let my body sink into his, and I quietly speak, my words muffled. "I don't understand how someone does this. How were those pictures even taken? I didn't tell anyone about our date."

He rubs his hand up and down my back, trying his best to remain calm and comfort me in the process. I feel his body vibrating with tension, but he is taking everything that has happened in stride while I'm barely clinging to my sanity.

He is trained for this kind of stress. Maybe not when it involves him personally, but he knows how to deal with stressful situations. Me on the other hand, I can deal with any situation dealing with teenagers. Tell me I'm some type of magical creature? Sure, ok, but stalkers? That is beyond my realm of coping. I have officially reached my limit. Don is definitely the only reason I haven't fallen into a heap of sobbing goo.

Looking up at him, he glances at Brent. Brent gives him a nod as if to say go take care of her, I've got the rest for now. Don doesn't hesitate to stand up with me in his arms and walk down the hall to the bedroom we shared.

"Where are we going?"

"We are just going to have some quiet time. The guys will get it sorted, and right now, I'm more worried about you."

"He knows where we live, Don. How can I go back to my house?"

"Don't worry about that right now. Just focus on being here with me. I've got you, and no one is getting up to Brent's house without tripping alarms. That's half the reason we come out here; it's safer for all of us to shift while we are here because it's so secluded and protected."

"I feel so out of control, Don. There is a sick man out there thinking he has the right to invade my privacy. My body isn't even my own anymore. Why would you even want to be with me after all the mess I brought to your doorstep?"

"Hey, none of that now. You listen to me. None of this would ever make me think you weren't worthy of my time. You are worth so much to me. I will not abandon you. Do you hear me? This is not your fault."

A small sob leaves my lips as I nod in understanding.

He is too good for me, but I don't even fucking care. He is mine.

DONOVAN

That small sob kills me. My beast is raging inside me. I would like nothing more than to shift and go on the hunt with my Clan brothers. I've dedicated my life to protecting others, first as a soldier and now as an officer of the law, and that doesn't even touch the surface of how I help my people. I should be able to keep Kinley away from harm, but I haven't. Those pictures have now tainted a moment between us that should only contain the pleasure we found in each other. Someone violated us both, and I'm trying my damndest to not lose my temper. I don't need Kinley seeing that. I won't have her fear me. I can't have her doubt my ability to provide what she needs. The fact that I'm failing to keep her safe fills me with enough shame already.

This woman has brought so much into my life in such a short time, and I can't help but feel an unwavering need to protect her at all costs. She's been thrust into our world without any knowledge, and she has shown such poise and bravery, and now someone is coming for her–trying to take her away from me when I only just found her. I can't, no, I won't let that happen. She is mine. My mate. I will keep her safe, no matter the cost. My beast and I are in utter agreement: when we find this fucker, we will feast.

I set Kinley on the bed, going to turn the lights off and draw the curtains, but Kinley scrambles up, clinging to me as she starts ripping at my clothes.

"Kinley, what..."

"I need to feel in control, Don. I need to know I have a choice...I need you... please."

Her beautiful eyes begin to glow that unearthly violet, her beast trying to push up to the surface. My beast rears up inside of me, wanting nothing more than to answer her. My voice deepens as we speak together.

"Whatever you need."

I help her in her pursuit to get us both naked. As soon as every piece of clothing is flung onto the floor, she pulls me down onto the bed with a strength that she hasn't displayed before. She scrambles to straddle me, but I still her. She snarls at me, her beast riding her hard.

"You will hurt yourself if you aren't prepared, I will not allow you to be hurt," I manage to growl back.

I grab her ass firmly with both hands and lift her up to my face, desperate to taste her.

"You will ride my face before you ride my cock."

She looks down at me, hearing the authority in my voice and nods. Her thighs spread wide on either side of my face. My arms curl around her thighs, anchoring her to me, and I satisfy another urge to feast. I groan as I get the first sweet taste of her pussy. *This female was made for me.*

Her body vibrates, overcome with that unknown force inside her. Her hands fling out, bracing herself onto the headboard as I suck and lick her center until she is shaking above me. My tongue thrusts into her weeping cunt, pleasure shooting up through her body. Her back bows just as an orgasm violently peaks through her.

Those black claws of hers extend from her fingers and they dig into the wood under her hands, her hips grinding down on my face. I growl with delight. She is fucking perfect.

I drive her wild, my tongue plunging into her core over and over.
Goddess, she tastes so fucking good.

A scream of pleasure bubbles up from her throat, and a dam bursts inside her. I feel a shift in energy spread through her body, but I want one more of her releases on my tongue.

She has other ideas, obviously. Reaching down for my hair, she pulls my mouth away from her core. Her pleasure coats my face, my eyes bright with hunger.

I unwind my arms from her thighs, seeing the silent command in her eyes to release her. She is ready to claim her prize, and I am more than willing. A wicked feral grin spreads across my face as I let her claim me.

Our mate, my beast rumbles inside me. *Yes… our mate.*

She glides down my taunt body with a grace and sensuality I haven't seen before. Her claws scrape gently down my muscles, and hungry growls rumble through my chest as her soaking core nudges my hard shaft.

"Are you mine?" A voice not quite her own asks me. It's deeper, more primal. *I fucking love it.*

"Yes."

My answer is all she needs as she reaches between us, lines up my cock, and sinks down onto me until she is fully seated.

Goddess, she is so fucking tight.

Sounds, scents, and sensations flood into my body as she rides my cock. Everything is brighter, louder, more heightened. Growls of pleasure leave both of our bodies as we unleash ourselves onto each other.

What little control we have snaps, and we fight for dominance. Our bodies writhe against each other in a furious and frantic rhythm. Her hips move in a rhythm that drives me to insanity. She feels so fucking good.

I can't help but thrust my hips up to meet her downward strokes. She is fucking everything. My beast is quickly growing restless. We need more.

Unable to stop myself, I flip her, putting her on her hands and knees. Grasping her round ass in both of my hands, I growl at the sight of her dripping pink pussy. I thrust back into her in one stroke, her cries of pleasure music to my ears as I pound into her.

My grip on her is bruising as I force her body into another climax.

My teeth grip onto her shoulder as my pace picks up. My thrusts are hard and fast as I pump through her inner muscles' strangling hold.

My own release is so close. My balls tighten, and I clench my teeth harder on her shoulder, growling my pleasure into her perfect skin. But before I can reach my climax, she breaks free of my hold.

As she fucking scrambles off the bed, confusion and sexual rage burn through me. *Where the fuck does she think she's going?*

Snarling, I lunge for her, but she is too quick. A feminine voice breaches my mind. *If you want me, you have to earn me.*

My mate wants to be chased…then I will fucking chase her. She leaps for the door, but I'm hot on her heels, steam snorting out of my nostrils.

You are ours. You won't get away.

I taunt her in our mental link as the predatory nature of my beast fully takes over.

She tries to dodge my pursuit, but my quick lunge is a success. Tackling her to the ground, I flip her onto her back. I'm thrusting back into her hot wet core before she can attempt to escape me again, pinning her under me as I take what is mine.

She writhes under me as I unleash myself, dangerously close to shifting. I watch in amazed wonder as her teeth elongate into fangs. Her claws dig into my shoulders as she pulls herself up my body to get as close as possible to me. My thrusts never break rhythm as power rolls off of her.

I can tell she is nearing another orgasm, but what I'm not expecting is for her to bite down onto my shoulder. I fucking love it, feeling her fangs sink deep into my flesh. I roar in pleasure as her teeth sink in further, drawing blood. The copper tang of my blood mixes with the delicious perfume of our mating.

A link snaps into place within us, and my hips stutter briefly.

Could it be?

A song builds within our very souls, weaving the threads of our lives together, the strands humming in perfect harmony. The song builds and builds, increasing in momentum to match the pace of our bodies, the pleasure like nothing I have ever experienced before. We are both helpless to stop it as the crescendo crashes into us.

But beneath the waves of immense pleasure, something else is building. I shout in alarm as I feel my body begin to shift.

Fuck, no! I will kill her if I shift now!

"Kinley, stop!"

Panic lacing my every word, I try to pull away, but still her magic continues pushing into me where our bodies are joined.

"No! baby, I'll hurt you, please!"

I can't stop it; she is overpowering me. A scream of my stallion breaks free from my throat as my body begins to shift.

I make one more attempt to pull away, but it's no use. Muscles ripple, black fur coats my body—but my body doesn't shift fully. A new form emerges.

My shift triggers both of our orgasms, bringing everything to a blinding completion. We cling to each other, breaths heaving out of our chests as the power recedes back into Kinley's body.

Kinley is the first to move, disengaging her canines from my shoulder and cleaning the wound she left with her tongue, a contented rumble bubbles up from her chest. I'm too stunned to move. There is something wrong with my shift, and I'm almost afraid to look.

Shouts and the crashing of the door being broken down push me past that fear. I have to protect my mate. I whirl up and around, preparing to defend her, but seeing Brent, Aiden, and Camden standing in the door instantly makes me freeze.

"Holy Fuck," Cam whispers out as they all stare in awe at me in this new shifted form. Not seeing any looks of horror, I glance at the mirror close by. I can't believe what stares back at me.

I have in fact shifted, but I'm completely different. My head is that of my Kelpie form, but smaller than what it would have been had I fully shifted. My neck and torso are more humanoid, but thicker and more heavily muscled, covered in my black-as-night coat along with human-like arms. My legs mimic the hind legs of my Kelpie, but more heavily muscled as they taper down to two large cloven hooves. A tail swishes behind me. It's as if my human form and my Kelpie have merged together in perfect harmony.

Will I even be able to fully shift? Is this my new form?

A part of me hopes not; I love my Kelpie. There is nothing like the power I feel racing across an open field or swimming at top speed in my lake. I pray to the Goddess that I won't have to give that up.

I turn to look at Kinley sitting on the floor below me. Her eyes still shine that bright ethereal purple. The shadow of a great beast hovers just behind her as if she still can't finish her shift.

"Mate," I rumble aloud.

Kinley smiles and nods, but her smile slowly melts away. A look of immense pain and sadness washes over her. Tears pool in her eyes. I crouch down to her, my large shifted hands cupping her face as gently as I can.

"What is wrong?"

"Don. I think I'm starting to remember."

CHAPTER 18

KINLEY

P ain wracks my body.
The smell of blood fills my nose, and a dark voice whispers in my ear.

"You bleed so prettily, Chosen. I can feel the power in your blood. You will be mine once and for all. You're mine, Kinley!"

It's as if my name is the key to unlock what I have been missing. Untapped power bursts from me, my entire being changing into something powerful and menacing.

My vision clears, the pain that had overcome my body now a mere memory. I whirl to face what attacked me. This new body is lithe and agile. I don't know what I have transformed into, but I'm no longer on two feet. My wounds stitch back together and the bleeding stops entirely. I'm finally whole.

I bring my eyes up to the cloaked creature, a growl ripping from my throat. Surprise and anger flashes across its eyes.

"How! You should not be able to transform yet!"

I bare my teeth, a deep rumble of fury comes from deep within me. The creature's power coils around me, preparing for action.

Before it can lunge at me, I lunge first. Instincts I didn't know I had take over as my beast leaps through the air. My powerful jaw opens wide, preparing to meet flesh. I'm mere inches away, my sharp teeth so close to ripping into this creature, but I'm halted midair.

Suspended and paralyzed by a power I do not know. I try to break free, but nothing I do can release its grip over me. I rage within these new bonds, howling my anger, until I'm silenced as well.

The Crone steps between us.

She no longer appears as she did before, but I know her instantly. Gone is the polished, docile crone that held my hand and whispered that everything was going to be ok. She now gazes at me with eyes of electric purple and elongated claws of black. No longer is her body hunched but standing tall, power rolling off of her in waves.

"You were banished! You dare disrupt our sacred rite! You cannot have her, and you are a fool to think you could."

The cloaked creature struggles against the Crone's hold but is only able to hiss. "You can't keep her from me. No matter where she is, I will find her. It is what I'm owed!"

"You are owed nothing! You greedy, foul beast! It is because of you that we are broken! It is because of you our Clan suffers so!"

The creature roars in fury at her words, thrashing harder in his magical bindings. The Crone begins chanting, and from her mouth a chorus of hundreds chant with her. The creature rages and screams but cannot break free. I'm helpless to do anything but look on in horror as the creature turns into mist. The screaming is unbearable to my sensitive ears when a portal opens in the very ground it once stood on. The portal sucks what remains of the creature into it, snapping closed when nothing of the creature remains on this side.

The chanting slows and comes to a halt. My body slowly gains feeling, and I'm lowered to the ground.

The Crone then turns to me, "Turn back child; release the hold on the beast. It is not time for the two of you to unite."

No, that can't be right, this form finally makes me feel whole. I don't feel empty any longer.

She must sense my unwillingness to obey. A sad smile coming over her face.

"I'm sorry, child; it is not your time. You are still not ready."

Power pushes into me, and it's beyond my ability to fight against it.

A howl unleashes from my throat. Pain washes over my entire body as I feel the tugging and pulling of my beast being shoved back into a deep locked away place within me.

Gasping for breath, I find myself once again on two legs. Every muscle in my body is shaking from the exertion of changing so rapidly, and against my will. Tears pour down my face as my eyes meet the Crone's, and I want nothing more than to beg her to give me my beast back. But then I glance just behind her, and I'm stunned to see the destruction and hysteria that is left behind. My beast will have to wait for now; there are more troubling problems to be dealt with.

"How can one creature do all of this?" My voice is raw and raspy.

People are cowering and sobbing; others are frozen in horror. The ceremonial altar is destroyed; crystals have been shattered, and the flowers and greenery are burned to ash. All the beauty is gone; blood and debris are everywhere. Members of the clan are lying still on the ground, and I can't tell if they are unconscious or dead. My parents are nowhere to be seen. That thought makes me frown.

My parents? Had they been here?

The Crone touches my arm, bringing my shattered attention back onto her. Her mouth opens in preparation to speak.

I jolt awake, gasping, unsure of my surroundings until I feel the comforting warmth of Don's body lying next to me. I inhale his scent, grounding myself to the present. That lingering touch of the woman, the Crone, echoes off my skin, making me feel like I'm forgetting something. Something that I shouldn't have, something that is important but just out of reach.

Is this just a dream or is it a memory? Nothing feels real anymore. How the fuck am I supposed to make sense of any of this?

Broken images flit through my mind but still nothing makes sense. I can remember a ceremony of some sort, but then there is blood, pain, and despair, and the memory fades away. Is this ritual where it all changed? And that woman, the Crone, is she even real? Did I know her? Some part of me recognized her, and remembered that night, but why I was there and who all of those people were are still beyond my recollection. I wish I had the answers; I wish this all made sense.

I know I'm not getting back to sleep with my dreams plaguing me, so I leave Don sleeping in bed. Not wanting to wake anyone else, I go out onto the back deck, soaking in the comforting presence of the moon. It's always brought me peace, but now I'm starting to realize maybe it's because of my hidden past.

Seeing Don in that form earlier was alarming, but he's pure perfection in any form he takes. There was a lot of confusion and questions from all of the guys, but I had no answers for them. I had no idea how I had done it. It had just felt right in the moment, and I couldn't stop my body from taking over.

Don finally got a hold of his grandmother, just like he said he would. What I had done was beyond all of their knowledge. I didn't understand how she would have been able to help, and I had been right.

Not even she could shed any light on the situation. She told Donovan that she would have to see me in person to get a better idea of what we were dealing with. Even when he had asked if it was possible for a Maiden to be missing and have no memory of her life within a Clan, she had scoffed and said that wasn't possible. Hearing that put me right on the edge. How could she be all knowing? Something had obviously gone wrong for me to be in this position.

A trip to see Don's family made me want to throw up. I'm not any good with families. My parents left a lasting impression on me for the worse, and all I wanted to do was hide at the suggestion. I'm lost in a sea of doubt, but Don has become a beacon for me. If he is by my side, then I will do whatever needs to be done.

Mate is what he had called me, and I know that is exactly what he

184

is to me. Even now I can feel his presence within me, like a bridge has been linked between us. It's comforting, knowing that I'm not alone.

I should really go back inside and try to get back to sleep.

I'm just about to go snuggle up to Don when my phone lights up; it's Megan. My stomach sinks. I answer it immediately. There is only one reason she would be calling me this late at night.

I walk quickly back into the house, going straight to where Don is sleeping. Sitting on the edge of the bed, I reach over to touch him.

"Don."

His eyes instantly open, "What's wrong?"

"I have to go. It's Megan, she needs me."

He sits up quickly. "Baby, it's not safe."

I cut him off before he can go further.

"In this, I won't budge. She is my family, and right now she needs me. All of the rest can wait."

Seeing the look of determination and sorrow on my face, he does the only thing he can do. He pulls me into his arms.

"I'm not sure I can be away from you right now."

"I don't know if I can either, but I can't ask you to take off more work than you already have. You have done so much already."

"The hell I can't. What do you need me to do? Tell me, and I'll do it, unless you ask to go alone. That I can't do."

I lean forward, snuggling further into his arms.

"I need to go home and pack, figure out where to put Beretta, and then drive up to Megan's."

"One of the guys can watch her. What about your cat?"

"Oh, Indy will be fine at home as long as he has food and water."

"Do we need to leave now, or are you ok getting a few more hours of sleep?"

Sighing, I whisper softly, "I haven't been asleep for a while."

He gently pulls me away from his chest to look at me properly. His brow furrows with worry. "Why didn't you wake me if you couldn't sleep?"

"I just needed some time to process."

He nods in understanding. "Ok, let me go talk to the guys."

"Thank you," I murmur quietly, "for everything."

"Anything for you."

He slips some pants on and walks out to talk to the others.

We leave an hour later. Brent promised to go pick up Beretta later and to make sure my house was locked up tight. Aiden offered to house sit, but I vetoed that immediately. I'm seriously against anyone else showing up on my stalker's radar. Taking Don's truck, since he will be considerably more comfortable in it—he's a big man—we waste no more time getting on the road.

We make a quick stop at my house, to pack and give my sweet pets some love. I've missed them and missed my house.

A sadness washes over me. It's such a violation that someone has tainted the safety of my home, but I can't dwell on that now; I need to get to Megan.

All packed, I make sure that Indy has plenty of fresh water and food. I also leave out Beretta's food for Brent to find. I give each of them a kiss on their heads, cuddling Indy close and quietly telling him to guard the house while I'm gone. I have spent entirely too much time away from both of them, and I'm going to make sure that doesn't continue to happen when I get back.

I meet Don outside by his truck. He wanted to keep watch. When we got out of the car earlier, I could tell he was on alert. He made sure to go through my entire house first, and then once it was clear, he left me alone inside.

"I'm ready."

He opens my door, helping me in, before taking my bag to place it in the back seat. Before I get a chance to close my door, he stops me, leaning in and kissing me softly.

"Do you want a blanket for the road? I can run back in and get you one."

My heart melts; this man is all mine. I still can't believe it. "Yes, please."

"I'll be right back."

Shutting my door, he lopes up to the door, enters quickly, and soon exits with one of my cozy blankets I keep on my couch. He locks the door and quickly comes back to the truck, hopping into the driver's side. He tucks the blanket around me, placing another sweet kiss on my lips and then gets us on the road.

I'm exhausted, so once Don starts driving, the warmth, safety, and motion of the car quickly lulls me to sleep.

The truck coming to a stop wakes me. I'm not sure how long I slept, but the sun is up now. Don, noticing that I'm awake, leans over the console and smooths some of my hair off my face.

"Hey baby, I've got to get gas. You want to get out and stretch your legs or run to the restroom?"

God, I'm so fucking lucky.

I lean into him, putting both of my hands on either side of his face to kiss him. He groans as I run my tongue over his lips, sneaking it in as his lips part. Our kiss deepens, one of his hands coming up to cup the back of my head. Breathless and beginning to ache, I reluctantly pull away first. He stares deep into my eyes.

"There you are. Don't get lost on me. I know a lot is going on, but don't get lost, baby."

A breath shudders out of me. *How had he known?* We barely know each other, but our connection already runs so deep. He knows that I have been starting to close in on myself. I haven't been this stressed since the summer before I went to college, but somehow he knows my mental struggles. My lower lip trembles, and he cups my cheek.

"I've got you, baby; you can lean on me. My beautiful mate."

A single tear slips from my eye, and he brushes it away.

I promise, baby, I've got you.

Hearing that reassurance in my mind bolsters me.

I'm so thankful for you...mate.

A grin spreads across his face.

I like being able to hear you in my mind. And I love hearing you call me "mate".

I give him a small smile.

Out loud he asks me, "You ready to get out of the truck?"

"Yes, I do need to pee. Did you notice any place to eat around here, or is it a gas station breakfast for us?"

"I passed a McDonald's if you're down for that."

Eh, it isn't my favorite, but I'm hungry enough to make an exception. "That's fine."

"Alright, I'm gonna fill up the tank. I'll wait for you to come back out before I go in."

True to his word, he waits for me to come back so I can sit in the warmth while he goes inside to also use the restroom. I take that time to check my phone. I have one message from Brent letting me know he has Beretta safe at his house. He even includes a picture of the two of them on his couch. I reply back my thanks, and for him to not spoil her too much.

I figure out where we are on my map app and send Megan a message letting her know when I should arrive. I also give her a heads up that Don is traveling with me.

I still haven't told Megan any of what has been going on with me, and I'm feeling guilty about it. But now is definitely not the time to unload on her, and I probably can't tell her half of what happened anyways. Plus, I don't want to worry her. Megan has enough to deal with, and I will protect my best friend from the craziness that is infiltrating my life.

After grabbing breakfast we make good time. I offer to drive a few times, but Don is insistent that I rest. Which works out, because I'm really tired still and fall asleep shortly after we get moving every time.

While I sleep, vague dream-like images brush through my mind. Wolves racing through fields, giant eagles, large saber-toothed cats, an assortment of animals both real and mythical traipse through my mind. But one stands out—a lone wolf, fur as dark as chocolate, eyes a vibrant purple, with horns spiraling out of its head between erect ears. Its head tips back and a mournful cry sings from its mouth, but no other creature joins its song. It is utterly alone.

CHAPTER 19

KINLEY

Dressed in a sensible black knee length dress, I hold Megan's hand tightly as the casket is lowered into the ground. It's a somber affair, and very few people are present. It's sad really; no one is here to mourn his life, they are all here for Megan. The funeral is short and to the point, no one to drone on about what a great man he was, no overly ostentatious floral arrangements that will just go to waste. The cloudy day sets the mood. A life was lost, but in turn, a life is being regained. Megan is free; finally.

When I reached Megan's house a few days before, Megan took one look at me and crumpled into my arms. No words were said; we didn't need them. I knew exactly what Megan was going through.

It's the release of a burden that has held on a little too long that causes the onslaught of emotions breaking free in Megan. Like an old weathered dam that can no longer hold back the flood.

I know because I have been right where Megan is, a long time ago. But while Megan has me, I had been all alone. A scared eighteen year old, no family to help as I buried my parents. An accident took them both, and as a result I was also freed. Freed from the disdain, disapproval, and toxic narcissism of my parents.

But that freedom also came with uncertainty. I was so young and naïve, and without anyone to hold me back, it was overwhelming. College allowed me to explore. I had originally set my major as business management and communications, but had quickly determined that was not for me. With some trial and error, I found my place, found my friends, and found my path in life. But that was then. I guess that's life. It's always changing, always evolving into something new. Only time will tell if those changes are good or bad.

Later that night, after everything is cleared away, we sit in front of a warm fire in Megan's sitting room. Travis' snoring fills the silence, his paws twitching sporadically from whatever he's dreaming of. Don had gone to the hotel, knowing we needed the time alone. I miss him already.

"So, are we gonna talk about how the man you just met drove you all the way here, that there is something very different about you, or that you haven't mentioned any of this any time we've talked in the past few weeks?"

I sigh, rubbing my face. It has been a long few days and I'm feeling the effects of the stress and lack of sleep.

I'm sure I also look like shit under all this makeup.

"I didn't want to worry you, or bring my drama into the picture when you had so much to deal with. Plus, I'm still processing some things of my own."

"That's bullshit, Kinley. My drama is nothing new. You could, and should have told me. The tension that's been rolling off of you and Donovan since you got here has already told me that something serious is going on, so spill."

I take a good long look at Megan, sadness and exhaustion still lining her face.

Should I really burden my friend with this? Am I even allowed to tell her? Fuck, I should have asked Don.

"I don't even know where to begin, or if I can even tell you everything. It's so complicated, and doesn't involve just me."

191

Megan scoots over and takes both of my hands in hers. A vibration slowly begins to build where our hands are connected. It spreads, twining its way up my arms until it settles right on my chest. My eyes widen as I look from our hands up to Megan's face. Megan smiles sadly at me.

"I always knew you were special. I've felt the draw between us, how our magic seemed to weave together, but you just never were able to notice it back."

What the actual fuck.

I'm speechless, but I don't draw my hands away. Even if I hadn't been aware, I always knew that Megan was meant to be in my life. There has been a connection between us from the very beginning.

Is this why?

"Are you like me?"

Megan shakes her head, and my heart falls a little.

"I never knew what you were, just that our magic was complimentary. It's never been this strong, though. Is Don the reason your magic is suddenly this vibrant?"

I nod, because, as far as I know, he is the reason.

"But what are you if you're not like me?"

She raises her eyebrow at me. "Do you think there is only one type of magic?"

"I didn't even know about magic until a few days ago, so don't give me that look."

"Fair enough. I'm a witch. My whole family are witches."

"Witches? Really?"

"Why do you seem so surprised, don't you change into an animal?"

My eyes widen. *How the fuck could she know that?*

An embarrassed blush spreads across my face.

"Actually, I can't; there is something wrong with me."

A concerned look sweeps across Megan's face. "What do you mean? It doesn't feel like something is wrong. In fact, your magic finally feels complete. You feel whole, Kinley."

I shake my head.

"There is something wrong. I can't access my magic or shift. The guys can feel it, but something is blocking me from fully following

192

through. I also have no recollection of why. I am apparently a mystery, but somehow, even though I'm a dud, I still managed to mate Donovan."

A squeak brings my attention back to Megan, who is gaping at me.

"Wait, you're mated? You dirty bitch! How could you and not fucking tell me!"

Her high pitched squeal, rings sharply in my ears. It also causes Travis to snort awake, he lets out a disgruntled growl when he quickly realizes it's nothing important. He flops back down just as Megan tackles me in the tightest hug.

"Megan, too tight," I manage to get out with a gasp.

She releases me, but doesn't take her hands away.

"I didn't know that I could tell you. With the whole not a human thing and what you were going through…. And just everything. I couldn't burden you with this."

"Kinley, you never have, and you never will be a burden to me. You're my best friend, my sister."

Tears fill my eyes, and looking at Megan I see that hers are also.

"I understand why you didn't tell me. If your magic has been sequestered away this whole time, you wouldn't have known what I am. But now that you do, you better spill everything."

"Wait, did you know what the guys were? And how have I never even gotten a hint that you were magical?"

She blows out a breath, giving me a guilty look.

"They are Clan, right?"

I nod.

"Clan are kind of hard to read magically, at least for most witches. We can usually sense the females, but the males only feel a little magical, unless, of course, they are shifted. So, while I thought I was picking up some hints of magic, it was impossible for me to actually tell what they were. I just knew they weren't witches, and I didn't get any threatening magical signatures off them so I knew you would be safe."

"But what about you? How have I never known about you?"

She gives me an apologetic look. "Most Covens are very strict on who we can and can't tell. Mine especially, the only real reason I'm even allowed out on my own is because I was married to Todd, and

I visit my brother frequently. Also, my magic doesn't do well around others in my Coven. Anyways, we can talk more about that later. To answer your question, I wanted to many times, but even though I knew you had some type of magical signature, I didn't want to put unwanted attention on you. My Coven would have made me put a gag spell on you. Because for all they know, you are human, and there are very strict circumstances in which humans can know about us. But hey, now that you are officially not a human, we can talk magic all day long."

She smiles widely at me, while I'm still kind of reeling from all of the information she just gave me. She takes my hands back, squeezing them comfortingly.

"It's going to be so nice, being able to talk to you about everything now. But speaking of talking, you have some explaining of your own to do."

"I think we are going to need wine for this, or at least I am."

Megan raises an eyebrow.

"That good?"

With a guilty look, I shake my head.

"No, it's actually pretty bad. Donovan is the good part."

"What the fuck, Kinley. It's only been less than a month, how is it bad?"

"Wine, first. I need courage."

"Goddess, help me, fine. I'll go get the wine, but then you're telling me everything. No more secrets. That is going to be our new motto, for the both of us."

While I wait for Megan to come back, I text Donovan.

> Me: Did you know that Megan is a witch???

> Don: No...but that kinda makes sense. You doing ok? I keep getting moments of sadness and stress down our bond.

Hmmmm, that's interesting. I wonder why I don't get anything like that from him. I'll have to remember to ask him about that later.

Me: I'm ok… it's just a lot. Is it OK if I tell her everything?

Don: You can tell her whatever you want. If you trust her, then I trust you to make the right decision. You gonna stay the night there?

Me: I'm not sure, it's getting hard to be away from you honestly.

Don: Just tell me when and I'll come get you, ok?

Me: ok

I set my phone down when I hear Megan coming back. Megan notices and smiles.

"Bet it's not easy being away from him, huh?"

With a sheepish smile, I nod in agreement.

"It's really not. It's still really new."

"How new?"

I blush, "Ummm two nights ago new."

"Oh my Goddess, Kinley! How are you even functioning? I've heard it's so bad to be away from your mate the first few weeks or even months."

"You needed me."

"Shit, that asshole sure does have terrible timing."

Having just taken a sip of my wine, I snort and almost choke. "Jesus, Megan the dirt hasn't even settled."

She just shrugs. "Still. Ok then, let's make this quick so you can go jump his bones."

My eyes roll. "Ok, but you can't interrupt me no matter what. Even

195

when you get pissed at me for not telling you, got it?"

She nods in firm agreement, and I spill everything. I start with the incident at the cabin and keep going. Megan almost makes it the whole way through without interruptions, but she's able to get herself back under control, and I'm able to finish.

We both sit in silence, and I'm slightly worried that Megan is about to blow up, but all she does is pull me into a hug. I blow out the breath I hadn't realized I was holding and relax into my friend's arms.

"I can't imagine what you're going through, or how you are even handling all this, but you aren't alone, Kinley. You have me, Don, and it seems like the rest of the guys."

I nod against Megan's shoulder.

"Thank you."

"Don't thank me. I'll always be here for you. But right now, I think you need your mate more. You look a little pale. Tell him to come get you, so he can sex you back to life."

I snort, and I give her a light shove, but I do what she tells me and send Don a message. He responds immediately, letting me know he will be right over. While we wait, we clean up our wine glasses and Megan talks about random things that are going on with her. It's getting more and more difficult for me to pay attention the closer I feel Don get. Because I do feel him, and my patience is unraveling. Megan tentatively touches my arm, and a rumble bubbles up from my chest.

"Geeze girl, tomorrow bring him with you. It's not good for you to be away from him, especially with your magic being this new."

Why did she sound so far away?

Megan's cool fingers touch my forehead.

"Goddess, you're burning up."

My eyes focus enough for me to glance at Megan, and I barely notice her eyes widening.

"Oh goodness, your eyes. Here, sit right here, before you fall over."

She steers me over to a chair.

"I'll be right back ok; don't move."

My breathing has become ragged. I really am getting hot. My skin itches and my clothes feel so tight and suffocating. Growls and whines escape me. *Where is Don? I need him….I need my mate.*

A cooling touch brings some clarity back. "Baby, I'm here. Goddess, I'm sorry, I should have come sooner."

"Damn right you should have. You shouldn't have left her at all. You know she doesn't know about how it is with mates, Don. She's flying blind."

"You're right."

"Of course, I'm right. Now go, get out of here and take care of my friend."

If I hadn't been so out of it, I would have laughed. But all I can do is concentrate on Don's soothing touch, his scent, his voice. He sweeps me up into his arms, and I can't contain the growl that slips out. An answering growl rumbles under my cheek where it lays against his chest.

"Don, do you think you guys are going to make it to the hotel?"

"Shit, I don't know."

Unbothered by their conversation, I reach up and pull Don's neck down to my face, breathing in his scent. He smells so good. I moan and try to climb up to get even closer, vaguely hearing him groan.

"Baby, you have to hold off on doing that; just wait a little longer."

Not caring at all what he is saying or where I am, I twist in his arms, wrap my arms and legs around him, and grind my pelvis into him. I'm so desperate for relief.

Don curses and Megan tells him in an exasperated tone.

"Oh, just go into one of the guest rooms. I'm not going to have you crashing on the way back to the hotel. Try not to break my furniture."

Megan must have pointed him in the right direction, because a moment later he is slamming me into a wall as he begins frantically removing my clothes. It takes me a moment to catch on, and when I finally realize what he is doing I start helping him get us both naked.

"Don… need you now," I whine breathlessly.

He wastes no more time. Ripping my soaked panties off, he spares only a moment to line himself up to my entrance before thrusting into my drenched core. Even as wet as I am, I can't take him fully in. He's too large, but that doesn't deter him one bit. He growls at my tightness, working himself in and out of me, gaining further entry with each thrust.

My desperate whines grow louder before he places a large hand over my mouth to muffle my cries. I'm beyond full, but I know that he still isn't fully in me. The angle is wrong and I desperately need to feel him filling me, I need to feel my body stretch for him. I need him to own my body; I need him to be so deep, that even when he is gone, I will still feel him within me.

A growl rumbles in my chest, spurring him to thrust into me harder and faster. He takes his hand away from my mouth to grab my hip and tilt my pelvis at a better angle. His next thrust sends my neck and back arching into the wall behind me.

I don't know I'm screaming until his hand surrounds my throat, tightening just enough to cut off my scream. I don't even care that I'm growing light headed from the lack of oxygen. I can only cling to him and take what he gives me. *And I want it all.*

His growls are guttural as he hikes one of my legs up so that my ankle rests against his shoulder, and he buries himself even deeper. My vision grows hazy, black spots swimming in my periphery, when he unclenches his hand on my throat.

The oxygen that roars in my lungs is almost as glorious as the feeling of him bottoming out in me.

"Come for me, Mate. Come all over my cock. Now."

I didn't think it was possible for me to come on command, but I do. My release barrels through me, my mouth open wide on a silent scream as my world detonates around me.

When I blink my eyes open, I'm no longer against the wall, and Don isn't inside me anymore. I must have blacked out for a moment because I'm now on a bed.

"What happened?" I manage to croak out.

He chuckles, but it holds a note of darkness, and when I focus on his face I notice his beast is shining brightly through his eyes.

"You came, just like I told you to. But we aren't done. You're going to come again and again, until you take every drop of my cum like a good little mate."

A part of me wants to fully submit to his incredible dominance, but another part of me wants to growl and snap at him. He must see it in my eyes because he doesn't give me a chance to fight him.

He has me flipped and pinned down with my ass in the air before I can even think to snarl at him. My attempts at wiggling out from under him just pin me further beneath his weight.

His hand burrows into my hair at the base of my neck, weaving deep, ensuring he has a firm hold. Pulling my hair, my head tilts back so my eyes meet his blazing blue depths.

"Who owns this pussy? Who is this pussy dripping for?"

His growled words make me pant and whine.

Pulling my hair tighter, my back and neck arch so far my muscles scream in protest.

"If you want my cock buried deep in you, you will answer me."

His cock glides through my wetness, bumping into my throbbing clit, teasing me, denying me what I need.

"You...my mate."

He gives me no warning as he thrusts fully into me, my inner muscles burning with the sudden intrusion.

"Donovan!"

He pins my face in the bedding, muffling my cries as he claims my body, burrowing himself further into my very soul as he drives deep.

Heavy breathing and the sounds of sweat slicked flesh pounding against each other fill the space. Our pleasure builds to an inferno.

I can't do it; it's too much. I can't come again.

"You can, and you will."

He smacks my ass sharply. My inner muscles clench down tightly on him, making him snarl.

"Please, I can't!"

I'm practically wailing. My body is too sensitive, there is no way I will survive another orgasm.

Thrusting deep as he smacks my ass again, his hips flush against my ass as he rolls them against mine. Pushing into me with a mind blowing friction.

The change in sensation drives me straight to the edge.

"Give it to me."

He groans his words against my neck. His canines lengthen, scraping against my skin, making me shiver and clench around him. He growls deeply, slowly pulling out of me until just the head of his cock is nestled in my entrance.

"Come for me again, baby."

With a slow, powerful thrust he is seated in me again, hitting my cervix and making me cry out. It's a different type of pleasure, sharp and intense every time he plunges so deep that he is ramming against me. I'm babbling with each steady thrust, my legs shaking and my back aching from the arched position I'm in. His thrusts are so powerful that I scramble to gain purchase on something, but I can't keep myself from sliding across the bed.

I hear his frustrated growl, before both of his arms lift me off the bed until my back is flush with his chest. I'm practically sitting on his thighs, his hips not thrusting upwards but still just as deep. One arm bands across my breasts, his hand loosely wrapped around the front of my throat. The other arm wraps around my waist. My body is too hot, and I need something but I can't name it.

Don knows my body. He knows what it craves, what it requires to reach that blessed peak. He's just taking his time, savoring this heat.

I sense how close you are, how much your body craves the madness. You're going to submit to me, mate. Submit to me as I fill you with everything I have.

"Yes, Don! I need it, I need your cum filling me. God, I need…I need more!"

He rotates us until we are facing the headboard, loosening his hold enough to allow me to lean forward.

"Grab the headboard."

I obey, and he gives me more.

His hips slam into me so hard and deep that I see stars. I cry out, pleading for him to not stop. My head bows between my shoulders as my arms brace my body against the onslaught.

So good...so good....So deep.

His fingers reach down to circle my clit, the rough pressure making me detonate.

I scream, my orgasm almost painful, and then I feel him join me in bliss. He roars his release, his sharp teeth clamping down on my shoulder as he pumps his seed into me.

I'm delirious, barely able to hold myself up, but the fog from earlier begins to fade. On the verge of giggling, I can't help but wiggle back against him making him groan into my shoulder.

I wonder why his bite doesn't hurt.

Because, Mate, you are meant to submit to me.

Hearing him say that sends a shiver down my spine as I also roll my eyes at him. He gives my ass a playful tap.

"Are you feeling better?"

His voice is scratchy.

We should really get some water after this.

"Kinley, focus. Are you still feeling anything like you did when I first got here?"

I think for a moment, assessing my body. "No, I'm not. I still feel a little on edge, but nothing like I was earlier. Will that happen anytime we are away from each other?"

He nuzzles into my shoulder, pulling us down onto the bed until we are lying on our sides. His body curls around mine. "It doesn't happen the same with everyone, but I've heard the first few weeks are rough for new mates if we are apart for too long."

I turn around in his arms to face him. "Don, I was straight up feral. I don't like being that out of control."

He tucks me in close, resting his chin on my head. "Now that we know how strong your reactions can be, we can be proactive and take steps to make sure you don't get to that level."

"Let me guess, it involves your monster cock."

A surprised laugh bursts out of his mouth. "No, not always. Just touching can also help."

I hum in contemplation, shifting closer to him for warmth now that my body doesn't feel like an inferno. That little shift of my body tells me exactly how sore I'm going to be in the morning.

Will my body ever not be sore after we have sex? Is it even possible to adjust to that?

Donovan chuckles breathlessly. "Baby, your inner thoughts are killing me."

I gape at him. "You heard that?"

"Yes, you are great at projecting all of your thoughts."

"Oh, what the hell, how do I make it stop? And why can't I hear yours?"

"Baby, I don't mind. Your inner thoughts are very honest, and it's refreshing. Now as to why you can't hear me, I have blocks in place so I don't overwhelm you. We get taught how to shield our minds at an early age."

"Great, another thing that I don't know how to do."

He brushes a kiss on my forehead.

"It's something we can work on; don't stress about it."

"Easy for you to say. You don't have all of your thoughts projected at your mate."

I'm full on pouting. I'm sure I'm overreacting, but I'm getting really tired of how my lack of knowledge is hindering me. I'm not mad that I don't know the information. I'm used to learning new things; it's a part of my profession. What I'm not ok with is not having a way to figure it out myself. I'm wholly reliant on others to inform me and teach me.

Well shit, this must be how some of my students felt. I'm too tired for this. Shit, am I getting horny again?

Donovan remained quiet while I puzzled out my mental state, but my last thought is obviously too much for him to ignore. He snorts with laughter, which makes me feel a little violent, so I smack him in his hard stomach, which just makes him laugh harder. I growl in frustration, because that made my hand sting, so I attempt to pinch him next, but he isn't having any of that. He flips me on my back, pinning my hands down at my sides.

Ugh, he's so big, and strong; so sexy.

He just grins down at me as he leans in to nip at my neck. I shiver and feel my body instantly give up my fight to get free. His tongue licks along my neck, and my breath stutters out of me.

"Mmm, there's my good girl. I will have to remember this when you get horny and bratty."

His hips bump against my mound, letting me know that he is hard again. My legs open to wrap around him, my feet digging into his ass. All thoughts of being too sore flee from my mind as the hot ache builds back up in my center.

"Ahhh, Don, I need you again."

His lips meet mine, and as he kisses me his hand finds its way between my legs, testing my wetness. I groan in his mouth as two of his fingers penetrate me, gliding in effortlessly with how soaked I am with my release and his.

Deepening our kiss, he smoothly replaces his fingers with his hard length. His tongue mirrors the movement of his cock, languidly thrusting into me. He is in no rush, and I have no objections. This time isn't about two bodies frantically coming together. It's about two beings finding themselves within each other.

Our bodies move in harmony with each other, our hips moving in tandem. We revel in each other's bodies. We touch and taste, our sighs and moans intermingling in the space between us. His thrusts are slow, but hold an edge of the power in which he took my body just a short time ago. The long push and pull of his hips against mine, the way he rolls into me at the last moment and grinds himself against my clit is exquisite.

I'm swimming in pleasure, but I'm utterly unprepared when I orgasm. It catches me completely by surprise. There is no slow build up; it's just suddenly there, roaring through my exhausted body.

As I climax, Don speeds up his thrusts, chasing his own release. I cling to him, fearful that my body will drift away. His lips return to mine, kissing me hard as his own climax rolls through his body. He groans deep against my lips, his muscles tight as his hips jerk with the force of his release.

Our breathing calms slowly as we both come down from the intense pleasure. I snuggle into Don's body, not even caring that his skin is warm and slick with sweat. I'm just as sweaty.

He groans as he rolls us both, him on his back and me draped over his front.

"Mmmm, this is nice."

I murmur as he smooths his hands down my back, cupping my ass.

He chuckles breathlessly.

"Now I know why some Clan females have more than one mate."

He leans in to kiss me, but I stop him with a hand on his mouth.

"They do what?"

A mischievous gleam flares in his eyes, he licks me. My nose scrunches in disgust as I move my hand and wipe it on his chest. He chuckles before explaining further.

"Strong females have been known to take more than one mate."

I roll my eyes at that. *Here we go again with how powerful I'm supposed to be.*

"First off, are you telling me you would even let another male touch me, let alone put their cock anywhere in my general vicinity?"

He frowns and opens his mouth to speak, but I cut him off.

"Second, I'm not a strong female. I can't access my magic, can't control my need to be around you, and can't even shift."

"Are you done?"

I give him a pissy look, or as much of one as I can muster after being sexed within an inch of my life.

"Yes."

"I have grown up around the strongest females in my Clan, so I have it on good authority the criteria of one. Even with only a portion of your magic free, you rival some of those females, Kinley. You pulled a mid-shift out of me. I've never heard, nor have I seen such a thing happen. So yes, you are a very strong female, and I'm proud that you have claimed me as your mate."

He kisses me sweetly and lazily swipes his tongue along my bottom lip. "Now as far as another mate, if you ever felt the pull to have another mate, I'm not really sure how I would feel about it. Ultimately, it is always the female's choice. There is a good chance my beast would probably fight that male for dominance, though."

"I think we can agree to disagree on that. Plus, I don't think I could handle another mate if he's anywhere close to your size. Do you shift your cock during sex, because I swear it gets bigger."

He roars with laughter, making me smack his chest.

"I'm being serious." I really do pout this time, causing my bottom lip to protrude slightly.

Still laughing, he rolls so we are both on our sides and pulls me in tight so I'm cocooned in the warmth of his body. I give his abs a firm poke for him laughing at me though.

I really want to know if he did. I don't think it was that funny.

I continue to grumble to myself about dumb men and their enormous cocks, when I distract myself by tracing the tattoos on his chest and upper arm. Donovan's laughter slowly stops as I realize that under his tattoos are scars.

How have I not noticed these?

"Don?"

"Hmm?"

"Where did these come from? If you don't mind me asking?"

He glances down to where I'm gently tracing a raised scar.

"Well, some are from dominance fights, but most are from when I was touring in the service. I'll tell you about them some day if you still want to know, but right now we should both get some sleep, before it starts back up again."

"Now what are you talking about?"

He groans. "I seriously keep forgetting how little you know about Clan shifters. It's really common for new mates to go into a sort of mating frenzy shortly after. It's why it's so hard to be away from each other. I'm thinking it's just now setting in because of everything that happened with Megan needing you so it got repressed for a little bit."

"And how long is this supposed to last? "

He chuckles. "Honestly, it just depends. Could be a day, could be a week… maybe a month."

My eyes widen and a horrified look crosses my face. "Don…I won't survive if we have that much sex. You'll break me!"

"Kinley, you won't break; we heal pretty quickly. And it's not me that is going to be demanding it."

I huff at him and roll over onto my other side so I face away from him. I'm not going to be able to sleep with my face smooshed against his chest. He drags me back against him and a contented rumble vibrates in his chest. I feel my entire body relax in response, and a rumble of my own answers him.

"Go to sleep, baby."

He kisses my neck and inhales deeply, as if he's savoring the blending of his scent with mine. "You smell so fucking good."

I smile to myself and wiggle a little closer. Soaking in his warmth, I soon drift off to sleep knowing that no matter what, my mate will be here when I wake.

Of course, he is right; after just a few hours of sleep, my body begins to heat and tension spreads through every muscle. I groan and feel Don stir behind me. His lips caress my neck with soothing kisses as his hands stroke and cup my breasts. My core clenches, instantly ready for him.

It wasn't the last time we came together that night. Sometimes it's fast and hard, our bodies burning hot. Other times it's slow, and we savor each other's touches. I completely lose track of how many times we climax. We both got very little sleep that night.

CHAPTER 20

KINLEY

When my hunger for food outweighs my hunger for my mate and my need for sleep, I creep out of the bedroom and downstairs in search of sustenance. Don is in a deep sleep, and I can't wait for him to wake up. Also, he is sleeping so peacefully that I just don't have the heart to wake him. I, on the other hand, need to eat, and I need to now.

The sun is still low, so I know it isn't too late in the day. Thankfully, I know my way around Megan's house, so if she isn't around, I can fend for myself. I'm almost hoping that Megan isn't around. I'm a little embarrassed about the way I behaved last night. I know it's apparently natural for me to have these needs but goodness, I certainly hadn't planned on climbing Don like a tree and dry humping him in front of Megan.

I turn a corner and stop short. Welp, looks like I'm destined for embarrassment. Megan is standing in her kitchen, cup of coffee in hand. She's looking out the window, but she must sense me approaching because she gives me a sidelong look over her shoulder.

"Well, you're up earlier than I thought you would be. Is he dead?"

I snort and roll my eyes at her as I pour myself a cup of coffee. "No, not dead, just sleeping."

Megan grins at me.

"Maybe I need to get myself a Clan boy. They sound like they are givers."

I almost choke on my coffee, my face heating as a blush quickly spreads across my face. "You heard everything?"

Megan gives me a look that says, of course I did. "You were both anything but quiet. Is the furniture still intact?"

"Yes, the furniture is fine," I grumble, as I gingerly sit down onto a kitchen chair.

Megan laughs at me, her eyes twinkling with mirth. "Bet you're hungry, huh? Want me to make breakfast?"

"Yes, please, I'll love you forever."

"You already will, but I'll still take pity on you and make you food. You think Don will be up…for breakfast?" She snorts at herself.

"You're such a child."

Don does indeed get up for breakfast. The tempting, mouthwatering smells of bacon and waffles infiltrated his sleep, and his stomach demanded food. As he walks into the kitchen, looking fresh and well-rested, I wonder how he managed that. *Ugh, he looks perfect…*

Walking straight to me, he places a kiss on my forehead.

"Good morning, baby."

Ugh, who fucking cares. He's mine…Shit, am I getting turned on? Dammit, I just want to eat….

I glare down at my lap.

Stop it, you hussy.

"You ok, Kinley?"

I shoot my eyes up at Don.

Hmmm, maybe he didn't hear that.

"Yes. Just trying to talk myself down."

He gives me a confused look, but when he inhales, he catches my scent and grins. "Eat first, baby."

"Kill me now," I mumble under my breath.

"You two better not stink up my kitchen with your pheromones."

I groan and bang my head on the table. Don just laughs on his way to the coffee pot.

I don't know if it's because of my heightened senses, or if it's because I'm one moment away from jumping onto Don's lap, but the waffles and bacon taste amazing. I'm halfway through my waffle when I notice Don and Megan staring at me. Don looks like he wants to feast on me, and Megan has a horrified amused expression.

"What?" My question is muffled by a mouthful of waffle.

"You keep making those noises, Kinley, and I'm not going to be responsible for what I do next," Donovan rumbles. Which gets my inner hussy all fired up.

Megan gags and points a finger at Don. "Please, don't! And yeah, Kinley, it sounds like you're having sex with your food."

I swallow, and a mortified expression engulfs my beet-red face. "What the hell, I was not!"

"Yeah, you were. I know I'm a good cook, but seriously."

"Ughhhh, what is wrong with me? It just tastes so good. Wait, did you do something to it? I've never reacted to your cooking like this before."

"No, I didn't do anything to the food." She rolls her eyes. "Maybe it has to do with all your new magical abilities."

Still embarrassed, but too hungry to not eat, I shrug and reluctantly pick my fork back up. Don rests his hand on my arm and strokes his thumb along my skin. I grumble, but start eating again, being extra mindful about not making any more noises.

"It's ok, baby. Everything is new to you. Speaking of magical abilities though, I have a question for you, Megan."

She looks up from her plate, and I eye them both as I keep eating. *God, I'm so fucking hungry.*

"Sure, Don, ask away," Megan replies openly.

"I'm sure Kinley told you everything that has been happening lately." Megan nods.

"I hadn't mentioned this before now, but knowing now that you are a witch, I'm hoping you can shed some light on a ward that was in place at your lake house the night of the intruder. Aiden picked up the scent of it, but hadn't noticed it previously. Was the ward your doing?"

"I do have some wards on the property, but they would have only activated if there was a serious threat. I find spells to be more reliable than security systems."

She eyes me. "Kinley, did you feel anything while you were in the house?"

I shake my head, quickly swallowing my food before answering. "No, was I supposed to? Honestly I was so scared that I was more focused on getting myself and Beretta somewhere safe. I didn't notice anything magical. Not that I would have known to look for something like that."

Megan looks thoughtful before she continues. "My wards would have made it impossible for anyone to enter that had sinister intent. All entrances would be impenetrable, including the glass on the doors and windows. They aren't specific to magical signatures, they just protect against intruders."

Don seemed to be satisfied with that answer.

"You know, it would have been nice to know we were in a witch's domain, Megan. I'm sure you knew we weren't human."

She rolls her eyes at him.

"Yes, I did know that you weren't human. But males of your species have subtle magical signatures unless you're shifting, so I didn't know exactly what you were. Plus, I thought Kinley was mostly human. I couldn't just go parading around that I was a witch in front of her. Though, I'm pretty sure Aiden knew what I was."

"Hmmmm, well, he has a much better nose for those things than I do."

"So, Don, now that you are mated to my best friend, I expect you to protect her with everything, and I mean everything you have. I know you Clan boys have useful powers when it comes to defending your mates. So make sure you and whatever beast you have lurking within you, are vigilant when it comes to keeping her safe."

He rumbles, like his beast is insulted that she even brings that up. "Megan, with my very life, my mate will be protected."

She nods, her eyes boring into him as if she's making sure he's being one-hundred percent truthful.

"Don takes very good care of me. Everything is so new, but I know without any doubt that he would do anything for me."

Don's hand gives my thigh a gentle squeeze at my admission. His thumb strokes my inner thigh, as his deep voice fills my mind.

My mate, you are my life.

"You're talking to her mentally, aren't you?" Megan asks with a soft smile on her face.

Don nods. "My words were only for Kinley."

I blush, as deep emotions stir within me.

Megan sighs wistfully. "I'm truly happy for you both. I know how rare matings are among all of our kinds. The fact that you found each other so randomly is really a blessing."

That piques my interest.

"So you could have a mate too, Megan?"

She shrugs. "It's even rarer for witches, so it's not likely."

That brings sadness to my heart for her. Just thinking of what I'm beginning to have with Don, the idea that my best friend may never get to experience something similar, breaks my heart. She deserves all the happiness in the world. She deserves to be loved and cherished.

At the thought of love, my brow furrows slightly.

Did I even know what love was? I mean I loved Megan like a sister, but did I know what love between partners felt like?

Don's hand, still on my thigh, squeezes with a little more pressure until my eyes meet his.

Mate, you are capable of so much love. Your heart and soul sings with it. It's what makes the threads of our bond so vibrant.

My eyes get misty at his heartfelt words.

Megan, ever the keen observer, reaches out and touches my hand.

I clear my throat, not wanting to get all wrapped up in emotions, at least not right this moment. I need to steer the conversation to something less emotional.

"Megan, I bet you can't guess what Don's beast is."

Megan's eyes twinkle with the challenge as Don snorts in amusement.

I know what you are doing, mate, and I'll allow it. We can talk in private later.

Megan rubs her hands together in anticipation, as she loves a good bet.

"Ok, if I guess correctly, what do I get?"

"Hmmmm, what would you like?"

Megan taps her chin in contemplation. "A rain check of whatever I want."

I snort. "Deal, because I seriously doubt you're going to guess it correctly."

Don chuckles, crossing his arms across his chest, as if he, too, doesn't think she will guess correctly.

With a flick of her wrist, a burst of air sweeps right through Don. I sit up, alarmed, my beast perking up as well. An angry bellow from Don's stallion bursts from his mouth, his eyes blazing from the sheer power of his Kelpie.

The table rattles as Don slams his hand down on it as he glares at Megan. She just smirks at him.

"Oh, that is a good one! Kelpie, right?"

Before Don can speak, I beat him to it. "What the fuck was that, Megan?" My voice deepens with the growl of my beast.

"Magic, duh. You didn't say I couldn't. He's fine, I promise. Go on, tell her Don."

He does not look amused, but he answers me quickly. "I'm fine, baby. Megan, you're very lucky I have exceptional control over myself and my beast, or you would be getting an in-your-face look at a pissed off Kelpie."

"See, all fine." She cackles at us.

I shake my head at her. "Don't do that again. I didn't like it."

She assesses me, noticing quickly that I'm being serious. "Of course, won't happen again."

Breakfast finishes without me making an even bigger fool of myself, or anymore theatrics. I give myself a mental pat on the back for accomplishing that. I'm still exhausted, and several days in a row of very little sleep is quickly catching up to me. Don suggests that he take me back to our hotel room to rest, and then we will both come back over later. Megan also thinks that is a good idea, and I sleepily agree.

I hug Megan while Don goes to warm up the truck.

"I know this is all scary, Kinley. You are handling it really well, though. I'll do my best to help you in any way I can. Now, go get some rest...actual rest."

I laugh quietly, getting one more squeeze in before I go outside. "Megan, I'm truly thankful for you. Being able to finally tell you everything has lifted a weight off my soul. It didn't feel right keeping it from you."

"I know exactly what you mean. How do you think it felt all these years to not be able to share a part of my life with you? At least I was able to help in small ways without you knowing it."

I push back from her, my eyebrows raised in question. "You're going to tell me everything, but after I go take a freaking nap. God, I'm so fucking tired."

I end on a huge yawn, and Megan steers me out the door where Don quickly takes over, boosting me into the truck. I wave goodbye to Megan and snuggle into the heated seat.

"Well, that was really wild," I murmur quietly.

Don hums in agreement. I turn to study him as he drives, taking in everything. "Can I ask you something?"

He glances at me sideways. "Of course you can."

"I know we are mates, but what does that mean in the grand scheme of things? Are we as good as married? Is it normal to just know that we are mates? Is it supposed to happen this fast?"

He reaches out his hand for mine across the console, linking our fingers together before answering.

"True mates, when they first meet, almost always have an instant connection. It is two souls recognizing their counterpart. For my people, a true mate is beyond marriage, because a mating can't be as easily broken. It would take an act of a god for a mating bond to break, but a marriage can be severed with paperwork. Does that make sense?"

I nod, because it does. Our connection feels monumental; it feels like the planets aligned just so we could meet.

"When I call you my mate, I'm calling you that because you have claimed my very soul. Everything between us is profound."

"I believe every word you are saying in my heart. My mind is still playing catch up. I wish I could instantly have your outlook on it and not question if what I'm feeling is real."

"You are allowed to feel that way, Kinley. I never expected you to just fall in line and not have questions. You were living your life as a human until a week ago. I would find it odd if you didn't question everything."

I give his hand an affectionate squeeze.

Am I brave enough to take a deep look at my feelings?

As soon as we get up to our hotel room, I kick off my shoes and head straight for the bed. Don laughs as I flail my arms at him in a "gimme" gesture. He removes his clothes, but keeps on his boxer briefs, climbing in next to me and wrapping me up in his arms. I sigh as I bury my face in his neck, throwing a leg over his hip.

"Don," I mumble, half asleep.

"Yes, baby?"

I am so warm and comfy, mmmm he makes me so happy..

"I do love you, Don," I mumble into his neck before my breathing deepens, and I'm asleep without even realizing I said it out loud.

DONOVAN

As Kinley lies wrapped in my arms, peacefully sleeping, I stare at her. *How could I not stare at her?* She is ridiculously beautiful. She's my fucking mate, and she loves me. My beautiful mate loves me.

My soul feels like it's singing. If she hadn't been so tired and desperately needed the rest, I would have woken her up and let her know exactly how I feel, with words and my body. I know she's struggling with figuring out how she feels about our relationship. I also deduced that her childhood wasn't the best and emotions don't come easy to her.

But her sleepy admission makes my heart leap. My beast roars in excitement; he also wants nothing more than to show our mate that we are worthy of her love. Later, we will show her. My beast knickers in agreement. *Later*.

CHAPTER 21

KINLEY

Mmmmm, I love when I wake up warm and comfy. My cheek rises and falls with the rhythm of Don's breathing. I hum to myself, basking in my mate's closeness. I'm getting the best sleep lately, and it all stems from Don being present. I just sleep better when he's next to me. It's like his presence keeps the dreams away, and my mind can actually rest along with my body. Don stirs, and I tighten my arms around him, not wanting to move just yet.

His hips shift and roll us both over without warning. One second I'm lying on top of him, the next, I'm underneath him. I have no objections. I definitely like where this is going. I look into his smiling face, and I can't seem to keep the butterflies in my stomach at bay.

This man has my whole heart.

"Sleep well?"

I stretch, purposefully rolling my hips into his while I run my hands down his sides, gliding along the ridges and valleys of his muscles. "Yes, I always sleep better with you near."

My hands reach his lower back, and I glide them up along his muscles, scraping my nails lightly, causing him to shudder and groan with pleasure.

His eyes are closed, his neck arching slightly, grinding his hips into the apex of mine. I pause my exploration of his body but keep my hands at his shoulders.

When he opens his ocean blue eyes, I see the desire written plainly, but there is something else there I can't put my finger on. He brushes a strand of hair away from my face, leaning down to kiss me.

I want to wake up like this every morning.

Mmmmm, that can be arranged, baby.

His kiss and response sparks the hunger that is already slowly building, and I moan as his tongue enters my mouth. It strokes against mine, matching the strokes of his pelvis, long and languid. Pressing up against me, stokes the heat of my desire even higher. He breaks the kiss, too soon in my opinion – I could spend hours kissing him. He makes me want to make out like a horny teenager, and I'm not mad about it. Our breathing is heavy, our chests brushing up against each other's, my nipples hardening at the friction.

"We have on too many clothes," I tell him as I attempt to shimmy out of mine.

Grinning, he helps me out of them until I'm naked under him. He looks up and down my body, and if I didn't see the undeniable hunger in his gaze, it would totally make me self conscious. But the way he takes in all my curves, how my softness draws him in, and how he groans as he zeroes in on my chest— *Yeah I have nothing to be self conscious about with Donovan. At least not where my body is concerned...*

With his hands and his mouth, he worships them. My gasps and moans guide his movements. His hands knead them as his mouth continues lavishing my breasts. His boxer brief clad hardness grinds firmly against my dripping pussy, making me realize he isn't naked. He really needs to be naked.

"Don...please," I groan as he bites my nipple then soothes the sharp sting with his tongue.

He lets go of my hardened peak and looks up at me. His eyes are so bright, his beast so close to the surface.

"I need you naked. I need you inside me."

He leans up to strip off his briefs but pauses as he looks down. Wondering why he is staring at his crotch, I prop myself up on my elbows to look down. Like a cold bucket of water, embarrassment washes over me. *Oh fuck, Oh shit! Noooooooooo. Fuck my life!*

"Oooooh nooooo. I'm so sorry!"

I want to bury myself under the covers and not come out.

Blood is streaked across the front of his white boxer briefs. I freaking started my period. I flop back onto the bed and cover my face with my hands. I'm mortified.

As I'm wallowing in embarrassment, I hear Don chuckle darkly. The bed shifts, and his hands grasp mine, pulling them gently away from my face. "Hey, it's ok. A little blood isn't going to stop me from fucking you."

My mouth drops open.

Did I hear him right? He doesn't care that I'm bleeding?

A very primal growl escapes his throat.

"Did you forget I'm a carnivore, baby? I'll lick, suck, and fuck your pussy, and not even a little blood is going to stop me."

I go from horrified to molten hot in an instant. The speed at which he went from sweet to downright filthy is awe-inspiring and makes me ravenous.

I'm transfixed as his tongue swipes across his upper lip. He stares at my red tinted wetness, his chest rumbling with desire. He rips that final layer of clothing off and gets comfortable between my thighs.

I weakly protest; I still am not sure how I feel about him eating me out while I'm bleeding. Hot in theory, but in actuality I'm still on the fence. My protest falls on deaf ears as he proves his point by licking the entire length of my pussy. *Oh my god.*

My toes curl as my moans intermix with Don's hungry groans and growls. His tongue thrusts deep into my core over and over, wringing cries from my lips.

My fingers grip the sheets, and my thighs try to clamp down around him, but he has pinned me down thoroughly. His eyes meet mine as he sucks my clit into his mouth. My mouth gapes open in a silent cry as my body bows with the force of my climax. Donovan doesn't even wait for me to come down; he lunges up and thrusts his cock deep into me, groaning as his hips become flush with mine. His long tongue licks the remnants of my climax from around his mouth.

God why is that so fucking sexy?

DONOVAN

My beast is urging me to dominate our mate, and in this we are in agreement. My biceps and shoulders flex as I bring her hips higher onto mine, and I grip her ass tight as I pound into her.

Goddess, she feels so tight, and she is soaking me.

The scents of her pleasure mixed with iron brings me into a frenzy that only her tight heat can cure.

When I tasted her sweet nectar mixed with her blood, it took everything in me to not explode with that first taste. Never have I tasted something so delicious. The fact that she lingers on my tongue makes my pleasure reach higher than I thought possible. This female is wrecking me, and I never want her to stop.

Seeing her tight pink pussy taking my entire length makes me growl. She was made for me.

"Goddess, baby, you take me so fucking well."

Her sweet cries spur my thrusts on. I need to feel her clench tightly around me. I need to feel her cum all over my cock. I'm barely hanging on, but I need to feel her cum one more time. I know she is close from the way her muscles tighten and those sweet cries she makes. Reaching down, I rub her clit in tight circles, helping her climb to her peak faster. My hips speed up, and the force of my hips meeting hers makes her beautiful breasts sway. *Goddess, I love her breasts.*

"Don, I'm gonna cum, please."

Her cries are the sweetest fucking sounds that I have the pleasure of hearing. With a final brutal thrust we climax together. I roar as I fill her to the brim.

When my breathing is under control, and I can stand being out of her body, I get up and walk to the bathroom. I wet a cloth, cleaning myself off, and rumbles of pride escape me as I see the evidence of my mate's pleasure on my shaft and thighs. *Fucking perfection.*

Throwing the used cloth into the sink, I wet another and go clean my mate.

As I approach Kinley's sprawled body, I can't help the grin that spreads over my face. She has hardly moved since I got up. Her beautiful body is on perfect display, our collective releases coating her inner thighs. It almost makes me want to throw away the wash cloth and clean her with my tongue. Her breathing has slowed, her eyes slitted, perfectly content to just lay on the bed while I gently clean her.

"Did I make a big mess?" Kinley mumbles.

I chuckle as I peer down at the mess we have made all over the sheets. "We made a mess, but it's fine. Nothing that can't be cleaned."

That makes her groan and sit up. She scoots herself back until her back rests on the pillow up against the headboard. She frowns down at the sheets, "Don, it looks like we murdered someone on the bed."

"No, it doesn't. There would be way more blood."

She grumbles under her breath as she gets up, going to take a drink out of the bottle of water by the TV stand. As she passes me, I can't resist the temptation, I swat her bare ass, watching it jiggle with delight. *Goddess, I love her body.*

As she drinks, she eyes the bed, choosing to ignore that I smacked her ass.

"Well, at least we know I'm not pregnant since we are both awful at remembering to use protection."

Her words make me pause. *Shit, have I really not talked to her about this?* I go over to her, wrapping an arm around her waist.

"We don't need to worry about that."

She whips her head up to me, smacking me in the face with her hair. "We certainly do!"

"I keep forgetting that you don't know these things, but for one I'll be able to smell when you're fertile. And two, you're Clan…females don't cycle every month."

Her mouth gapes open, then she scoffs at me, "Then why do I have a period every month? And don't you think that is something we should have discussed? I can't keep track of all the things I should know but don't!"

I don't know about that one, but now that she mentioned it, there is something else I need to tell her. I spin her around so she's facing me, my hands grasping her hips. Kneading her soft flesh as I lean down and kiss her tenderly.

"Alright, how about this one? I love you, Kinley."

Her eyes widen and her mouth drops slightly, then her lips draw into a line and the bottom one quivers the tiniest bit.

"You love me?" Her voice is small and unsure. I don't like that she has doubts, so I continue.

"Love doesn't seem big enough for what I feel for you. My very soul craves you. My heart beats for you alone. The threads of my very existence glow and pulse with the sweetest symphony all because of you. You are my everything. Of course I love you."

Moisture gathers in her eyes before she throws her arms around my neck. Moving my hands, I boost her up by cupping her ass, and she grips my waist with her thighs. My beast knickers in my mind in agreement with my words. *She really is all of that and so much more. My heart would cease to beat without her.*

Burying her face in my neck, she whispers, "I love you, too. I thought I was going crazy. I've never been in love before – the very thought always terrified me. With you everything feels so big, and all these feelings, they honestly scare me to death."

I sit down on the edge of the bed, keeping her pressed against me, not willing to give up any space between us.

"No, baby, you're not going crazy." I stroke her back, cradling her on my lap. "You can feel it in our bond, just like I can. Don't doubt yourself."

She lets out a deep breath that tickles across my skin. Her hands play with the hair at the back of my neck. I feel the moment she looks within at our bond, the brush of her mind gentle and sweet. Looking deep within herself, she feels along our mate bond. It is truly a beautiful thing that I never thought I would ever experience. Mate bonds are not a common thing anymore, and I will thank the Goddess every day that she gifted me mine. Kinley continues to mentally brush against our bond. She is just as much in awe of it as I am. The threads are intricately woven, glittering with love, desire, and so much more.

CHAPTER 22

KINLEY

We finally make it back to Megan's right around dinner time. Megan, not having the desire to cook, ordered take out for all of us. I literally would have eaten anything she put in front of me, I'm ravenous. While we eat, Donovan gets a phone call, so he excuses himself to answer it. This gives Megan the opening that she has apparently been waiting for.

"Well, you are looking much better than you were this morning. You still doing ok?"

"Yeah, a nap and some more amazing sex was just what I needed."

We both can't help but laugh.

"Enough about me. How are you doing?"

Megan gives me a tired smile, and I can't help but feel like a shitty friend.

"It's different not having to worry about him anymore. My brother wants me to come stay for a while, but I'm not sure I'm ready for that. I think I'm ready to be alone first."

"I'm sure he will understand. You are allowed to think of yourself and do what you need. And if you need an excuse, you can always just pretend I need you now that my life is upside down and crazy. Keegan loves me, he'll happily agree that you need to be with me over him."

"That's not really a lie; you do kinda need me."

"I promise I'll be ok, and I swear as soon as I'm not, I will call you, and you can rush to my rescue."

The sound of Don's hurried footsteps makes me pause, and his guarded expression fills me with dread.

"What happened?"

His inner turmoil filters in from our bond, he's at war with himself, his need to protect me fighting with his need to keep me informed. "Just tell me Don, please."

"There was a break in at your house."

Dread pools in my stomach, my hands fly up to my mouth, "Oh my god, Indy is still there! Did someone find him? Is he ok?"

The sharp edge of my panic spears towards him. Crouching down in front of me, he takes my hands in his, giving me some of his strength.

"Baby, he's fine. Brent and Aiden got him out, and he's perfectly safe at Brent's. Whoever broke in very clearly got injured. Brent said there was a good amount of blood at the scene, but none of it was Indy's. I'm not sure the extent of the damage to your house yet, but I swear to you, Indy is fine."

Megan gasps in anger, drawing both of our attention. "How the hell did they get in? I put charms on your house years ago, since you insisted you didn't need a security system. There is no way a normal human would have made it in. And there is definitely no way, if the intruder was human, that they would have made it out of your house alive. When Indy attacked them, he would have surely killed anyone non-magical."

I'm ashamed to admit it takes me longer to process Megan's words than I'd like to admit, but holy shit did she really say that? "Whoa, whoa, whoa, what the hell are you talking about? Charms on my house? Indy killing people?"

Megan sighs, and I steel myself for the truth bomb she is about to drop.

"Obviously, you had to expect me to have made sure you were safe. I can't have my best friend not being safe in her own home. So I took some steps to ensure I wouldn't worry about you."

"Ok, that explains why you put the charms on my house. But what the fuck did you mean about Indy?"

Megan gives me a sheepish look, shrugging her shoulders. "I might have made a bargain with a familiar to watch over you."

Don growls and I give him a startled look.

"You did what? Familiar bargains are dangerous. Why would you do that when Kinley had no idea about magic?"

Megan waves him off, more concerned with watching my reaction. I'm utterly confused and there is that panic again, slowly creeping back.

"So my cat isn't a cat?" My bottom lip wobbles and I suck in several shaky breaths. I'm going to start crying, I just know it. *I'm too hormonal for all this shit!*

"Oh, honey, he is! He's just a little more than that. I resolved the bargain a long time ago, but he wanted to stay with you. Honey, he's there by choice! So is Beretta."

"What the fuck, Megan! My dog, too?"

Maybe I'll smash something instead. Damn my hormones!

Megan holds her hands up quickly. "I swear I had nothing to do with her! She found you all on her own."

Growling, I push up and start pacing, breathing deeply, trying to calm myself down. I'm so mad and hurt, and I don't know what to think anymore.

"Kinley, I swear this isn't a bad thing. You are theirs as much as they are yours. They have an unwavering loyalty to you. A familiar that is with you by choice is a powerful thing. They will protect you with their lives if that is what needs to be done. They love you, Kinley."

"So you're telling me my pets are magical."

Megan nods.

"Goddess, this just keeps getting more complicated," Donovan mutters. "Megan, is there anything else we need to know?"

"No, that's it. I tried not to interfere with your life, Kinley. I just wanted to make sure you were safe. Just talk to them; they will reveal themselves to you if you ask. A bond with a familiar is incredibly valuable, and when freely given, it's priceless."

"What even is a familiar? Do you have one?"

Megan's eyes shift first to me and then to Don. His eyes narrow at her, as if he is telling her that this is her mess and she is in charge of clean-up.

"Ok, again, it's important that I stress they are loyal to you and would never do anything that would hurt you. Familiars are guardians of certain dimensions of the underworld. They can ferry souls to their afterlife destinations, and they can also torture evil souls, it just depends on their capabilities. Sometimes familiars will come to our realm to serve and bond with magical beings, protecting and aiding them whenever they can."

My mouth slowly closes. It has been hanging open the entire time Megan talked. *Holy fuck.*

"Megan, please tell me that my dog and cat aren't demons."

"What, no! Kinley, familiars are definitely not demons. Honestly, it's pretty offensive to call them such. Some familiars are even known to hunt demons."

Well, that is a relief...I guess.

My eyes shift to Don, narrowing slightly.

"Did you know what my pets were?" I ask him suspiciously.

"No, baby. Familiars are very secretive, and are very good at disguising themselves so only their bonded know what they are."

"But I'm not a witch, so how do I have not one, but two familiars?"

Megan smiles. "You don't have to be a witch. You just have to be powerful."

Bombshell after bombshell kept dropping on my head, and a less mentally stable person would probably be rocking in a corner. Megan and Donovan manage to calm me down, but really, it was mostly Donovan distracting me with his magical cock.

I was on edge and being a snappy brat, until Donovan threw me over his shoulder, swatting my ass hard, and proceeded to fuck the brat right out of me in the first room he found. He had me bent over the bathroom sink so fast I didn't know what was happening. When he was done with me, he pulled my clothes back on and sent me back to finish talking with Megan with his cum pooling onto my pad. It really isn't fair.

We ended up staying until late the following day, much to my frustration. I understand why we waited, the mating frenzy was riding us hard—figuratively and literally. And that overwhelming desire took precedence.

Under normal circumstances I would have been ok waiting, but I need to get back, and I am just not going to be satisfied until I see that both of my pets are safe. I still haven't wrapped my head around the fact that they are familiars. The word holds no meaning to me, even after Megan explained. They have been my pets, my babies, for years. Nothing is going to convince me that they are more than that until I lay eyes on both of them.

This time away was supposed to be about me supporting Megan and it's really turned into her and Donovan consoling me. *Everything is so messed up.* I haven't felt this helpless since I was eighteen. And just like then, my world is crumbling apart. I don't know who I am anymore. My best friend has been lying to me for years. My pets, my babies, aren't even from this world. They are fucking demon hunting, soul eating creatures, and have been living in my home for years!

I don't know what is real anymore. How do I even begin to put my life back together when the pieces I thought belonged don't fit back into place? Or maybe they do and it's me that never fit the mold.

I just want to go lie down in a dark room and not think. Maybe eat my weight in peanut butter slathered chocolate bars. But I know if I try, if I give into the dark places my mind will go, I'm not sure I'll be able to climb out this time. I crave to be somewhere safe, and not have to experience any more groundbreaking, life-changing revelations. I want to hide. I realize I need answers, but at what cost?

Things also now feel off with Megan. I love her, but it's hard to get behind all the secrets. Megan can feel it, too, and I know she feels responsible. Thinking about it logically, I can start to understand, but my heart aches with the many things that have been kept from me.

Before we leave, I make a point to wrap Megan in a hug and whisper, "We are ok, my brain and my heart are just in too much turmoil right now. I love you. I will always love you, ok? I'm just upset with everything that is going on."

Megan's eyes swim with tears, but she takes a deep breath, squeezing me back.

"I understand, I really do. Please tell me if you need me, though. I know you're upset, and you have every right to be. I'll give you some space, but don't push Don away. I know how you can get."

She knows me too well, but I don't think even she realizes I can never pull away from Don. I sigh. My soul feels so weary.

As I pull away from Megan, I nod in confirmation. "I'll talk to you soon."

Walking toward Don's truck, my eyes lock on the sight of him waiting for me just like I knew he would be, it brings a little bit of calm to my anxious heart. He watches me, looking for anything amiss, and he doesn't miss anything.

A lot has gone wrong, but even I can admit that I'm incredibly lucky. I have people who love and support me. Many people don't have that. I know what it's like to not have what I have now, so I make a vow to myself, that I won't fuck it up by running away. I will stay, for myself and for them.

CHAPTER 23

KINLEY

When is this mating heat going to end?

I'm so uncomfortable. I'm hormonal, horny, and seriously on edge.

We are only an hour into driving back, and I don't know how I'm going to last without pleading with Donovan to pull over and fuck me. This whole mating frenzy thing is really messing with my head and my body.

"You want me to pull over and fuck you?"

My head jerks to face him. "What?" I squeak out.

Don chuckles. "Baby, you're thinking very loudly."

Fuuuuccckkkk.

"Really?"

"Yes, love. Do you need me to pull over? Because I will if that's what you need."

I think about it for a brief moment, and decide that I'm going to ask for what I need.

"Can you? I'm so uncomfortable."

He quickly nods and takes the next exit, noticeably shifting in his seat. I stare hungrily at his growing erection.

Is my mouth watering? Yes, yes it is, and I'm not ashamed.

Thank goodness we are in a heavily wooded section of the highway, and lucky for us there are frequent pull offs to allow for travelers to stop and appreciate nature. I giggle to myself. We are really about to appreciate nature.

Don parks quickly, and ever the gentleman, he ensures that he angles his truck so that anyone who passes by won't get a look at what we are about to be doing. I whip off my seat belt, hopping out of the truck as Don strides around from the other side. I lick my lips as I eye his hard cock straining against his zipper. Reaching for me, he kisses me hard before spinning and bending me over so my chest is flat against the passenger side floor board. I gasp and moan as he pushes up against me.

"This is going to be fast and hard, baby, so hold on."

I can't help but wiggle my ass; I'm beyond ready for him.

He smacks my ass and wastes no time pulling my leggings and panties down to just below my knees, not allowing me to spread my legs.

"Shit, Don my tampon," I gasp out.

"Got it."

He pulls it out quickly, before entering me in one long hard thrust. I scream out, unable to keep myself quiet. His large hand immediately covers my mouth, muffling my needy cries.

True to his word, it's fast and hard, and all I can do is hold on and take it as he ruts into my body. I'm almost too sensitive, but my body welcomes his brutal thrusts.

My inner beast stirs; she revels in his passion filled grunts and growls as he pushes my body to the limits. But she remains just out of reach. His hands tighten on me, the hand on my mouth barely giving me room to breathe. He can steal all my air, as long as I get to cum right now.

With a shift of his hips, his cock strikes my g-spot, and I'm a goner. We climax together, shouting our pleasure.

Our breathing is heavy as the frenzy slowly ebbs away. Don removes his hand from my mouth and gently turns my face up so his lips can capture mine in a tender kiss.

"Don't move, I'll get some wipes to clean up," he murmurs against my lips.

He eases himself out of me, and I shudder as the cold air meets my bare body. But I stay put, my ass completely exposed to the wilds, smiling a little as I think how wild my life has gotten recently. If someone were to tell me that in just a few months I would go from single and celibate to having magic, being mated to a man that turns into a carnivorous mythical horse, and willingly having outdoor sex, I honestly would have laughed in their face. Yet, here I am. It's truly mind-boggling just thinking about it.

A chilly wind brushes my skin, and I shiver some more, but I don't have to wait long before Don comes back behind me. I hear a soft growl of approval and his warm hand caresses my backside.

"I've certainly made a mess of you."

He brushes cool wet wipes over my swollen flesh and goosebumps pebble my skin from the chill and pleasure. When he's finished cleaning me, he lays a gentle hand on my ass, giving me a little squeeze before he says.

"I got your bag out so you can grab another tampon, so you don't have to hobble over to the back seat."

Standing up, I turn around and thank him before I dig in my bag to find what I need. Thank goodness I always travel with period supplies. Not finding a tampon, I settle for my back up pad. Which is probably a better idea, because if we have to do this again at least he won't have to be pulling more tampons out of me.

I quickly pull up my pants and, on wobbly legs, climb back up into the truck. Don gets in shortly after and looks over at me with a satisfied grin.

"Feel better, baby?"

"Yes, thank you."

"Baby, you don't need to thank me. If you need me, just say so. I'm happy to stop as many times as we need to, but I'm not going to be happy if you're hurting."

Leaning over the center console, I kiss him.

"I promise I'll let you know if I can't wait."

"Good girl."

Why did those words make my pussy clench?

"If you say things like that, we aren't going to make it back home."

He just smirks at me. "Put your seatbelt on, baby."

I eye him as I do so, and then cheekily reply, "Yes, Sir."

A hungry growl rumbles through the cab, eliciting a giggle out of me. Out of the corner of my eye, I notice him shaking his head as he puts the truck in gear and pulls out of the lot.

Settling into my seat, I remember something I've been meaning to ask him. "Don?"

"Hmm?" He doesn't look over at me as he's focused on merging back onto the highway.

"There is something that I have been wondering that just doesn't make sense to me."

"What's that, baby?"

"How is this "mating" frenzy happening if I'm on my period? Doesn't that defeat the purpose of mating?"

"Well, I'm no expert, but the mating frenzy doesn't have anything to do with making babies. It's about solidifying the mating bond."

"Oh, so it doesn't matter that I'm not ovulating?"

He chuckles. "No, baby, not at all."

"Ok." Seems weird to me, but I guess I'm just thankful our sexathon isn't going to get me pregnant.

I never really thought about having babies before. When you have shitty parents, you get kind of skittish about having kids of your own. Though, the thought of having sweet little babies that look like Don does make my stomach all fluttery.

Reaching over, he takes my hand, stroking his thumb over my knuckles. "Don't forget to let me know if you get too uncomfortable. I'm sure you are extra needy since you are bleeding as well."

That's definitely something I can do. I nod and give his hand a little squeeze. Cuddling under the blanket, I do kind of hope that we don't have to stop too many times. I'm ready to be home.

"I love you, Don." It feels good to say it and seeing his bright smile lays to rest any fears I still had.

"I love you, baby, so much."

We have to stop two more times, much to my chagrin, before we pull into Brent's driveway. The sun had set over an hour ago, and I can tell Don is just as tired as I am.

"Can we just sleep right here? Too tired to move," I mumble.

"You know the guys are going to come out here as soon as they realize we aren't coming in."

I whimper, but find the strength to make myself get out of the truck. I trudge about halfway up the front stairs when the door opens and Cam walks out. His nostrils flare and he quickly comes towards me.

"Are you ok, Kinley? Are you bleeding?"

Ugh really, he could smell that?

Too tired to explain, I pat him on the chest. "I'm fine, Cam."

"But I smell blood," he inhales deeper, "and sex?"

Oh come on...seriously.

Don chuckles. Of course he would think this is funny.

"Cam, she's fine."

Cam makes a deep hissing sound, reminding me of a very large pissed off bird, and eyes Don.

"Did you hurt her?"

"Cam, seriously?" Don asks incredulously.

"What's going on out here?" Aiden appears, followed closely by Brent.

"Kinley is hurt." Cam hisses out.

"Oh my god, I'm not hurt! Cam, I swear I'm ok. Thank you for being concerned; it's very sweet. It's just that time of the month." I interject quickly before anyone else can jump to conclusions.

A bright blush spreads across Cam's face, and Aiden and Brent snort.

Too tired for this...

I push past Aiden and Brent and they both get a whiff of my scent. They both close their eyes and inhale deeply, making me grumble about no privacy, but Don growls in protest. They both give him a sheepish look.

ƁRENT

"You can't blame us, she smells amazing. Mating frenzy?" I say with a shrug. Because, Goddess above, she smells fucking fantastic. My beast agrees wholeheartedly, and I get a mental image of him rubbing himself all over her.

Donovan nods his head, but I notice how on edge he is. A muscle in his jaw ticks. "Yeah, it hit her pretty hard while she was with Megan. It was definitely interesting getting back. Now, if you will excuse me, I'm going to go pass out with my mate until it builds back up again."

Donovan goes to find Kinley, and I call out to his back from the doorway, because I just can't fucking help myself, "Hey, if you need an assist, feel free to give us a call and we can tag in."

Donovan flips me off without even turning around. Aiden and I look at each other and laugh.

Cam, still a light shade of pink mutters, "But clan girls don't get periods."

That makes both of us turn to look directly at him. Aiden walks up to him and wraps an arm around his shoulders.

"Bud, don't think too hard about it. Don't want you to hurt that big brain of yours."

Camden shoves Aiden and grumbles under his breath as he walks into the house.

Chuckling, I go to follow him, but I'm stopped by Aiden's hand on my arm. My eyebrow raises in question. He gives me a stern look, and my humor diminishes.

"If you're saying that shit to fuck with Don, you need to cut it out." He holds his hand up to stop me from interrupting. "But I get the feeling that there is more behind it, so if that's the case, you need to talk to Don. He needs to know if you are also getting urges from your kitty cat."

A growl rumbles out of me. "You know we fucking hate when you call us that."

"My bad...Tigger."

I shove him, and give him a pointed look down at his crotch.

"What's your excuse...puppy?"

Aiden just shrugs.

"What? They both smell like sex, and Kinley smells like Megan."

"What is with you and witches?"

"It's not all witches...just that one."

I pat him on the shoulder, because I've seen the way he looks every time Megan is mentioned.

"Well, she's technically single now. It's pretty wild, though, how Kinley has been surrounded by magic this whole time and knew nothing about it. The wards around the lake house make so much sense now. I wonder if Don found out anything else useful while he was with the girls."

He gives me a pointed look. "Stop trying to change the subject. You need to talk to Don."

"Yeah I know, but at the end of the day, it's still Kinley's choice."

"Have you talked to her?"

"Of course not. I'll talk to Don, see what he thinks. She's been through a lot, and I'm not going to add to it just because my beast is interested."

Because at the end of the day, a clan female is the ultimate decider on mate bonds. Running a hand through my hair, I sigh. *Would it even be worth mentioning?* It isn't like Kinley knows anything about our culture. She will probably think I'm crazy for even bringing it up, and then that will just piss Don off.

CHAPTER 24

KINLEY

It takes another four days for the mating frenzy to subside enough that I can stand to be away from Don for more than a few hours. Our mating bond is vibrant and full of life after the need between us calmed.

It still boggles my mind that I can be magically linked to someone, and that if I look within myself I can see it, actually see my soul's threads woven with his. It is wild. I'm in awe.

It feels wonderful. It did even in the beginning, but now there are no words to describe the confidence and comfort I get from our unbreakable connection.

I'm still hiding out at Brent's. In fact, we all are. I haven't felt comfortable going back to my house, even if I could have stomached to be away from Don. There is no way I want to be alone at my house after someone broke in.

Cam and Aiden have even stuck around, what little I see of them. I feel like the worst kind of house guest, eating their food, barely coming out of the room I've been given, having wild and crazy sex with their friend at all hours of the day. *I'm the worst.*

Not wanting to be a space invader, I mention it to Brent one morning after Don and Aiden run into work to help with one of their ongoing cases.

Wanting to not feel like a total mooch, I'm busying myself making pancakes when Brent strolls in, shirtless.

Of course he's shirtless. Why do I want to suddenly lick down his chest and abs? Trace every line of his many, many tattoos.

Down girl, you literally just had your insides rearranged by your mate not even an hour ago…Stop ogling the man…that's not yours.

A tiny growl slips out as I furiously whisk the pancake batter. He sidles up close to me, so close I can feel his body heat. Trying desperately to distract my hormonal and horny inner beast, I figure now is a good time to make sure I'm not overstaying my welcome.

"Brent."

"Yes, princess?"

"Is this ok? You know, all of us being here at your house? I just feel like…I mean I don't want to take advantage of your hospitality."

A raised eyebrow on his face makes me pause, my head unconsciously cocking to the side slightly in question. *Why is he looking at me like that?*

"What? I'm serious. I don't want to take advantage…this is your home."

His expression doesn't change, he just keeps looking at me and my body fidgets under his scrutinizing gaze.

"Do you not like being here, Kinley?"

There's an edge to his tone that I can't figure out. The hairs on the back of my neck rise, like I'm being stalked by a very dangerous predator. And if I'm being completely honest with myself, I like it.

"Of course I like being here. Brent, your house is beautiful, and it's so peaceful."

"Good, now stop asking stupid questions. You're part of our Clan now. You belong with us, and right now, it is safer for all of us to be together."

He moves a little closer, his body almost flush with mine, the heat radiating from his body makes me want to rub up against him like a cat. *Jesus, am I still in heat?* So focused on his warmth and his delicious scent, I don't notice him leaning down until his mouth is next to my ear.

"I like you being in my house, Kinley. I like your scent spreading throughout, mingling with mine…and Don's. I can't get enough of it."

He breathes deeply into the crook of my neck, taking in my very essence. I freeze, because I have no idea what I should be doing.

"You smell so fucking good, princess, covered in your mate's scent. Were you a good girl for him? It sounded like you were."

My mouth gapes open at his bold words. *Holy shit…Oh my god.*

I'm so flustered, I don't know what to do.

Should I be aroused? Should I be mad? What the fuck am I supposed to do with that?

My beast takes that moment to perk her head up. *Oh shit, is she interested?* I shake myself out of it and push him away, scolding myself for noticing how firm his chest is.

"What are you playing at, Brent? I'm with Don. I don't know if that means anything to you, but it means something to me, and I don't appreciate the come-ons. It confuses the hell out of me, and I just need this…" I motion between the two of us, "to be less confusing. I need to feel safe, Brent…this doesn't make me feel safe. It puts me on edge."

Ok, I wasn't being completely honest; Brent does make me feel safe. But wanting him on top of being with Don makes my stomach cramp with anxiety. I feel the energy in the room decrease, and I'm able to take in a much needed calming breath.

I cautiously look up at him, afraid to see that I hurt or made him angry. But I don't see that at all. Brent's face softens and he nods as if he understands.

"I'm sorry for making you feel that way. Kinley, I…" The rest of what he is going to say dies as Camden strolls into the kitchen, seemingly oblivious to the tension in the room.

"Ooo, are we having pancakes for breakfast?"

And like the coward I am, I take the much needed distraction and snap back to finishing the batter. I smile a little too brightly at Camden.

"Yeah, I needed to do something productive, and cooking helps."

Brent moves away, turning to start coffee, and I get the griddle ready. The three of us chat companionably as we finish off the mound of pancakes I made, drinking coffee, and relaxing in the morning sunlight that streams in through the windows of the breakfast nook. And as I drink from my steaming mug, I make the conscious effort to not allow things to be weird between Brent and me. I like Brent a lot; I like them all, but I love Don, and nothing is going to take that away from me. So to keep the peace and smooth everything over, I'm going to push the weird feelings he stirs in me and make sure that there aren't weird vibes between us. Because that is the right thing to do. Right?

BRENT

Kinley going off to take a shower leaves me and Camden to clean up. She had been ready to start, but we insisted. As soon as she is out of earshot, Cam elbows me hard making me grunt.

"You're welcome for that."

Glaring at him, I ask, "What is that supposed to mean?"

Cam just gives me a knowing look.

"That shit you're pulling with Kinley. Brent, she just got through her frenzy with Don. She doesn't know that what you're doing is common within the Clan. If you are feeling the urge to join them, you have to talk to Don and he can help ease the path."

I growl in frustration, my shoulders sagging slightly. "I know. I can't fucking help it. It was literally all I could do not to break down their fucking door this week."

Cam pats me on the shoulder. "Trust me, I know, but thankfully, I don't feel the pull that you are feeling. You haven't even talked to Don yet, have you?"

I shake my head, feeling ashamed. "No. I know I should, and I keep meaning to, but the right time just hasn't come up."

"Dude, if your beast is riding you this hard that you practically pin her against the kitchen countertop and look like you are seconds away from mounting her, you need to talk to Don. What if it had been him that walked in and not me."

Grabbing fistfuls of my hair, I snarl. "Goddess, I fucking know."

"Good. Now, I'm going to work for a few hours."

"Hey! I thought you were helping clean up?"

"Nah, buddy, that's all you."

Camden dances out of range as I try to swat him with a kitchen towel. I stare at his retreating back for a minute, thinking about what Cam said, and know that I can't put off talking to Don any longer.

Closing my eyes, I take a deep breath and pull out my phone from the pocket of my sweats. I shoot a text off to Don, letting him know that I need to talk with him when he gets back.

CHAPTER 25

KINLEY

Swiping my hand across the steam covered mirror, I take a good long look at myself. I feel so different, but my appearance is still the same. After all the changes and craziness that have occurred over the last few weeks, I guess I just expected some outward evidence to be present– Something to show for what I have gone through, the good and the bad. But I still look like I did before I met Donovan and began this journey of discovery. Why did that make me so disappointed?

Dressing in some comfy leggings, a baggy shirt, and twisting my hair up into a messy wet bun, I exit the bathroom. I come face to face with both Indy and Beretta lounging on the made bed. My eyebrow quirks up at the sight of them. I have yet to confront them both on the whole familiar thing, but I guess now is as good a time as any. *Why am I so anxious?*

Beretta's tail begins wagging, and she makes as if to get up off the bed and approach me. *Nope, I can't have this conversation if she gives me cuddles.*

"Beretta, stay."

The wagging stops, and she cocks her head at me.

I sit down in the chair facing the bed and watch them, and they watch me back. I take a deep breath. *Here goes nothing.*

"So are you two just going to sit there and keep on pretending you are real animals?"

The unnatural way that Beretta glances at Indy is unnerving, and then Indy's eyes narrow slightly at me, but still they sit there.

"I know what you are, so you might as well come clean."

A deep and raspy voice comes out of Indy's mouth, and I watch in fascinated horror as he answers me.

"So, the witch finally confessed?"

Composing myself so I don't freak out, I count to ten in my mind and then answer him.

"Yes, Megan told me what you both are, and how you came to me. Care to elaborate?"

"Well, if she told you all that, then there is no need to elaborate. You know what's important."

I fight the urge to roll my eyes. It feels silly to do so at a cat, even though he isn't really a cat.

"I would like to know more about you both. You have been with me so long, and now I feel like I don't even know you."

A voice that sounds a little too sweet answers me from Beretta's toothy jaws.

"She has a right to know, it's not like we didn't know this day would come. Especially now that she is mated to the water horse."

I can't help but grin at her name for Don. Indy grumbles a little too quietly for my ears to pick up, and Beretta nudges him with one of her front paws. Clearing his throat and giving Beretta a side glare, he speaks a little louder.

"We will answer whatever questions you might have, Mistress."

Mistress? Nope, don't get distracted. "I have so many, but I guess the one that means the most is, do you both actually want to be here? I couldn't bear it if you thought being with me is an obligation."

They blink at me. I think it's a look of bewilderment. Indy is the first to answer. "Obviously the witch didn't tell you everything. We have no bindings to keep us here with you, we could have left at any time. We choose everyday to stay."

Tears swim in my eyes. I have been dreading this answer. Even though Megan assured me that they want to be with me, I still had my doubts. It is still hard to believe that people choose to be with me, even after all the years that have passed.

A gentle lick swipes over my hand, and my attention draws back to what is before me, the sweet face of my Beretta.

"Mistress, please don't cry. This is a good thing, now we no longer have to hide our true natures. It was very hard remaining as we were, seemingly ignorant to the world around us. While it was a simple life and you cared for us deeply, it was difficult not to interact with you in the way we truly crave." I move to pet Beretta's head, but my hand pauses.

Can I still pet them? Will they even want that?

As if sensing the reason for my hesitation, Beretta bridges the gap and nudges my hand with her head.

"You may still touch us as you did before. Your touch is comforting to us, just as ours is to you. It also gives us a power boost and keeps us grounded on this plane."

Taking comfort in that, I stroke Beretta's head, and begin to process her words.

"How have you been surviving all this time, though? I didn't have power."

Indy takes that moment to jump up in my lap, nudging Beretta over slightly. He stretches his body up, placing both front paws on either of my collarbones, and peers deeply into my eyes. His eyes shine like the most vibrant emeralds, the colors now rolling in waves.

"Mistress, you have power enough for a hundred familiars and not feel the drain. Even with those annoying geas, power leaks from your very pores. It's why we were drawn to you in the first place, and only partially why we remain."

He bumps his head onto my chin and rubs his cheek against mine.

"Do not trouble yourself with these feelings of sadness and

243

inadequacy. You are worthy of us, and we shall remain. Even if you did mate with a water horse."

I snort. "I really do love you both, and I'm so thankful that you really want to stay."

"We shall not be parted with you." Indy murmurs through a loud comforting purr.

"So, Megan mentioned that familiars lived in the underworld, or a different plane. Why did you decide to come here?"

"It can get quite boring in our realm, so when we feel a pull towards this plane we generally don't ignore it. This is my first time being in this realm, and while I do sometimes miss being in my true form, it is nice to have a true purpose as your familiar." Beretta comments quietly, it's so weird hearing words come out of her mouth when the movement of her lips are off. Like a badly dubbed foreign film.

"But you don't really do much, how is being here not boring?" I ask skeptically.

"Oh Mistress, being here with you is quite entertaining and fulfilling. The slow pace is a novelty that I very much enjoy. Yes, we don't do much, but protecting you is a worthy purpose. Plus, now that your powers are slowly unlocking, I'm sure we will have more to occupy us. Indy certainly has been busy. He got to have all the fun without me." Beretta sounds so enthusiastic that I decide, even though I don't understand their reasoning for being here, I'm not going to question it.

"Wait, that reminds me. Indy, what happened at our house?"

He growls in fury. It alarms me hearing such a fierce noise come out of what looks like a house cat.

"An intruder broke in. I'm ashamed to say that they took me by surprise at first. I have become complacent, even though I knew of the dangers that lurked around you." He sighs heavily before continuing. "I was outside, enjoying the sunshine, when I heard the noises. At first I thought they were from that old bat next door. She makes a god awful ruckus on a weekly basis, but then I heard glass breaking."

"You weren't hurt, right? Don said you weren't, but I don't know how fast you heal."

He scoffs. "Of course I wasn't hurt. My pride is a little wounded, though. I am ashamed I allowed that creature to enter your home, Mistress. I am also furious with myself that it escaped me."

"What got in?"

"A foul creature; it had a tainted soul. I was so close to devouring it, but it escaped me." His fur stands on end as he recaps what happened.

"So they weren't human?"

He nods. "No, or at least not entirely. They were completely covered, but their scent was full of decay. Like a demon possessing its host, but not quite."

Beretta hums. "I wish I had been there, I would have loved to devour them." She giggles, and I'm torn between finding it adorable and downright terrifying.

"Well, I'm just glad you are safe, Indy. That is really all I care about."

He grumbles as I stroke my hand down his back.

"You don't happen to know anything about my powers, do you?"

A deep rumble sounds from Indy.

"That is a very complicated question, Mistress. I have not encountered many of your kind in my lifetime, and the power you possess only holds small similarities. But even with our minimal knowledge, we were still able to break most of the geas surrounding you."

My eyebrows raise in surprise.

"You were the ones to break my powers free?"

They both nod.

"Yes, Mistress, though we must apologize for how long it took us. The spells were very intricate, and we couldn't risk your safety by rushing it. You might have been able to find your mate sooner if we had been able to break them faster."

Beretta looks slightly forlorn.

"I wouldn't have met Don if the spells were still present?"

Indy shakes his head.

"It is highly unlikely. The geas repelled Clan magic. I believe its intent was to protect you, but it mostly left you vulnerable."

My head is reeling. If Indy and Beretta had never come into my life would I have been alone forever? The thought of never meeting Don, or any of the others, leaves my stomach in knots. Now all I want to do is curl up and not think about the what ifs.

"Would it be weird if we cuddled in the bed like we always do?" I ask quietly, hoping that even though they are not actual animals, but sentient beings, they will still continue to indulge in my need to cuddle them.

Beretta wags her tail and gives my hand another lick before leaping on the bed. A smile filled with joy and relief spreads across my face, and I look down at Indy, still on my lap.

"What do you say, big guy, can we still cuddle?"

"Only for you, Mistress."

I stroke my hand down his back, and even though he technically isn't a cat, he still arches his back in enjoyment. Before he can hop down, I scoop him up in my arms and carry him to the bed, not wanting to let go for a minute. Indy was my first true love, and it brings me so much comfort that he knows how much I really do care for him. How much I care for them both.

As I lay down and cuddle up to my two familiars, I take the time to truly thank the Goddess for bringing them into my life. I don't know who this Goddess is, but in the short time that I have known of her existence, I have been blessed with things I never thought were possible for me. So I thank her, and I will keep thanking her for the blessings that I have been given.

I breathe in a shuddering breath. My emotions are still all over the place. My body curls around them both out of habit, extremely grateful that I can still have these moments with them. Even if at first it was because of my best friend wanting to ensure I was protected, and that they were drawn to whatever power I supposedly possess. It's a relief that comforts my very soul to know that they stayed because they truly care for me. I know how precious that truly is.

Sensing my deep thoughts, like he always seems to do, Indy nudges my chin.

"Rest. You are still weary from your heat, and I'm doubting your mate's ability to truly care for you."

"Yes, but at least her mate is actually tolerable. The other males she subjected us to were just dreadful." Beretta mutters haughtily.

I groan. "Oh god, now I'm really embarrassed. Wait, did you both watch me when I brought dates over?"

Beretta eyes me over her shoulder, "Do you really want us to tell you that?"

Nope, no I did not.

I smother my face into Beretta's neck and mumble curses. Indy takes that as the conversation is over and sprawls himself on top of me, beginning to purr loudly, soothing me into a deep, dreamless sleep.

DONOVAN

I rub at my tired eyes, gripping the steering wheel a little tighter to keep the truck steady. It was an unnaturally long shift, and I'm absolutely certain it has to do with being away from Kinley. *Goddess, I miss her.* The mating frenzy hasn't been over long, but our bond is an anchor pulling me home.

My phone flashes with a text alert and I grab it out of the cup holder, hoping it's her. I'm only slightly disappointed when my mom's name pops up on the screen. I've been putting off talking to her and I have no good reason to not answer. Swiping open my phone, I call; this is not something I should be texting, and sometimes even I need to just talk to my mom. The ring tone is loud over my truck's speakers but it doesn't take her long to answer.

"Well, this is a nice surprise."

There is just something about hearing her voice that eases some of my lingering tension, and the tight grip I had on the steering wheel loosens.

"Hey Momma…You got a minute?"

Her sweet laugh rings in my ear, "I always have a minute for you, sweetheart. Does this have anything to do with the rumors that have been flitting about the Clan?"

I push out a deep breath and figure out how best to put into words what I'm feeling. I can only imagine what she has been hearing, and I love her even more for not badgering me to talk these last few weeks. "Yeah, a lot has happened since we talked last." I rub a hand on the back of my neck as I steer my truck one-handed into a mostly empty lot.

"Don, sweetheart, are you ok?"

"I'm ok, I promise. Momma…" I rub my clammy palms onto my pant legs, steadying myself as I find the right words. "Momma, I found her."

"Sweetheart, what do you mean? Who did you find?"

I want to speak, but I have to clear my throat first. *Goddess, I'm getting all choked up.* "My mate. Momma, I found my mate. A real mate with a soul bond "

Her gasp is louder than I was expecting "Donovan Hayes! When did this happen? Who is she? Do we know her?" The shrillness of her voice causes me to flinch.

She probably would have rattled off a plethora of questions if I didn't stop her. "Momma…Mom! Take a breath, before you pass out and Dad tears into my hide."

"I'm calm…" I can just imagine her smoothing down her clothes as she reels herself back in. "Please continue, sweetheart."

"Her name is Kinley, and she's no one you or Dad knows. But Mom… she's amazing, and so fucking beautiful."

"Donovan! Language!" She scolds loudly.

I put my hand over my mouth to smother my laughter. She always was a stickler for no cussing.

"I'm sorry Momma, but she's perfect. Goddess, you're going to love her. I love her."

A happy squeal sneaks out before she reins it back in again. "Don, you love her?"

I rub my chest as the warmth seeps in just thinking about how much

I love her. Our bond tingles, almost as if she knows I'm thinking about her. I'm sure I have a sappy smile on my face.

"More than anything, Goddess I love her."

There is a long pause and I check to make sure she's still connected. "Momma?"

"I'm still here." Her voice is thick with tears. *Shit, I didn't want to make her cry.* "My baby is in love"

I can't help but sigh and shake my head. "Momma, Rowan is the baby."

"Oh hush your mouth, you boys are both my babies. It doesn't matter how old you are or what order you came into this world."

"Whatever you say, Momma."

"Oh, Don!" There is a faint sniffle from her end before she continues, "A true mate…the Goddess has blessed you both." Her voice is still thick with emotion, "And now I have a daughter! You know I love you boys more than life itself, but you and your brother were a handful and a half. Sweetheart, I'm so happy for you! I can't wait to tell your father!"

I grin widely just thinking about Kinley meeting my Mom; she's not going to know what hit her. My mom will wrap her up so tight and make her feel so loved, just like she's always done for us. I can't fucking wait. Kinley deserves to know what a mother's love truly is; she deserves the world.

"Thank you, that means everything to me."

"Does your grandmother know? She will be beside herself with joy, I just know it. A mate!"

At the mention of my grandmother I still. *Should I tell her? She usually tries her best to stay out of Council business.*

"Grandma knows, we've been asking her and Aunt Willow for help. Kinley has no history within a Clan that she knows of, and we haven't had much luck getting any new information. But they either don't know, or they won't tell us, and they keep insisting they need to see Kinley in person."

"They won't tell you?"

"No, it's been a real pain in the ass."

"Don! Language!"

This time I can't help the chuckle that slips past. "Sorry, Momma."

I can just make out her quiet huff, and her mumbling about how she raised me better.

"Wait....Don? Does Kinley not know what she is? Sweetheart! Does she know you are mates?"

"Yes, Momma, she knows. It was quite a shock for her, and it took all of us to convince her we weren't crazy. That wasn't a fun moment, but she's so strong and has taken everything in stride. I can't believe she's real sometimes." My voice wavers and I have to stop. I clench my hands to stop them from trembling. *I can't lose her.*

"Don, what's the matter? You sound like you have the whole world on your shoulders."

I rub my face, I feel even more drained than I did a moment ago.

"She's been through so much, I honestly don't know how she's gotten so far without anyone but her friend. There are so many unanswered questions, and I can only assume this is just the beginning. How am I supposed to protect her from what I don't even know she will face? I'm terrified I'll lose her. I'm afraid that I won't be enough to help her through what comes next."

"Donovan, the moment I laid my eyes on you I knew you were destined for more than what our Clan could provide, and when you were thirteen and the Kelpie claimed you, I saw in your eyes the hunger for a path that was not easily taken. You have never strayed from the difficult, and you won't now. Sweetheart, you were meant to find Kinley. She's your destiny. You were molded to be everything she needs. You won't fail her."

The breath I didn't know I was holding whooshes out of me, and just like that my mom manages to do what I can't, dissipate the doubt. It doesn't matter how old I get, she always seems to know what to say. *I should have called her sooner.* My mom makes me promise to bring Kinley to see them soon before I'm allowed to hang up. It's been too long since I've seen my parents and my brother, and I should make more of an effort. Being with Kinley has made me appreciate my family even more .

As soon as I pull into Brent's driveway, I go in search of my mate.

She hasn't responded to a few of my texts, but when I run into Cam he mentions that she's probably napping. I enter our room quietly and smile at the sight that greets me.

Kinley has her arms wrapped around Beretta, her face buried into her furry neck, and Indy is sprawled on top of them both. She looks so peaceful which is a look that I haven't seen too much of since she came into my life. I need to make sure that happens more often.

I'm about to turn and leave them to their nap when Indy's raspy voice halts me in my tracks. Familiars aren't common in Clan communities; they tend to bond with witches over us. I'm not sure of the protocol for interacting with them, but the fact that he is communicating with me now leads me to believe that Kinley has talked with them about knowing what they are.

"Water horse, I will only say this once. You will guard my mistress's heart and soul with your very life. As long as you do that, I won't eat your heart and burn your entrails."

I turn back toward the familiar, my eyes gleaming with my beast's presence. He does not care much for being called a "water horse".

"That, you won't need to worry about, familiar. The same can be said to you. Now that my mate knows what you are, if you abandon her, me and my Clan will hunt you down and feast on your carcasses before sending you back to the Underworld."

Indy perks his ears before giving me a very feline grin.

"Good, then we understand each other. My mistress is precious to us. I sensed the deep well of power in her the moment I laid eyes on her, and when I knew that I alone could not ensure her safety I called upon Berethial to aid me."

I glance down at the dog lying in Kinley's arms and notice that she too is eyeing me, assessing my worthiness, no doubt.

"Is that your true name? Berethial?"

"Yes, but I prefer the name my mistress gifted me with."

I nod, Beretta is definitely easier to say, and then ask Indy.

"Do you prefer the name Kinley gave you as well?"

Indy nods. "Yes, my true name is foreign to your tongue, and I'd rather you not butcher it with your attempts. Indy suits me just fine. I know how much it means to her. She spent a considerable amount of time coming up with our names, taking such care to ensure the names fit us just right. Little did she know how similar they were to our true names."

I smile down at my mate. I can imagine her making a list and taking the time to go over each option until she found the right fit.

"She is truly one of a kind; a pure soul. I just wish I knew what I could do to help her unblock her powers and memories. Do either of you know how to do that?"

Beretta responds quietly so as not to wake Kinley.

"We have searched for that knowledge and have come up mostly empty. We managed a few things without the necessary knowledge. But we do not have access to a Clan council like you do. Clan magic, especially female clan magic, is a coveted and secret thing, as I'm sure you are aware. Whatever or whoever put these geas on our Mistress did so a very long time ago, long before we came into her life. But thanks to us, parts of the geas will dissipate over time. How do you think she came to you and you to her? That was not mere luck; it was meant to happen."

My mouth parts, but I find myself at a loss for words. Meeting her had been too much of a coincidence, and now I know that it was truly meant to be.

"Then I am truly grateful for what you have done. I couldn't imagine what my life would be like without her, and it has only been a short time. I am also glad that she had you both. I can feel the echo of the loneliness that she experienced when she was younger, and I'm sure you both had a hand in banishing it from her."

The familiars both nod their heads in agreement.

"I have a few more things to take care of. Do you mind waking her in an hour or so for dinner? I don't want her to get hungry."

I'm just turning to go to the door when Indy speaks one last time.

"It's good that you can share her, because you might have to share her with more than just us." His eyes glow a vibrant green and his tail twitches with humor.

A soft rumble vibrates my chest. *What is that supposed to mean?*

But before I make the poor decision in getting into a verbal tussle with a familiar, I walk out of the bedroom door and shut it behind me quietly.

I keep thinking about what the cat said. *Is he talking about sharing her with another mate?* I already had suspicions that my Clan brother's are interested in Kinley, and one in particular needs to have a talk with me, according to the vague as fuck text he sent me earlier.

Is this what he wanted to talk to me about? I mean it makes sense, and it's stupid for me to think that as powerful as Kinley is turning out to be, that I would be her only one. That thought riles my beast. The cat has gotten under our skin, and now he's thinking we might have to share her with another male. He is begging to be let out.

As I walk down the hallway to Brent's office, I work to calm myself. I don't need to go trashing Brent's house by stomping around in here with my hooves. This is my Clan brother, and if Brent wants to talk about what I'm beginning to guess, then it isn't really up to me. It's up to Kinley. *Will she even want that?*

CHAPTER 26

KINLEY

I'm going stir crazy being in this house with nothing to do, and I'm running out of clothes. Yes, technically I could do laundry now that I actually know where the laundry room is in the house, but I want to get out. No, I *need* to get out.

I'm almost thirty years old. I'm perfectly capable of going and doing things for myself. It will be simple. I'm just going to grab some things from my house, and have a little alone time. Plus, it's really past time for me to face the damage that the intruder did to my house, even though Camden has assured me that it has all been repaired and cleaned up.

I need to reclaim my independence, or at least try to. I'm not a damsel in distress, and I'm getting tired of being sequestered away for my safety.

Yes, I relished the protective nature of my mate in the beginning, and I still do. It is ridiculously hot when he gets all protective and dominant. But at the end of the day, I'm used to being on my own, and not asking for permission to do what I want.

So I'm going out. I'm going to get dressed in something other than sweats or pajamas and get out of this house. I have already accomplished the getting dressed part, so the next step is leaving the house. Of course, I then realize I don't know where my car keys are. Sighing and grumbling to myself, I go off to find Brent. Surely he will know where my missing keys are.

Well, shoot.

I can't find him, or anyone for that matter. Of course, when I actually need someone they are nowhere to be found. I know Don and Aiden have gone to work, but I didn't think they had all left. *Had they?*

I don't even see Camden.

What the hell, did they leave me here and not say anything? Fine, I'll use one of their cars.

I probably should text Don and ask, but he is at work and I haven't gotten around to getting the other guy's numbers. It hasn't really come up. They are always around, except, of course, for now.

My mind is made up. I'm just going to borrow a car. I'm a good driver.

I walk through the house back to the garage where I know Brent keeps a few vehicles. I have to admit I'm getting a little excited. I have been eyeing one in particular. I can't wait to drive that baby.

With the flip of the light switch, I walk down the few steps into the large four car garage. Two cars and a motorcycle are still parked. *They really did leave me here alone, what the hell.*

Brent's SUV that he normally drives is missing, which solidifies my decision to borrow one of his other cars. With the keys hanging in plain sight, I snatch the ones to the sleek, blacked out BMW that I have secretly been drooling over.

With the push of a button, I'm seated in the plush leather driver's seat. I inhale deeply, closing my eyes for a moment as I take in the luxurious smells. Brent's scent permeates the car's interior, and I can't deny that his scent does something to me. It's incredibly potent, and sitting in his sleek sports car, I'm finally brave enough to admit to myself that I like his scent just as much as I like Don's. *What does that even mean?*

Adjusting the seat and the mirrors, I smirk to myself because I just know that will irritate him. I start the car, reveling in the growl of the engine. A thrill shoots through me, and a wide grin spreads across my face. The garage door rolls up, and I take off down the driveway. I'm going to have fun today.

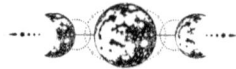

Cruising around town in Brent's car gives me so much joy. A little bit of that joy comes from stealing his car, and I'm big enough to admit that. No one has called my phone wondering where I am, so I assume that they don't even know I left. I grin mischievously.

I wonder if I can make it back without anyone figuring it out.

I get a few texts from Don asking how I'm doing, and I just happen to not mention what I'm actually getting up to. I only feel a little guilty. There is just something about driving a powerful expensive car that puts oneself in a great mood. I can definitely see why Brent has this car, even though I don't think he drives it often. But it also makes me wonder just how much money he has, and what he actually does for work.

I don't go to my house right away. Instead, I spend the next few hours doing a little shopping, making sure to stop and grab a much needed latte, and then I drive by my house to grab a few things that I have been missing.

I mentally prepare myself to expect the house to be trashed, but when I pull into the driveway nothing looks out of place.

Without having my keys, I have to climb over the side gate, and walk around to the back door. Lifting the garden gnome that sits next to the door mat, I grab my spare house key. *Good thing the intruder didn't find this.*

"Well, here goes nothing."

Unlocking the back door and replacing the key, I walk into my house.

I haven't been here in over two weeks, and it feels weird. The house has been cleaned, but I notice immediately that some of my furniture is missing. My bottom lip quivers slightly. It had taken a lot of careful consideration and time to get all of the items in my house.

I shake myself out of my funk, not wanting to get upset over furniture that can easily be replaced. That's if I even want to replace anything. The most important things to me are already safe at Brent's.

Walking through to my bedroom, I notice that even more of the furniture is missing, and I'm starting to think that this trip has been a waste of time. The clothes that had been left are no longer present. *Why hadn't I even asked anyone what kind of damage was done to my house?* I should have asked, but I had been too relieved just knowing that Indy was fine. I hadn't cared in that moment; it just hadn't seemed important.

Realizing there is nothing for me to grab pisses me off. My fists clench and a growl bubbles up and out of my throat. This was my home! Someone had come in and wrecked it! I want to throw something, but there isn't anything for me to throw. That realization makes the anger slowly ebb. Taking in some deep breaths, I try to calm myself. It's no use dwelling on what I can't change.

I exit my bedroom as my phone begins to vibrate in my pocket. Pulling it out, I see it is Don and quickly accept the call.

"Hi, babe."

"Kinley, what are you doing right now?" His careful tone immediately puts me on edge.

"Why?"

"Baby…why did I get a notification that you are in your house?"

Looking around suspiciously, I answer.

"Seriously, Don, did you have cameras installed in my house?"

"Baby, we told you we installed a security system."

"Don…I just walked in. There is no security system."

"Yes, there is, but that is beside the point. How did you get there? Are you by yourself?"

"Why does it matter, Don? It's my house, and besides, you all left me at Brent's by myself."

My irritation grows further, hearing his next response.

"Baby, you could have messaged or called me."

"Don…I love you, but I'm a grown ass woman that doesn't need permission to leave the house and run errands for myself."

Muffled curses answer me before he responds more clearly.

"Kinley, I absolutely know that, and I wouldn't even bring it up if you didn't have someone gunning for you who knows where you live."

Pinching the bridge of my nose, I take in a deep breath to calm my frustration.

"Well, I'm not going to be here for much longer. Had I known that there wasn't anything salvageable, I wouldn't have bothered coming here to get some of my stuff." Hearing him getting ready to say something, I quickly continue, cutting him off. "And before you say anything, I didn't ask one of you because I needed to get out of the house. And just so you know where I'm going next, I'm going to get a few things to make for dinner tonight and then go back to Brent's."

A deep exhale of breath answers me.

"Ok, be safe, call me if you need anything. Even if it's something small…please."

Still not mentioning that I have Brent's car, I agree that I will and end the call. Locking up my house, I quickly get back into Brent's car and drive over to the grocery store. Trying not to let the conversation with Don irritate me further, I concentrate on making a grocery list in my head of the food I will need to make dinner.

Making it to the store, I carefully park in a spot far away from other cars, not wanting to add getting the car scratched to my list of transgressions for the day. Though thinking of Brent's expression when he realizes I took his car does cheer me up a little. *Why does it give me so much pleasure irritating him?* I shrug and grab a cart. I'm not going to worry about that.

I don't know what it is about grocery shopping, but it just has a way of relaxing me. The only thing that could have made it better is if I had my ear buds and could listen to an audiobook while I did it. I wander the aisles, occasionally grabbing something I need, but I'm in no hurry to get back.

All checked out with a cart full of groceries, I push the cart out to the waiting BMW. With the parking lot almost empty it's easy to spot the lone black sports car, but as I draw closer a pit in my stomach begins to form. I quickly realize something is very, very wrong. Glass litters the ground all around the car, and it takes a few moments for my brain to process what I'm looking at.

258

The car's windows and windshield have been thoroughly smashed, the supple black leather upholstery has been shredded, and that is just the tip of the iceberg. Spray painted in red, garishly written along the side of the car is the word "WHORE". And splayed out on the hood is the worst thing of all, a dead white cat is nailed down to the hood, splayed out and cruelly mutilated. A cat that looks eerily similar to Indy.

I stare transfixed at the gruesome scene, and a numbness sweeps through my entire being. But I'm thankful for the emptiness, because it shields me from the panic and despair that has become all too familiar these past few months. Through the quiet, I can think. I know I need to get help, so I reach into my pocket and dial Don. He answers on the second ring, his deep voice pushing some of the numbness back, leaving me vulnerable.

"Hey baby, did you need something?"

Keeping my voice as calm as possible, and trying as best I can to mute our bond, I ask for him to text me Brent's number. I know he senses the turmoil circulating in our mate bond, I can't completely shut it down.

"What's wrong, Kinley?"

"Um, there is something wrong with his car, and I need to ask him a question. So can you please send me his number."

"Shit, Kinley, what car did you take?"

"The BMW, now can I get his number?"

I hear him chuckle, and mutter something about the m6 finally getting out of the garage, but he lets me know he will send it. Murmuring that I love him, I quickly end the call before I lose all restraint I have on my emotions. As soon as the text comes through, I call Brent.

"Well, hello, princess, what can I do for you?"

My breath wavers, and my throat closes in on itself as I try to form the words. Hearing my choked response gets him dropping all traces of humor. "Kinley, what's wrong?"

"Brent...I-I need..." I can't form the words, as I continue to stare at the horrifying scene, praying no one else comes up to witness this.

"Where are you, Kinley?"

"G-g-grocery store."

Brent curses, "Which car Kinley?"

"B-b-bmmm-w."

"Fuck! I'm on my way. Are you hurt?"

I so badly want to answer him, but I can't find the words, and it isn't until I hear his snarl over the phone that I'm spurned into responding. "No…just the cat."

"What cat, Kinley?"

I zone out, helpless to bring my eyes away from staring into those dead sightless eyes of the poor creature, I can't get it out of my mind that it could be Indy. As if in a trance I say. "We need to bury it; it didn't deserve this."

I hear Brent respond, but his words don't register. I have to bring that innocent being some semblance of peace; there is something in me urging me to lay it to rest. I'm about to set the phone down, when I pick up on Don's name being mentioned. "What?"

"Goddess, Kinley, does Don know?"

"Does Don know?" My voice is so monotone.

"Yes, princess, does Don know where you are? What has happened?"

His words are confusing me.

"I'm not sure. Brent, I need to take care of the cat, no one needs to see it like this."

My voice trails off as I focus back on the gory scene on the hood of the car. The pooling blood contrasts brightly against the black paint of the car, and I can't seem to make myself look away.

"Shit, Kinley, you better not hang up the phone."

Setting the phone down on the shopping cart, I walk up to the once beautiful car, and reach out to try and gently remove the small body. Quietly murmuring to myself that I need to help it, I carefully work to remove each nail. So focused on my task, I'm completely oblivious to the high pitched wails of a police siren. Only when strong, gentle hands grip my shoulders does my focus shift. The beginnings of a snarl quickly die in my throat when no sense of additional threat comes from the figure holding me. Cradling the lifeless cat in my arms, I turn around to face the owner of the hands that is touching me so gently.

"Aw shit" a deep voice exclaims as they take in the sight of what I'm cradling, blood covering my hands and arms. A deep voice I recognize. Through the haze of pain and fury, my mind begins to register that Aiden is standing in front of me, gently holding onto my shoulders. I stare deep into his eyes, letting him see the emotions that swirl in mine.

"I couldn't leave it like that. How could they? What gives them the right to do this?"

Too many emotions cross Aiden's face, and I don't even attempt to decipher them. "When does it stop, Aiden?"

"I don't know, Kinley; I really don't know."

Looking down at the frail creature I'm cradling, I whisper sadly. "Can you help me?

"Yes, hun, I can."

Gently, he leads me to the back of his work issued car. Popping the trunk, he takes out a blanket and carefully takes the cat out of my arms, wrapping it up before placing it in the backseat.

"Kinley, why don't you have a seat in my car, and I'll get you cleaned up a little, ok?"

"Ok."

My voice is an aching whisper that I almost don't even recognize.

With medical grade disinfectant wipes, he gently cleans off the blood on my hands and arms. He doesn't break the silence between us, and for that, I'm grateful.

He is almost finished when quick, heavy footsteps sound behind him. My beast, who prowls in the back of my mind, instantly knows who it is, the scent and the cadence of their steps a dead give away. Brent walks into my line of sight followed quickly by Don. They both stare down at me and all I can do is stare back. No words come to me; I just stare, taking in their tense postures and the rage that threatens to boil out of them. My mate and my friend, both my protectors, but they couldn't protect me from this.

I wish I knew what to say. I'm so tired of feeling like this. I hate feeling scared, angry, and numb.

Don is the first to talk. "Is she hurt, Aiden?" They can smell the blood that still remains on me.

"No, it's not her blood," Aiden reassures him.

My eyes continue to look from Don to Brent. I have to say something. Swallowing the lump in my throat, I manage to croak out,"I'm sorry; it was selfish of me. I should have never left the house."

My lip quivers, and I look directly at Brent next.

"I shouldn't have taken your car. I'm so sorry, Brent."

His face is unreadable. He doesn't speak, he just stares back, looking me over thoroughly to reassure himself that I'm not physically hurt. I wait for him to speak, but after a moment he nods his head, as if accepting my words, and then walks off in the direction of his car. His reaction makes me sick, and I can't help but think that I deserve this treatment from him. Forgiveness might be too much to ask for.

Seeing that exchange, Don attempts to go after Brent, but Aiden pulls him to the side. I can't hear what they are saying, and I don't even try. My heart is so heavy, so I do the only thing I can do at that moment, because I can't keep feeling like a complete failure. I lean my head back on the headrest and close my eyes. Shutting out the world for just a moment, so I can try and put some of the pieces back together.

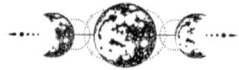

Camden arrives at some point, and all four of them stand in front of Aiden's car blocking my view. I'm not sure how long I close my eyes for, but some of the haze lifts from my mind.

Any curious onlookers are quickly shooed away. It's a crime scene after all.

I notice that someone has collected the groceries from the cart I abandoned. I also vaguely wonder if someone grabbed my phone. A tow truck arrives at some point, and the operator gets busy loading up the BMW. The four powerful men continue to look on. Don's hand is clasped to Brent's shoulder. Aiden and Camden rest on the hood of the car I currently sit in.

I feel so far away from them, so helpless and alone. I don't belong here. They are good men. I keep bringing them into my messes. My mind continues to spiral down, down into a dark sad place, but I don't resist, even as my beast snarls at me.

*I'm so stupid. They are trying to keep me safe, and what do I do...
steal a ridiculously expensive car and joy ride around. I need to get out
of here, go back where it is safe and never leave. Then maybe no one
else will get hurt because of me. I'm such a shitty mate, such a shitty
person.*

As if he hears that last bit, Don whirls around, staring at me through
the windshield. My eyes refuse to meet his, I can only take in his heaving
chest. I don't even know if I'm blocking him or not. For all I know, I'm
blasting my thoughts and emotions at him.

I'm just too ashamed, and I don't know how to stop myself. I need
help, but do I even deserve it?

A gentle whisper caresses my mind, but I push it away.

Fuck...I'm fucking this all up.

My eyes meet his for the briefest moment, just long enough to see
the pained look that crosses his face. But then the pain melts away and
he turns to speak to Aiden, who gets up off the car and walks around to
the driver's side.

Oh god. Oh god, no, Please don't let him turn away from me.

My panicked words suddenly stop as I feel him, my mate, push past
the block I put up in my mind. His stern, deep voice soothing some of
the panic.

*That's enough, Kinley, I can't let you berate yourself anymore. This is
not your fault, none of this is your fucking fault. Aiden is going to take
you home to Brent's and we will all meet you there once we are through
here. I love you so damned much, Kinley, do you hear me?*

Yes.

I see him nod, and for the first time since he arrived, I truly let myself
see him fully. I see his strength, I see his desire to protect me, even from
myself. He is truly everything I need.

Aiden getting into the car breaks our eye contact. Aiden looks me
over before he quickly starts the car and drives us away from that scene
of hate and despair. The silence is almost deafening, but I endure it
because it's what I need. Because deep in that silence, I find the answers
spoken to me in a calm and assertive voice. I open myself up to it. I

don't question why it speaks to me, I just listen to the words that give me what I desperately need. It pries open that inner strength that I yearn for and the knowledge to accomplish what I must do next.

CHAPTER 27

KINLEY

As Aiden pulls up to the house, I waste no time getting out. I have an important task that can't wait. Quickly opening the back door, I lift the bundle gently from the floor board. I don't pause. I just begin walking towards the back of the house so focused on my task, I don't even stop when Aiden calls after me. The voice is calling for me, guiding me, to what only I can do.

Come, dear heart, I will show you what must be done.

Reaching the backyard, I am met by my familiars. They are waiting for me, just like I knew they would be, my silent sentinels. The whispers in my mind tell me that with their help I can begin to ease the suffering and right a small part of the wrong that has been done.

Indy and Beretta stare deeply into my eyes, into my very soul. With a nod of their heads they turn and lead me deep into the trees. As we pass through the deep shadows of the surrounding vegetation, my familiars' bodies transform from my beloved pets into their true forms.

Dark shadows weave around each of them. They are both hauntingly beautiful.

Indy, now more than double in size, stands as tall as my hip. His white fur is gone; he is now black as the deepest depths of a shadow. His eyes glow an eerie milky white, and in the center of his forehead between his upright ears is the mark of a crescent moon, glowing as brightly as his pale orbs.

Beretta almost towers over me, and as she turns her head to look at me, a skulled face with swirls and runes carved in intricate detail stares back at me. Anyone would have been terrified, but I have nothing to fear from her. I know this beast, know that I'm utterly safe in her presence. Beretta's coat is an inky black, and fluid-like shadows drip from her skin. Deep in the eye sockets of her skull are glowing orbs of the most hypnotizing red.

With a hand now covered in blood again, I reach out to tenderly caress her bone snout leaving behind a smear of crimson. Her unnaturally long tongue snakes out of her open maw, licking off the blood, savoring the offering.

I glide silently through the dark forest with them at my sides, until we reach an opening within the trees, and we all come to a synchronized stop. I take in the clearing that seems so welcoming, as if it formed just for us.

Indy steps away from my side into the center, then turns to face me.
Follow the Guardian's lead, dear heart. I will aid you for the rest.

That hauntingly beautiful voice whispers deep in my mind. I don't even question it; I just do what they ask of me.

"Mistress, place the fallen at my feet."

Carefully, I stride forward, kneeling in front of Indy as I gently lay the bundle at his feet. I gingerly unwrap the blanket, uncovering the innocent creature. With a gentle hand, I stroke the cat's fur, and a sorrowful hum begins from deep within me.

Build it, let the song free, dear heart. I am with you.

A flood of power washes over me, and I give myself over to it. With the guidance of my familiars and that ethereal voice, I unleash my power from deep within myself. I begin to cleanse the creature's soul of all the pain and grief from their life cut short.

The power bubbles up and up until what bursts from me is a heartbreaking melody. The song that spills from my lips is ancient and powerful, and I willingly give myself over to it.

As the song builds within me, my familiars' shadows swirl around me, caressing my skin as if asking permission to join. Arms outstretched wide, I eagerly welcome the shadows of my familiars into my body, welcoming the strength they offer. Welcoming the transformation that sweeps through me.

The song is hauntingly beautiful, my emotions rising with each note. A single tear glides down my cheek, glimmering in the dark of the woods. The tear slows its descent on my skin as that ethereal voice quietly calls to me again, just loud enough to be heard over my song.

Place the tear on the creature, Chosen. Let your tears heal its soul.

With a claw-tipped hand, I brush the tear onto the tip of one lethal claw, letting it slide down the length. The single tear glows faintly, and as it leaves my claw, the glow strengthens as it draws nearer to the once white fur.

Still my song continues, not once faltering as a deep baying howl of my hound joins me along with the mournful yowl of my feline.

The clearing bursts with light. My song, the ancient song of my ancestors, harmonizes with the song of my familiars. It grows and grows, echoing into the trees, echoing into the very souls of any being that is near.

As the song draws to a close and the light begins to fade, a sense of peace and hope fills me. My eyes are drawn to the once bloody bundle, now pristine, the body now whole but still unmoving. And as the last note fades away, a tiny ball of light rises from the small body. It hovers and bobs in front of me, as if in greeting, before shooting up into the night sky.

With a wave of Indy's paw, the remains fade from existence, but the ground is no longer barren. What now grows beneath, is a single deep red dianthus.

For a brief moment I feel whole. *Is this how I'm meant to feel? Is this what I have been missing?*

But before I can fully grasp what that power truly feels like, it fades back into the depths, where it becomes untouchable again. I want to yell my frustration, but I lack the energy. I sigh, and bring my attention back to my familiars, and what we have accomplished together.

Beretta leans down and sniffs the flower, and as if she gleans something from it she looks to Indy for confirmation. A nod so small I almost miss it crosses between them before they turn back to me. Beretta straightens to her full height.

"Come, it is late and you have expended more power than you should have. We will lead you back to your mates."

I nod because she is right, I am exhausted, but then I pause, registering that very last part.

"I have one mate, Beretta, and I'm not even sure he's going to want to see me. I really messed up." My head drops in shame.

Beretta and Indy scoff at that, not acknowledging what they deem as me being stupid. Not saying another word, they nudge me forward and lead me back through the dark woods. We walk for a lot longer than I realize, and it's so quiet. A large shadow crosses our path from overhead, making me freeze in my tracks.

"What is that?" I whisper nervously, my voice sounding so small.

Indy swivels his large ears before nudging me forward again.

"It's just the big bird, being nosey."

"What big bird?" I hiss. *They really need to work on their communication skills.*

Beretta sighs in exasperation. "She hasn't seen that one shift; she doesn't know who you're talking about."

"The golden haired one…I can't be bothered learning their names."

What the fuck? "Cam…is a big bird?"

Indy only responds with a tail flick. I'm too tired to unpack that, so I decide to put a pin in that one for later, because as we near the edge of the trees, the energy shifts. My guard instantly goes up, the hairs on the back of my neck rise. Grunts and growls of large animals meet my ears, coming just beyond the tree line.

"Don't be frightened, Mistress. If they threaten you, we will feast on their entrails." Beretta says a little too cheerfully.

What the hell?

They keep me moving forward, and as the trees thin further, my attention is immediately drawn to the three enormous beasts that prowl the back lawn, watching, and waiting for me.

CHAPTER 28

KINLEY

I watch, completely captivated by my mate's anxious pacing, his Kelpie form magnificent in the moonlight, but his agitated movements worry me.

Is he worried...or is he angry?

That's when I realize I can't sense him, which sends my mind reeling.

Did I block him out completely?

But then I look closer at all three of the powerful beasts. The prowling wolf and the large saber-toothed cat sitting silently, the only thing giving him away that he is real, is the slight twitch of his tail. None of them are looking my way, as if none of them can sense me, smell me, hear me.

"Can they not sense me?" I ask my familiars, worried that something else has happened.

Indy chuckles. "No, Mistress. I put up a ward so those busy bodies wouldn't interrupt us performing that delicate ritual. But they will the moment you step out of the tree line."

Now understanding why they are all so agitated, I quickly step out from the shadows, breaking the ward and hoping that they aren't too mad. Along with the ward breaking comes the weight of the shame I thought I shed. I walk quietly out of the woods, my shoulders sagging and my head drooping.

Indy swats at my thigh, making me stumble slightly.

"Hold your head high. You have nothing to be ashamed of. They are lucky to be in your presence. You do not cower before them."

I look at him, seeing the confidence and pride he has for me. Beretta nudges me gently, and my shoulders straighten. My head tilts up in time to see the startled gazes that focus on me from across the lawn. All their movements still, taking in the sight of me and my familiars.

With their gazes on me, the last echo of that ethereal power recedes from my body. I feel utterly exposed standing beside my guardians, both having chosen to remain in their true forms.

A large dark shadow passes overhead, a whisper of wings on the wind brushes my ears as a huge eagle lands softly on the ground next to the wolf I know is Aiden. And then there are four.

As if an invisible tether snaps, Don barrels towards me, his four legs eating up the distance between us. I stand my ground, confident in the fact he won't trample over me. Our bond unfurls the closer he gets to me.

Hot steam snorts out of his enlarged nostrils. His wide mouth gapes open, showing off his sharp teeth, and still I don't move. He skids to a stop, his front four-toed feet digging into the ground as his hind hooves slide along the slick grass.

"Where have you been, mate?" His voice is incredibly deep and powerful in this form.

Holy shit he spoke out loud.

I'm so in awe of his deadly beauty, but I find the words that he needs to hear.

"I was cleansing the fallen's soul. I had to do it before it was lost to the darkness." My voice is quiet but calm.

The Kelpie's head dips, further assessing every part of me, deeply inhaling my scent. His long pointed tongue snakes out of his wide mouth, licking up the length of my neck, tasting the magic still lingering on my skin. I shiver at his touch, my heart beginning to race, not from fear, but from desire. "I heard your song—we all did—but I couldn't get to you."

A rumbling snarl breaks through before he continues. "My mate, my beautiful mate. I couldn't reach you, and it enraged me."

I can't stand still any longer. I need to touch him, feel him. My hands creep up the smooth silky coat of his wide muscled chest, trailing them up the sides of his massive curved neck. His muscles ripple in my hands' wake.

"I'm sorry for worrying you."

My voice comes out breathy with a slight waver.

"Are you angry with me?"

A frustrated snort is all he gets out before Brent's dark growl answers me instead.

"Are we angry, princess?"

A snarl rumbles through the air between them, and suddenly the feeling of being prey creeps up my spine.

"Are we angry that you left the house without telling one of us? Are we angry you put yourself in unnecessary danger? Are we angry that you shut us out and let us wonder what was happening to you?"

His voice quiets to a deep, dark whisper right into my ear, making a small gasp leave my parted lips.

"If you were my mate, I would paddle your ass so hard you wouldn't be able to sit for a week."

My spine stiffens as Donovan's voice barks out. "Brent, that's enough."

But Brent isn't done, and his next words make a burning ache build deep inside me.

"In fact, I might still, just for taking my car and scaring the shit out of us." The feelings that rush through my body leave me feeling confused.

What is he doing to me? Why am I feeling this way? He's not my mate.

Donovan, having enough of Brent's threatening, snaps his teeth at him causing Brent to quickly sidestep out of the way.

"I said, that is enough."

The energy in the air shifts, and Brent's black saber-toothed beast bursts out of his body in a shift so fluid that I almost miss the change. I back up slightly, and a brush of a shadow lets me know that Indy and Beretta aren't far behind me.

This is the first time I've gotten a true look at Brent's beast, and I stare in awe at the sight of him. His beast rivals even Donovan's Kelpie in size; he's that massive. Eyes the brightest of emerald greens contrast deeply with his dark black coat, and silver stripes run down the length of his spine up to the tip of his long tufted tail. Muscles ripple under his fur. He looks soft, and a part of me wants to run my hands through his thick coat. I frown slightly at that thought.

He's not a house cat for Christ sake.

That urging, I'm beginning to realize, is my beast deep within me. I thought she had gone too deep for me to feel her, like the rest of my power, but she is still present enough for me to be aware of her. That brings a sense of calmness to my inner turmoil.

I've felt her gaining strength over these last few months, but in the presence of these men, these beasts, my inner self feels as if she will finally burst from my skin. Especially after all that power pulsed through my body earlier.

A deep snarl leaves Brent's beast, causing the hairs on the back of my neck to rise, and I brace myself for the fight that seems to be imminent between the two powerful predators. As their muscles bunch in preparation to battle, an even deeper snarl echoes through the night causing us all to pause. Having enough of their posturing, Beretta and Indy, still in their true forms, step out of the shadows. They flank me, eyes glowing, assessing for threats to me, their mistress. Don and Brent both eye the familiars, doing some assessing of their own.

"If you are quite done with your posturing nonsense, our mistress is weary and needs rest and care after the day she has had. The behavior you are lowering yourself to is distasteful. I would think you would put all this energy into finding the being that continues to taunt and threaten her and you all instead of questioning her." Indy hisses out.

Beretta growls her agreement before gently licking my cheek. I touch her skulled snout, feeling the power vibrating underneath. It's strange, I would have expected that my skull-faced hound would have hot rancid breath of something decaying, but it's pleasant. Like a comforting fall morning, warm and spiced with a hint of herbs. She nudges my hand and swipes it with her tongue as well, and I can't help the tender smile that touches the corner of my mouth.

Camden clears his throat behind Don and Brent, having shifted during the argument.

"Guys, he's right. Don, your mate is dead on her feet, and we need to get a better angle on this whole situation. This has gone beyond just us. We almost got exposed today, and I know both you and Aiden can't afford to have your positions on the force questioned with everything that has gone on. We need to reassess and possibly call in backup."

Brent and Don shift back simultaneously giving each other a nod of understanding and forgiveness. Brent turns briefly towards me, eyeing me warily. I don't like him looking at me like that.

"Don't do that again, Kinley. You scared all of us; you have to take your safety seriously. You're too important."

He doesn't wait for me to reply; he just turns on his heel and quickly strides back to the house. My heart aches at the sight of his retreating back.

I slept fitfully that night. Even wrapped in my mate's arms and being utterly exhausted, my dreams are plagued with images that I find both confusing and terrifying. I toss and turn, but every time sleep claims me, my mind is assaulted.

Chanting fills my ears, the words unknown, but I feel the urgency and desperation behind them. I keep trying to call out, but the voices don't answer. They never do; they just continue to chant. If only I could find them and ask what it all means, but my limbs are so heavy, and I never know what direction to turn.

And then there is that voice.

"My little doe...I will find you...they can't keep me from you... you're mine," It growls at me, but soon the chanting drowns the voice out, like always.

Why can't I see anything? Why can't I move?

And then the ground disappears and I'm falling, falling so fast, and there is nothing for me to grab onto. I try to scream, but no sound leaves my throat. My fall seems to go on for eternity, but I'm halted by hands reaching out and jerking me abruptly. I get pulled through a rift in space, into a void where no light or sound exists. I'm alone, all my senses deprived.

And just when I think I can't stand it any longer and that I will surely go mad, brightness assaults my eyes, and my other senses engage.

I find that I'm facing myself, but my appearance is strange.

My eyes glow from within and my clothes are so odd; it's me…but not.

"Where am I?"

The other version of myself just smiles knowingly, but says nothing.

"I don't understand what any of this means. Can you help me?"

Again my counterpart says nothing.

"Please, why am I here?"

It's no use. I never get the answers I need. Without saying a word the other turns and begins to walk away. Seeing her walk away makes my desperation climb, but before she gets too far away she turns and beckons me to follow.

I follow her endlessly through fields, forests, across a little bridge with a trickling creek below, but still we reach no apparent destination.

I don't bother calling out anymore. She remains silent and doesn't look back.

I lose sight of her as she disappears around a structure that appears out of nowhere. *No, I can't let her get away!*

I try to speed up, but my legs are now heavy and uncooperative. It takes so much time to finally make it around the structure. Fully expecting to find the weird version of myself waiting for me, I'm shocked when I am met with a new figure, cloaked in fabric that seems to shimmer and flow around them on a vacant wind. The figure reaches out a delicate feminine hand, beckoning me closer.

"Can you help me?" I ask as I approach the figure slowly. "I can't make sense of anything that is happening; I need help."

An ethereal voice, both young and old, answers from deep within the hooded cowl. "Dear heart, your journey has been long…longer than any others. None before you have faced what you have and made it before me. I only hope you continue to do so for what lies ahead."

"Why do these things keep happening to me? Why don't I remember who I am supposed to be?"

"Events occurred long before your birth into this world, setting in motion the obstacles you have been asked to face. You have done so well, even without the necessary knowledge."

"But why can't you tell me? Why does no one seem to know where I came from, or what I am?"

"Not even I can reveal that."

My head bows in defeat.

"I don't even know where I belong."

A cool gentle touch tilts my head up, and I stare mesmerizingly into the face of ultimate beauty, the face that only a goddess could possess.

"My dear Chosen, you are exactly where you are meant to be, with the ones that are meant to aid you in this journey. Stay the path, and all will be right in the end."

I try to respond, to ask anything more, but time has run out. It always runs out.

My vision dims, and my body slowly fades away. I try to fight, to remain in the presence of the woman, but I can't keep myself present. I try so hard to reach out and anchor myself to the figure, but my body no longer connects with my mind. The figure steps away, not attempting to help me stay in their presence, but just before they fade away from me completely, they say one parting comment.

"Thank you for guiding the fallen to me. They made it safely."

"Baby, wake up, you're dreaming."

Don's voice jolts me awake, breaking through the fog of my mind, pulling me back into reality. I blink blearily at him, trying to make sense of where I am and what I saw within that dream. Our eyes connect, and I see the worry written all over his face.

"Do you want to talk about it?" He asks softly.

"Can we talk about it later? I'm still so tired."

His lips gently kiss my forehead, lingering for a moment.

"Of course, baby. I will be right here when you're ready."

I don't even know if I will be able to fall back to sleep, but I don't want to dredge up the pain and confusion of everything that occurred the day before. I also don't want to try and decipher what my dreams are about.

So, I close my eyes, bring my body as close to Don's as is feasibly possible, and try to push the bad feelings away for the time being.

In the morning, when the sun is shining, I will talk. Maybe in the light of day, the events of yesterday will be a little less traumatic, and I can finally make sense of what is truly happening.

Maybe, I will tell them all what I felt and saw in those woods, in my dreams. Maybe, they will be able to help me make sense of it all. Maybe, I can trust Don and his clan brothers with a little more of my heart and soul. Maybe, I can let them in and finally accept that I'm not alone. I just need the courage to let them in. *Can I do it?*

CHAPTER 29

KINLEY

"I can't do this."

Aiden laughs at me sprawled on my ass.

"Of course you can, we just need to figure out what triggers your powers. We all feel them getting stronger, but something is holding them back."

I glare up at him as he holds his hand out to help me up off the ground. I take it, but grumble at him as he assists me.

We have been at this for more than an hour. The guys insisted that I should try and access my magic. That is a lot easier said than done apparently. Aiden is my instructor for the day, and while he is good natured about it, he still doesn't go easy on me.

We have tried meditation techniques, but the only thing that helped was being able to block some of my thoughts from Don. While pretty helpful, it isn't what we are trying to achieve. Which then led to Aiden throwing me around on mats that he and Cam dragged out from the gym.

Cam had come up with the idea. His reasoning was that I tended to show my powers during moments of stress. So, they thought it would be a good idea to make me fight them.

And by fight, it was really them putting me in holds and me trying to get out of them. I took basic self defense years ago, but they are all much stronger than I am. My rusty defense moves are no match for well-trained men.

All Aiden has accomplished is making me incredibly frustrated. Cam had been helping, but he had to leave to get some work done. So here I am, sweating my ass off, and sore as hell from not being able to dodge Aiden's strong holds.

"Maybe we should get Don and Brent out here, get you riled up in a different way." He winks at me, and I let loose a growl.

"Shut up, Aiden."

He smirks at me, wiggling his eyebrows.

"What, you wouldn't want a Don and Brent sandwich?"

My jaw drops. *What the hell is he playing at?* My eyes narrow. *He is being an ass on purpose.*

"Is this about some bet you have with Cam?"

He looks at me innocently. "Nope, no bet. Just trying to nudge things along."

"There isn't going to be any type of sandwich, you perv."

He chuckles darkly. "Never say never, Kinley."

Fine, if he wants to play like that, then I'm going to play dirty, too.

"Why don't you worry about yourself, Aiden? You know, I bet Megan would love to hear about how helpful you're being." I see him blanch and it makes me grin.

"You wouldn't," He says nervously.

"Hmmmm, I'm not sure."

"Are you two done sparring with words? I thought the wolf was supposed to be training you, Mistress, not whatever this is." Indy's dry, disdainful voice interrupts us.

We both turn to face my familiars, who have decided to become spectators to today's training sessions. I look at them sheepishly.

"Well, do you have any suggestions, oh wise and mighty Guardians?" Aiden says in a joking tone.

Indy yawns widely, obviously not amused with Aiden's tone. "You obviously don't make her feel threatened, wolf; you don't instill fear. Maybe it would be wise to call in more terrifying beasts."

Aiden frowns hard, and I laugh. Indy has a very amusing gift of insulting the guys in a roundabout way, and I find it hilarious.

"Oh, you think that is funny, do you?" Aiden's eyes gleam as he stalks towards me. His body begins to pulse with power. *Oh fuck.*

"Aiden, this isn't funny." I laugh nervously.

He growls, his body vibrates in the way they do just before they shift, and I bolt. I race towards the trees, a scream leaving my lips as his snarl bellows just behind me.

"Aiden!" I cry out, on the verge of panic.

I hear his teeth click together just behind me. *Fuck, he wouldn't hurt me, right?*

I'm running as fast as I can, and it's still not fast enough. His hot breath blasts against my neck. He's chasing me down like prey. *No, no, no, no, I'm not prey.* A deep growl rumbles in my chest, my beast finally deeming to make her presence known.

A deep, growling laugh fills my ears. Aiden hears it, too.

"Is she finally coming out to play…little mouse?"

Oh, my beast did not like him calling her that. I feel her anger spark, just as she commands me to stop running.

I leap to the side, whirling as I do, just in time to watch Aiden skid to a stop just feet away from me.

His tongue lolls out of his mouth as he pants. A wolfish grin spreads his mouth wide, showing every sharp tooth.

"What's it going to take to really get her to show herself? Hmmmm, should I leave my mark on you…stake a claim?"

"You are not worthy to claim anything." I snarl at him, my voice lanced with dominance.

His ears perk forward. He hears her pushing towards the surface, so he pushes back.

"What if I bit down on that pretty little neck of yours? It's not like you can do anything about it. Your mate isn't even here to protect you."

My body snaps into motion before I even know what I'm doing. I lunge at him, not even phased that I'm still in my delicate human form. My claws push out of my finger tips, and I go after him with pure rage.

As I'm mid-lunge, I hear him utter one word. "Shit."

Did he not think I would? Well, he's about to find out what I'm willing to do, even without my beast fully present.

I slam my body into his. He grunts as I land on top of him, my claws digging deep.

"Kinley!"

My name is roared in the distance, but I pay it no heed. My sole focus is beating this dumb wolf. Aiden must have seen that glint in my eye, the one that promised pain. I'm not seeing him any longer; all I see is a male that has no right to me.

He manages to shake me off, but not without my claws dragging through his hide. Yelping, he spins out of my reach as I go to lunge for him again.

I don't even make it one step before I'm lifted off the ground, steel-like arms banding around my body.

I kick and thrash my body, my mind consumed with feral rage.

"Enough!" A deep voice snarls in my ear.

I almost manage to thrash free, when I'm pinned against a tree. A hard body presses against me fully from behind, a muscled thigh wedging between my legs. I'm completely at the mercy of this male. I growl deep, voicing my displeasure, when an even deeper growl answers me. It vibrates through my whole body, making me stir in a completely different way.

"Be a good mate, and stop fighting me," The deep voice rumbles.

His words begin to clear the angry fog from my brain.

Mate?

This time my growl doesn't hold the rage it had a moment ago; my growl holds a sensual note. I push my hips back into the male, and I feel his teeth take hold of the flesh at the base of my neck.

Mate. His voice rumbles through my mind as my body goes pliant in his grasp. *That's it.*

"Don?"

Who else would be calling you that? Are you going to be my good girl if I release you?

The rage hasn't fully dissipated, but my beast is preening now that our mate has us pinned. We like him being all dominant and bitey. I nod, feeling the skin on my neck pull as his teeth grip a little tighter before he releases me.

I miss his warmth immediately, but he doesn't release me entirely. His hand takes mine, turning me towards him as he leads me back to the house.

A small crowd has gathered on the back deck.

When did everyone get home?

Don leads me up onto the deck, placing me right in front of him, his arms coming back around me.

"Would someone like to explain what was going on back there?" Don's voice rumbles, sending vibrations into my back, making me shiver.

Aiden looks sheepish and a little worse for wear. He shifted back, his shirt being used to put pressure on the worst of my claw marks. I wince, feeling slightly bad about the damage I inflicted. *He deserved it though.*

"Well, I thought I might try a new tactic, since what we previously have been trying wasn't getting her beast to perk up. I might have underestimated how she would react when I led her to believe you weren't around to stop me from claiming her."

Don's snarl and mine blend together, creating a harmony of fury. Aiden quickly holds his hands up in surrender.

"I wasn't serious! I just couldn't think of anything else to rile her beast."

His apologetic expression eases my anger.

"I also might have let the cat get the better of me. He is remarkably well-adapted at manipulating me." He rubs his hand on the back of his neck sheepishly.

The cat in question scoffs at him. "Maybe if you used your supposed intelligence, you would be more of a challenge."

This exchange is entirely too amusing, but Indy isn't being very nice.

"Indy, we are guests; be a little nicer," I scold gently.

His piercing green eyes fall on me as he nods slightly. "As you wish,

Mistress."

His eyes are filled with mischief, so I won't hold my breath that he won't continue egging the guys on at every opportunity. My eyebrow rises, but all he does is blink slowly at me.

"Aiden, maybe next time we don't do that again. I wasn't going to stop. She had control and had a one track mind of punishing you."

He looks startled. "Really? Hmmmm, I guess we will just have to keep trying then. Maybe have Brent try next time."

There he goes again suggesting Brent. I smirk at him. "That reminds me, I need to go talk to Megan." I wiggle out of Don's embrace and stride purposefully into the house.

"Fuck, Kinley! I'm sorry." Aiden calls out after me. Hearing him coming after me, I sprint to my bedroom. He's hot on my heels; I try slamming the door in his face, but he plows through. The door slamming into the wall, I shriek into a fit of laughter as I lunge for my phone on the side table. Aiden snatches it right out of my hands. Holding my phone high over his head, way out of my reach.

"Give me my phone, Aiden."

He shakes his head. "Nope, not going to happen, not until you say you won't tell her."

I growl and go in for the kill, and by kill I mean tickling him to death. Cam let it slip one day that Aiden is incredibly ticklish and will howl like a baby. I lunge at him before he realizes what my goal is, and tickle his sides mercilessly. I do avoid his injuries, I'm not that cruel. His eyes widen in shock and horror just before he begins howling.

I cackle maniacally as he trips trying to get away from me and I pounce on him. I show no mercy.

"Stop, stop, please stop, Kinley!" He cries out, and still I laugh.

This is too fucking funny.

"You know what I want. Give it to me, and I'll stop," I say between laughing my ass off. It's getting pretty difficult to keep my place on top of him and tickle him. He's strong, but with only one hand to try and stop me, I still manage.

"What the hell is going…" Brent and Don's loud voices cut short, as they see what is happening.

"Shit, princess, you're ruthless."

"Baby, let the poor guy up."

They are just enough of a distraction that Aiden is able to shove me off of him and hide behind Brent.

"Brent save me; she's gone feral," Aiden pants, knowing that Don won't protect him against me.

They both tower over me, from my position, sprawled on the floor. Their eyes gleaming with laughter. *Why did I like them both looming over me so much?*

Aiden peeks out from behind Brent, his eyes narrowing. "Who told you I was ticklish?"

I just smirk at him, miming zipping my lips. He growls and I growl right back.

In my sweetest, syrupy voice I ask. "Brent, could you please get my phone from Aiden?"

His eyes light up. "What's in it for me, princess?"

All sorts of sordid things flit through my mind at his suggestive tone. *Nope, nope, nope, not going there.*

Not even justifying him with a response, I ask the one I know will help me. I brush myself off as I stand, and walk to my mate. My hips sway more than usual. His chuckle full of amusement and a hint of arousal as I approach him. His hand snaps out, snagging my phone out of Aiden's fingers, placing it in my hand as I lean up to kiss his waiting lips.

"Thank you, baby," I whisper against his mouth, nipping his bottom lip playfully.

He smirks, side-eyeing the other two, before saying, "Anything for you, mate."

I stick my tongue out at Aiden and Brent. *Am I being childish? Yes, yes I am. Do I care? Absolutely not.*

"Looks like your mate could use something else to occupy her mouth with, Don," Brent says darkly.

I roll my eyes at him, but I smirk at Don, licking my lips as I eye him up and down. Aiden coughs loudly before I can do anything further.

"Well, this is getting entirely too heated for me, so I'm gonna go patch myself up. Brent, could you give me a hand?"

Brent looks like he wants to do anything but help him, but he lets Aiden lead him out of our room.

Don shuts the door behind them, leaning against it, eyeing me hungrily. "You like pushing his buttons, don't you?"

"What? He has been such a dick lately. Yes, I get that I was being stupid, but I've apologized multiple times, Don. If he is going to be an ass, then I'm going to push his buttons."

The heavy sigh that leaves him makes me pause.

"What's wrong?"

"Just a long day at work, baby. I missed you."

"I missed you too, Don."

I go up to him, wrapping my arms around his waist, snuggling my face into his chest, inhaling his scent."So, there is something I wanted to talk with you about."

His hands brush up and down my back, giving me all sorts of warm fuzzies. "What's that?"

"Well, I've been thinking about going back to work."

Resting my chin on his chest, I peer up at him.

"I'm not sure that is the best idea; it's not safe."

"I'm pretty sure I'm going to get fired if I don't go back."

His hands travel down until each cups my ass. He boosts me up, making me squeak with the sudden change of height. Resting my arms on his shoulders, I'm now directly in front of his face.

"Are you trying to distract me?"

"I'm trying to hold my mate. Wrap your legs around me, baby."

I do as he asks, and he starts walking towards the bed. My mouth opens to protest. I still want to talk about going back to work.

"We can talk about you going back to work later. Right now, I want to lay you down and lose myself in you for a little while."

I soften in his arms. "Ok, we can talk later."

I kiss his lips, pressing mine into his, letting him feel the desire that is always present for him.

Laying me down gently, he begins removing my clothes. My nose wrinkles as I remember just how sweaty I still am.

"Don…I'm all sweaty and gross."

"Mmmmmm, more flavor."

I snort. "Gross."

"Hush, I'm concentrating. I've been craving you all day."

My cheeks flush. "I always crave you, Don."

He hums in agreement as he finishes removing my clothes. Quickly, he divests himself of his own clothes until we are both bare. Seeing my mating mark on Don's shoulder, the scarring from my teeth shining in the low light, brings up an uneasy feeling.

"Don…what would have happened if Aiden hadn't been joking and he really did bite me? Could he have actually claimed me?"

"Baby, he would never do that. Are you worried he will?"

"No, I just need to know if a claim can be forced."

"No, baby, a mate bond has to be accepted by both."

"Why would he say that then?"

Don sighs, propping himself up on his elbows. My hands come up to rest on his sides.

"For one, he wanted to get a reaction out of your beast, which he did, by the way. But, there have been stories of bonds being broken and forced when dark magic is involved. That's not something you need to worry about, though."

Then why do I keep thinking about it?

"Will I ever have control over my magic?"

"Kinley, of course you will. You have to remember it took us all years to fully control our powers. The fact that you can even do the things you are already doing, even if it's not a conscious effort, is beyond what anyone should be capable of. Baby, you are a marvel. The control will come in time. Your powers are just starting to unfurl."

His touch on my face is reverent, and he's so sincere. His open honesty and willingness to share anything I ask is rare and something I will cherish. His faith in me makes me believe that I will be capable of controlling my powers, one day. I know it's silly to just expect to have full control, but I really want to understand my powers and use them.

Don's gentle kiss brings my focus back to him.

"Now, I'm going to need you to stay right here and let me make you come. Then, I'm going to fill this perfect pussy with my cock."

"Well, when you put it that way…yes, Sir."

A grin spreads wide on his face. I love it when he smiles like that.

"I fucking love it when you call me that, baby."

"I know…Sir."

His eyes darken with lust and it makes my core clench with anticipation. I'm not expecting him to flip me over though. My gasp quickly turns into a throaty moan when his tongue dives into my wet heat.

"Ahh, Don… baby…so good."

His beast must have been close to the surface because his tongue feels so long. Spreading my cheeks wide, he devours me from top to bottom. Feeling his tongue on every part of me feels depraved and so, so good. I pant and plead until I'm screaming through my orgasm.

He lays me down, shoving my hips into the bed, his powerful thighs bracketing mine. Taking my hands, he brings them above my head, his fingers weaving between mine as he lays his body atop mine. Shifting his hips back, he notches the head of his cock at my opening, my slickness easing his way into me. He pushes deep until his hips are flush with my ass. I moan at the fullness of him sheathing himself to the hilt.

"You grip me like a fucking glove, baby."

"Don…so full."

I'm completely at his mercy, fully pinned beneath his large muscled body. His thrusts are shallow but still hold power behind each one. The friction of his movements builds my next orgasm so quickly, each thrust gliding right against my g-spot.

"Don, please…I'm so close."

"Kinley…you're everything…baby, I love you so much."

When his teeth clamp down over his mating mark, I detonate, and we climax together.

I scream his name into the bedcovers as Don empties himself deep within me, his roar muffled against my neck.

He rolls us onto our sides, and we both try to calm our breathing.

I pat his arm, "Good game."

He snorts. "Smartass. You know, the memory of you tickling the shit out of Aiden is going to be one of my favorite memories."

I look over my shoulder at him as he laughs.

"Really? Not the memory of this morning when I did that thing with my finger, while I sucked your cock?"

His chuckling stops immediately.

"Ok, you're right, that is a way better memory. And...now I'm hard again."

I can't help the laughter that bubbles up. He rolls me onto my back, seriously contemplating going for another round, but my stomach growls with hunger.

"Feed me first?"

His forehead comes down to rest on mine.

"Yes, food first...then we are coming right back to you being underneath me again."

CHAPTER 30

KINLEY

I'm going back to work.

It has been over a month, and I'm pretty sure that I'm going crazy. Last time I felt this stir crazy, I stole a car and disaster struck. So I'm trying to be proactive and take some steps to not let bad shit happen again.

I missed the normalcy of it, and if I'm honest with myself, I need the distraction with everything that has been happening. I need something to go my way.

So, like I said, I'm going back to work. Not just to get back some control over my life, but because I'm not going to be any good to anyone if I don't get back into the right state of mind.

Work has always been a safe place for me; it centers me and gives me focus. There is just something calming about interacting with my students on a day to day basis and teaching them the wonders of life sciences.

What can I say: I'm a science nerd. Is that why being magical is a real mind fuck? Hmmmm, I will circle back to that later.

When the guys protested me going back to work, I explained that mentally, I needed to do this, and they had begrudgingly relented.

I think they saw that feral gleam in my eyes and knew I wasn't going to back down from this. They insisted that Cam put a few apps on my phone to help track me, and to give me immediate access to each one of them if something happened with just a touch of a button.

I'm not too thrilled about them all knowing my every move, but after what happened the last time I went rogue, I understand the need for them to know where I am and if I'm safe.

When everything keeps spiraling, with my lack of consistent powers, lack of memories, and a crazed stalker that keeps popping up in my life, work is something I can control. *Right?*

Now, while parts of not working have been nice, I have bills to pay, and I have officially run out of days to burn. Don has been so sweet and assured me that he could help me out, but I'm not sure I'm ready to be fully dependent on a man to support me financially.

While I have claimed him as my mate, it's hard for me to switch my mindset over to thinking that means we are as good as married.

I mean, I don't even have a ring...not that I'm asking for one, but I wouldn't say no to one.

Thankfully, Don is understanding, but I could tell it hurt his feelings a little.

Don and the guys have all been so supportive with everything, and I know that without it, I would have spiraled into a dark place. A dark place I haven't visited in a very long time and have no interest in returning to.

Are things perfect? Absolutely not. Brent is still somewhat standoffish with me after the car incident. I still don't blame him. I'm determined to mend that hurt, though.

He has become just as important to me as Don. They all have. Don and Aiden have assured me that Brent couldn't care less about the car; it's replaceable. I do know that he isn't really upset about the car. Even though the BMW M6 is a really expensive car, he is more upset about how I left the house without telling anyone, but he has yet to tell me that. I'm pretty sure I'm going to have to corner him if he keeps avoiding me every time I try to talk with him.

Even though they are completely different from what I have with Don, they still feel like they are my family, even with the short time that I have known them, and nothing is going to make me give that up. It has been a very long time since I've had anyone other than Megan. I'm determined to keep them all, and I'm going to do whatever it takes.

I have all of their numbers now, and an ongoing group chat has been established. The group chat is rather amusing. The way the four of them interact with each other is pretty entertaining. I found out really quickly that Cam likes to send memes, and most of them are incredibly inappropriate, but they never take it too far.

I'm not sure why, but getting all four of them to agree to my terms feels like an accomplishment.

What doesn't feel like an accomplishment is how behind I am at work. So behind, in fact, that I call my teaching partner Cory and plead with him to meet up with me so I can plan with him and catch up.

There is nothing like a good plan to get your head on straight.

Which is where I'm headed now. Cory agreed to meet me at a local coffee shop, so we can figure out what we are doing, and of course gossip, because I have pretty much fallen off the face of the Earth. I mentally go over my story, snorting at just how much I'm going to have to omit or lie about. *This might be a terrible idea.*

I beat him there, so I grab us a table big enough to spread out our stuff and not be too crowded. With the table thoroughly claimed, I get in line and am ordering coffee and something to eat when Cory walks in.

I wave at him, motioning to the table I claimed. He gives me a thumbs up, and goes to set his stuff down before joining me in line.

He moves in close and gives me a side hug. My skin tingles with discomfort, making me wonder if my body doesn't like other guys touching me now that I'm mated. Or, is it because I'm not actually human? *Ugh, more questions.*

"It's so good to see you. You had us all worried."

His tone is slightly off. He doesn't sound like his usual happy self. *Has he really been that worried for me?*

"I know, the last few weeks have been rough."

I'm sticking with the story that I have been very ill and then a death in the family required me to go out of state. *I mean it was partially true...*

"Well, you look good for being on death's door."

He gives me a once over, which again makes me feel weird. The way his eyes slowly track over my body. I'm not sure why I'm having this kind of reaction to him.

We have never been interested in each other romantically. He is bi, and he usually leans more towards being attracted to men. He is also dating a really great guy. So why the hell does it seem like he eyed me with a look of hunger.

God, Kinley, you are going certifiable.

"My friend, Megan, took really good care of me."

"Is that where you were?"

"Yeah, I was with her since her husband just passed. And then I got really sick."

"Man that sucks; at least you were with someone who could take care of you."

"Yeah, I don't know what I would do without her."

Time to change the subject, Kinley.

"Hey, thank you so much for meeting me. I'd really be lost without you."

I give him a warm smile because, even though I'm feeling weird around him, I am really grateful he is taking time on the weekend to help me.

"No problem, I'm happy to help. What are partners for?"

Drinks and food in hand, we get busy planning. It doesn't take long for us to catch up with work and get a general idea of what units to cover for the rest of the semester. It helps that everything is digital now, so we easily pull from previous years and create a cohesive plan. While we work, I ask him about how things are going on campus.

"Well, apparently, Allen had a nervous breakdown in the middle of class a week and a half ago. Raving about demons."

My stomach drops.

"What the hell, really?"

"Yeah, I saw the whole thing. It was rather alarming."

"Rather alarming? Seems like an understatement. So, where did he go?"

"Not sure, the resource officers dragged him away."

"Jesus, and that's it? Cory, you are literally the nosiest person I know. You would normally have all the details. Are you feeling ok?"

"Yes, I'm feeling ok. I've just been wanting to focus on reaching my own goals lately. I can't be bothered to deal with people that aren't pivotal to my success."

I frown. He doesn't sound like himself at all.

"Cory, are you doing ok? You just don't sound like yourself." I reach out to touch his arm, but I stop just before I physically make contact. Something just isn't right. *Was it me?*

He chuckles, but again it sounds off.

"I'm great, Kinley. I just relieved myself of some unnecessary baggage, and I'm feeling refreshed."

Unnecessary baggage? And then it dawns on me.

"Oh my gosh, did you and Will break up?"

"Will? Oh yeah, but I don't really want to talk about it."

He isn't acting too heartbroken over it, but I still give his hand a comforting squeeze. Just from that small touch, my body wants to shudder in revulsion. I fight to keep my body still, but I quickly remove my hand. I'm so confused why I'm having this reaction.

"Ok, but if you need to talk, you know I'm a good listener."

He smiles at me, but it doesn't reach his eyes. I guess maybe he is upset by the break up after all. *Just goes to show what I know.*

We chat for a little bit longer, while we finish up working, before he gets up to get a refill on his tea. *I wonder when he started drinking tea. When did I get so suspicious of people? Oh right, when I suddenly got a stalker.*

My thoughts are interrupted by a text from Don.

Don: What time do you think you'll be done? I was going to swing by to grab some take out, but if you're almost finished I'll wait for you, and we can go in and get it fresh.

> Me: What take out? I think I'm about finished.
> Less than 30 minutes for sure.

Seeing the dots signalling he is typing has me staring at my phone waiting for his response. So, of course I don't notice when Cory comes up behind me.

"Who's Don?"

I jump slightly, covering my phone.

"Oh goodness, you scared me a little. Oh, Don is a guy I'm seeing."

"What? When did this happen?"

"Well…I met him a month or so ago. We really hit it off…it's been really great so far?"

"That's it?"

"Well, it's still really new, and with you going through a breakup, I didn't want to make you sad by talking about my boyfriend."

"I thought you said you just met?"

"Ugh, Cory, he's really great, and we are exclusive so yes, my boyfriend…because it would be weird if I called him my man friend."

I snort, but then I stop when I see the look on Cory's face. *Why does he look angry?*

Guess he really is upset about his breakup. I need to get out of here before I make him sadder.

"So, do you think we need to do any more work? I think we are in a good place, at least for the next two or three weeks."

"Sure, yeah, I think we are good for next week."

"Ok, great. I'm gonna head out then. I'll see you on Monday."

I quickly pack up, but notice he isn't.

"Are you gonna hang out some more?"

"Yeah, I'm going to hang out and finish my tea."

I know I'm oblivious sometimes, but I'm not that oblivious.

"Cory, when did you become a tea drinker? I swear you've said tea drinkers are stuffy assholes."

"Well, maybe I'm a stuffy asshole."

My laugh is slightly strained.

"Right, sure. Well I gotta go, see you at work."

I feel weird about that entire exchange, but I think I'm jaded now after the last few months. I still walk out quickly. There is a slight drizzle now, so I don't waste time getting into my car. I get buckled in, but take the time to read Don's response first. Smiling at his sweet message, I almost miss the figure staring at me from the corner of the coffee shop, their hands clenched. Even with their face completely shadowed by the hood they are wearing, I just know they are looking at me. I feel their eyes, staring.

What is going on today?

I don't stick around to find out, driving away quickly to meet Don.

We walk into Brent's with bags of take out. Don told me at the restaurant that we are feeding everyone tonight. We are going to have a quiet night in with movies. I can't wait; I don't even care what movie they picked, a movie night sounds perfect.

Setting the food bags on the kitchen island, I don't even pause to say hi to anyone. I'm on a mission to get into something comfy. I race to the bedroom, quickly stripping out of my slightly damp clothes. I sigh when my bra comes off, the girls don't like to be confined.

I'm practically skipping into the kitchen a short time later. Aiden spots me first, and he grins seeing how good of a mood I'm in.

"Someone's excited."

I nod, smiling widely.

"It's been so long since I've had a movie night with friends, I can't help it."

Aiden chuckles, responding to my happiness.

"Then you are going to love what Cam is doing to the living room right now." He nods his head in the direction of the living room. "Go on and look."

Intrigued, I leave Aiden to his task of making drinks, and go to investigate. My grin spreads even wider across my face as I take in the sight of Cam putting sheets on blow up mattresses. I must make a noise because Cam looks up from what he is doing and laughs as he takes in my excitement.

"Wanna help?"

"Absolutely!"

I hastily climb over the couch to help him with the rest of the sheets and blankets. When we finish, we both stand back and admire our handiwork. The living room has been converted into one large bed, a large projector screen has been rolled down, and the space is ready for an epic movie night.

Cam and I grin at each other, high-five, and then I proceed to do the silliest happy dance ever. I'm not a dancer, but I can't help but wiggle my body in excitement. Cam raises an eyebrow at me and a throat clearing makes me pause my dancing mid wiggle.

A blush spreads across my face and neck as Brent stands there, hands laden with our take out food, eyeing me critically.

"If you got time to dance, then you got time to help me grab all the food, princess."

I blow out a heavy breath, navigating around the moved furniture, walking past Brent to head back into the kitchen. I spy another tray and get busy putting the rest of the take out on it, grabbing utensils and extra plates. I just finished getting everything set on the tray and am going to head into the living room, when a hard warm body presses up against my back.

"Don't you think it's a little cold for you to be wearing that, princess?"

Brent has leaned down and whispers those words directly into my ear. I growl, as I turn around, shoving him off me. I've had just about enough of his attitude, and it's going to stop right now.

"What is your problem, Brent? Is this still about the car because you are the one that keeps insisting that the car doesn't matter any time I apologize. So please, tell me what your fucking problem is because if I'm not welcome here anymore, I will leave. Right fucking now."

I'm seething, my temper boiling hot. I have noticed since the guys have been trying to push my powers into manifesting that my beast is quicker to rise and so is my temper.

I expect him to be angry, but shock is what is written on his face. He also stares a little too long at my tits before his eyes come up to meet mine. My fists clench, and I wonder if I will have a better chance of punching his face or punching him in the dick. He must see the violence that glitters in my eyes because he finds his words and gets to talking.

"Fuck, no, I don't want you to leave. Goddess, Kinley, you are always welcome in my home."

"Then what is the problem?"

He growls, running his hands through his hair, pulling it free from the top knot he put in. When he looks at me next, his eyes have that eerie glow that lets me know just how close his beast is to the surface. His mouth opens, but he stiffens and looks over his shoulder, directly at the audience we now have accumulated. Don, Cam, and Aiden are all staring as if they too are waiting for him to answer.

"Fuck, can I talk to you in my office? Please?"

My eyes narrow, I peer around his large frame until my eyes meet Don's. He nods his head at me.

Is he encouraging me to go talk with Brent?

Go talk to him, baby. It's fine.

My head rolls back onto my shoulders until I'm staring at the ceiling. I sigh heavily.

"Fine, let's go, but if you don't answer my question, I will punch you in the dick."

A choked off laugh comes out of Aiden and Cam, and I turn my glare onto them.

"I swear to all things holy that there better be food left when I get back or I'm siccing Beretta and Indy on you all."

I stomp off down the hall towards Brent's office. And to think I had been in such a great mood. Fucking men.

CHAPTER 31

₿RENT

I watch Kinley's round ass bounce down the hall. I know she is mad at me—her body vibrates with it—but for the life of me, I can't stop staring at her delicious body. I start after her, but Donovan pulls me short before I get past him.

"Make this right, or I'll do worse than dick punch you."

I nod. I didn't need to tell him; he knows how I'm feeling. He isn't thrilled about it, but I'm his Clan brother; it didn't come as too big of a surprise when I confessed my feelings to him.

Now, I just need to tell Kinley. I'd let it go on for too long without saying what I needed to. Now she is busting my balls because I'm being a raging asshole. It isn't her fault that I can't think straight around her, but seeing her in that crop top and shorts that just barely cover the curve of her ass, leaving the rest of her curvy body on display? Seeing that, and then her wiggling in happiness, it's too much.

Yeah, I fucked up and snapped at her; I deserve her anger.

She is waiting in my office for me, her tiny bare foot tapping on the rug, her body vibrating with frustration.

Would groveling help? Would getting on my knees for her make her anger fade? Well, that can always be my plan b.

Closing the door gently behind me, I steel myself for the truths I need to admit. I pray to the Goddess to give me strength and to make Kinley listen to everything I have to say.

"Well, I'm here, so spill."

"Ok, ok. Shit, this is harder than I thought it would be."

"Ughhh, Brent quit stalling."

This female is going to be the death of me.

"I wasn't lying when I said the car didn't matter. Hell, you could have crashed it yourself, and I'd have gotten over it as long as you had been safe. I care about you, Kinley. That's all I care about. Well, and the guys. You are all that matters to me."

I can see the wheels turning in her mind as my words start to make sense to her.

"I don't know if Donovan has told you much about Clan life, but hopefully what I tell you doesn't freak you out when I'm done."

"Brent, you're already freaking me out."

"I get that. You've gone through more than anyone should in a very short period of time. I know it's a lot. But my beast and I both want you, Kinley. It's not something I can help. I've been a surly bastard because it's been taking everything in me not to fall at your feet and beg you to take me as your mate, too."

There I said it. A weight lifts off my chest, but my heart falls a little at the look that graces her face. *Is that pity? Fuck.*

"Brent...I don't know what to say. I'm mated to Donovan."

I move closer to her, taking her hand when she doesn't move away from me.

"Kinley, Donovan wasn't lying when he said that Clan females frequently take more than one mate. It is ultimately your choice, and I'll respect whatever decision you make. But I can't stand not telling you that I want you so fucking much."

"But...Don."

"He knows; he knows everything. Princess, we grow up knowing that if we mate to a Clan female, there is a good chance we won't be the only male. Mating is rare, and females that do mate are always powerful enough to warrant more than one. Hell, if you decided you wanted all four of us we wouldn't deny you."

Her nose wrinkles at that, and I can't help but chuckle. I know just by seeing how she interacts with Aiden and Camden that she has no such interests. My thumb strokes her hand, I love being able to touch her.

"Brent, this is a lot."

"I know, but I can't keep this from you anymore. I don't want to keep hurting you. You don't have to do anything about this; it is one-hundred percent your decision. But every time you look at me the way you do, and the way your arousal perfumes the air..." I growl just thinking about it. Her pupils dilate and her breathing quickens. "I just need you to know that it is ok that you are feeling that way. You aren't a bad person if you want Donovan and me."

"Brent, I need to think about this and talk with Don."

"You absolutely can. I won't pressure you; take as much time as you need. I might be a grumpy asshole sometimes when my beast is riding me hard, but that's on me, ok?"

She nods and squeezes my hand, but then she shocks the hell out of me and wraps her arms around me. My arms automatically draw her in closer, I breathe in her scent and it takes everything in me not to claim her.

"Thank you for telling me. I'm glad you aren't mad at me and want me to leave."

"Never, princess."

Her stomach takes that moment to growl loudly, I lead her out of my office feeling lighter. But I'm not a saint, so I follow behind her so I can watch that juicy ass sway back and forth down the hallway. *Goddess, I hope she picks me, too.*

KINLEY

His eyes are on me, and for once I don't feel wrong for liking it. I know I need to unpack that whole conversation, but I'm so hungry and all I want to do is eat, curl up with Don, and have movie night with the guys. Because, even if I choose none of them as mates besides Don, I know that they are still mine. They are family. They are my Clan.

I eat entirely too much Asian take out, and have to push the containers away when the guys keep offering me more. When they finally realize I am indeed full and can't eat another bite, they devour the rest, and I watch with fascinated horror as they eat until everything is gone.

I guess being big guys and being able to shift into really large magical creatures makes one need to eat a lot.

Aiden won rock, paper, scissors so he got to pick the movie, some sci fi flick that I completely zone out to after I finish eating. The pillows and makeshift bed are so comfortable that I find myself lying down with my head in Don's lap. His hand idly running through my hair.

Don?

His hand doesn't stop, as he answers me in my mind.

Yeah, baby?

What do you really think about Brent wanting to be my mate?

I think that it's your decision. If you feel an urge towards him that you can't deny, then he is also your mate. I will not sway you either way if that is what you were hoping for.

Ugh, that is no help at all.

Sorry, baby. All you can do is think on it. I can feel how conflicted you are about this. You don't have to make any decision now. If you decide to make him work for it, though, I won't be mad at all. In fact, I can help you ramp up his frustrations.

And that's how I find myself straddling Don's lap as he kisses me senseless. That is until Camden decides to interrupt.

"Don, seriously, some of us are trying to watch a movie, not get a weird hard on watching you two make out."

I choke out a laugh, pulling my head away from Don's mouth, looking at Camden incredulously. He wiggles his eyebrows at me and I roll mine at him. I do climb off of Don's lap though. I don't really want to put on a show, nor do I really want to make Brent uncomfortable. As I lay back down, I grab a few pillows and stretch out next to Don instead of laying down in his lap. Don't need to encourage him any further.

I must have fallen asleep shortly after because I can't recall what the movie was about. I also can't remember how I ended up in the middle of a cuddle pile with all four guys. My front is up against Don, my head resting on his chest. My legs are being cuddled, a head resting on my calf. My arm that is stretched over Don's side is touching someone's back. But whoever is behind me is spooning me, their arm draped over me to rest on Don's stomach, their very hard cock nestled against my ass.

How did I end up like this? And do I want to know who is where? Fuck it, I'm warm, comfy as hell, and I have never felt safer. And I also haven't been dreaming.

That shocked the hell out of me, I haven't gone without a crazy dream in weeks. And here I am, surrounded, cuddled in the middle of these males, and suddenly no dreams. Just that alone would have made me stay right where I am. So like any smart, red blooded woman, I snuggle back down and go right back to sleep.

CHAPTER 32

KINLEY

I have only one more class period and then I can start my weekend; it's a shortened week to allow students and teachers the time to attend the football team's playoff game, and I couldn't be more thankful. It has been a struggle to return to work after everything. I have only been back two weeks, and I still feel weird being here and attempting to act like my world hasn't been uprooted, and I'm not aware that magic exists. It's truly weird being around normal people, but I was so excited to see my students and get back into a routine.

Don is working late, and I'm taking myself to the game.

See, doing normal shit, while my man is at work.

I'm meeting coworkers, and it's public. The notes and tokens my creepy stalker left stopped after the car incident, so I feel ok going out.

None of the guys could go with me. They have lives too, and they also needed to get back to work. I'm definitely more aware of my surroundings, thanks to my beast being a little more present.

I have also started carrying a handgun in my car. I'm stronger than I had previously been, but I still can't shift. We have yet to figure out what my powers can do, because they are so intermittent that I might as well not have them. It's frustrating, but I need to be able to protect myself, hence the gun. I know how to shoot and after a thorough lesson from Brent, he begrudgingly gave me a gun from his arsenal in his secret basement. Yes, he has a secret basement, and I'm beginning to realize that his line of work is probably not really legal.

The guys still hadn't wanted me to go alone. I get that. Everyone is on edge, and the guys are so moody when it comes to my safety.

It's like a switch flipped after our movie night cuddle fest, making them even more protective. It can get a bit exhausting.

Cam even hacked my phone and put even more trackers on it, and not even Aiden would tell me how to get them off. Don and Brent just brushed me off, saying they didn't know any of that techy stuff. I'm pretty sure they were lying.

The final bell for the day rings, and I text the group chat to let them know I'm headed to the game now that school is over.

Sometimes, it feels like I'm dating all four of them. And there is a primal part of me, probably my beast, that wants to taste them all, especially now that I know how Brent feels. Aiden and Camden just don't instill that kind of need, thank goodness. The logistics of having four partners makes me want to run. *A girl doesn't even have that many holes!* I shudder at that thought.

Even though Brent stirs up all kinds of feelings, I'm still on the fence about that. Don is my mate, and he is more than enough. *I don't really need another one, right?*

I text Cory and Trina, letting them know that I'm headed out and that I will meet them there. They offered to carpool, but there is no way that I'm going to be without my own transportation. The game is an hour and a half drive, and if anything comes up I need to be able to leave. Once all my texts are sent, I don't waste time getting on the road, only stopping for a quick drive thru dinner.

Don calls me while he is on a break, his call ringing loudly over my car speakers. He knows I'm still driving, but he can't help the need to check in before he has to get back to work. The way he cares about me gives me warm fuzzies. He's telling me about how they tricked some Johns in their bust earlier, and I'm laughing when my wheel jerks hard.

"Fuck!"

"Kinley, what's wrong?"

"I'm ok, I just think I have a flat. It startled me."

"Shit, where are you?"

The fact that he thought I needed help is sweet but misguided.

"Oh, hold your horses," giggling at his unamused snort. "I'm a big girl, Don. I know how to change a flat tire. There is a gas station right up ahead. I'll pull in and change it."

Telling him I will call him back, I get my car into the parking lot. It's small, but it's safer than being on the side of the road. There are also lights, because the sun has almost set and I wouldn't want to attempt to change a tire in the dark. I'm not going to even think of all the creepy horror movies that start out in a tiny run down gas station in the backwoods. *Stay positive, Kinley.*

I walk around my car looking to see which tire is the culprit. It becomes very obvious which one it is. The back left is shredded.

What the hell did I hit?

Giving myself a brief pep talk, I get to work changing my tire, thanking my foresight to get a car that actually has a spare and not that useless fix-a-flat kit.

I'm working up a little sweat, and have just gotten the new tire on when the gas station attendant comes out, asking me if I need help. Rolling my eyes at his timing, I blow hair out of my face and peer up at him with a raised eyebrow. He's a tall skinny man, and he definitely looks like he's seen better days. I don't know if he would even have the muscles to crank the wrench, let alone heft the tire off.

"Nope, I got it. As you can see, I'm basically done."

He shrugs and walks away, but I do hear him mutter that I'm an uppity bitch. *Sometimes I really wish it was acceptable to throat punch people.*

Without any further interruptions, I finish quickly and get back on the road. If I don't have any more mishaps I can still probably make it in time to see kick off.

Not wanting Don to worry, I call him back to let him know I successfully changed my own tire and am back on the road. I can hear the relief in his voice, and I totally get it. I will for sure be locked up in a bubble if the one time I go out on my own, something bad happens again.

His radio crackles over the phone just as I notice I'm getting another call. "Hey Don, Cory is calling, I gotta let you go. It might be about the game."

"Ok, baby, talk to you later."

He hangs up, but I'm not fast enough to connect with Cory, so I quickly call him back. He answers after a few rings.

"Hey! Sorry, I'm almost there, I had to change a flat tire."

"Really? Well I'm glad you got it fixed. Unfortunately, my car is stalled. Do you think you could swing by and pick me up?"

"Oh my gosh. Are you ok?"

"Yeah, I'm fine. It must be the night for car problems."

"No kidding, where is Trina? She might be able to get to you quicker. I think I'm at least another 20 minutes out."

"I think she is already there. Cell service is kind of spotty, and she probably can't hear her phone anyways."

"You're right, she is so bad about answering her phone. Ok, send me your location, and I'll swing by. If she does call you back, let me know."

"Ok, I'll send it as soon as I get off the phone."

"See you soon."

He disconnects the call and soon after, I get his location through text. Not even a minute later a call from Brent comes through.

Jesus, these guys are gonna drive me nuts.

"Yes, Brent?"

A dark chuckle answers me.

He has no business being that sexy over the phone.

"I like hearing you tell me yes."

"You're incorrigible. What do you want?"

"A lot of things, princess."

"Brent...seriously."

"Fine, I just wanted to let you know I might swing by the game and keep you company."

"Did Don put you up to this?"

"No, he doesn't know. But I know he's seriously stressing about you being alone."

"Brent, I'm not going to be alone. I'll be anything but alone. I'll be perfectly safe."

"I know you're perfectly capable, but your safety is our number one priority."

I take a deep breath and count to ten in my head. I don't want to fight, because I know he will ultimately do what he wants and get Don involved if I don't just let him come with me.

"Ugh, fine…you're so annoying."

"I can make it up to you if you want, princess"

"Stop, you're ridiculous. I'm going to tell Don how ridiculous you're being."

"Who says he doesn't already know and has no objections?"

Ugh, not that again. I swear that male is relentless, and I still don't know how I feel about that.

"Shut up."

He chuckles. "When will you be at the stadium?"

"Don't tell me you're already there."

"Smart girl."

"Fucking hell, Brent. Well, you're gonna be waiting a little longer, I'm still fifteen minutes out and I have to pick up Cory. His car broke down at the park."

"Why are you so behind?"

"I had a flat tire."

"What? Why didn't you message the group chat?"

"I was already on the phone with Don, and I'm perfectly capable of changing my own tire."

"So hot. I love a female who can really work a wrench."

I groan. He really is ridiculous. He is lucky he's cute because he's seriously pushing his luck.

Brent is a pleasant distraction while I drive with his silly commentary of all the people that are already at the stadium. I can't deny that I'm secretly glad he will be there. I already consider him a good friend, and I'm not too put out by him showing up to the game to make sure I'm safe. I do wish he had asked first.

He's in the middle of describing a small toddler throwing a fit about wanting a hot dog, and I giggle at that image. I'm trying really hard to also concentrate on where I'm going as I pull up to the park. There's a large sign blazoned with Springville Park across it, so I know I'm in the right place, but the sun has fully set and there are hardly any street lights. A frown creases my forehead. I don't see any cars.

"Where is he?" I thought I said that in my head, but I actually mumbled it out loud.

"Who? Cory?"

"Yeah, he said he was at the park because his car broke down."

"Are you sure you got the right park?"

"Yessss…I got the right park. He sent me his location, and I think this is the only park in town anyways."

I drive a little further into the park, scanning the area, trying to find any evidence of where he might be. The wind picks up, scattering random pieces of litter across the parking lot into the path of my car. My eyes jerk at movement to my left, but it's just the swings moving back and forth in the wind. I almost tell Brent that I need to hang up and call Cory when I finally spot his car, but I don't see him.

"You find him?" Brent's deep voice sounds a little too loud over my car speakers, and I jump. I must have squeaked or made some sort of undignified sound because he chuckles.

"I found his car, but I'm not sure if he's still in it. I'll be right back, Brent."

Leaving the car running, I hop out before he can object, but I'm pretty sure he said to keep my ass in the car. Which just makes me smirk.

My smile fades as I get up to Cory's car and find he isn't in it.

Where is he?

The wind whips my hair around as I search the vacant park for any sign of him. *Did Trina pick him up, and I missed his call? Maybe he ran to the bathroom.* The creaking of the swings makes the hairs on the back of my neck rise. He said he would be here.

"Cory!"

Maybe he isn't too far away.

I call out louder, but I still don't hear a response, just that incessant squeaking as the playground equipment moves with the breeze. I really dislike that sound, it grates on my nerves and makes me think of all kinds of creepy shit. I'm going to give Cory an earful when I find him. I should go back to the car and wait, make sure I don't have a missed call from him or Trina.

A pit settles into my stomach. I'm getting a bad feeling. Lately my bad feelings happen for a reason, but then I hear him call out to me. I turn back, away from my waiting vehicle and search for where I hear his voice. He is just coming out of the tree line. A sigh of relief leaves my lungs. *Why was he way out there?*

I walk towards him but still remain within the light of a street lamp. "Cory, what are you doing over there? I was getting scared something happened to you."

"Oh Kinley, something did happen to me." His voice is all wrong and alarm bells begin ringing.

I don't even get a chance to question him before a foul smell of decay mixed with sulfur assaults my nose. Holding back a gag, I cover my nose and mouth. *Holy fuck. Don't get sick. Don't get sick.*

"Cory, what is that smell? Are you ok?"

I'm so fucking stupid. Brent is going to kill me, and then Don will take a turn.

As he draws near, the smell grows, the howling wind blowing it directly into my face. But that isn't enough to distract from the way he's walking at a disjointed, erratic pace, which quickens the closer he gets to me. *What is going on?*

"Oh my god, Cory, did someone attack you?"

There's a small part of me that wants to go closer to him and help, but a voice inside me demands I not go any further. In fact, it gets louder in its demands that I flee. It's my beast, roaring for me to run, but I'm frozen in place as she pushes and pushes, trying to break free.

If only she were able to.

A menacing snarl snares my attention straight to Cory's face, and I gasp. Black fluid oozes from his nose and eyes, and his teeth are stained black. He sneers at me, mocking my horrified expression.

"Don't you like my new look? I did this all for you, so we could finally be together."

Oh fuck, is he my stalker? Shit! Fuck!

No longer rooted in place by my beast, I start slowly backing away. *I have to get to my car.*

"Cory, what have you done?"

"I can't let them take you from me, my little doe. I gladly sacrificed myself, opened myself to the great God, and now it's time for you to join me. Like it was always meant to be."

This is madness, could a poison do this? Did he take drugs? What is wrong with him? Wait, the great God?

He has gone completely insane.

Just keep him talking. I have to get to my phone and get him an ambulance, I have to tell Brent. Just keep him calm.

I continue to slowly back away.

"Cory, did you take something? You look really sick. I'm going to get you help, ok."

"Oh, my sweet doe, I don't need help. I just need you. You have everything I need."

Dark energy leaches out of him. It swirls around him menacingly. That swirling dark energy triggers the fleetest of memories.

I have seen that before; I know I have. Where have I seen that before?

He continues to advance. My own powers, minuscule that they are, pulse in response to the danger. That makes him pause. A look of confusion followed quickly by devastation and then fury crosses his face.

"Did they force you? They could not have done so again. Whose scent is woven into your magic?"

I shake my head and quicken my pace. He isn't making any sense.

If I can just get to my car...I'm so close.

"Tell me!"

"I don't know what you're talking about! Please, Cory, let me help you; you're sick."

Panic is nearly taking over my logic. I want Don; I want my mate. I will be safe with him. I need to get to Don. Or Brent.

I turn my head to see how close I am to my car. I'm almost there. When I turn back to face Cory, I instantly regret having turned away. Somehow he moved so quickly and silently that he is now right in front of me.

He moves so fast, I can't do anything to get away. His hands grab me. Dark power zaps through me, shutting down what little power I'd managed to push forward.

I can't help the scream that claws up my throat. The pain is immense as it invades my body. Tears leak from my eyes as my body seizes.

I'm beyond helpless. I can't break free. He is strong—unnaturally strong. I desperately try to reach for my magic, to push him out. Every part of my being struggles to get away from him.

"Whose magic is this! Tell me now!"

My screams continued. I'm going to be sick. The smells, the magic, the fear and pain, everything is too much. *Someone, help me, please.*

He grabs my face, wrenching it to the side, exposing my neck. His putrid breath fills my nose as he inhales and licks up my neck. My scream becomes blood curdling. My skin. It's burning. I thrash in his hold. I have to get free. As I struggle, my arm is released.

Riding on instinct, not allowing myself to think, I punch at his face. My only thoughts are to inflict pain and get away. I hear Cory grunt, but he doesn't release me until my claws find purchase and dig deep into him.

I slash and dig into wherever I can reach, frantic to get away. A lucky strike gets him in the face, and he shoves me away.

Falling to the ground, I push myself through the pain, scrambling to get up so I can run, sobbing when I realize I haven't been fast enough. *Brent! He will help me, I just have to get to my car and then everything will be ok.*

Cory is right there, in front of me, blocking my path.

"No!" I sob. I can't let him grab me again.

He snarls at me, black blood running from the multiple wounds I was able to inflict on him. The worst runs the length of his face all the way down his neck. Seeing him like this is hard for my brain to accept. The guilt of hurting him is strong, but my self preservation is stronger, and I know that Cory isn't really here anymore.

"No one is coming to save you, my vicious Chosen. Not even your mate."

He snarls and snaps his teeth at me. Dread pools in my stomach and my beast snarls in fury.

How does he know I have a mate?

He chuckles menacingly, black spittle flying from his lips.

"I left a little present for him, but had I known that he mated you, I would have left him something else."

A sinister grin spreads across his face. It's made even more horrifying by the black blood covering him.

"What did you do?"

I pray he didn't kill anything else, but I get the feeling that isn't the case.

"Oh, just keeping them all busy with a body."

A dark chuckle leaves his bloodied lips. My hand comes up to cover my mouth. I'm too terrified to ask whose body he means.

"You see, Allen couldn't leave well enough alone, and be thankful that I no longer needed his service. So, I used his body for a different purpose, as a distraction. I couldn't have him getting in my way and ruining everything I have worked so hard for."

Oh god, he killed Allen? Is he the reason that Allen wouldn't leave me alone?

"Why are you doing this, Cory? You're my friend."

"No, say my real name when you speak to me. Say it like you used to."

His voice deepens to a growl.

"I don't know what you want me to say."

His eyes become crazed and he leans closer, but I still manage to keep just out of reach.

"You know my name. Say it."

"I don't know your name. I only know Cory."

A deep rumble reaching my ears is my only warning before he lunges at me. I barely manage to sidestep him.

I can't let him get a hold of me again.

I just know if he does, I won't be strong enough to break free again.

I silently beg for my beast to show herself. *Please help me! Take over my body and shift, please! Don't let him hurt us anymore!* She growls and snaps, lunging to break free of the bonds that still hold her, but she's not strong enough and neither am I.

We circle each other, and I just manage to keep him in my line of sight, and my body out of reach. It's a deadly, dangerous dance, and I want no part of it. I try again to plead with him.

"I'm sorry. I don't know you. I don't remember. Please, stop this."

My beast still has yet to fully emerge, and I'm losing hope that I will be able to protect myself if he attacks me again.

"You stink of another male, and now you lie to me!"

His words, along with the barest of brushes along my mate bond distract me enough that I hesitate a moment too long, and with his next lunge I'm in his grasp again.

I fight with everything I have, but his strength is otherworldly. *How is he so strong?* His foul breath, filled with putrid decay, makes me want to retch. As he leans in close, black saliva drips from his open mouth, burning my skin where it lands. I snarl in pain.

"I will obliterate this bond. You will not be taken from me again. I have the power of the great God now. A mate bond can't stop me this time."

Claws burst from his hands and dig in deep to my sides. I cry out and tears glide down my blood speckled cheeks. His face begins to stretch and elongate. The very breath is stolen from my lungs, the pain short circuiting my mind.

It is horrifying, and I'm frozen, unable to break free as his claws rip into the soft flesh of my stomach and back. The pain is unending, but what's even worse is seeing his jaws open with razor sharp teeth advancing toward my shoulder.

He's going to bite me!

"No!" A rage filled snarl bursts from me. I have to protect my mate bond. Don said only dark magic could break it, but Cory oozes darkness.

I can't let him try to break my connection with my mate. It's the one good thing in my life, the one thing that is solely mine. Don is mine, and I will fight to protect the intricate threads of our souls woven together.

The creature that was once Cory, rips his claws from my side to wrap them around my throat, lifting me off the ground and trying hard to subdue my struggles.

I gasp for air, desperately trying to break his hold. All my training flits away from my mind; I'm completely useless. And still his jaws loom closer. My vision begins to blur, the lack of oxygen making my body sluggish, but I keep struggling.

Where is my magic? Why can't I get away? Help me!

The imminent threat to the mate bond triggers my beast one more time. Weak snarls burst from me as I feel her try to push through the darkness that is keeping her leashed. If I could just get his hand off my throat.

I continue to put everything into breaking free from him, but even I can't make my weakening body obey. Not when I'm faced with a lack of oxygen and blood loss.

His burning tongue licks up my skin yet again. I scream in my mind, desperate to reach out to my mate, to tell him how much I love him, but he is too far away. I can't feel him. I'm all alone. Not even my beast is present enough to save us.

It isn't supposed to happen like this. I have only just found happiness.

The edges of my vision darken. Anger, despair, and hopelessness cycle through my mind. And then I feel something shatter. Deep in my mind a dam breaks and memories flood my mind, but it's too late.

The sob that escapes me is filled with monumental regret. I should have told Megan I loved her one last time. I should have hugged Beretta and Indy more. There are so many things I didn't get to do.

My brain races and Don's face appears in my mind. If only I could tell him how much light he has brought into my life, how much I wanted to live mine with him. And Brent…I wanted the chance…I wanted to learn what it would be like to let him in.

A lonely tear, filled with all my heartbreak, slides down my cheek as I shut my eyes. If this is my last moment, I don't want to be faced with evil. I wrap myself in the memories of everyone that I love and let them shield me.

I want to block out this dark entity and save myself, but I can't, so with the last of my strength, I send out a prayer to the Goddess. The Goddess that called to me, that assured me that I was on the right path. I plead to her, begging for her to aid me once more, but it's not her hauntingly beautiful voice that I hear.

"My sweet Chosen, soon you'll be mine." His wretched words whisper into my ear just before his teeth sink deep into my shoulder.

To Be Continued…

ACKNOWLEDGMENTS

To my readers, thank you for taking the time to read my debut novel. I put my heart and my whole ass foot in it. I hope you loved Kinley as much as I do. I'm sorry for the cliffhanger! I promise the wait will be worth it!

To Kayla, without you this book would still probably be rotting in the vast abyss of my Google Drive. Thank you for reading, and reading, and re-reading my ideas and listening to my crazy musings. And thank you for being the very best friend I could have ever asked for.

To my husband, thank you for your quiet encouragement. Thank you for listening to my crazy plot ideas, and giving advice when you could. Even though you probably won't be reading this book, just know I couldn't have done this without you. Love you, babe!

To my editor, Alexis, you were the first bright light in this publishing journey. You took this manuscript and pushed me to take it beyond what even I thought it was capable of. You also became a wonderful addition in my life.

ABOUT THE AUTHOR

Lexi Macqueen, is a plus-size girlie, living her best life in North Texas with her husband and their adorable son. Being a voracious reader of all things romance, fantasy, and the paranormal, she couldn't not write about magical love stories. When she's not writing or reading, she's probably consuming too much coffee.

If you want to connect with Lexi, follow her on social media, or join her Discord.